SUN WOLF

SUN WOLF

SPACE UNBOUND BOOK 2

DAVID C. JEFFREY

Sylvanus Books

Sun Wolf
Copyright © 2020 by David C. Jeffrey.

ISBN: Paperback: 978-0-9986742-2-3
eBook: 978-0-9986742-3-0
Cover design by Rafael Andres
Interior design and illustration by Phillip Gessert

Published by Sylvanus Books *www.davidcjeffrey.com*

First printing: 2020 Printed in the United States of America

For Ann

CHRONOLOGY

1929: Edwin Hubble confirms that the universe is expanding.

1998: Observations of Type Ia supernova reveal the expansion of the universe is accelerating. The term "dark energy" is coined for the force responsible for this cosmic acceleration.

2012: The Higgs boson is discovered.

2031–2040: Human population approaches 10 billion, and catastrophic effects of climate change accelerate. Global order deteriorates, resource wars commence, limited nuclear and biological warfare spread.

2040–2082: The Die Back. Total collapse of Earth's ecosphere and infrastructure of civilization. Over one half of the human population perishes. Dissolution of nation states and governments. All scientific inquiry virtually ceases. Historical records of this period are scant.

2082: The United Earth Domain (UED) begins to rebuild global order through military and political intervention. Sustainable power and food production are enforced.

2082–2113: The post–Die Back "twilight" period. Global living conditions improve, but distrust of science lingers. Institutions of higher learning gradually reemerge. Scientific inquiry and technological innovation resume.

2113: First post–Die Back space flight ushers in the New Age of Space.

2121: The first human colony is established on Luna.

2123: Terra Corporation dominates space-based resource mining and grows into an autonomous superpower. The New Industrial Revolution commences as resource extraction expands from Luna to the asteroid belts.

2132: First human colony on Mars is established, initially by scientists and technicians and later by a diverse proletariat population.

2147: Mars declares independence from United Earth Domain under the governance of the Allied Republics of Mars (ARM). Expands military and industrial prowess.

2153: The graviton is discovered jointly by ARM and UED scientists.

2162: The first G-transducer is developed to minimize forces of acceleration in space travel and induce synthetic gravity.

2169: The solar system's voidoid is discovered and recognized as a portal into nearby star systems. The Holtzman effect is developed for instantaneous communication between the voidoids of other stars.

2170: The first manned voidship jumps from V-Prime into another star system, establishing V-Prime as the gateway into star systems within Bound Space.

The Ganymede Pact of 2170 is signed by the UED and ARM to declare free and open access to all of Bound Space for resource extraction and research.

2170–2216: UED and ARM colonies proliferate within the solar system. Exploration and resource mining accelerate throughout Bound Space. Search for Earth-like exoplanets continues, but none are found.

2197: The Cauldron is founded by Elgin Woo in the Apollo asteroid group.

2208: First void flux detected at V-Prime. Void fluxes throughout Bound Space increase in frequency and duration.

2217: Silvanus, the first Earth-like exoplanet, is discovered in the Chara system. Military conflict erupts between ARM and UED over its possession. Total war is narrowly averted. First alien intelligence is discovered on Silvanus, dubbed the Rete.

The New Ganymede Pact is signed by the UED and ARM to declare all resources within Bound Space as Common Heritage, including Silvanus and any other habitable worlds.

2218: The present. An uneasy peace between the UED and ARM is threatened by nationalist factions within both governments. Rapidly increasing voidoid fluxes threaten to shut down access to Bound Space.

The planets in their stations list'ning stood,
While the bright pomp ascended jubilant.
Open, ye everlasting gates, they sang,
Open, ye heavens, your living doors.

—John Milton, Paradise Lost

1

HD 10180 SYSTEM
Domain Day 150, 2217

THE STAR SPOKE to Elgin Woo.

He peered at it through the *Starhawk*'s forward viewport, smiled, and leaned forward as if to hear more clearly. Even at this distance, just under two billion kilometers away, the star shone impossibly bright, a tiny hard point of thermonuclear violence piercing the death-black emptiness of space. An unblinking eye peering into his soul.

The star was the first thing he'd seen after regaining consciousness from his improbable voidjump into this sector of space, into a region that should have been impossible to reach. But Elgin Woo—the ship's sole occupant, its captain and creator—had indeed accomplished the impossible. He had jumped far beyond the 36-light-year boundary of the V-Limit and was now racing directly toward a star cataloged as HD 10180, the center of a planetary system 127 light-years from Earth. Woo smiled at the star, absently twirling one side of his long, braided moustache between finger and thumb. Among the many superlatives that could be applied to his life's work, the 63-year-old Nobel Prize–decorated astrophysicist could add one more: he was the only human being ever known to have successfully jumped beyond Bound Space.

But known by whom? No one knew he was here. He hadn't brought along a Holtzman device, so he had no way to communicate his whereabouts to anyone back in Bound Space. Yes, he had divulged his intentions to Aiden Macallan and Skye Landen back in the Chara system just before attempting the impossible. But now they had no way of knowing if he had succeeded.

Woo turned away from the viewport and set about brewing a cup of tea in the *Starhawk*'s small galley. He had stocked the vessel with only the bare essentials before he and Skye departed the Cauldron in great haste on their mission to Silvanus, and Woo considered his current favorite tea more than essential. He carefully coaxed the dark leaves of Keemun black tea into his antique silver brewing ball, feeling their dry but still pliant texture between his fingertips, a process that liberated a faint orchid-like fragrance. This particular variety of Keemun was still grown exclusively in Anhui province and had been a gift from his father. Woo smiled as he placed the ball into a ceramic mug of hot water. *Rest in peace, Bàba.*

It was not yet perfectly clear how he'd arrived here. Finding the gateway voidoid, of course, had been the key. His theories about its existence, and where to find it, had proven correct. But the exact mechanics of it—the *quantum* mechanics, to be more exact—still mystified him. Apparently, it had nothing to do with the *Starhawk*'s revolutionary zero-point drive. He'd made the jump using only the ship's conventional matter/antimatter drive, proving that any standard voidship in Bound Space could do the same. But now that he was here, those questions were no longer of immediate interest to him. He was more fascinated by what came next.

Elgin Woo was a man consumed by the singular state of mind that had propelled his career into unparalleled scientific accomplishment: curiosity. The pure and simple curiosity of a child, combined with the will, courage, and intellectual gifts to pursue it wherever it led him. Hence his present location. The tight-beam microburst of neutrinos emitted by Chara's voidoid and aimed directly at HD 10180 had compelled him to investigate, ignoring the very high probability of losing his life in the process. Now he was here, and the star had *spoken* to him upon his arrival. Curious...

Woo removed the brewing ball and took his mug of steaming Keemun back to the viewport, hypnotically drawn to the sight of the star. He sat on a narrow bench built into the bulkhead and took his first sip, feeling the hot liquid slide down his throat to warm his core. The tea's smoky aroma filled his nostrils. He took a long moment to delight in its malty flavor, a nonastringent taste reminiscent of unsweetened chocolate.

Then, of course, there was the matter of the nine planets here in the HD 10180 system, or as his sensors had revealed upon arrival, 10 planets. The tenth one was a surprise. It had never revealed itself to astronomers back at Sol and therefore had never been cataloged. Plus, HD 10180 was a G1V-type star, similar to Earth's sun but slightly larger and about half again as bright. That held intriguing possibilities for any of the planets orbiting within its habitable zone.

There appeared to be only two such planets. One was well documented—HD 10180g, a Neptune-sized gas giant sitting 1.4 AU from the star. The other, however, was none other than the previously undetected planet, the one that wasn't supposed to be here but now showed up bold as daylight on the *Starhawk*'s optical screen. At a distance of 1.2 AU from the star, it lay smack in the middle of the system's biohabitable zone. And unlike most of the other massive planets crowding the inner system, it appeared to be a terrestrial world with tantalizing hints of protective atmosphere. The moment it showed up on his sensors, Woo had named it Shénmì, a word meaning "mystery" in his native Mandarin. The planet was less than two billion kilometers away. His jump from the voidoid had already put the *Starhawk* on a heading straight toward it. Shénmì was his obvious next destination.

Woo turned away from the viewport, humming softly to himself some mindless little melody, set a course for Shénmì, and prepared to engage the *Starhawk*'s zero-point drive. If the inertia-altering device worked as well as it had up to this point, it would deliver him into Shénmì space in about two hours, no need for prolonged acceleration followed by deceleration. No G-forces. Virtually instantaneous transition to 92 percent light speed, a clever trickeration of the laws of physics.

He entered the command to engage the drive and sat back in the pilot's chair, awaiting the next revelation in this most extraordinary excursion. The viewport flickered once, obscuring the view outside, then cleared again. And...

Nothing happened.

The ship did not change course or velocity. Woo tried again, adjusting the electromagnetic field generators to a slightly different set of resonant frequencies. Still nothing.

Uh-oh...

Woo sat back in his chair, looking out at the emptiness of space he knew was not empty at all. What made the zero-point drive work, basically, was the elimination of inertia. Without inertia, acceleration to relativistic velocities could be attained almost instantly, free from the forces of acceleration and requiring only modest initial thrust. He and his colleagues at the Cauldron had found a way to manipulate zero-point fields with tuned EM generators to control the phenomenon of inertia itself. The trick was finding the right combination of interacting EM resonances to produce the effect on any given scale. But the frequency settings that worked perfectly well in Bound Space were apparently not working out here in this sector of space. He thought he knew why—a slight variance in the cosmological constant predicted by his own nascent theory of living voidoids. The same theory that also predicted the problem would be virtually impossible to correct in his current situation.

Woo took another sip of tea and stood up. At least he could keep trying. With the aid of his Omicron-3 AI, who he addressed as Mari, he spent the next two hours testing different settings on the EM generators. None of them worked. There were too many variables, and he didn't have the necessary equipment to narrow them down, instruments that existed only at the Cauldron. And even if he did have them, the ship needed to be at complete standstill to accurately recalibrate the field generators. Right now, he was zipping along at 2 percent light speed.

He sat back down and sipped the last of his tea, now cold but still delicious. The drive was, after all, an experimental prototype. He couldn't expect perfection this early in the trial period, but the timing of the malfunction was so...unfortunate. He could almost hear Skye Landen's admonitions. She had warned him of the folly of his little jaunt into the unknown, for reasons exactly like this one. She had, of course, been right.

He took a deep breath and reviewed his situation. The *Starhawk* was currently on a straight-line trajectory toward the star's inner system at a velocity of around 6,250 km/sec, the same velocity with which he'd entered the voidoid. He could not use the zero-point drive, but the vessel's conventional matter/antimatter drive still worked perfectly well and could deliver up to 1 G constant acceleration. At least until he ran out of antimatter fuel, which would happen sooner than later. The good news was that the *Starhawk* had a virtually inexhaustible life-support system operating on superbly designed recycling technologies developed at the Cauldron. The bad news was that it couldn't churn out all the bulk nutrients his body needed to survive for an extended period of time, and his stored food supply had dwindled.

Given all of that, and his inability to communicate with Bound Space, it would appear he had only two options now. He could either turn around, head back to the voidoid, and attempt to jump back into Bound Space. Or he could continue onward into the system to investigate whatever secrets it held, including Shénmì. If he wanted to head back to the voidoid, he couldn't just stop where he was and turn around. Conventional rocket science didn't work that way. Given his current velocity of 6,250 km/sec, he'd have to decelerate and come to a full stop before turning around. That would require seven and a half days at 1 G thrust. From there, getting back to the system's voidoid nearly two billion kilometers away and to approach it at a sane velocity—highly recommended when attempting a voidjump without a Licensed Pilot—would take another 10 days at 1 G. Total: 17.5 days continuous thrust before he could even attempt a jump back into Bound Space.

The problem was he had only enough antimatter fuel reserves for about 11 days of 1 G thrust. Technically, it would still be possible for the *Starhawk* to reach the voidoid after turnaround. But without continuous acceleration throughout, the new calculations would add over two months to the trip. He would surely starve to death well before then.

Option number two, however, required only the first part of option one—start decelerating now at 1 G, and in seven and a half days when he came to a standstill, he would find himself close enough to the planet Shénmì to slip easily into orbit around her. His food supply, if strictly rationed, would be sufficient. So, it was a no-brainer. Option number two, setting course for Shénmì, was the only one that made sense.

He gave Mari instructions and felt the *Starhawk*'s engine shut down just long enough to turn the ship 180 degrees about-face and begin deceleration toward Shénmì. Satisfied, he moved to the viewport again and sat, admiring the beautiful star, its brilliant point of light ruling over the cold emptiness of space. He felt content, even happy, that the decision he'd wanted to make in his heart was now backed up by cold, hard facts. Shénmì called to him like a siren from the deep. He would go to her, and even if he ended up starving to death in orbit around her, he would die in peace.

It all made perfect sense to him now. If he was going to die here anyway, why not have some fun first? Why not continue the quest that brought him here in the first place? So many intriguing questions had emerged during his mission to Silvanus. Why had the Chara voidoid emitted that microburst of neutrinos aimed directly at this very star system, HD 10180? And why had it happened at exactly the same time that Silvanus, the only other living planet known to exist in Bound Space, became sealed within a protective energy field? And why had both phenomena occurred right after the planet had been threatened by destruction from outside agents? It couldn't be a coincidence. The neutrino emission was clearly not some sort of signal intended for this star; it would take over 150 years to get here from the Chara system. No. It made more sense that it was a beacon pointing the way here. Intended for him. An invitation?

To Woo, an undeniable element of purpose—of *intelligence*—was apparent in these phenomena. It supported his hunch that the voidoids themselves were alive and were in fact integral parts of a larger web of life in a vast galactic ecosystem. The obvious best place to look for answers was right here, in the HD 10180 system, and he was determined to start looking.

Woo smiled, feeling unusually lighthearted, and instructed Mari to set a course for Shénmì. Seeking knowledge was far superior to seeking safety. But there was another reason he felt at ease with his decision to go onward toward Shénmì. The planet's sun, the star, had *spoken* to him. He heard it even now. Not words, and not heard through his ears. More like music or a subtle little melody running through his head that he couldn't shake. A message both simple and deep with meaning, yet profoundly enigmatic. Not words, but the translation was just as clear: *Welcome. You are always here.*

2

HAWKING STATION
Domain Day 80, 2218

"You are always here."

The voice seemed to come from inside Aiden Macallan's head, but the words were not his own. The hair on his neck prickled and a reflexive shudder jolted up his spine. He took a deep breath to calm himself before realizing the voice had come from behind him. Turning from the observation window, he found Roseph Hand standing at the entrance of the dimly lit observation suite, his tall silhouette backlit by the outer corridor lighting. Ro held two mugs of steaming coffee, one in each hand. The rich aroma of ground beans freshly brewed filled the quiet chamber. As Ro stepped forward, faint starlight from the observation window brought into focus the mischievous smile on his face.

Aiden cocked his head and asked, "What did you say?"

"I said, 'You are always here.' That's how I know where to find you, especially when you disconnect from the station's comm-net." Ro glanced at the deactivated p-comm on Aiden's wrist, then shrugged. "You are always here, Aiden. In the observation bubble."

Aiden leaned his back against the window and crossed his arms, feigning annoyance. "A bit of an exaggeration, don't you think? I am not *always* here. Is one of those cups for me?"

"No. I'm drinking both." Ro Hand, master of the straight face. Aiden smiled and extended his hand. "Give."

Had anyone else on Hawking Station other than Ro interrupted his contemplation, Aiden's annoyance would not have been feigned. As it was, his mood lightened with the unexpected entrance of his closest friend. Since his return from Silvanus, Aiden's moments of stillness had too often turned to melancholy, a deep blue current of loss he hadn't been able to rise above since his departure from that extraordinary world.

Ro approached, his movements smooth, catlike, and handed the mug over. He stood next to Aiden but faced the observation window, staring out at the blackness of space, relaxed, quietly sipping his coffee. Aiden turned back to the window as well. "Okay, wise guy. How did you know I would be in this *particular* observation suite? There're four of them here on the station."

Ro stayed silent for a while, then, without moving his gaze from the stars, said, "Right now, it's the only one on Hawking Station facing in the direction of the Chara system. And Silvanus."

And in the direction of Skye Landen, who was currently stationed there, over 27 light-years away, heading up the Silvanus Project. Doctor Skye Landen, Aiden's mate, his other half. He missed her now more than he could admit, even to Ro.

But Ro knew already. He squinted and pointed to a spot outside the window. "That star right there. Chara. In the constellation Canes Venatici. It's always in your window, Aiden. Right along with your planet, Silvanus."

Ro was playing him again, trying to lighten him up. Aiden shook his head slowly, playing along. "Sure, I can see Chara from here, if I wanted to. But Silvanus? Totally invisible."

"Absolutely right. Totally invisible...to anyone who's never been there." As usual, it was impossible to decipher precise connotations in many of Ro Hand's pronouncements.

Aiden glanced at Ro's serene profile—at the Canadian's square jaw, clean-shaven, and his close-cropped sandy hair—and heard the rest of what his friend left unspoken: *invisible to anyone except the only person alive to have experienced a soul-altering neurolink-age with an entire living planet.*

Ro always had his number. Was that a comforting thought or a disturbing one? Aiden had never decided for sure. "So, why were you looking for me?"

Like flipping a switch, Ro was all business. He looked directly at Aiden for the first time since entering the room, his pale blue eyes unblinking, intelligent, unreadable. "Your mission briefing has been moved up, Commander. Vice Admiral Stegman just got in from Luna aboard the *Argo*, and he wants to get down to it now. Sounds like some serious business."

It had been over 10 months since Aiden was promoted and given command of the *Sun Wolf*, the Science and Survey Division's new flagship, and being addressed as "Commander" almost sounded natural now. Almost.

He warmed his hands around the mug of coffee, realizing how chilled he'd become in the darkened observation bubble. "And Stegman enlisted you to track me down?"

Ro nodded. "Correct. And he wants me to join the briefing."

Aiden smiled. "Good. I was hoping you'd be included. Maybe now we'll find out what the *Sun Wolf*'s first real mission is all about."

After one last shakedown cruise out in the vicinity of Jupiter, Aiden and his new crew—including his acting Science Officer, Roseph Hand—had returned the *Sun Wolf* to Hawking Station for the ship's final fitting and to "await further orders." That was 10 days ago. For Aiden, whose natural response to idle time was dark introspection, 10 days of waiting was far too long.

He took his first sip of coffee, tasting the subtle harmony of organic bitterness played against floral sweetness. "Hmm. Tasty. African?"

"Ethiopian."

Aiden wanted to ask Ro how he'd scored such an exotic commodity, just to see how artfully elliptical the answer would be, but said nothing and returned his attention to the star-studded blackness outside. Hawking Station's slow spin had brought Earth's luminous orb into view. The oceans of humankind's home planet shone dull blue, filtered through a persistent global haze. Its land masses still looked faded brown and scarred, the devastating, long-term effects of the Die Back. He knew enough about himself now, after Silvanus, to recognize how his recurrent melancholies were fed by contrasts. Like the contrast between the world he could see very well from here but whose life he could not feel inside, and the other world he could *not* see but that lived inside him. Silvanus, forever blossoming. A contrast between the dying world where he'd been born and the vibrantly living one where he'd been reborn.

Aiden sensed the other man reading his thoughts. Ro pointed to the globe of Earth moving slowly across the upper half of the observation window and said, "Have you checked out the South American subcontinent lately?" He spoke as if they were standing together in an art museum, musing over some subtle nuance of a painter's brushstroke. "Look closely around where Old Brazil used to be. See those little green smudges? Areas of hyperaccelerated reforestation in the Amazon Basin. All because of that crazy fungus you brought back from Silvanus. The mystery mycorrhizae. Amazing, eh?"

Aiden nodded but did not look where Ro pointed. Of course, he had heard all about it, how the fungal samples he'd brought back from Silvanus, living pieces of the Rete's own body, had been applied to the nascent reforestation projects on Earth with startling results in remarkably little time. And he'd heard more than enough about how he, Aiden Macallan, was the hero of the story, a savior even, for bringing to Earth the gift of renewed life. A gift given to him by the Rete.

When he finally did look up, he saw only his own reflection in the observation window lit by Earth's shining orb. He saw a pale, lean figure and a face dominated by dark eyes that burned a little too intensely and underlined by faint semicircles, remnants of his past struggles to kick the Continuum habit. The effect would

have added years to his face had it not been for the mane of black
hair, overly long by spacer's standards, hanging lank to his shoulders. Its length had once been useful in obscuring the letter *T*
laser branded on his neck, just as the dark beard, also unconventional but now closely trimmed, had once hidden the long scar
below his right cheekbone. Both marks had been painful sou-
venirs of his nightmare incarceration at Hades nearly two decades
ago. Both marks had been erased by the Rete on Silvanus, but
they were gone from the surface only.

Aiden spoke to Ro's reflection in the window. "I get it, Ro. You
can back off now."

Ro's pale eyes softened, but he said nothing. Aiden took a deep
breath and straightened his back. "So, what's the new start time
for this briefing?"

Ro made a show of looking at his chronometer. "At 20:00."

Alarmed, Aiden looked at his own chrono. "That was 10 minutes ago!"

Ro smiled again in silence.

"What the hell! Why didn't you say...?" But he knew the
answer before finishing the question. Ro had his own priorities,
mostly obscure but always for a greater good.

Not bothering to wait for a response he knew wasn't coming,
Aiden clapped Ro on the shoulder and said, "Well, great gods,
man. Let's get going."

They set their coffee mugs on a nearby service tray and headed
for the door.

"There's something else you might want to know before this
meeting," Ro said. "I got this straight from Stegman. He's
received word from Dr. Maryam Ebadi. The *Sun Wolf*'s first stop
from here will be to pick her up at Luna."

"Maryam Ebadi. Elgin Woo's codirector of the Cauldron."

"That would be her, now the acting director in Dr. Woo's
absence."

Aiden paused at the corridor entrance, his interest piqued.
Dr. Ebadi and Elgin Woo were close associates at the Cauldron,

both specializing in zero-point energy and quantum gravity theory. He looked at Ro. "If anyone in the System has a clue to Elgin's whereabouts, it would be Maryam Ebadi."

No one had heard from Elgin Woo in the 10 months since his brash attempt to voidjump beyond Bound Space, from the Chara system toward a certain star 127 light-years from Sol. Aiden feared the worst, but less so than most others familiar with the circumstances.

Ro nodded. "I'm guessing she'll also have information extracted from the top-secret cryptochip Woo gave you to deliver before his vanishing act. Dr. Ebadi was his intended recipient, right?"

"Yes, she was." As requested, Aiden had hand-delivered Woo's cryptochip to Ebadi the day after his return from the Chara system. "Let's get going, Ro."

They strode out of the observation bubble into Corridor A3 to find the quickest way to the station's conference suite. Hawking Station operated under the jurisdiction of the UED, United Earth Domain, and was the largest combined docking and construction shipyard in all of Bound Space. It was located at the Earth-Moon Lagrange point L5, a stable position about 384,400 kilometers from Earth. Composed of four massive U-shaped structures joined at their apexes, their open arms facing outward, Hawking Station offered external docking for spacefaring vessels of every known size and configuration. This was where virtually all Domain voidships were constructed, repaired, or refitted. Hawking also provided internal docking facilities for freighters, personnel transport vessels, and military fighters assigned to enforce station security.

Perpendicular to the docking arms, the station's central hub supported a huge, city-sized cylindrical assembly that housed smelters, fabrication factories, hydroponic farms, personnel habitats and research facilities, and was topped by an armored control/command pod. The station's powerful gravity transducers conferred a steady 1 G to all habitable sections, allowing its designers to depart from the cumbersome rotating-ring structures of the past. The slow spin of the central cylinder was maintained now only to enhance the viewing enjoyment of its inhabitants.

Aiden and Ro decide to take a short cut and caught a freight elevator that tracked down the station's outer hull. Noisy, hot, and smelling of oil and raw metal, the lift was not intended for personnel movement, but it was the fastest way down to Level 7 where the conference rooms were located. Aiden had to yell to be heard over the clanging of the track rollers.

"Ro," he shouted over the racket. "Now that Stegman brought the *Argo* back with him, I expect you'll want to take command of her as soon as possible."

It was more a loaded question than a simple statement, and they both knew it. After the smoke cleared from the Chara crisis, Ro had been awarded command of the survey vessel SS *Argo* at the same time as Aiden's promotion to command the *Sun Wolf*. They had served together as crewmates on the *Argo* under Ben Stegman's command, leading up to the discovery of Silvanus. After Stegman had been promoted to vice admiral and given leadership of the Service's new Science and Survey Division, the *Argo* was left without a captain. Aiden had been the expected choice for the position, but he'd been moved up to command the *Sun Wolf*, and Roseph Hand got command of the *Argo*.

But the *Argo* had remained in the Chara system, tasked with overseeing the foundation of the Silvanus Project, leaving Ro in limbo awaiting *Argo*'s return. Aiden had seized upon Ro's idle time to sign him on as temporary Science Officer aboard the *Sun Wolf* for its shakedown cruises. During that time, Aiden kept up his campaign to persuade Ro into postponing his command of the *Argo* to sign on as Executive Officer of the *Sun Wolf*.

Aiden had a strong argument for it too. Things would be a lot more interesting on the SSD's newest flagship, especially under what many in the Service considered the hot-shot rookie command of Aiden Macallan. The lure was set even deeper when, just before his audacious jump into the unknown, Elgin Woo had reaffirmed his offer to have the Cauldron's zero-point drive installed aboard the *Sun Wolf*. If that happened, things would be *a lot* more interesting aboard the *Sun Wolf* than any other ship in the System. Aiden believed it would be the final factor in swaying Ro to ship with him as XO. But now, in Woo's absence, the zero-point drive proposal remained on hold, and Ro continued to put off his decision.

It was no different now. In response to Aiden's question, Ro nodded thoughtfully and remained silent. Aiden shrugged it off. Impatience was the wrong approach with Ro.

As the elevator continued tracking downward, its full-length viewport afforded them a vista of the station's docking arms below and the surrounding star-studded blackness of space. Luna's iridescent orb had just slipped past the left margin of the viewport when, halfway down the track, Dock Arm 2 came into view. The *Sun Wolf* sat there, poised for flight.

Even after his many months aboard the *Sun Wolf*, Aiden's initial wonderment over her elegantly powerful design had not abated in the least. He and Ro stopped for a moment and gazed at her in silence. Ro was the first to speak. He nodded in the ship's direction and said, "Nice ride."

Aiden grinned back at him. "No shit."

The *Sun Wolf* was similar in size to Science and Survey vessels like the *Argo* and smaller than a Military Division's standard battle cruiser. But functionally it was designed to operate equally well as both. At 210 meters in length and 26 meters at its widest cross section, it was constructed with super-light, super-strong materials, weighing in at 8.7 kilotons. Its sleek design presented a less aggressive appearance than a battle cruiser. But looks could be deceiving; it was equipped with the most up-to-date weapons systems, artfully concealed, and its shielding capabilities were superior to those of most military ships.

Lacking the ungainly central ring structure of survey vessels, its slender fuselage had a slightly hexagonal cross-section and tapered forward to a narrow point. The design had nothing to do with aerodynamics and everything to do with battle defense, offering minimal targeting profiles and only beam-deflecting angles. The aft section bulged with a protective cowling that encircled the beamed core matter/antimatter engines. And unlike in popular sci-fi dramas, its command bridge was buried deep inside, heavily shielded against both enemy weaponry and the intense gamma radiation yield of its beefed-up propulsion system.

Matter/antimatter engines—M/AM for short—had been around for a long time, but in the beginning they were fuel-hungry systems, and early technologies for producing and storing antimatter had limited their power. All that changed with the advent of the Bickford Process for harvesting large quantities of antihydrogen from the magnetospheres of Jupiter and Saturn. That, along with vast improvements in Penning trap technology for antimatter containment, allowed the development of immensely powerful beamed core M/AM drives. They utilized antiproton annihilation to directly generate thrust after deflection by electromagnetic nozzles, making them ideal powerhouses for a torch ship. The newest and most powerful generation of the drive had just been perfected and the *Sun Wolf* had four of them. Mounted astern on stout heat-radiating blades inside the cowling, only their magnetic nozzles protruded beyond to protect the ship's superstructure from their star-hot exhaust plumes.

As the elevator shook and groaned to a halt at Level 7, Aiden glanced at Ro for a long moment, wondering if the *Sun Wolf's* impressive visage would finally have a positive effect on his friend's decision to sign on. The heavy metal doors slid open with the invisible question mark still hanging in the air between them. The two men emerged into the relative quietness of the circular lobby at the hub of the conference suites. Now that Aiden could lower his voice to conversational levels, he stopped in front of Ro and faced him.

"Look, you know I want you as my Executive Officer on the *Sun Wolf*. Once this briefing is over and the mission gets launched, things are going to move fast. I'll need to complete my crew roster and XO is the last position up in the air. You've got to make a decision."

Without hesitation, or a hint of annoyance, Ro said what he always said when the issue came up. "We'll see."

Aiden nodded as he started toward the door marked Conference Room Four. Without looking back, he said, "Right. And I think we *are* about to see."

3

HAWKING STATION
Domain Day 80, 2218

HAWKING STATION'S FOUR conference rooms occupied one entire floor of the station's cylindrical habitat assembly. Like a circle divided into four equal pie slices, each one a 90-degree wedge, the rooms shared a common lobby at the circle's center. The primary seating area of each conference room was located at the outer perimeter of the wedge, where the gently curving outer wall supported an elongated observation window spanning its entire width. When the window's protective duranium shield was withdrawn, opening like a sleepy metallic eyelid, the room's occupants were offered a 90-degree view of local space. Given the station's unique position at Earth-Moon L5, situated within the moon's orbital plane, the design was intentional. The station's slow spin treated each conference room to a momentary view of Earth and Luna within the same window, both roughly equidistant from the station.

It was precisely at one such moment of visual splendor that Aiden and Ro entered Conference Room Four. And they were late.

Vice Admiral Benjamin Stegman, Aiden's former commander on the *Argo* and now chief of the Science and Survey Division, a branch of United Earth Domain's Space Service, sat at the head of the circular conference table. He was accompanied by two other men. Aiden recognized one of them, and the other he'd never seen before. Stegman stood as Aiden and Ro walked in, his bushy gray eyebrows raised and twitching with barely concealed annoyance. "Nice of you to join us, Commanders."

Aiden made a slight bow of contrition, then straightened, shoulders back. "I apologize for the delay, sir." Under other circumstances, he'd be tempted to offer an excuse for their tardiness, but this was clearly not the time for it.

Stegman made a gruff utterance, then turned to the others seated at the table. "Gentlemen, this is Commander Aiden Macallan of the *Sun Wolf* and Commander Roseph Hand, of the *Argo*. They will be our primary operatives in the field." He turned back to Aiden and Ro. "Be seated, gentlemen and I'll introduce you to the others."

Aiden and Ro exchanged a quick glance as they settled at the table. Ro was now included as an operative in a mission ostensibly assigned to the *Sun Wolf* alone? Curious.

Stegman gestured to the straight-backed, gaunt figure sitting to his left. "You may already know Admiral Drew Prescott, chief of the UED Military Space Service."

Aiden nodded. He did indeed know Prescott, primarily from his role in the military conflict over Silvanus in the Chara system. The man looked no different now than he had on the *Argo*'s comm screen nine months earlier during that fateful incident. In his late sixties, Prescott's craggy face, steely eyes, and buzz-cut gray hair were archetypal military. Aiden exchanged polite but curt nods with Prescott, concealing his surprise over the presence of the UED's highest ranking military officer. He felt an indistinct foreboding creep into his gut, a sensation amplified by the sour expression on the admiral's face.

Stegman turned to his right, gesturing toward a tall man, probably in his early forties. "And this is Colonel Victor Aminu. He's from DSI."

Uh-oh. That indistinct foreboding suddenly became distinct. DSI stood for Domain Security and Intelligence, UED's central intelligence agency. Spy types. And Colonel Aminu looked the part. To call him serious-looking would be a vast understatement. Lean, fit, with luminous ebony skin, immaculately cut hair, classic high-cheek-boned features, he would have been extremely handsome if his face had shown any signs of having ever expressed humor or affability. There was, however, nothing cruel or menacing in that face, and his eyes were those of a highly intelligent and inquisitive investigator. While his posture remained erect, it revealed no tension as he made graceful nods to Aiden first, then to Ro, unblinking.

Stegman sat, folded his hands on the table, and turned his attention to Aiden. "This briefing is about your first mission, Aiden, as commander of the *Sun Wolf*. I'll get right to it with the basics. As you know, voidoid fluxes have been a problem in Bound Space for nearly a decade now. We've seen periods when fluxes ceased altogether, followed by periods of increased activity, like last year during the Chara crisis. As you'll recall, three of Admiral Prescott's voidships were temporarily lost and dislocated in a voidoid flux during that period."

Aiden nodded and checked his impulse to glance at Prescott. He already knew what he'd see in the man's face. Three battle cruisers under his command, on their way to combat missions in the Chara system, had disappeared into V-Prime just as the voidoid fluxed out. It was the longest flux event ever recorded, lasting 3 hours and 21 minutes. Fortunately, all three ships reappeared safe and sound back in the Sol system after the flux ended but found themselves nearly two billion kilometers due south of Sol, at the system's polar opposite point. Not all vessels caught in a void flux had been that lucky, including the ARM battle cruiser that most recently disappeared into V-Prime.

"After a brief lull in void flux activity following the Chara conflict," Stegman continued, "it has now increased to an unprecedented level, to the point where governments of both the UED and ARM are seriously considering the recall of all vessels currently in Bound Space and barring any further outward-bound traffic through V-Prime."

Aiden glanced sideways at Ro. Shutting down V-Prime, even temporarily, would be a drastic measure. Unprecedented. It meant barring access to all of Bound Space, anywhere beyond the Solar System.

For almost 50 years now the voidoids had served humankind as reliable, albeit enigmatic gateways into the other star systems within a radius of 36 light-years from Sol. Even though voidjumping to stars beyond that radius had proven impossible, realtime travel to any of the nearly 5,000 stars or starlike bodies within Bound Space was now a reality. It had enabled human enterprise to expand widely and rapidly. It had also led to the discovery of Silvanus.

Then void fluxes started happening. Voidoids blinking in and out of existence was a recent phenomenon and had put the entire human population on edge, not just spacers. All the gains that had come about through the voidoids, and the promise of so much more, now seemed threatened.

Stegman let the possibility of a V-Prime lockdown sink in before continuing. "Now to some specifics. You all know about the ARM battle cruiser that vanished two weeks ago while attempting to jump from V-Prime during a brief flux event. That was the RMV *Markos* and it hasn't been heard from since. The *Markos* was the new flagship of ARM's Militia. According to our intelligence reports, it was the most powerful warship in their fleet, operating with the most advanced technology in the System, probably second only to the *Sun Wolf*.

"But the latest incident is most interesting. A Domain survey vessel, the SS *Arcadia*, out in the Alpha-2 Hydri system, reported sighting an unidentified vessel parked in close proximity to that system's voidoid, generating some kind of energy field directed at the voidoid. At one point, according to the *Arcadia*'s report, the voidoid became visible and displayed peculiar optical effects before collapsing and vanishing completely. It reappeared about an hour later but remained unstable.

"Alpha-2 Hydri is 36.3 light-years out. It's the most distant star system reachable by voidjump, at the extreme edge of the Frontier. The *Arcadia*'s crew feared they'd get stranded out there and made a high-velocity run toward the voidoid, hoping to jump out of the system before it fluxed out again. They repeatedly hailed the unidentified vessel, but it fled as they approached. The last Holtzman transmission we received from the *Arcadia* reported the voidoid growing increasingly unstable as they approached. That was the last we heard from them. Their whereabouts remain unknown."

"How long ago was this?" Aiden asked.

"Four days. And that's not all. We've also lost the SS *Conquest*, the latest addition to the Domain's military fleet. It was on a shakedown cruise out at Zeta Tucanae for a drive-system upgrade and happened to be making a voidjump at about the same time as the incident at Alpha-2 Hydri. Its captain reported the sudden onset of a void flux just before the ship passed into the Tucanae voidoid. The *Conquest* hasn't been heard from either."

Aiden knew the SS *Conquest*. Terra Corp's most potent warship during the Chara crisis, it had been commandeered by Cole Brahmin on his twisted quest to destroy Silvanus. After the Chara Treaty, Aiden had been charged with returning the *Conquest* to Sol to be refitted for service in the UED's Military. Now it was missing too.

Aiden leaned forward. "And you believe the two incidents are related, occurring as they did simultaneously in neighboring star systems?"

Stegman's eyebrows went up a fraction of an inch. "Yes. That is now the opinion of both the military and Domain intelligence agencies."

Stegman said this as he glanced at Prescott and Aminu. Both men nodded, but before either could comment, Aiden continued.

"And you also believe the unidentified ship spotted by the *Arcadia* may somehow be responsible for triggering both void fluxes."

"We've agreed that it's highly suggestive," Stegman said, then fell silent. Aiden had rarely seen such a grave expression on his former captain's face. He sat back and thought for a moment. The notion that a void flux in one star system could trigger one in a neighboring system had become less difficult to accept as evidence for it grew. Aiden knew the Zeta Tucanae system, where the *Conquest* had disappeared. He'd been there years ago on a survey mission with Terra Corp. An F9.5V main-sequence star over 28 light-years out, it was in the same general vicinity as Alpha-2 Hydri, separated by about 12 light-years. That was relatively close, as star systems go. It had become more apparent, to him at least, that all voidoids in Bound Space were dynamically interconnected, but in ways no one understood. No one except maybe Elgin Woo.

But the notion of someone *attacking* the voidoids? Deliberately causing them to flux out? It was insane. "Who would want to do that? And why?"

"That's exactly what we want to find out," Prescott blurted, his face red, fists clenched. "That's part of your mission, Commander Macallan. We need to find those bastards and put 'em away. The *Conquest* was our flagship, top-of-the-line. My son was a serving officer aboard."

Aiden heard the raw emotion in Prescott's voice as he spoke. But he also heard the other part loud and clear. *Part of your mission.* He was now fully alert.

Stegman intervened before Prescott could get ahead of himself. "We don't know who's behind this attack, Aiden, but at least we have some ideas of where to start looking. We all know that not everyone in the System loves what the voidoids have given us. There are several powerful activist groups, both from Earth and Mars, who have their own skewed narratives for why the voidoids should be blocked or shut down altogether. And they've been empowered in recent months by the isolationist backlash taking

hold in the System since the discovery of Silvanus was made public."

Aiden felt his face burn. The discovery of the Rete, the alien
intelligence he had encountered on Silvanus—the first true
extraterrestrial contact in human history—had not been met
with universal wonder and optimism, and he'd been naïve to
assume that it would. Despite the enormous promise for a bright
future offered by the Rete, there would always be a segment of
the human population that reacted to such discoveries with fear
rather than with hope, with the impulse to withdraw inward
rather than to explore outward. And there would always be formidable, charismatic figures rising up in such times to harvest
the fear as a way to consolidate their personal power over others.
It was already happening on Earth as a xenophobic nationalist
madman was seriously challenging President Michi Takema for
leadership of the UED. A previously unknown midlevel customs
official rising out of nowhere, barely literate but a brilliant liar, he
gained more popular support every day. His name was Hugh Daw
Thunck, but all of his followers called him Houda Thunkit. It was
such a fitting sobriquet that now almost everyone called him that,
his birth name all but forgotten.

And it was happening on Mars, too, as members of the reac-
tionary Red Party, the so-called Ruddies, were poised to take
control of the Directorate, the governing body of the Allied
Republics of Mars. The Directorate's current leader, Vol Charnakov, had been in power for nearly three decades. As a pragmatic
moderate, Director Charnakov had stabilized ARM's economy
and, with the recent exception of the Chara crisis, had maintained a peaceful coexistence with the UED. As Charnakov was
aging and ailing, the Ruddies, with their isolationist saber-rat-
tling, were ready to pounce.

Aiden shook his head slowly as he listened. Even in light of
the recent shifts in public perception and political reaction, he
still couldn't fathom any plausible motive for annihilating the

voidoids, for driving civilization backward so drastically. That was beyond extreme. There was an evil to it.

"Assuming it's even possible to destroy a voidoid," he said, "who in the System has the knowledge base and technology advanced enough to attempt it?"

Stegman said, "You're asking the right questions, Aiden. We're hoping you can find answers to some of them. That's partly why Admiral Prescott and I have asked Colonel Aminu to join us here, to give you some relevant background as to who might be responsible and why they're doing it. As to the question of advanced technology, I'm bringing aboard a preeminent expert in the field of voidoid science, Dr. Maryam Ebadi. She is an associate of Dr. Elgin Woo's. She'll be joining you tomorrow."

Stegman turned to Victor Aminu. "Colonel. Please proceed."

4

HAWKING STATION
Domain Day 80, 2218

Victor Aminu remained still for a long moment before responding. Then, like an elegant bronze statue reanimating, he uncoiled and scanned the faces of everyone in the circle around him. "This incident at Alpha-2 Hydri is not the first we've known about. Over the last decade, there have been rumors, vaguely substantiated reports, of voidoid disruptions in other systems that coincide with sightings of unidentified vessels in the vicinity. These have mostly been hearsays from private enterprises plying the Deep. This was the first well-documented incident reported officially by a Space Service vessel, including visual recordings."

Aminu's voice projected a deep resonance without relying on volume to be heard. He spoke precisely, with a measured cadence and a distinct musical lilt that seemed out of place with his severe demeanor. "There has been speculation that these sightings are directly related to the recent increase in void fluxes over the last several years. But I'll leave speculations of that nature to Dr. Ebadi. That is her field of expertise, not mine.

"What we do know at the DSI is the field of players most likely to perpetrate these attacks. At this point, we don't suspect foreign government involvement, meaning the Allied Republics of Mars. The DSI has good sources inside ARM, including its intelligence agencies, and we've ruled out any direct government connection. That leaves nongovernment players, and of those, the One Earth movement stands out. Specifically, its most radical wing, Green War."

Aiden was well aware of the One Earth movement. Its primary tenet was that humans belonged on Earth and nowhere else for the foreseeable future. They believed that humanity's only chance of survival was to turn their energies inward, back to Earth instead of outward to other planets. To focus on the work of healing planet Earth. To atone for the errors we made that caused the Die Back. They viewed exploration of space as a fatal distraction and opposed all colonization of off-world habitats and planets, including the current colony on Mars. To them, those activities were misguided diversions that distracted people from their responsibility to repair Earth first.

Aiden had engaged a few One Earthers in heated arguments. He agreed with their basic premise regarding humanity's duty, individually and collectively, to help repair the damage they'd done to the planet. But he disagreed with their blind dismissal of all the alternative ways it could be accomplished. Couldn't they see, for instance, how the reforestation projects in the tropics had miraculously accelerated due to the gift the Rete had given them? A gift that would have been impossible without space exploration. But Aiden's arguments had gotten nowhere. Even the most intelligent among them seemed surprisingly closed-minded. But that was always the way inside belief systems placing self-perpetuation above seeking the truth.

"The majority of the One Earth movement is relatively benign," Aminu continued. "They're grassroots idealists, loosely associated, mostly young and well intentioned. But their radical wing, Green War, is hardcore. They cause the most trouble and we monitor them more closely. Green War uses violence and sabotage to advance the goals of One Earth. They've destroyed launch sites on Earth, bombed orbital space installations, and trashed a few lunar facilities they thought were draining resources away from planet Earth. Agents of Green War have even been apprehended on Mars attempting to destroy ARM's terraforming projects, although not so much now after what happened when ARM's Militia caught up with them. They've openly demanded that V-Prime be shut down, even destroyed, to force people back to Earth, where they should focus attention on making the planet great again."

"What about the Zero-Pops?" Stegman interjected.

"Yes, I was getting to them," Aminu said. "The Zero-Population cells are a small subset of Green War, but they're undoubtedly the most dangerous of all. Self-described suicide terrorists, their credo is purely nihilistic and openly destructive. They believe humanity is a scourge upon the universe, literally a disease that needs to be eradicated before it spreads to other planets and throughout the galaxy."

Aiden had never met a Zero-Popper in person and was glad of it. They'd most likely kill him on sight after recognizing who he was. The Zero-Pop ideology was dark in the extreme, the ultimate perversion of the old Zero Population Growth movement, summed up in their motto: "Zero Population. Period," pointedly omitting "Growth." They saw the Die Back as incontrovertible evidence that humans as a species are innately rapacious and destructive, and if allowed to thrive, they will always devastate their environment, along with all other living things within it.

"Many of the experts who study them," Aminu continued, "characterize the Zero-Pops as a religious movement whose adherents have a sacred mission to simply kill as many human beings as possible. To virtually wipe out the human race. That includes themselves in the process, not to be seen as hypocritical. That's why all their acts of terrorism are suicide missions carried out by individuals who fervently believe they're acting to save the natural world, to spare it from the disease of humanity. They use weapons of mass destruction that have a minimal impact on the natural environment and other animal species, engineered specifically against human life. They see their own deaths, in the process, as a supreme sacrifice for Earth and for all other potentially habitable planets, by sparing them from the disease of humanity."

Stegman said, "Wouldn't they have the strongest motivation to see the voidoids destroyed? To prevent the spread of humanity into other systems. Keep the disease contained."

"Not necessarily." Aminu said. "The Zero-Pops focus more on the human population itself as the primary scourge, not so much on their means of migration beyond Earth."

Upon his return from Silvanus, Aiden had heard the news of the Zero-Pops' most recent attack. It had been a weaponized coronavirus unleashed at the heart of Mumbai, India, still one of the most densely populated spots on Earth. The death toll had been in the millions.

He turned to face Aminu. "Do any of the Green War groups have access to ships capable of voidjump?"

Aminu gave Aiden a long look, and not a friendly one. "We know only that Green War operates several privately registered craft. They don't employ Licensed Pilots—legally, at least—so their activities must be confined to the System. But Green War is good at concealment. It wouldn't surprise me if they'd found ways to operate elsewhere in Bound Space."

"V-Prime is the only way in and out of the System," Aiden pointed out. "And Friendship Station strictly regulates all voidjumps from V-Prime. Nobody makes a jump without going through them. How good is security at Friendship Station these days, Colonel?"

Aiden hadn't meant to sound accusatory. DSI shared security responsibilities at Friendship Station, along with its intelligence counterpart from ARM and special forces units from both ARM and the UED.

"Security at Friendship is as good as it can be, Commander Macallan." The tone of Aminu's response was cold as comet ice. "And after these last incidents, security measures have been dramatically expanded. Military presence around the station has doubled, and new jump protocols have been enforced. That includes mandatory boarding and inspection for all nongovernment vessels requesting clearance for voidjump."

Aiden sat back and returned Aminu's unblinking glare. He did not share Aminu's conviction that government involvement was totally off the table. "Good idea. What about government vessels? Are they generally given a free pass to jump, without boarding inspection?"

"What are you implying?"

Aiden felt the hostility directed toward him like a laser burn. He deflected it without letting it get to him, a valuable skill he'd learned the hard way. He'd endured far worse than the likes of Colonel Aminu. Still, the personal vibe of Aminu's animosity made him curious. "I'm not *implying* anything, Colonel. I'm asking a question, pure and simple. Information is all I'm after."

Aminu backed off, a transparent act of self-discipline. "For now, yes. Our own government's vessels—officially registered UED ships—and those from the Allied Republics of Mars are granted access to V-Prime without mandatory board-and-search restrictions. It's an issue of sovereign states, covered by the Ganymede Pact. An issue currently being questioned in light of these recent incidents."

"If that's the case," Aiden pressed, "then it is possible, theoretically at least, that clandestine activity could pass through V-Prime undetected, under the guise of Pact immunity. Are there any elements you know of inside our own government, the UED, or within the Allied Republics of Mars, that might have means or motive to disrupt voidoids?"

Aminu was clearly uncomfortable with the direction of Aiden's questions. A little too close to home, Aiden guessed. But the colonel made another admirable effort to maintain a semblance of objectivity. "I'm sure all of us here have witnessed the dramatic rise of nationalism and isolationist rhetoric in both the UED's Security Council and ARM's Directorate. Those factions may be advocating for more control of the voidoids, but not their outright destruction."

Aiden nodded. "That may be true, but even within the UED's Security Council, the Earth First Party is blatantly stoking the population's fear of alien invasion. They point to Silvanus as proof that alien intelligences exist and take every opportunity to convince people that V-Prime is nothing more than an open door inviting alien races to 'invade' the Solar System. Wouldn't they love to see the voidoids disappear?"

Aminu waved a hand dismissively. "You're referring to the fringe elements of the Earth First Party, led by this character Houda Thunkit. But the Earth First coalition is not in power and may never be. Even if they did succeed in controlling the Security Council, the long-established institutions of the UED would prevent any government-backed move to shut down the voidoids."

Aiden leaned back and folded his arms. He didn't share Aminu's confidence that UED's liberal institutions could withstand a populist tidal wave of fear, ignorance, and hatred. Yes, the Earth First Party was not in power, but they were powerful, and their "fringe" elements had become a rallying point for the party's majority. But Aiden decided to let it go for now. "What about possible factions on Mars, within ARM?"

"As I said, the DSI has assets on Mars," Aminu said stiffly. "Their reports are classified. But I can assure you, any information I find pertinent to this matter will be available to you."

"Need-to-know. Isn't that what it's called, Colonel?"

"Something like that, yes."

Wrong thing to say. Aiden felt heat rising to his face. "You're telling me I don't need to know?"

Aminu cocked his head in a conciliatory gesture. "At this point in time—"

Aiden interrupted Aminu, right hand held up to silence him, then turned to Stegman. "Vice Admiral, let's back up here. Is this a mission briefing?"

Stegman didn't smile, but Aiden knew the man well enough to know he wanted to. "Yes, it is, Commander Macallan."

"And you want me to head this mission, as commander of the *Sun Wolf*, correct?'

"That's right."

"But you haven't exactly told me what this mission is, what you expect me to accomplish. Can you do that now? Sir."

"Fair enough, Commander." Stegman must have known Aiden had reached a limit of restraint that only calm clarification could mitigate. "You will investigate these reports of deliberate voidoid disruptions, track down the perpetrators, and intervene with armed force if necessary. You will begin by taking the *Sun Wolf* into the Alpha-2 Hydri system, the location of the last known incident, in hopes of picking up the trail. Both Colonel Aminu and Dr. Ebadi will accompany you as specialists, in advisory capacities. You will be authorized to go anywhere else in Bound Space your investigation leads, will be given a full complement of military weaponry, and the authorization to use it at your discretion."

Holy shit. That was more than he'd expected. Aiden nodded, straight-faced. "And I, as ship's captain, will have the full authority in the field over all decisions made in service of those mission objectives?"

"That's correct. In the field. Second only to directives from myself or another officer from the Admiralty in my stead."

"And in order to make the best possible decisions in the capacity of ship's captain and mission leader, I will be given all available information I deem necessary. Is that also correct, Vice Admiral?"

"Yes, that is correct as well."

"And finally, am I correct in assuming that authorization for this mission comes from the top, from the president of the UED, Michi Takema?"

Stegman only nodded in confirmation while giving Aiden his "get-on-with-it" look.

"Thank you for that clarification, sir."

Aiden then turned to Aminu and said in a calm, even tone, "I need to know."

Colonel Victor Aminu was not a happy camper, but he matched Aiden's even tone in response. "Point taken. I will revise my response: any information I have that *you*, Commander Macallan, deem pertinent to this matter will be made available to you."

"Thank you, Colonel. I'm glad we understand each other," Aiden said, doubting that such mutual understanding would prevail anytime soon. "You can tell me about possible ARM involvement later. But for now, I'd like to ask the Admiralty why a mission like this has been handed to the Science and Survey Division. Sounds to me more like a job for the Military Space Service."

Admiral Prescott's expression soured even further at this observation. He obviously agreed and was unhappy that it was not so. But it was Stegman who responded. "Yes, we debated that point ourselves. But there are several reasons why it's SSD and not the military, the first of which is purely political. It hasn't been that long since hostilities ceased between the UED and ARM. Things got pretty hot between us and them, both in the Chara system and here in the System. The Chara Treaty put an official end to it, but it's still a delicate situation and suspicions remain. Any overt projection of military presence by either government, beyond basic home world security, is considered unwise at this time. Even though the *Sun Wolf* will be as heavily armed as any UED battle cruiser, it's still on the books as a Science and Survey vessel, and appearances are crucial right now.

"Another reason is the science part. This really is a scientific mission as much as anything else. In-depth knowledge of the voidoids, their relationship to the space we inhabit, could be critical to this mission. That's the primary reason Dr. Ebadi will be going with you. Her expertise in this area is unequaled, apart from Dr. Woo himself."

Yes, Elgin Woo. Aiden had just now decided that Woo's disappearance and his possible whereabouts might become another critical objective of this mission. It would be a hard sell, of course. Especially to the Admiralty. The timing had to be right. But

Stegman seemed to be paving the way in that direction, uninten-
tionally. Aiden let him continue.

"Regardless of who's behind these attacks," Stegman said, "the
more we know about the voidoids, the better chance we'll have
figuring out what kind of technology they're using. That knowledge could lead us directly to who's doing it and why."

"Understood, sir," Aiden said, eager to draw the meeting to a
close. "I look forward to having Dr. Ebadi aboard for this mission.
How are we hooking up with her?"

"You'll be departing with the *Sun Wolf* tomorrow morning
at 0800 hours on a short hop to Luna, where you'll pick up
Dr. Ebadi. But before you make your jump to Alpha-2 Hydri,
you'll be making a brief stop at Dr. Woo's research facility, a place
called the Cauldron out in the Apollo Group."

Interesting. The existence of the Cauldron, Elgin Woo's largely
undisclosed research facility burrowed into a remote asteroid out
in the Apollo Group, was not common knowledge. And while
many renowned scientists did tenures there, their stays were
ambiguously documented. Maryam Ebadi, for instance, was recognized as one of the Domain's leading researchers in the quantum physics of dark energy and cosmology, but her association
with Woo's merry band of geniuses at the Cauldron was deliberately obscure. She was currently working from her tenured position at Luna University.

"And why are we stopping there, sir?" Aiden asked, then
glanced at Ro, who had been sitting quietly without expression
but now showed a glimmer of anticipation.

Stegman paused just long enough for dramatic effect. "That
brings me to the final reason the *Sun Wolf* has become the logical
choice for this mission. Indeed, the only choice. Because it will
soon have an enormous advantage over any other ship in the System. Dr. Ebadi is now the acting director of the Cauldron. As per
instructions transmitted to her by Dr. Woo before his disappearance, a full-scale model of his zero-point drive stands ready at the

Cauldron to be installed in the *Sun Wolf* as an auxiliary propulsion system."

Stegman paused again and took a long breath before continuing. Aiden recognized the man's classic "may-god-help-me" gesture, one that always preceded decisions about which he was deeply conflicted. "And, as chief of the Science and Survey Division, I have authorized this action. After picking up Dr. Ebadi at Luna, you'll proceed to the Cauldron, where their technicians will install this new drive system."

Aiden maintained his straight-faced composure, albeit with some effort. But Ro was grinning ear to ear, a rare sight. Admiral Prescott sat up even straighter, looking resolute, while Colonel Aminu sat motionless, a doubtful frown spreading across his face.

Stegman folded his hands on the table. "Any questions, Commander?"

"Yes. I'll need full transcripts of the *Arcadia's* report on the incident at Alpha-2 Hydri, including all visual and sensor recordings they were able to send us."

Stegman nodded. "I had all that uploaded to the *Sun Wolf's* command log before coming over here today. Level One security. We'll be in contact with you via Holtzman transmission throughout your mission. Let us know if anything else comes up."

"Thank you, sir."

"Further questions?"

"None that can't wait until we're underway, sir. I've got enough to get started."

"Good. Is your crew roster completed yet? The last I heard, your Executive Officer position was still in question. Is that taken care of?"

Aiden turned to Ro, who grinned at him with a thumbs-up.

Aiden said, "It is now, sir."

"Excellent." Stegman smiled. "Briefing is concluded. Good luck, gentlemen."

5

AFTER LEAVING CONFERENCE Room Four, Aiden headed to his quarters, packed his personal gear into one medium-sized duffel, and met Ro at the personnel elevator for transit down to the docking level. He glanced at his chrono. It was just past 22:00 now. Their departure was scheduled for tomorrow at 08:00. Ten hours was plenty of time to ready the ship, brief the crew, then catch some shut-eye onboard before launch. In truth, the *Sun Wolf* was ready to go now, antimatter tanks topped off, all systems humming on standby.

The elevator door hissed open and Aiden and Ro emerged into the cavernous docking bay. It was cold down here, about 6 degrees C, Aiden estimated. The air was dry and smelled of welding fumes, ozone, and a hint of polycyclic aromatic hydrocarbons. After walking about 300 meters and passing through two security checkpoints, they reached the *Sun Wolf*'s docking port. Under Stegman's orders, the ship been moved up the line to the last dock on the arm, terminal 2D, in preparation for launch. They boarded through the forward personnel hatch.

Now that Ro had signed on as XO, Aiden had a full operating crew of seven. That was not counting Hutton, the ship's Omicron-3 AI, who in truth could operate most of the ship's functions perfectly well by himself. Adding his two advisory guests,

Colonel Aminu and Dr. Ebadi, made a total of nine human souls under his command. Nine men and women whose lives depended on the decisions he made. For Aiden, it was a responsibility keenly felt and one he'd only recently grown to welcome.

After stowing his gear in the captain's quarters, he made a ship-wide announcement for all crew to convene on the command bridge for a prelaunch briefing, to commence in 30 minutes. On his way up to the bridge, he ran into Colonel Victor Aminu striding resolutely toward him from the opposite direction.

"Commander Macallan," he said as he stopped and straightened. "I was on my way to see you in your quarters. Could we have a word before your crew briefing? In private?"

The colonel's demeanor had not warmed up one degree since their earlier encounter. If anything, he seemed more aloof and indignant.

"Okay, Colonel. But make it brief. There's a wardroom just up the corridor. Let's go there." Aiden led the way and Aminu followed.

Aiden sat at the small galley table and motioned for Aminu to sit as well, but the colonel remained standing. "What is it, Colonel?"

"I understand I'm here in an advisory capacity," Aminu began, his tone still formal. "But as an agent of the DSI, a branch of the UED's Department of Peace Keeping Operations, I do hold ultimate authority in some areas, even while aboard this ship."

Here we go, Aiden thought. This relationship was headed for trouble. The sooner he could straighten things out between himself and Aminu, the better. But he decided to remain in listening mode, to hear the man out. "And what would those areas include?"

"Part of this mission is to track down whoever might be responsible for deliberate attempts to destroy the voidoids. If and when such person or persons are apprehended, I have the authority to arrest, imprison them in the ship's brig, and deliver them to UED authorities upon our return."

Aiden nodded. "That is correct, Colonel. But you will do so only with my permission. I am captain of this ship, and unless directed otherwise by the Admiralty, I have primary authority over what happens onboard while in the field. That includes the disposition of any person who comes aboard as a suspect in a crime."

Aminu stiffened even more. His jaw muscles tensed. "Commander—"

Aiden held up his hand to interrupt. "Colonel, we're on the same side here. We're both agents of the UED tasked with the same mission. Our goals should be the same. If we both keep our heads about us and not let personal animosities diminish our objectivity, it's likely we'll both agree on most decisions made in pursuit of those goals. We just need to be clear about the chain of command here. Understood?"

Aminu raised his chin a fraction higher. "I understand what you say, Commander."

It was not the conciliatory response Aiden had hoped for, and he suspected the issue would come up again in the very near future. "What other areas of authority concern you?"

Aminu folded his arms across his chest. "Security."

Aiden could guess where this was going. "And...?"

"My *recommendation* is that your crew not be informed of all the details of this mission, including the acquisition of this zero-point drive, unless it is absolutely necessary. And that would be when a crewperson's job is to address a specific aspect of the mission, in which case they may be given whatever information they need to accomplish their task."

Aiden sat forward and crossed his arms on the table. Careful to keep any semblance of amusement from his voice, he asked, "What? You think we may have spies among my crew?"

"This is a serious matter, Commander. There are powerful forces afoot who will stop at nothing to keep us from succeeding in our mission here. And acquiring the zero-point drive will make the *Sun Wolf* a far greater threat to them than it is already."

Aiden immediately became more interested in what Aminu knew about these "powerful forces" and how much of it he'd failed to divulge at their briefing. The man's need-to-know obsession and his pompous tone continued to erode Aiden's patience. "I appreciate the gravity of the matter at hand, Colonel, believe me. But my crew?"

"Yes, your crew. What do you know about them?"

A hell of a lot more than I know about you, asshole! But he didn't go there. Yet.

"I've known and worked with four of the seven crewpersons aboard the *Sun Wolf* for nearly all nine of my years with the Space Service. I trust them implicitly. Three others are new to my command, but they were hand-picked by me from a short list of recommendations by Vice Admiral Stegman. They come with stellar and unblemished records, and I've been favorably impressed by all of them during our shakedown cruises."

Aminu's unyielding expression remained fixed like a mask. He stood silent for a moment before speaking again. "Tell me about them."

"My crew members? Are you serious?"

"Yes, Commander. If you would, please."

Aiden glanced at his chronometer. "You're going to meet them yourself in about 10 minutes. Maybe you should trust your own judgment of character."

"I'd like to hear it from your perspective. Humor me."

"By the looks of it, Colonel, I seriously doubt I could humor you. Now or ever."

Aminu said nothing and continued to glare at him, proving Aiden's point. As ship's captain, Aiden was under no obligation to grant Aminu's request, and he was about to say as much—probably with less tact than was prudent—when he decided to concede. Maybe it would pave the way to a more collegial rapport. "All right, Colonel. But we don't have much time, so I'll be brief. My Data Systems Officer is Faye Desai. She's as sharp as they come, hardworking and honest. My Comm/Scan Officer is Lilly

Alvarez. Same as Faye: bright and dedicated. Both were my crewmates on the *Argo*.

"My Drive Systems Engineer is Lieutenant Zachary Dalton,
the newest member of the crew. He's a brilliant young man in
his mid-20s with an impressive list of academic achievements
in propulsion engineering and five years of notable service in
the Military Service aboard the SS *Independence*, which you may
know had the most advanced drive systems in the Domain before
the *Sun Wolf* was commissioned. My Weapons Officer is Lieutenant (JG) William Hotah, also from the Military Service, also
mid-twenties. Bright and highly motivated. He served aboard the
SS *Endeavor,* the Service's flagship, under Admiral Prescott, and
saw action in the Battle of Chara. He was credited with a crucial kill against an ARM Militia battle cruiser, a near impossible
shot. It was textbook. Literally. A new chapter in the Service's
tactical manual is devoted to the incident. Hotah has some...atti-
tude issues, but that's improved as he's become more a part of the
team."

Aiden paused and looked again at his chronometer before
continuing. "Our pilot is Lista Abahem. She was the *Argo*'s pilot
for most of my tenure on that vessel. Aside from my observation
that she's a superb pilot, probably the most skilled I've ever seen,
I know as much about her as anyone could expect to know about
a Licensed Pilot, which is next to nothing. I'm sure you know
how little control Service ships have over which Licensed Pilot is
assigned to them. That's completely up to the Intersystem Pilots
Agency. But if you're going start doubting the integrity of the
Agency, or any of its pilots, you might as well jump ship now."

Aminu was not amused. Aiden continued. "On the *Sun Wolf*,
the position of Science Officer is mission-dependent. For this
trip, Dr. Ebadi will assume that role once she's aboard. You probably know as much about her as I do. My new Medical Officer is
Dr. Sudha Devi. She graduated top honors from Luna U. Medical
Center and has been a practicing physician for over 10 years, both
on Luna and aboard two different voidships, one from the Mili-

tary Service and the other a Terra Corp survey vessel. Coincidentally, she is a close associate of my XO's wife, Dr. Thea Delamere,
on Luna.

"Which brings me to my Executive Officer, Dr. Roseph Hand,
a man I would absolutely trust with my life and have done so on
numerous occasions."

Aminu held up a hand. "The DSI is familiar with Dr. Hand
and is in fact indebted to him on several accounts, none of which
I can divulge. So I agree with your assessment there. He is the one
member of this crew in which I have 100 percent confidence."

Aiden cocked his head, momentarily stunned, although he
shouldn't have been. Ro Hand was the most complicated and
multifaceted person he'd ever known, and Aiden found himself
continuously reminded of how little he knew about the man
he considered his closest friend. But it was the implication of
Aminu's last sentence that got his goat. He leaned back in his
chair, folded his arms, and fixed his eyes on Aminu's. "And you
can't say the same thing about me, can you? To give me your 100
percent confidence rating."

Aminu remained silent, sensing the rising temperature.

"Okay, Colonel, let's get this out here and now," Aiden said.
"You don't like me and I think I know why. Personally, I don't
give a rat's ass what you think of me. That's something I reserve
for people I actually know and respect. You? I don't really know
yet, and given what I've seen from you so far, the respect part is
going to take a while. If ever. But we're stuck with each other on
this ship with important work to do, the nature of which can only
be hindered by the kind of passive-aggressive shit I'm picking up
from you now."

Aiden straightened up in his chair, turned his head, and pulled
his hair back to show Aminu the left side of his neck. "Let's have
it, Colonel. It's about this, isn't it?"

Aminu reacted as if he'd been slapped. He stared at the spot
on Aiden's neck where the laser-branded *T* should have been but
was no longer.

"That's right, it's not there anymore," Aiden said. "The Rete took care of that. Basically rebuilt my body after the crash on Silvanus. No more facial scar either, and no more limp from the knee injury. Good as new. But the *T* brand is still there, isn't it? Even though it's gone from sight. Even after the official pardon from President Takema herself, the records expunged. But for me, it'll always be there. And apparently for you, too, UED's law man. To the man with the gold star, I'm still an ex-con."

The letter *T* stood for *treason*, the offense for which Aiden had been convicted at age 22. It was no secret, although no longer a matter of public record after the presidential pardon, that Aiden had served three years at the infamous Hayden Federal Correctional Facility, an orbital penal colony out at L4. Its name had been shortened and aptly referred to as Hades by those who knew anything about the horrors that went on there. On Aiden's first day at Hades, they knocked him out cold and branded him with the *T* using a surgical laser, a form of permanent punishment.

It took a moment for Aminu to recover his composure. But there was no sympathy in his voice when he spoke. "You broke the law, Commander."

Aiden was right. He'd struck a nerve. In Victor Aminu's book, Aiden's past crime constituted an indelible stain on his character, placing him several notches below Aminu himself as a human being. Aiden was genuinely disappointed in the man standing across from him, as he had been in other small-minded and self-righteous people who had judged him similarly, people who were deliberately blind to their own human nature and had no understanding of redemption.

Aiden let his hair fall back in place over his neck and turned to face Aminu. "That was 17 years ago, Colonel. I've grown way past the shaming phase. That won't work on me now; a waste of your time."

Aminu appeared to relax and sat down across from Aiden. "Commander, I am not without empathy. The DSI still has the particulars of your case on file. I understand it was a youthful act of vengeance against those you believed were responsible for your mother's death."

Right. The DSI. They had the dirt on anyone, anywhere. If Aminu had read the files, he would have known that when Aiden was 10 years old, his mother, Morgan, had been killed in a freakish construction accident on the lunar surface, attributed to Terra Corp's dismal adherence to common safety standards. The despair that consumed Aiden as a child grew steadily into a smoldering rage against the blind powers that had so carelessly taken his mother's life from him. While attending Luna University, he managed to hack into Terra Corp's computer records and discovered the true story of how his mother had died. Evidence of willful negligence was clear. Someone had *wanted* her to disappear. Her Gaian affiliations and high-profile advocacy for workers' rights were a thorn in the company's side, threatening its profit margin. So she'd been silenced. Permanently. That was when Aiden's rage had grown into an obsession for revenge.

He dug even deeper into Terra Corp's classified records and posted every scandalous factoid he could find on the FreeNet, including the company's efforts to suppress workers' concerns over safety issues and equal pay. But more damaging, Aiden uncovered documentation of widespread corruption, industrial espionage, and sabotage of Martian mining operations carried out by agents from Terra Corp *and* the UED. Technically, an act of war. He posted it on the FreeNet for all to see, not bothering to conceal his identity.

It wasn't long before federal agents came knocking on his door. He was charged under the Espionage Act for supplying intelligence to a foreign government and sentenced to 20 years in prison, to be served at Hades. But Aiden's revelations had fanned into flames an already smoldering popular outrage over Terra Corp's misdeeds. Now confronted with Aiden's evidence of UED complicity, Domain's lawmakers could no longer stand by idly. Aiden had been released after serving only three years. But for him the damage was done, as deeply as if he'd done all 20 years.

Aiden fixed Aminu with dark eyes, unblinking. "I'm not buying it, Colonel. You don't strike me as the empathic type."

Aminu spread his hands imploringly. "Even justified revenge is no excuse for breaking the law."

As excuses go, I can't think of a better one, Aiden thought. But he said, "Save your moralizing for someone else, Aminu. Someone who cares what you think. Maybe you can practice it on the lawbreakers you plan to arrest. If we ever find them."

Aiden was just gearing up to lay into Aminu with more venom when his comm chimed. It was Ro. "Commander, I've got the crew assembled here on the bridge waiting for your briefing."

Aiden looked at his chrono. He'd let his anger get out of control and forgotten the time. Which made him even angrier, at himself this time. "Okay, Ro. I'll be there shortly."

Aminu stood up to leave, but Aiden remained seated. "We're not done yet, Colonel. In the process of vetting me and my crew, you forgot someone. Yourself. How do *we* know you're trustworthy? What makes you beyond reproach?"

Aminu assumed a stance of military attention, as if he were about to salute. "Before joining the DSI, I served with *honor* as an officer in the Nigerian Armed Forces."

Aminu's emphasis on the word "honor" was more than pointed. He remained at attention and said nothing more.

"Ah. The honor ethic of the military." Aiden leaned back again. He was going to enjoy this. "Very impressive, although I believe the current view on that brand of honor concedes there's really no relation at all between honor and virtue. The two don't necessarily go hand in hand. As a result, the status of honor is sometimes bestowed on the wrong people."

Aminu stiffened. "What are you implying, Commander?"

"Only that telling me you served with honor in the military does nothing to prove you're worthy of our trust, or even that you're the right kind of person. Lots of soldiers in the field use honor as a substitute for having to genuinely believe in the cause they're fighting for."

"You're describing false honor," Aminu said, struggling to maintain an even tone. "True honor is internalized and always serves the public cause, not some personal end. *That's* honor, Commander. With virtue."

"Agreed." Aiden shrugged. "There's false honor and true honor. Which kind do you own? Right now, that's as unclear for me as my honor is for you."

"And just how *would* honor become clear to you, sir?" The acid in Aminu's voice had returned.

Aiden stood, his fists clenched at his side, and leaned into Aminu's face. "How? True honor comes from respect, Colonel. Let's say, for instance, if you had spent three years in the most brutal prison in the System, confined cheek by jowl with your enemies every minute of every day, not just engaging them momentarily on the battlefield in the company of your comrades. And if you had come out of that place alive without having to join any of the ruthless gangs for protection, that could mean only two things. One, that you are the most dangerous psychopath in the yard and everyone is scared shitless of you. Or, two, that somehow you'd earned genuine respect among the kind of people who, by circumstance, respect almost no one. Ever. People who judge you only on the strength of your humanity. If I knew you'd earned that kind of respect, *then* your honor would be clear to me."

Aminu had stepped back reflexively, as if Aiden's words had been physical blows. The tense silence between them seemed to explode with a thunderous boom—but it was the sudden and loud rumble of a very real explosion. The floor beneath them shook and tilted. Metal fittings in the wardroom vibrated wildly. Two coffee mugs bounced out of their rack and broke on the deck. The roar grew in volume then tapered off and was replaced by screeching alarms. Aiden steadied himself against the table. He and Aminu stared at each other, wide-eyed.

Aiden's comm beeped. It was Ro. "Commander? We've got a problem."

Aiden straightened his back, eyes still locked on Aminu. But his anger was displaced by a sickening dread. "We're on our way, Ro."

6

HAWKING STATION
Domain Day 81, 2218

It took Aiden and Aminu less than a minute to reach the bridge. The crew were at their assigned stations in Level One readiness. They looked alert but anxious. Ro sat at the Ops station, alert but calm. Hawking Station's general alarm sirens shrieked through the comm. The *Sun Wolf*'s own internal alerts howled, adding to the earsplitting cacophony. Aiden had to shout to be heard over the din.

"Alvarez, shut down all alarms!" The internal alarms went quiet first, followed by the station alarms when Alvarez cut the comm link. Aiden barked, "Status report, Ro!"

"An explosion. One moorage down from us, at 2C. The entire station is on Level One Alert. Security and Rescue Forces are on the way. There's no apparent damage to the *Sun Wolf*. At least nothing we know about yet. There's a small hull breach in the station's docking corridor adjacent to the explosion site. But the auto-mend bots are already on it. Decompression is minimal."

"Casualties?" Aiden kept his voice calm, but his gut churned.

"At least five fatalities confirmed so far, all dock workers. Fortunately, no vessel was docked at 2C."

Ro let that last statement hang in the air. Aiden knew why. The *Sun Wolf* had been docked at 2C no more than two hours ago, just before the ship was advanced up the line to 2D for launch prep. Aiden glanced at Aminu. The colonel nodded silently, like a man whose worst nightmare had only deepened upon awakening.

Aiden turned back to Ro. "Any details from Security?"

"The initial assessment from security cams suggests an explosive device concealed in one of 2C's magnetic docking assemblies. Detonated either remotely or by a timer."

"Right," Aiden said. "Exactly where it would cause maximum damage to a vessel moored there. What kind of bomb? Radiation?"

"No. It appears to be a conventional explosive, but with a very large, high-velocity shrapnel yield."

Aiden glanced up at the ceiling. "Hutton. Do you detect any damage to the *Sun Wolf*?" Aiden knew the fastest way to determine the ship's physical condition was to ask the Omicron-3 AI whose neural net extended throughout the ship.

"Only superficial scoring along the armor plating astern. From errant shrapnel strikes." Hutton's disembodied voice sounded perfectly human, even coming from the wall-mounted audio transducers. "Had our ship been docked at 2C, as it recently was, the damage would have been considerable."

"I don't like it," Aminu said, his head lowered like a bull ready to charge.

"Nor do I, Colonel. I think it's time to shove off. Ahead of schedule. Ro, ready the ship to disengage and drop to launch point."

Ro nodded and got busy. From the Comm/Scan station, Alvarez spoke up, her voice tight with tension. "Commander, we have a call from Admiral Stegman."

"Put him through, bridge-wide."

Stegman's face materialized on the forward view screen. His outward appearance remained stoic, but Aiden could easily read the anxiety in his eyes. "Commander Macallan. You now have orders to depart the station immediately, as soon as you can make ready."

"We're on it now, sir."

"Good. We don't know enough about this bombing to say the *Sun Wolf* was the intended target, but the sooner you're off this station, the better."

"Agreed, sir. We're ready to shove off now. I assume we're still on track to pick up Dr. Ebadi at Luna?"

"Affirmative. But now you'll be arriving about twelve hours ahead of schedule. We'll try to speed up her transport shuttle, but you may be parked in lunar orbit for a while before she can get to you. Admiral Prescott and I have agreed to give you a military escort from Luna onward to V-Prime. The frigate SS *Kepler* is currently inbound to Luna from outer-system patrol. She'll pick you up there and escort you to the Cauldron. We'll dispatch a battle cruiser from Friendship Station to meet you at the Cauldron. She'll escort you the rest of the way to V-Prime."

"Acknowledged." Aiden wasn't sure the escorts were necessary, but he was shaken enough by the bombing to be grateful for the company.

"Unfortunately," Stegman continued, "there are no flight-ready military vessels here at Hawking Station. You'll be on your own for the short hop to Luna."

"Yes, sir. We'll keep our eyes open."

"See that you do, Commander. Good luck." And with that, Stegman's face vanished from the screen.

Aiden turned toward his crew. They had heard from Stegman part of what he intended to tell them in his briefing, and more than anyone had expected until a few minutes ago. All seven crewpersons were present. Their reaction to being attacked by an unknown foe was written on their faces in as many different ways.

"I'll fill you in on the rest later," he told them, "after we're underway. For now, let's do our jobs."

He moved to the command chair, situated at center of the bridge's circular floor layout. He sat and turned to the Ops station on his immediate left, where Ro sat. "XO, inform the station's dockmaster of our departure and comply with their usual instructions."

He then faced forward to the three stations spread out in front of him. The Helm, the center station of the three, was occupied by Pilot Lista Abahem. Not yet in neurolinkage, she sat upright in her flight couch, intent on the control module in front of her. Without the linkage cap in place, her smooth, hairless head seemed to glow with pale luminescence. Her demeanor, as always, remained mute and serene. Aiden spoke to her in even tones. "Lista, bring the ship out of dock. When clear, set course for lunar orbit with turnaround at midpoint."

Aiden turned to Comm/Scan station, positioned to the right of the Helm. "Alvarez, do a broad scan of local space to identify all vessels in our immediate vicinity. Then cross-check that with the latest update from ISBS. Designate any vessels in our vicinity as threat potentials. Even registered cargo vessels and private yachts."

The Intersystem Broad Scan network had sensor scans positioned throughout the Sol System to track all registered vessels within its realm. Vessels that wanted to be kept track of, that is. Plenty of others flew under the radar—literally. Even the most advanced radar-based sweeps had limitations and could be defeated by even more advanced stealth technology.

Aiden then turned toward Tactical station, to the left of the helm. William "Billy" Hotah was focused laser-like on the tactical screen. It flickered with activity in front of him. Aiden had almost gotten used to Hotah's exotic appearance but was still struck by the young man's fearsome countenance every time he looked at him. His smooth, copper-toned complexion, and high cheekbones accentuated a gaunt, stern-looking face, punctuated by intense dark brown eyes. His black hair, considerably longer than Aiden's, was parted in the middle and fell shoulder-length at either side. But his most striking feature was a speckled band resembling red war paint tattooed across his face extending horizontally from ear to ear, passing beneath his eyes and over the bridge of his nose. It gave him a feral look that belied his razor-sharp intelligence.

"Lieutenant Hotah, bring our point-defense systems to Level One status. Offensive weapons to remain at Level Two. For now. Set defensive shields to Level two."

Hotah nodded once in a silent gesture that Aiden had come to recognize as both acknowledgement of the order and confirmation that it was already done. The point-defense system was a grid of phased-array plasma lasers positioned across the surface of the *Sun Wolf*. It was designed to intercept incoming enemy fire, including missiles and other kinetic projectiles at midrange and closer. The ship's defensive shield, when fully powered, could absorb both the kinetic energy of incoming projectiles and EM energy of laser weapons and particle beams.

He turned 90 degrees to his left to face Drive Systems station. Zachary Dalton had already swiveled his flight chair to face Aiden, awaiting orders. Dalton was older than Hotah, but not by much. He was sturdily built, trim, with squared shoulders and a square jaw. His light brown hair was cut short but styled in a casually rakish tumble-down covering half his forehead. He wouldn't have been considered particularly handsome were it not for the perpetual grin on his face, a sly but genuine expression, and the blue eyes that shined with good-natured mirth, even in the most stressful situations. He obviously considered himself a smooth talker, but in the short time Aiden had known him, Dalton had proven himself unusually prone to stunning faux pas in social situations. He was also extremely good at his job.

"Lieutenant Dalton," Aiden said. "What's the fastest way to get from here to lunar orbit?"

"The fastest *and* safest way, sir? Or just the fastest?" Dalton's face lit up.

Smiling inwardly at Dalton's folksy south Texan accent, Aiden said, "The fastest."

Dalton grinned and made a quick mental calculation. "Well, sir, being that we're starting out here at Earth-Moon L5, that makes us 384,400 klicks from Luna. Fastest way to lunar orbital insertion would be to initiate continuous thrust at 3 Gs to turnaround, then continuous thrust at 3 Gs deceleration the rest of the way. That'd be about two hours total time."

Aiden, of course, knew all this but wanted to give Dalton the chance to shine in the moment. "That's it? Two hours?"

"Yes, sir. This new beamed core M/AM drive can put out 300 mega-Newtons of thrust, 600 terawatts thrust power, with an exhaust velocity of over 5,000 KPS. No other ship in the System can do that."

That was a lot of juice, Aiden had to admit. "Very good, Lieutenant," he said. "When ready, make available to the helm 3 Gs continuous thrust, before and after turnaround."

"Yes, sir." Dalton grinned even wider at the prospect of lighting up the M/AM torch full blast. "Yahoo! Let's see what this baby can do!"

Dalton's enthusiasm lightened the mood and elicited smiles from some of the crew. Even Ro cast a droll expression toward Aiden. Colonel Aminu, who remained standing next to Aiden, did not look amused. Nor did Billy Hotah.

Data Systems station was situated on the opposite side of the bridge from Drive Systems, 90 degrees to Aiden's right. He turned in that direction. "All systems go, Faye?"

Faye Desai, Data Systems Officer, looked back at him. She was slender and dark-eyed, in her late twenties, of Israeli descent. Not your typical data-systems geek, she possessed a keen sense of humor, along with an alluring smile she seemed to reserve only for Aiden. She and Aiden had been crewmates on the *Argo* where, from the onset, an undeniable chemical attraction had ignited between them. Undeniable but never indulged. Aiden's fidelity to Skye Landen was the real deal and Desai knew it. Still, she couldn't help teasing him with it.

"Yep, all systems are go," she said with a coy smile. "The Omicron is humming along sweetly."

Hmmm. Sweetly. Aiden broke eye contact quickly and turned to Life Support station. Medical Officer Dr. Sudha Devi sat facing him, smiling calmly. The daughter of a long line of physicians from Delhi, she was stout and pleasant-looking, in her mid-fifties. Her dark hair fell in waves to her shoulders, with a long streak of gray running to one side. Aiden thought he saw a subtle gleam of humor in Devi's eyes after Faye's response.

Whatever it meant, Aiden knew it wasn't judgmental. Not from Sudha Devi. In the brief time Aiden had known her during the *Sun Wolf*'s shakedown exercises, he had found her to be one of the most tolerant, warm, empathetic, and insightful human beings he'd ever met. There was a gracefulness in her eyes, her voice, her movements, and in the way she regarded everyone she met. She could be brutally honest, but everything about her radiated compassionate enlightenment. He felt lucky to have her as part of his crew, for his own sake personally, and for the general health of his entire crew.

Before he could ask, Devi nodded and said, "Life-support systems are also humming along sweetly." She smiled at Desai, sharing a private amusement.

Aiden sighed and looked at his chrono. It was just after midnight, 00:17 to be exact. A long day was about to get even longer. He turned to Ro. "Launch."

He heard the dull clang of the magnetic docking latches disengaging and felt the momentary dropping sensation of the ship "falling" below the station under cryo-hydrogen thrusters. On the forward view screen, he watched in realtime as Hawking's superstructure passed out of sight above. The *Sun Wolf* reached its launch point two kilometers below Hawking Station, and the attitude thrusters turned the ship forward to face Luna. Without preamble, Pilot Abahem ignited the M/AM drive. A sudden ultralow frequency rumble filled the bridge, accompanied by a barely perceptible sensation of lateral G-forces along the axis of thrust just before the ship's inertial compensators kicked in.

As a function of the gravitational transducers, inertial compensation not only negated the G-forces the crew would normally experience, but it also allowed the ship's decks to lay parallel to the axis of thrust while providing a constant "downward" force of 1 G at deck surfaces. Laymen called it "artificial gravity." Spacers called it essential to life when working the Deep years on end.

After a postlaunch status check, Aiden gathered the crew in front of him on the bridge. "As you know by now, we're headed to Luna to pick up our second passenger, a prominent physicist, Dr. Maryam Ebadi. The other non-crew person aboard is Colonel Victor Aminu, who I have not yet properly introduced to you. He's from the UED's DPKO, the Department of Peace Keeping Operations, and is here to assist us in our mission."

Aiden deliberately omitted the finer detail of Aminu's position as an agent of the DPKO's security and intelligence service. No need to inject further paranoia at this point. He glanced at Aminu, now seated at one of the wall-mounted personnel benches. The man gave a small greeting nod to everyone in general and seemed relieved at Aiden's choice of omission. Aiden doubted Aminu would be as relieved when he heard the next part.

"The mission we've been tasked with is to investigate a probable hostile incident by an unidentified vessel out in the Alpha-2 Hydri system, resulting in the disappearance of a Domain survey vessel, the SS *Arcadia*. She vanished attempting to voidjump out of the system while the voidoid was in a state of flux. The circumstances are both suspicious and scientifically intriguing, which is why both Colonel Aminu and Dr. Ebadi are coming along.

"After picking up Dr. Ebadi, we'll be heading to V-Prime for a voidjump into the Alpha-2 Hydri system. But first we're taking a slight detour to a research station out in the Apollo Group to pick up some scientific equipment that'll help us in our mission. Due to the sensitivity of this mission, I'm invoking Delta priority protocol aboard the *Sun Wolf* as of now. That's as close to military protocol as it gets for a science vessel. It bestows upon me, as commander, powers of authority that extend beyond those of a normal science or survey mission, including enforcement and discipline. It also includes a personnel comm lockout. That means no personal communications, incoming or outgoing. Is that clear to everyone?"

He made eye contact with each of them in a semicircle, from left to right. Satisfied that his message had been received, he eased up. "Good. That's it in a nutshell. I know you'll have questions, but they'll have to wait until we have more information."

Aiden could tell by their fidgeting that the crew indeed had more questions, but they also had the good sense to heed the note of finality in his voice. Aminu looked unhappy with the details already given out but satisfied with the ones Aiden had withheld. It was a compromise Aiden could live with. For now.

When the *Sun Wolf* reached the halfway point to Luna, the M/AM drive powered down long enough for the attitude thrusters to turn the ship in the opposite direction before reigniting the drive for the deceleration leg. Travelling close to 106 kilometers per second, they needed to shed most of that momentum before reaching Luna for orbital insertion. It meant accelerating in the opposite direction with the same thrust and for the same duration—the classic brachistochrone maneuver torch ships had been using in space for nearly a century.

An hour later, Pilot Abahem shut down the drive and let the ship coast into orbital insertion at 3 km/sec. She maneuvered the *Sun Wolf* into a parking orbit 96 kilometers above the lunar surface over the southern hemisphere, not far from Tycho City. At 02:21, Lilly Alvarez notified the Orontus Space Port that they were in position and ready to receive passenger Maryam Ebadi. The port controller informed them that Ebadi was still in transit to Orontus. Every effort had been made to speed up her departure, but the soonest they could get their passenger aloft was 10:30.

So, they had some waiting to do. Most of the crew had been awake on-shift for nearly 20 hours. Aiden ordered split-shift duties all around—four hours on, four off—to give everyone a chance for some shut-eye before Dr. Ebadi came aboard. He assigned himself first watch at Command and had Ro hit the bunk for four hours. At 06:30, Ro was back on the bridge to relieve him. Looking surprisingly refreshed as Aiden passed him on the way to his own quarters, Ro glanced at him and said, "Sleep. The final frontier."

7

LUNAR ORBIT
Domain Day 81, 2218

ONLY AFTER AIDEN entered his quarters and saw his bunk off to one side, beckoning to him, did he realize how exhausted he was. He'd been up for 24 hours. A lot had happened in that time. He drew a glass of water from the small galley, sat on the side of his bunk and drank, feeling the clear water slide down his throat into his stomach, cooling his core, calming his nerves. "Hutton. Play 'Idle Moments,' Grant Green, please. Volume medium-low."

"Yes, Aiden," the AI said. "An excellent recording, from 1963 on the Blue Note label, composed by Duke Pearson. A true classic. There's an interesting story about that particular recording date—"

"Hutton. Enough. Just the music, please." Aiden knew Hutton's appreciation for the old American classics had grown far beyond his already prodigious social interaction algorithms. Ever since their extraordinary experience on Silvanus, where the AI had used the music of John Coltrane to conceive a common language for communicating with the Rete, Hutton's appreciation of that supreme art form had become organic. Aiden believed Hutton genuinely *enjoyed* the music, if such a thing were possible for a neural net AI.

As the slow, hypnotic tempo of "Idle Moments" began to fill the space around him, Aiden removed his shoes and lay back on his bunk. He felt the muscles in his shoulders relax. The tension around his eyes and in his jaw loosened. He began the breathing exercise Skye had taught him, slow and regular. The Flowform mattress under him gradually molded to the contours of his body, cradling him as he closed his eyes. He heard his own heartbeat slowing evenly to a ballad tempo, felt his blood pulsing through the vessels of his body with each ventricular contraction. He breathed in air that held a subtle aroma of sandalwood, emanating from a single bar of exotic bath soap sitting all the way across the room, another gift from Skye.

As Grant Green's guitar solo meandered through its melodic explorations, Aiden fell even deeper inside. He felt the water he had consumed reach his gut and sensed its molecules passing from his intestinal lumen into the plasma of his bloodstream, and from there to interstitial spaces and cells throughout his body. He felt the neurotransmitters in his brain's auditory system responding to the music as it reached his ears. He tasted the music, smelled it, saw its dancing colors beneath his closed eyelids. He felt the boundaries blurring between his sense of self and the spaces around him and sensed a valve in his consciousness opening up, allowing him to pass into a more fluid, hyperconnected space...

Then it all collapsed.

Back inside himself, he stared up at the cold, hard metal ceiling. The chrono at his bedside displayed time moving on, second by second. All the objects around him became crisply separate, harshly distinct. His breathing had grown more rapid but remained regular. He recognized the region of consciousness he'd just fallen from. Oh, yes. Recognized it all too well. Knew that it was, in part, due to the lasting effects of Continuum, the drug he'd struggled to wean himself from. But he also recognized it as the threshold to the same hyperexpanded consciousness he'd experienced on Silvanus during his neurolink with the Rete. A place he both feared and yearned to revisit with every fiber of his being. A place in time and space he would never forget or ever recover from. A reality so complete and inclusive, so egoless and positive with light and love, so intense with meaning, that its stark absence had left Aiden stranded on its cold shores, naked and alone. Shivering with loss.

He rolled onto his side and pulled the thermoblanket over his shoulders, feeling a sudden chill. He'd started taking low doses of Continuum soon after his return from the Chara system. It was the same drug the Licensed Pilots sometimes took to augment their talent for linking with a ship's Omicron neural net, an essential function for high-velocity voidjumps. It was a function that only Licensed Pilots trained from childhood could provide, and sometimes only with the aid of Continuum. Not surprisingly, Continuum was a genetically tailored derivative of psilocybin, the psychoactive ingredient of hallucinogenic mushrooms.

But what most people didn't know was that pilots often took low doses of Continuum *after* linkage, off-shift, to ease their times away from the Omicron's addictive embrace. It was a kind of therapy for what the Licensing Agency had originally called Post-Linkage Depression but later changed to Post-Linkage Syndrome due to the stigma around the diagnosis of depression. Regardless of its given name, the nature of PLS remained the same. It was a form of depression akin to bipolar disorders where the hyperconnected state of linkage with the ship's Omicron neural net represented the high-energy phase. The low-energy phase was precipitated by disconnection from the linkage. Whenever pilots talked about it—which was almost never—they described it as a profound sense of loss. In their profession it was considered an occupational hazard, and because Continuum could mimic that hyperconnected state, it was often used in carefully calculated doses to ease the precipitous drop from the heights of neurolinkage.

Aiden understood completely, probably more than anyone who wasn't a pilot. Maybe even more than a pilot. The linkage

he'd experienced with the Rete on Silvanus had been with a
neural net billions of times greater and more complex—and
evolved—than any man-made AI. It had extended to embrace a
whole planet. His linkage with the Rete had been a voluntary act
of salvation, a courageous and selfless one, necessary to save the
life of the planet. For that opportunity, he would be forever grateful. But its aftermath had left him with a malaise he couldn't quite
shake.

The Space Service physicians had suggested limited dosages of
Continuum soon after his return to the System. It had worked,
too, for a while. At least before he started to use it a little too
often. His usage had morphed into an escape from his pain rather
than a tool to help him confront it clear-eyed, to work through
the darkness on his own. It became a means unto itself, a denial of
the inner strengths he had acquired but could not fully acknowl-
edge. While Continuum was a unique derivative of psilocybin,
its pharmacokinetics were very similar. It activated specific sero-
tonin receptors in the brain, the same ones responsible for the
hallucinogenic effects of psilocybin. But it also activated certain
dopamine pathways in the brain, which made it potentially addictive.

And even though the effects of Continuum dissipated within
several hours, if taken often enough—too often—its secondary
effects could linger, leading to a perpetual state of low-grade disconnection from the real world. That, and its addictive potential,
began to trouble Aiden. He worried that it would interfere with
his judgment, with his ability to command a voidship. He could
not allow that to happen. Never. He was stronger than that. He
had choices. He only had to believe in himself enough to make
the right ones. Sudha Devi, his new Medical Officer, had helped
show him the way and to control a Continuum habit that threatened to ruin him.

Aiden wondered even now if his decision to take Dr. Devi on
as part of his crew had been prompted by some subliminal intuition he had about her, that she was uniquely qualified to help

him personally, as well as providing the emotional intelligence his crew would need to weather the storm they were about to face. Yes, she was a close associate of Dr. Thea Delamere, Luna's preeminent physician/healer, Ro's wife and Skye's close friend. But it was Devi's impressive resumé that had gotten her in the door for an interview. After one minute of their meeting, Aiden knew she was the one. He could tell right away that she *saw* him, effortlessly, noninvasively, compassionately. And if she could see him, the hidden and conflicted Aiden Macallan, then she could surely do the same for the rest of his motley crew. Bottom line: he trusted her. And the trust freed him to seek her help.

Devi had responded with the vision of someone who already knew his pain, recognized its source, and believed absolutely in Aiden's own inner strength to conquer it. Now, thanks to Sudha Devi, he had better control of the situation. He still had a bottle of Continuum in his cabinet, but now he made better choices. Almost always...

The tenor sax solo on "Idle Moments" was winding down, one of the most eloquent expressions of passion and musical intelligence in the history of recorded jazz. Aiden rolled over to lie on his back and fluffed his pillow. He needed sleep but couldn't persuade his brain to comply. Hutton, who monitored everything aboard the *Sun Wolf,* including the crew's life signs, had noticed. His voice gently intoned over the comm, "Aiden?"

"What is it, Hutton?"

"I noticed you were awake, otherwise I would not have addressed you."

"I know that. Thank you, my electromagnetic friend. What's up?"

"I wanted you to know that a personal communication for you arrived just before the comm lockdown. It's from Dr. Skye Landen. Do you want to open it now or after your sleep?"

Aiden felt his heart beat faster. A pang of longing settled in his gut, a sadness so akin to the loss he'd experienced leaving Silvanus it frightened him. Skye. The woman he loved and who had helped him find the answers he'd needed to save Silvanus. His separation from her opened up a black hole of darkness at his core, like the down phase of PLS hollowing into a bottomless pit. Just when the doors between them opened up, just as the integration of all his disparate parts grew within reach, he and Skye had been parted.

The inexorable currents of human events on a history-changing scale had pulled them in two different directions. Soon after returning to Luna with Aiden, Skye had departed again for the Chara system to head up the newly founded Silvanus Project. He'd been required to stay in-system as commander of the Service's new flagship and prepare for a mission he now feared might keep them apart for a long time. Or maybe forever.

"Aiden? The message from Dr. Landen?"

Aiden rose to sit on the side of his bunk and rubbed his eyes as the final chorus of "Idle Moments" whispered to a close. "Yes, now would be fine, Hutton. Thanks."

Hutton was surely aware that Aiden couldn't have slept a wink knowing a message from Skye awaited him. He no doubt knew that Skye and Aiden had agreed on exchanging messages every other day, and today was that day. Aiden got up, padded in his socks over to his comm desk, and faced the screen. He paused for a moment, preparing himself emotionally, absently fiddling with the gold ring on his left-hand ring finger. It was the twin of the one Skye wore, a simple gold ring with a Gaian symbol impressed into its surface. Skye had given it to him for his thirty-eighth birthday. "Open the message, Hutton."

The comm screen blinked once then resolved to frame the head-and-shoulders image of Skye Landen. Aiden felt an ache in his chest and took a deep breath to relieve it. She was, as always, beautiful. Not so much in a classic statuesque way, but blessed with a purely natural attractiveness that spoke of good genes, healthy living and a positive outlook on life. Still a young woman—she had turned 33 in the same month that Aiden turned 39—she was of Swedish heritage, a natural blond with clear blue eyes, fair complexion and a hint of freckles across her cheeks that had once (according to her) been far more prominent as a child. Of medium build and erect bearing, she stood almost as tall as Aiden. Her smile from the screen was like the morning sun banishing darkness from Aiden's soul. "Hey there," she said.

Their video messages came with a four-hour lag time, a delay that precluded normal dialogue. That was the time it took to get to and from the Holtzman buoy in their respective star systems. It didn't matter that they were 27 light-years apart because, like voidjumping, Holtzman transmission between star systems was instantaneous. Only the leg of transmission through realspace took time.

"I hope this message finds you well, my love," she said. "I'm doing fine, but I'll just say this right now because it's what I'm feeling most, then I promise I won't get all mushy after that: I miss you, Aiden. And I love you."

Aiden felt his eyes moisten and wiped at them before anything recognizable as a tear could develop. Skye paused and made the same motion before putting the moment aside and continuing. She was good at making that transition—far better than Aiden. "The Project is coming along full speed, and in several different directions at once. We're making incredible progress in understanding how the Rete has regulated the ecosphere of Silvanus over the last several million years and how it altered that process to include what it does *not* regulate, to allow a measure of chaos into the system. That last part came from your interaction with the Rete when you were there. We're learning how all that applies to restoring Earth's forests and oceans and to the terraforming projects on Mars. It's exciting and I've been busy. Too busy, maybe. Some real sleep once in a while would be helpful, I guess.

"The energy shield around Silvanus is still in place, of course, as it has been since you left. Not being able to visit the planet in person, to walk through its forests and to breath its air, is driving us crazy here. So far, you're the only human being to have done that, and for all we know, you may be the last. Our position here at the orbital station is still the closest we can get, and we have to rely totally on Hutton's ability to communicate with the Rete through the Omicron-3 hardware you left down there on the surface.

"On a positive note, progress in our work has been accelerated by some amazing advances in Hutton's linguistic connection with the Rete. As you know, the whole scheme is based on music. I honestly don't understand a word of what he tells me about it, but he said a new breakthrough happened when he combined elements of Liszt's Piano Sonata in B Minor with the modal improvisations of John Coltrane on his composition 'Miles' Mode.' He said you'd understand."

Aiden had to smile. He did understand, some of it at least. Both compositions were in B minor. Beyond that, they were totally different, which was probably why it worked. Bridging such a wide gulf between two brilliant pieces of music with one common strand, the B minor scale, would generate a more finely detailed template on which to base a common language between two vastly different but structurally similar intelligences. Between Hutton's neural net and the Rete's planet-wide neural net of mycorrhizae. It was an elegant approach, one that only Hutton could have conceived.

"As much as we're learning about the Rete and Silvanus as a whole, we still know almost nothing about this energy field surrounding the planet that prevents us, or anything with mass, from going down there. What is it? Why did it materialize when it did? And how long will it remain? The Rete itself either doesn't know or for some reason can't tell us.

"But something more immediate is beginning to worry us here," she said, shifting gears, "and I'm wondering if you know anything about it. We've picked up signs of multiple voidoid fluxes at the Chara voidoid occurring over the last several days. It's unusual activity, more frequent than anything on record. And now we're picking up rumors from Sol about a possible enforced lockdown of V-Prime. I don't need to tell you how anxious that makes everyone here. Including me. But I'm the lead person and I need to put a good face on it, to remain optimistic. Any information you have, that you're free to share, would help."

She paused and glanced at her chrono. "Anyway, there's so much more going on here to tell you about, but I have very little time right now. I've got a meeting with the principal terraforming researchers from Mars, new people who arrived here yesterday. That's in about 10 minutes, so I need to sign off now. I am *so* looking forward to hearing back from you. I hope you can send me something today. It feels like such a long time since I heard from you last, even when it's only been two days. I promise I'll record a longer message next time."

Skye stayed quiet for a brief moment, as if switching from left-brain verbal mode to right-brain meditative. She looked directly at him and, even as a digital image, Aiden felt himself fall into her clear blue eyes. "I'll say it again, Aiden. I love you. Be well."

The screen went blank.

The joy he'd felt being with her for those few moments came crashing down. The black hole in his stomach swirled again, sucking the light from the room. That he could not respond to her message only made it worse. He'd just invoked a Delta priority protocol aboard the *Sun Wolf* barring all crew members from incoming or outgoing personal communications. Skye's message had come in just minutes before that. As captain of the ship, he could certainly authorize himself to send her a response and not tell anyone. But that was out of the question. He couldn't do it. He would not betray the trust of his crew, even if they'd never know about it.

The thought of Skye not knowing why he didn't respond, that she might fear for his safety—or worse, doubt his love for her—made it hurt all the more. He felt himself on the edge of a precipice looking down into the abyss, teetering more precariously than he had in many months. He glanced across the room to the med cabinet, where the bottle of Continuum sat behind its mirrored door. He got up and walked toward it. He raised his hand to open it, then stopped as he saw his face in the mirror. He looked into his own eyes.

No. He had choices. He had a job to do. The lives of the crew, of people he cared about, depended on him. He had a mission to accomplish, one that a growing unease told him would impact the lives of *all* people. He had choices. And he made one.

Aiden dropped his hand from the cabinet and returned to his bunk. He lay on his back and, as before, began his breathing exercises. "Hutton. Play ocean sounds. Volume, low. Do not disturb. If I'm not awake by 10:00, wake me."

"Yes, Aiden. Rest well."

Aiden closed his eyes and felt his heartbeat slowing. He envisioned the sun rising again, burning away the darkness from behind his eyes. Its warmth felt like Skye's love, but its light was all his own. He drifted out into a clear blue ocean, its waters calm and deep.

8

LUNAR ORBIT
Domain Day 82, 2218

AIDEN RETURNED TO the bridge at 10:10 to relieve Ro. Three hours of sleep out of 24 wasn't ideal, but enough to recharge him. He sat at the command chair and looked around at his crew. Busy at their stations, some looked more rested than others. Ro gave him a status report.

"The transport shuttle with Dr. Ebadi aboard," he said, "is on schedule to launch from Orontus in about 15 minutes. No sign of hostiles. All scans are clear of any unidentified vessels in our vicinity. Our escort, the SS *Kepler*, is still en route but should be alongside around 13:00 hours. Nothing new from Admiral Stegman."

When Ro said nothing more, Aiden sat back. "Thanks, XO."

He looked forward to having Ebadi aboard. Her expertise in the study of voidoids would be critical to puzzling out what was happening with the void fluxes, and her seminal work with zeropoint fields would be invaluable once the ZPD was installed in the *Sun Wolf*. But equally important was her insight into Elgin Woo's work and how it might inform Aiden's unspoken plan to find the eccentric physicist. If indeed Woo was still alive. He was beginning to believe Victor Aminu's claim that larger forces were at work here. Dangerous powers that only Elgin Woo could help them defeat.

Lilly Alvarez interrupted his thoughts. "The transport shuttle has launched from Orontus. ETA 10 minutes."

"Good. XO, you have the bridge. I'm heading to the docking bay to greet Dr. Ebadi. Dr. Devi, would you accompany me, please?"

"With pleasure," Devi said. Just as they were exiting the bridge, the ship's tactical alarms went off, red lights flashing from all bridge consoles.

Hotah's head jerked up. "Incoming missile! Impact 58 seconds."

Aiden rushed back to the command chair. "Hutton?"

"Shielding is activated, Level One," the AI said calmly. "And point-defense is online."

The point-defense system was automated, controlled by the AI, and could respond within a millisecond of detecting enemy projectiles. It activated a grid of potent laser weapons that covered a 360-degree defensible zone around the ship. But it was a short-range system, best for close-in encounters.

"Has point-defense acquired the target?"

"Yes, Commander," Hutton responded. "But—"

"But the missile isn't aimed at us," Hotah interrupted before Hutton could finish.

"What?"

"It's targeting Dr. Ebadi's shuttle, not the *Sun Wolf*."

Holy shit! "Is it within range of our point-defense?"

"Yes, sir. But..." Hotah said nothing more, lost in concentration.

"But what?"

"Impact with shuttle in 30 seconds," Hutton said.

"Lieutenant?" Aiden kept his voice calm even as fear and anger jolted up his spine.

"Point-defense won't engage the target, sir," Hotah said.

"Won't engage? Why? Point-defense has more than enough time to target and fire."

"Yes, to protect *us*. But not the shuttle."

Aiden's heartbeat faltered.

"Impact with shuttle in 15 seconds," Hutton said.

Hotah remained silent, concentration focused on his console. Aiden saw his hand flick to tap the surface. An abrupt crackling sound rang though the ship like a lightning strike.

"Missile killed," Hotah said, poker-faced, eyes still fixed on the screen in front of him.

The entire crew had turned from their stations to face Hotah, eyes wide. No one had dared to breathe, including Aiden. Lilly Alvarez broke the stunned silence. "Confirmed. Missile destroyed. Dr. Ebadi's shuttle is unharmed, still inbound. Docking in eight minutes."

Aiden let out a slow, controlled breath. "Mr. Hotah. What happened?"

"I hit it with our long-range laser cannon. Sir." Hotah had finally turned in his seat toward Aiden. His face remained impassive, but his dark eyes burned with some inner storm.

"Weapons system was on Level Two standby," Aiden said. "How could the laser cannon power up so fast?" But he already knew the answer.

"Yes, sir, it was. I brought it up to full power, Level One, as we approached Luna."

"Without consulting me first." A statement, not a question.

"I thought it was prudent, sir."

"It *was* prudent," Aiden admitted. "Good call, Lieutenant. I assumed our point-defense system had broader parameters."

Hotah nodded his head once. "The point-defense system is superefficient at taking out incoming projectiles aimed at us. But if the incoming weapon is aimed somewhere else, not at our ship, it won't fire. The missile was headed toward the shuttle, not us, so the system tagged it as a nonthreat and ignored it. It would have taken out the shuttle. I had to use the cannon."

Aiden felt his face burn. Granted, he was not military, didn't have that kind of training, but he should have known that detail. It was a lapse that nearly cost the life of everyone aboard the shuttle, including Dr. Ebadi. He looked at the ceiling. "Hutton. Input on this?"

"Lieutenant Hotah is correct, Commander," Hutton said in his scholarly tone, the one he often used when gearing up for a long-winded theoretical dissertation. "The point-defense system uses a great deal of the ship's power when discharged. That is why it will respond only to situations it deems a direct threat to the ship. To conserve energy, it will target missiles in our vicinity but will not fire upon them unless they turn toward us."

"Thank you, Hutton." Before the AI could carry on, Aiden turned back to Hotah. "Okay, Lieutenant. You saved the day with quick thinking and initiative. But for future reference, I do value your input, especially related to your job. If you have good reason to question any of my directives, I want you to do it. Without hesitation. We've all got our areas of expertise here, and we can all learn from each other, including me. Respect the command chain and I'll respect your input. You have my word on that. Deal?"

Hotah nodded again. If it was humanly possible to appear humble, relieved, and defiant all at once, Billy Hotah had perfected it.

Aiden accepted the gesture with a nod of his own and added, "I'd like you to work with Hutton to correct the system's algorithms for situations like this."

"I'll do that, sir." Hotah seemed back on even keel, but Aiden couldn't tell for sure.

He sat back in the command chair and took another deep breath. Colonel Aminu had come to stand next to him, arms crossed. "It appears someone doesn't want Dr. Ebadi to join us."

Aiden ignored the "I-told-you-so" tone in Aminu's voice. "Yes, it does. Maybe the same someone who didn't want the *Sun Wolf* to leave Hawking Station in one piece. But we'll talk about that later, once Dr. Ebadi is safely aboard. We'll convene in Conference One. You, her, me, and the XO."

Aminu gave a curt nod and resumed his seat to the side. Aiden asked Ro to inform Admiral Stegman of the incident and to query Luna's security services for any information they had on the missile's launch location and who might have fired it. As he headed toward the lift to join Dr. Devi in the docking bay, he overheard Lieutenant Dalton complimenting Hotah.

"Hey, nice shootin' there, chief!"

Hotah froze. Without looking at Dalton, he said in a low, dangerous voice, "What did you call me?"

"Whoa, partner," Dalton said, grinning wide, blue eyes smiling. "Just givin' you a compliment, s'all."

Hotah stood up slowly and faced Dalton, rage in his eyes. "And I'm not your partner either, *cowboy*."

Dalton, struggling to maintain his good-natured expression, stood up and held out his hands in apology. "I didn't mean nothin'..."

Hotah leaned forward and took a step toward Dalton. Ro, who had been sitting at Ops not far from Dalton, shot up instantly and stood between the two men. No taller than either man but more powerfully built, Ro stood like a solid rock wall facing Hotah, with Dalton at his back. "Gentlemen?"

The rest of the crew froze. Hotah's breathing came hard, his fists clenched, eyes wide. The look on Dalton's face showed genuine shock and not just a little fear. No physical contact had been made between the three standing men. Yet.

Ro spoke in a calm, even voice, addressing Dalton but still facing Hotah. "Mr. Dalton, you're the newest member of our crew, and obviously the most talented at inserting foot-in-mouth, so I'll cut you some slack. But you'll do well to remember that names matter. So does history."

Dalton shuffled his feet, now looking more embarrassed than confused. "Yes, sir. I wasn't thinking..."

Ro remained standing between the two of them, his chin lifted slightly, arms held at his side, relaxed but ready. Hotah looked past Ro and stared Dalton down in dark silence. Then he stood back, straightened, and mastered his anger, transforming it into something equally intense. Aiden thought he recognized it: a self-awareness that transcended pride.

"Are we done here?" Ro said, still facing Hotah.

Hotah's fists unclenched and his breathing slowed. He nodded once. "I'm good, sir."

Ro stepped aside, opening the space between the two men. Dalton had the good sense not to resume his perpetual grin, and though he looked as if he wanted to extend a hand to Hotah for a goodwill handshake, had even better sense not to try.

Ro moved closer to Dalton, looked him in the eye, and spoke quietly. "I know you're a good guy, Lieutenant, but for others to see that more clearly, you need to practice the art of thinking before speaking. It works. Believe me."

Dalton nodded as if he'd just now understood some intricate algorithm of human nature. Ro waited to see if he would keep his mouth shut, then looked around at the crew. "We're still on Level One alert, people. Back to work."

Ro made brief eye contact with Aiden. Hutton's voice entered the scene like nothing out of the ordinary had happened. "The Orontus shuttle has arrived and is executing docking maneuvers."

"Good. Thank you, Hutton," Aiden said. "Ro, you have the bridge."

He made his way to the docking bay, glad again for the umpteenth time that Roseph Hand was his XO as well as his friend.

Aiden and Dr. Devi met Maryam Ebadi as she emerged from the shuttle's airlock into the ship's docking bay. She was visibly shaken by the missile attack, and not just in the way people who devote their lives to the betterment of humanity are dumbfounded by deliberate acts of violence between members of their own species. Dr. Ebadi had taken the attack personally.

"Good to see you again, Dr. Ebadi," Aiden said with a modest bow, referring to his first meeting with her on Luna to deliver Woo's cryptochip. As with that brief encounter months ago, Aiden was struck by the woman's regal bearing. Her long black hair, olive complexion, finely featured facial structure and light green eyes all accentuated an alert self-assuredness that held not a hint of conceit.

"Glad to be aboard, Commander Macallan, safe and sound. That was quite an exciting shuttle trip."

"Exciting, yes," Aiden said, admiring how well she'd maintained her composure. "But troubling. We're looking into what it was all about."

"I believe it was all about what I'm here for. What all of us are here for."

It was both an artfully vague and rather pointed observation. He said, "Yes. I'm beginning to see that now. Once you've settled in and feel up to it, Dr. Ebadi, I'd like to convene a meeting with you and my team to discuss exactly what it is we *are* here for."

Ebadi tilted her head to brush an errant strand of hair from her face. Her fingers were slender, delicate. "Ready when you are."

Aiden gestured toward Devi, who stood at his side. "This is my Medical Officer, Dr. Sudha Devi. She'll show you to your quarters and can assist you with anything you need to get comfortable here. We'll meet in the ship's main conference room in, say, one hour?"

"Very good. Thank you."

When Aiden returned to the bridge, Ro informed him that their military escort, the SS *Kepler*, had arrived in Luna space. It had begun deceleration while making a loop around Luna and would be coming up to the *Sun Wolf*'s position with a residual velocity of 5 km/sec.

Aiden figured it would take a couple hours for the *Kepler* to complete the loop before reaching them. "Helm, take us out of orbit, set course for the Cauldron, but hold steady at five klicks per second. When the *Kepler* comes alongside, match her velocity and maintain formation until I speak with *Kepler*'s captain. Ro, any info from Luna Security on the missile attack?"

"They're still sifting through their data, but the missile was probably launched from somewhere on the far side, in the vicinity of the Van der Waals crater. There're no settlements out there, the closest being a small mining colony in the Vallis Planck. Security's got a Special Forces team swarming the area now. Their sensor network indicates a high probability of a nuclear warhead aboard the missile, driven by a fast antimatter drive."

"And using a very sophisticated guidance system," Hotah added. "It was locked on solid to the shuttle the whole way."

"That sounds like advanced military-grade weaponry," Victor Aminu said. "Highly restricted. No way it can get into private hands. Legally, at least."

"A nuke?" Aiden said. "Isn't that overkill for a shuttle?"

"Unless whoever launched it wanted to take us out too," Aminu said. "If it detonated close enough, the electromagnetic pulse could've fried our electronics and disabled the ship."

Hotah shook his head. "It'd have to detonate within a kilometer of us to pose any threat from EMP, and even then, our defensive shielding is strong enough to neutralize most of it."

"They knew they couldn't take out the *Sun Wolf*," Aiden said. "Because of our point-defense system. So they didn't even try. The shuttle was the intended target all the way."

"Yes, sir. The missile's trajectory was configured to strike the shuttle well outside our point-defense zone, and they probably used a nuke because it's an easy kill against a standard transport shuttle. Wouldn't even have to make impact, just detonate in the vicinity. Radiation and EMP would do the rest. They wanted zero margin of error."

"But the attack still could've succeeded," Aminu said, frowning at Hotah, "if the warhead had detonated when you hit it with the laser cannon. It's damn lucky it didn't."

Hotah shook his head again. "Not luck, sir. Detonation devices can be destroyed before they trigger if hit hard and fast enough. Our main laser cannon's got wicked muscle."

Aiden detected a note of youthful bravado in Hotah's voice. He couldn't blame him. "Again, Lieutenant Hotah: good work."

Hotah looked back at him with a hint of a smile, a rare sight, but his tone sounded genuine. "It's why you hired me, sir."

Indeed, Aiden thought. *You'll do.*

9

LUNAR ORBIT
Domain Day 82, 2218

AN HOUR LATER, Aiden met Dr. Ebadi at her quarters and led her to Conference Room One. She had changed into one of the *Sun Wolf*'s standard-issue jumpsuits, dark blue with the golden Space Service insignia above the left breast. She appeared relaxed and refreshed. Ro and Aminu were already seated in the conference room when he and Ebadi entered. Aiden showed her to a chair across the table from him, looked at the other two and said, "Gentlemen, this is Dr. Maryam Ebadi, professor of quantum astrophysics and a member of Dr. Elgin Woo's research team at the Cauldron."

"Good to see you again, Dr. Hand," she said to Ro with a tilt of her head.

"Likewise, Dr. Ebadi," Ro said.

Aiden glanced at Ro quizzically. He hadn't known the two were acquainted. Was there no end to what he didn't know about Roseph Hand?

"Dr. Ebadi," Aiden said, "can you tell us what you already know about this mission? That'll give me an idea of how to fill in the blanks for each other, as needed."

"Fair enough, Commander." Ebadi placed her folded hands on the table and leaned back. "I probably know as much as you do now, or as little. Prior to my departure from Luna, I was given a summary of the situation by Admiral Stegman, including a general transcript of your meeting with him yesterday."

Colonel Aminu's eyebrows went up. "I do hope that was done through secure channels."

"I believe it was, Colonel," she responded, looking at him directly. "Or else it wouldn't have been approved by your superiors."

Aminu looked vaguely mortified but remained silent. Aiden was liking her already.

"Good," Aiden said. "The way I see it, we've got three questions to pursue: Who is carrying out these attacks on the voidoids; why are they doing it; and how are they doing it? The more we learn about any one of them, the more we'll know about how to pursue the others."

"Agreed," she said. "I may have some special insights into all three of those questions."

Aiden stroked his beard absently and wondered if the "special insights" she possessed had anything to do with why someone out there wanted to silence her before she could share them. "I'm all ears."

Aminu leaned forward and said, "Don't forget, two other glaring questions have arisen over the last several hours: Who is trying to stop us from this mission, and how did they even find out about it?"

"I think it's safe to assume," Ebadi said, "that whoever is attacking the voidoids are the same ones trying to stop us from investigating their activities. Yes, the radical group Green War is the most obvious culprit. They hold a special loathing for V-Prime, and the voidoids in general, blaming them for humanity's increasing movement outward into space, away from the work of rebuilding Earth. They'd love to see the voidoids shut down, and they've proven over and over how willing they are to use violence to advance their goals. Assassinations and sabotage are part of their toolbox."

"They apparently also have access to ships capable of void-jump," Aminu added. "Without Licensed Pilots, of course. And they've got money. Lots of it. The DSI has been trying for years to trace their sources of cash, but it's all very well concealed."

Aiden had been watching Ebadi closely and said, "I get the impression you're not sold on Green War as the prime suspects."

She smiled. "That's right, I'm not. Green War satisfies the obvious 'who' and 'why' part of the equation. Maybe a little too conveniently. But when it comes to 'how?' That's where it falls apart for me."

"Explain."

"Have you had a chance to examine the report sent by the *Arcadia* before she vanished?"

"Not yet. We've been a bit busy since we left Hawking Station. But that's next on the list. Have you?"

"No, I haven't. But I'm guessing we'll find evidence that the mystery ship they spotted out at Alpha-2 Hydri was using gravitational fields to affect the voidoid. This isn't the first incident of someone attempting to disrupt a voidoid. There have been many over the last few years, in several different star systems. Dr. Woo and I have been compiling all the information we can get, from hearsay reports to remote sensor data gathered from research drones. And in the few instances where detailed data is available, we've seen evidence of powerful gravitational fields generated by some unknown method and directed at the voidoid."

Aminu looked at her, brows knit. "You and Dr. Woo have been carrying on your own investigation into this?"

"Yes, Colonel," she said. "It's called scientific research. It started out that way, at least—an investigation into the void fluxes, what's causing them, and why they've increased dramatically over the last few years. But when we started to get hints of deliberate human intervention, we voiced our concern directly to President Takema."

Aminu tried not to look scandalized at being left out of the loop and remained silent. Aiden looked at him, reluctantly impressed by the man's restraint.

Ro spoke up for the first time. "The last I checked, the ability to generate point-source gravitational fields of that magnitude is purely theoretical. It's outside the realm of the graviton-based technology we use for shipboard G-transducers. There's no known technology for it yet, and most physicists believe there never will be."

Ebadi nodded appreciatively. "Exactly my point. Green War may have the money and other resources to throw a few monkey wrenches into the works, but there's no way they'd have access to technology of that kind, if it even existed."

"Unless they're doing someone else's dirty work for them," Aiden said. "Someone who does have the means but wishes to remain incognito."

Ebadi nodded. "Possible," she said. "But who? To find that out, we need to look into any center of highly advanced research and technology focusing on gravitational theory, then follow where that leads us."

Ebadi said nothing more, leaving a self-conscious silence in place of where she must have known this line of reasoning would lead.

Aiden understood. "I assume you and Dr. Woo have examined that angle and came to the same conclusion I would. The only place I know of fitting that description is the Cauldron."

Dr. Maryam Ebadi did not flinch from the obvious implication. But her green eyes took on a sadness and, Aiden thought, a hue of genuine disbelief. "Yes, I'd have to agree with you. The Cauldron is the only place we know of in the System that has the brain power and resources to pursue gravitation technology to that extent. But that doesn't mean another place like it doesn't exist. And, in fact, if it did and its goal was to manipulate the voidoids, it would do everything it could to remain hidden."

"Dr. Ebadi," Colonel Aminu said, leaning farther forward across the table. "I have to ask this: How good is your security apparatus at the Cauldron?"

A flash of irony lit her eyes before she answered. "Colonel, we are a research facility, not a military compound. And while we prefer to remain out of the public eye, purely for reasons of academic freedom, we are not a clandestine operation. Prominent researchers and engineers from all over the System spend stints there ranging from one to seven years pursuing their particular area of interest. They're free to come and go as they please, limited only by the constraints of intrasystem transport, and our remote location favors the freedom from distraction they enjoy. Up until recently, we've had no need for a dedicated security apparatus."

"Are transmissions to and from the Cauldron monitored?"

Ebadi took in a deep breath then let it out. "Over the last year, yes. Dr. Woo became increasingly concerned about the possibility of intellectual theft at the very least, or at worst, of nefarious collusions involving resident scientists. He employed some of our communications experts to install monitoring protocols for all incoming and outgoing transmissions. It was quite unpopular among the staff."

Aiden wasn't surprised. A significant portion of the resident scientists at the Cauldron were Nobel Prize winners, or close to it. As a group, they'd become infamous for their fussiness and cantankerous ardor for absolute independence.

"And last year," she went on, "Dr. Woo beefed up the Cauldron's physical defenses."

"Weapons? To protect the entire asteroid?" Aminu asked.

"Yes." She sighed. "Some exotic ones, I'm afraid. Based on his zero-point research. And sensor arrays. All purely defensive measures."

Aminu sat back in his chair. "When we arrive at the Cauldron, I will want to conduct interviews with all of your residents."

Ebadi nodded, visibly unhappy. "Of course, Colonel. Just be aware, that will be highly unpopular. And therefore difficult."

"Nevertheless, necessary. I also advise you to hire a professional security service to handle these issues independently. I have contacts in that area if you're interested."

"Thank you. I'll think about it."

"Please do. I must caution you, if this matter grows more alarming on an intrasystem scale, the UED may require its military to step in."

Now Ebadi made no attempt to hide her anger. "An occupation force?"

"That would be an overstatement, Doctor. More like a security precaution."

Aiden stepped in to redirect the discussion. "Getting back to the 'how' question, do you know why the perpetrators might be using gravitational fields to disrupt the voidoids?"

"Yes, we do," she said, clearly relieved to change directions. "We know a lot, in fact. It's an area of research in which Dr. Woo has made some startling advances. I'm happy to go into more detail at a later time if you wish, but time is of the essence at this point, so I'll give you the short version."

She paused for a moment, looking to Aiden for a go-ahead. "Go on," he said.

"We believe that whoever is doing this may actually be attempting to control the voidoids. Not to destroy them, per se, but to learn how to turn them on and off. You can imagine the power that would give anyone capable of doing it. Exclusive power."

Aiden shivered. He could imagine it, and he knew from the expressions of those around him, they could too.

"Even if they succeeded in doing it," Ebadi continued, "that would be the least of our problems. Because the method they're using to accomplish this will almost certainly result in the terminal shutdown of *all* voidoids in Bound Space. Permanently. Forever."

Ebadi had their undivided attention now. "And that's *still* not the worst of it," she said. "If it stopped there, we'd at least be no worse off than before we discovered the voidoids. We'd still have our Solar System, for richer or poorer. But if the voidoids cease to exist, so will we and the entire universe as we know it."

"What?" Aminu said in disbelief. But Ebadi forged ahead before he could say more.

"Dr. Woo's research indicates that the voidoids are very old, at least six billion years old, emerging just when the expansion of the universe began accelerating. He's shown that the voidoids are responsible for creating and continuing to maintain local conditions within our universe that allow everything we know to exist—from atoms to molecules, to stars, planets and galaxies. Everything including organic life. They do this by actively controlling the density of dark energy within their domain. Without the voidoids doing what they've been doing for billions of years, our universe would have expanded explosively long before it had a chance to form. It's what physicists used to call the Big Rip. And it's exactly what would happen now if the voidoids cease to exist.

"It would start at the macro level—galaxies, stars, planets— and proceed all the way down to the subatomic level, elementary particles, quarks, all flying away from each other at light speed. The effects on organic life forms like ourselves would occur somewhere in between. It wouldn't take long to happen, and you can bet it would not be pretty."

10

LUNAR ORBIT
Domain Day 82, 2218

Maryam Ebadi's disturbing pronouncement resounded inside Conference Room One like a death knell. Even Victor Aminu fell silent, his skepticism paralyzed. For a long moment afterward, only the deep subliminal rumble of the M/AM filled the room.

Ebadi finally glanced at Aiden again for the green light.

"Tell us," he said.

"We've known for three centuries," she began, "that the universe is expanding and have known since the late 20th century that it's not only expanding, but its *rate* of expansion is accelerating. That led to the concept of dark energy to represent the unknown force field causing the acceleration. In some ways, it's a resurrection of Einstein's cosmological constant, representing a cosmic repulsive force that he inserted into his equations to account for why the universe is *not* collapsing under its own weight. Some physicists believe that the cosmological constant and dark energy are one and the same, but that remains hotly debated.

"Dark energy is thought to function as a kind of antigravity. Where gravity pulls things together on a local level, dark energy pulls them apart on a more cosmic scale. Physicists have called it different things, including vacuum energy of space and zero-point energy. But it's mostly still called dark energy because scientists know as little about it today as they did when they first coined the term. We at the Cauldron believe that dark energy is more specifically a special case of zero-point energy."

The blank expressions she saw around the table caused Ebadi to pause. She rubbed her forehead. "Sorry. I digress. It's difficult for me to simplify these concepts, but important for us to understand the basics of what we *do* know about dark energy. For instance, it comprises about 69 percent of all the energy and mass-energy of the universe. It's not very dense and was originally thought to be homogenous throughout the universe, but that notion has changed. The evidence now indicates that dark-energy density is dynamic, that it can vary with time and space. Dark energy is not known to interact with any of the fundamental forces of nature other than gravity, a very important distinction. But for about the last six billion years, dark energy—whatever it is—has increasingly overpowered the sum total of the universe's gravitational forces, causing the universe to expand at an ever-increasing rate. Dark energy is, in fact, growing denser and stronger over cosmic time.

"To understand what dark energy has to do with the voidoids, we can represent dark energy as the vacuum energy of space. We know that the vacuum of space is not empty at all. Far from it. It's actually a seething ocean of virtual quantum particles popping in and out of existence, matter and antimatter pairs, releasing energy in the process. That energy is the vacuum energy of space. It's derived from the constant emergence and destruction of virtual particles in empty space. And based on long-established quantum field theory, we can accurately calculate how much energy that process should generate. But here's where it gets crazier.

"When the calculations are done—as they have been repeatedly for centuries—a huge problem arises: the resulting value is always absurdly higher than what we observe in the real universe. Higher by an order of 10 to the 120th power. Meaning the universe should be expanding at a rate *that* much greater than what we observe it to be. The discrepancy has been called the worst theoretical prediction in the history of physics."

Ro nodded. "The so-called Cosmological Constant Problem."

Ebadi smiled at Ro. "Yes. What Einstein called his 'biggest blunder' after learning of Hubble's discovery of the expanding universe. It turns out that, in fact, it may have been one of his greatest insights. But all inquiries into this problem ceased during the Resource Wars leading up to the Die Back and didn't resume until the Neo-Renaissance, about a century ago."

Aminu shifted restlessly in his chair. "And this is important because...?"

"Because, Colonel," she said, "if the quantity of dark energy was as high as quantum field theory says it should be, its force of repulsion would be so immense that not even atoms could cohere. Matter itself could not exist. Stars, planets, galaxies— everything we know in the universe— never could have formed, leaving nothing but a soup of quarks, all flying away from each other at the speed of light, or greater. Nothing left but an emptiness full of dark energy."

She made eye contact with everyone around the table before continuing. "But this is obviously not the case in our universe, is it? We *do* live in a relatively stable universe, with ordinary matter and energy, with atoms, molecules, stars, planets, galaxies and all the rest. A universe that apparently contains exactly the right amount of dark energy to allow even the evolution of organic life. So, the big elephant-in-the-room question for the last few centuries has been *why* does the universe we live in exist at all when the best laws of quantum physics say it shouldn't?"

"I thought the String Theory folks had that one figured out," Aiden said. "With their multiverse hypothesis."

Ebadi waved her hand. "Yes, the multiverse theory was once a popular explanation, but since our universe is the only one we live in and will ever know, it can never be proven. It's a nonproductive theory and now largely ignored by leading people in the field. Still, no other theory has superseded it to explain why our universe *is* when it shouldn't be. No one has come close to figuring it out. Not until Dr. Elgin Woo came along, and I do think he's got it right. The answer has everything to do with the voidoids."

She looked around the room again. Aminu, while still impatient, sat up in his chair a fraction higher. Ro, on the other hand, leaned back with a faint smile. Aiden, fascinated, had an inkling of where she might be taking them. "Continue."

"Thank you, Commander. I know all this seems a bit erudite, but I promise you, it's essential to the problem at hand. We believe that, in fact, the voidoids are actively reducing the level of dark energy in our universe, keeping its exponential expansion in check, which in turn has allowed everything we know, from atoms to ourselves, to exist and evolve. Without the voidoids, the cosmos as we know it would have disintegrated long ago. This view predicates a vast multitude of other voidoids existing throughout our observable universe, all of which are collectively responsible for reducing the cosmological constant to the precise degree we observe it to be today. To a level that has allowed matter to come into being and endure."

"Other Bound Spaces like ours?" Aiden said. "Each with its own group of interconnected voidoids? There'd have to be billions of them throughout the known universe to accomplish what you're suggesting."

"Yes. Dr. Woo, at least, is convinced of that very thing. But don't get me started on why he believes this. It's fascinating stuff, but we need stay focused here."

She drew in a deep breath before going on. "All the voidoids taken together work to maintain the cosmological constant at the level we observe today, and they do this by drawing dark energy into themselves from around them. They may be syphoning it off into some alternative dimension, or maybe they're consuming it as an energy source. We don't have a clue."

"An energy source?" Ro said, delighted by the idea. "Like they're alive? Just like Woo predicted. Eating dark energy to live and in the process, allowing us to live. Brilliant."

"Maybe," Ebadi said. "We don't know yet what the voidoids do with the dark energy they remove from our universe, only that the process is precisely controlled to maintain the right level of dark energy to keep things as they are. The mechanism they use to accomplish this balance appears to be mediated by the relative strength of gravitational fields that they sense in their vicinity. Dr. Woo has developed a complex theory about the origin, evolution, and life cycles of the voidoids to explain why this is so. And whoever is experimenting on the voidoids apparently knows this, too, which is probably why they're using gravitational fields to manipulate the voidoids.

"The problem is, they're playing an extremely dangerous game by shutting down voidoids like this. Assuming their goal is to control the voidoids for ultimate power, political or otherwise, they may be totally unaware that in the process they're also threatening the very existence of...existence."

A dubious look spread across Aminu's face. "Dr. Ebadi, we're talking about manipulation of a single voidoid, or a few at most. Not *all* voidoids in Bound Space, or any of the countless others you say might inhabit the universe. If they exist at all. How could that possibly cause this...Big Rip of the entire universe?"

"It wouldn't at first," Ebadi said. "But as predicted by the current theory of dark energy—something called quintessence—the Big Rip phenomenon can occur locally, inside discrete regions of space like Bound Space, leaving adjacent regions unaffected. Dr. Woo's work shows that all voidoids in Bound Space are interconnected, as in a family unit, and the prolonged shutdown of even one will eventually lead to the shutdown of all others. We already know that when one voidoid undergoes a flux event, so do some of its neighboring voidoids. Simultaneously. We've been seeing this for years now. So, repeatedly shutting down even a single voidoid inside Bound Space could very easily lead to a Big Rip of the space we inhabit."

"Even so," Aminu said, folding his arms across his chest, "surely any noticeable effects of an increase in this dark energy you speak of can't be immediate. Not on a human scale at least. What are we talking about here? A billion years? Five billion? Ten? Our own sun could die out before then."

If Aiden could detect the patronizing tone in Aminu's voice, he was sure Ebadi picked it up loud and clear. Her eyes flashed green fire, but she kept her voice steady.

"There's no shame in struggling to understand advanced quantum physics, Colonel, but quite a lot in presuming you do when you don't. Do you have any idea how immense the difference is between 1 and 1 times 10 to the 120th power? Does anyone? That's how steep the gradient is between the level of dark energy as it is now in our universe and the level that it wants to be and *will* be without the voidoids keeping its expansion in check. With nothing to stop it, a gradient that steep will correct itself rapidly, even explosively. We're not talking about billions of years here. Once it starts, Bound Space would disintegrate completely within a year."

Ebadi let her last sentence hang in the air like a black cloud, a dark wraith Aiden struggled to vanquish by remaining inquisitive. "And what will that look like?"

"Assuming this destruction is at first confined to Bound Space, when the entire family of voidoids within it dies, things inside Bound Space will start falling apart. The least bound structures will go first. All the stars in the sphere of Bound Space will begin to move away from each other at an ever-increasing rate. The stars farthest from the center, out on the Frontier, will move away faster than those closer in. Our sun, Sol, is at the center, so it will stay put. At least for a while. But it won't be long before things on a smaller scale get messed up by the next phase of the Rip.

"Planets within star systems will start moving away from their stars as rapidly increasing dark energy overcomes the gravitational forces that hold those systems together. Then, for us, the really bad stuff starts happening. Matter itself starts to disintegrate, all the way down to the Planck scale. Molecules become unbound. Then individual atoms begin to fly apart, dissociating into electrons, protons, and neutrons. Then those particles dissociate further into fermions and bosons. It won't stop until there's nothing left. Organic life, of course, will have ended somewhere along the way. And quite gruesomely, I would imagine."

Victor Aminu leaned back, still unmoved, and spoke. "Am I right in assuming that this whole scenario is mere conjecture at this point? Based on admittedly exotic theories? There's no solid proof that something like could actually happen or has ever happened. Correct?"

Ebadi regarded him for a long moment. Aiden could almost hear the decision-making motors whirring away inside her head. How well would she keep her cool?

"Colonel, these 'exotic theories' you refer to are the best we have in a field of science that's evolved carefully and with highly verifiable success over centuries of work by the best minds humanity has produced. Theories that are no more exotic than the laws of gravitation or of thermodynamics. And yes, there is good evidence that this type of catastrophic event has happened before, elsewhere in our own galaxy. But only astronomers seem to know or care about them. No one else seems to remember the Big Fade that occurred back in 2032 when all the stars surrounding HD 23079 began flying away from it.

"The event was well documented by Earth-based and space-based telescopes alike. And being only 113 light-years away, it was relatively easy to see. Within 14 months after it was first noticed, most of the stars within a 28-light-year radius around HD 23079 disappeared altogether, and by month 17, so did HD 23079. The star began to expand, as if pulled apart from the inside out, until it disintegrated into nothingness. But not in the way a star does when it dies a natural death, expanding outward through its 'red giant' phase before collapsing. This was something altogether different, and most of the theories to explain it had to do with some kind of 'runaway' dark energy phenomenon. It remained a curiosity among astrophysicists for a long while, until the Die Back happened, then it was virtually forgotten.

"And that's only the most well-documented event of its kind. At least two more have been observed since then in regions of the galaxy much farther away than HD 23079. Whatever caused it to happen out there, natural or otherwise, it's a very real thing, and it's almost certain to occur here in Bound Space if our voidoids die."

All traces of smugness had finally disappeared from Victor Aminu's face. He sat back and said nothing more.

Aiden's growing sense of unease thrashed inside his chest like a dangerous arrhythmia. "How close are we to setting off something like that?"

Ebadi nodded. "Dr. Woo's latest models, completed just prior to the Chara crisis, predict that when the frequency of void fluxes, and the number of locations in which they occur, increase beyond a critical level, all voidoids in Bound Space will shut down, then die soon after. When that happens, not only will we be unable to visit other star systems but, as I've explained, our corner of universe will literally begin to disintegrate."

"And Dr. Woo believed we're approaching this critical level?"

"Yes, he did. And I do too. Approaching it rapidly, I'm afraid. I've seen the work. It's concrete, brilliant, and frightening. Void fluxes are happening more often, in more places, and for longer durations than ever before. Whoever is doing these clandestine experiments may have already set off a chain reaction that's impossible to stop. But we must try, Commander. We have to find them and stop them. Barring that, we'd need to learn exactly what they're doing, how they're doing it, and use that knowledge to reverse the damage before it's too late. I have some ideas on that account. But either way, I fear we have very little time."

Aiden tried to swallow down the roiling helplessness surging in his gut. If ever there was a time when they needed Elgin Woo alive and well, at their side, it was now. He straightened his spine. "Then let's get moving. Once we're under way to the Cauldron, we'll reconvene to review the incident report from the *Arcadia* and strategize on how to proceed. And I'll want to hear the ideas you referred to, Dr. Ebadi."

He looked at Ro. "XO, anything to add?"

"Like you said. Let's get moving."

Aiden turned to Aminu. "And you, Colonel?"

He nodded curtly toward Maryam Ebadi. "Like she said. Find them and stop them."

Lilly Alvarez's voice came through the comm. "Commander, the SS *Kepler* has pulled alongside, ready for escort duty. Captain Jacqueline Hidalgo would like to speak with you at your soonest convenience."

"Tell Captain Hidalgo I'll hail her in 10 minutes." He stood up from the table and the others followed suit. "That's all for now. Let's get back to the bridge. Dr. Ebadi, before you leave, a word please."

11

MARYAM EBADI SAT down again at the conference table as Ro and Aminu left the room. After the latch clicked shut, Aiden sat across from her, leaned forward, and spoke quietly. "Dr. Ebadi, I take it you believe Elgin Woo is still alive."

She looked back at him and said nothing for a moment, unblinking, jaw still tense from her exchange with Aminu. "I do, yes. And I take it you do too."

He kept a straight face. Could he be that transparent? Or was she unusually perceptive?

When he didn't respond, she smiled and asked, "Have you asked your friend Hutton what he thinks?"

After the epic events of the Chara crisis, it seemed that everyone knew all about his empathic connection with Hutton, the personified subroutine of the Omicron-3 AI he himself had created years ago and nurtured into an uncanny alter ego. But Ebadi's question took him by surprise. He hadn't considered discussing the matter of Woo's disappearance with Hutton.

"No, I haven't. Why would I?" he said, still attempting to appear clueless.

But Ebadi's expression told him he'd failed. She looked at him for another long moment before speaking. "Hutton is still linked to the Rete on Silvanus, isn't he?"

"Yes, he is."

"And the Rete has some special knowledge of the voidoids, some kind of…relationship with them, right?"

"Yes, Hutton has suggested as much, at least related to the Chara voidoid. But the nature of the relationship, if there is one, remains a complete mystery even to Hutton. What does this have to do with Dr. Woo's whereabouts?"

She faced him directly. "You know that Elgin believes the voidoids are alive, right? He also believes they're conscious and intelligent. Granted, that part isn't supported by evidence. Yet. But neither is it disproved. It's a hunch of his, and Elgin's hunches have a way of becoming fact. If he's right, if the voidoids are in some way sentient, maybe the Chara voidoid could provide a clue to what happened to Elgin when he passed through it. And if the Rete on Silvanus can communicate in some way with the Chara voidoid, maybe—"

"Maybe we can learn something from the Rete, through Hutton."

"Exactly."

"That's a lot of 'ifs,' Doctor."

"Yes, I know. But…can we just ask Hutton? Now?"

Aiden looked at his chronometer, then leaned back in his chair and looked at the ceiling. "Hutton, are you following this?"

"I am, yes." The voice from the comm speakers sounded perfectly human. The AI's personality algorithms had evolved far beyond Aiden's original tinkering. "And I find Dr. Ebadi's question an intriguing one."

Hutton had, however, been slower at learning to curb his inclination to elaborate endlessly on any topic presented to him. Ever vigilant in keeping that tendency in check, Aiden interjected quickly, "Based on everything we know about Dr. Woo's disappearance, and your association with the Rete, what's the likelihood of him still being alive?"

"There are many ways to approach that question. But I assume you want only a summary conclusion." Hutton sounded vaguely disappointed.

"Correct."

"I would say the probability is quite high; 93 percent, to be precise."

Aiden and Ebadi exchanged wide-eyed glances. "How the heck did you come up with that figure, Hutton?"

"I thought you wanted the short version." Was there a hint of annoyance in Hutton's response? Or anticipation?

"I did. And I do. I'm just surprised. But tell me this: Does your estimation involve input from the Rete?"

"Yes, absolutely. It would not have been possible without the Rete's historical knowledge of the Chara voidoid and of its interactions with other voidoids. While the nature of this interaction is unknown to me, I believe it is ancient and elemental. In fact, the most interesting and insightful work on this subject comes from Dr. Woo's own Synchrony Theory of Consciousness, based on the synchronization of shared resonances among many small constituents of a larger whole. It's a brilliant extrapolation of panpsychism, an ancient perception of universal consciousness—"

"Hutton! Enough. I just want to know if the Rete has any specific knowledge of Dr. Woo's existence."

"Yes, Aiden. Just now, as we were talking, I queried the Rete about Dr. Woo's current whereabouts, and it does sense the voidoid's recognition of his presence."

Aiden sat up, now fully engaged. "The Rete knows where he is?"

"Not with absolute certainty, but the probability is high that he is currently in the star system he intended to visit when he jumped out of the Chara system."

"The HD 10180 system, 127 light-years from Sol."

"Correct. Well beyond the V-Limit, where it should be impossible to reach via voidjump. However, I cannot accurately represent the logic of the Rete's conclusion—"

"That's fine, Hutton. Thank you." He turned to Ebadi. "So, to answer your original question: yes, I do believe Elgin is still alive. And now it's more than just a gut feeling. After hearing what you've said about the voidoids and the dangers we face, I also believe that Elgin Woo might be the only person who can help us now. In more ways than one."

Ebadi nodded vigorously. "Yes. Which means we have to find him. And soon."

"I couldn't agree more. The only problem is, if he's still out in the HD 10180 system, there's no way we can get to him. We can't use the voidoids to jump beyond the V-Limit, and we don't exactly have time for the two centuries it would take getting there. There's no way."

"But there must be a way, Commander. If Dr. Woo did it, we can too. We just have to figure out how he did it."

Aiden had to laugh. "That's one tall order."

"Yes. I know. But with all of Dr. Woo's documented research at my disposal, and with the brain power we have aboard this ship, it's not an impossible task."

"It would help if Elgin just came back and told us how he did it," Aiden said. "Isn't that the big question? If he got there in the first place, why hasn't he come back? Even just to say hello and 'look what I did'?"

She shrugged once, hands held out. "I don't know. It's a good question. There could be any number of reasons, most of them disastrous, I fear."

"Then probably disastrous for us, too, if we tried doing the same things he did."

"You may be right. We just need to start following his trail, his line of thinking. It's the only chance we have of finding Elgin where he's most likely to be. It's a risk worth taking."

Aiden smiled. He liked her style. She had balls. "I suppose we'll have to cross that bridge when we get to it. But I'm glad we're on the same page here, Doctor. Not everyone involved will agree, you know. A search for Dr. Woo isn't exactly a part of our official mission plan. It is, however, rapidly becoming a priority for me, even if I choose not to openly express it at this time. I wanted you to be aware of that, and to know I'll pursue that priority at the appropriate time. Until then, I'd appreciate it if you keep what we've discussed here to yourself. Understood?"

Her eyes softened and some of the tension in her shoulders eased. "Understood, Commander. You know I'll support that decision. And please, call me Maryam."

"All right, Maryam. Thank you. And I'm good with Aiden. But only under circumstances like this." Aiden glanced around the empty room.

"Agreed," she said.

"Good." Aiden stood, went to the door, and opened it for her. "Shall we?"

~ ~ ~

When they returned to the bridge, Ebadi assumed her place at the Science station as the mission's designated Science Officer. Aiden sat at the command chair. "Alvarez, hail the *Kepler,* please."

The main screen transitioned from a forward navigational view to the figure of a middle-aged woman with short chestnut hair, a strong, rectangular face, and wide-set eyes that looked tired but alert and intelligent. She wore the standard field uniform of an officer in UED's Military Space Service and stood erect at the bridge of her ship. "Greetings, Commander Macallan. I'm Captain Jacqueline Hidalgo of the SS *Kepler.* We're now in position to begin escort duty. I understand you've encountered some hostile actions against your ship and that your current destination is a research station out in the Apollo Group, a place called...the Cauldron? We have the coordinates logged into our nav computer. Our tactical systems are armed and we're ready to proceed."

"Greetings to you as well, Captain. Yes, apparently someone's trying to stop us from doing our job, so I appreciate your company. At least for the limited time we'll have it. I'm afraid we'll be parting company shortly."

Hidalgo's expression shifted from weary but resolute to quizzical and slightly annoyed. "Parting company shortly? My orders are to provide you with armed escort all the way to your destination, which according to our nav computer is about 1.6 AU from here. That's a three-and-a-half-day journey at 1 G constant accel with turnaround. Isn't that right?"

"Part of it's right, Captain. But there's been a change of plans. Turns out that our mission has become more urgent than previously assumed. The *Sun Wolf* needs to get to the Cauldron as quickly as possible. We'll be under full power, about 3 Gs constant accel. That'll get us there in two days. Just under 50 hours."

"Three Gs? Constant accel? Over 1.6 AU? I didn't realize that was even possible. What kind of rocket have you got there, Commander?" It was a good imitation of comradely banter between two ship captains, but Aiden saw the tension behind it.

He smiled disarmingly. "Yes, she's a real hot rod."

Hidalgo was not amused. "Look, Commander. There's no way we can keep up with you at those velocities. Which means there's no way we can give you the protection we've been ordered to provide."

"But there is a way, Captain." Aiden felt a need to put a good face on his decision. He knew Admiral Stegman might not be happy with the change of plans; now would be a good time to start working on his rationale. "The way I see it, the faster we travel, the less vulnerable we are to attack. Targeting becomes less accurate. Missiles and other kinetic weapons struggle to keep up. Even laser cannons are less effective against shields moving away at high velocities. We are, however, most vulnerable during the time it takes us getting up to those speeds. That's where the *Kepler* can help us most, offering protection during our initial acceleration. By the time we outpace you, our own velocity will be our best protection."

Hidalgo had placed one hand on her hip while she listened, her head cocked to one side. A classic posture of the unconvinced. "Hmmm. I see, Commander. And what about your equally vulnerable period during deceleration as you near your destination?"

Aiden nodded, her point taken. "A UED battle cruiser has been dispatched from Friendship Station to join us at the Cauldron. It will provide military escort from there to V-Prime."

Aiden said this knowing full well it probably wouldn't play out that way, especially if the Cauldron succeeded in fitting the *Sun Wolf* with a fully functional zero-point drive.

Hidalgo shifted stance, but her expression stayed the same. It reminded him of the way his grade-school teacher would look at him as a young boy late to class once again. "I assume the Admiralty is aware of this change of plans? I certainly wasn't told about it."

"It was an operational decision made moments ago, Captain. One that I've been given the authority to make. But I will inform Admiralty once we're under way."

Captain Hidalgo pulled back. "Very well, Commander. I'll need to log it from my end. The *Kepler* is ready to support your mission in any way it can."

"Thank you. My XO will establish a navigational link between our ships to synchronize our course settings. We'll engage primary thrust in five minutes. Confirmed?"

"Confirmed. We'll have all eyes open for hostiles and weapons powered up for as long as our engagement zones coincide. Good luck, Commander." The comm screen went blank.

Ro turned to Aiden and said, "You realize, of course, that if we're starting out at 3 Gs and the *Kepler* is starting out at 1 G, it won't be long before she'll be of no use to us?"

"I know." Aiden didn't exactly smile. "Her protection will be effective for about an hour and a half. Lieutenant Hotah, does that sound about right?"

Hotah had been following the conversation and responded immediately. "Yes, sir. That's based on a 300,000-kilometer combat engagement envelope. About one light-second separation between opposing vessels. Beyond that, targeting and weapons efficiency drop off dramatically."

Aiden sat back in the command chair feeling oddly exhilarated. "Well then, after an hour and a half we'll just have to depend more heavily on Mr. Hotah's expertise."

Hotah glanced over his shoulder with a confident grin. "Yes, sir."

Ro dropped the subject and checked his console again. "Nav systems are now synched with the *Kepler*," he said.

"Thank you, XO. Helm, set course for the Cauldron, 3 Gs accel."

Pilot Abahem, sitting directly in front of the command chair and facing forward, did not speak but raised her right hand in affirmation, thumb and index finger forming an "okay."

"Onward and upward," Aiden said, using his customary phrase for "launch." The millisecond of G-forces tapping him in the chest and the subsonic rumble of the M/AM drive growling through the ship told him that his command had been executed. Within seconds, Luna and her weary but resilient Mother Earth were left far behind. In front of them, displayed on the main screen, lay the endless ocean of stars, each one a hard point of diamond fire burning in the infinite darkness.

12

HD 10180 SYSTEM
Domain Day 158, 2217

ELGIN WOO COULDN'T take his eyes off the *Starhawk*'s sensor screen. What he saw there could easily be described as beyond incredible, even by a man with his boundless capacity for imagination. But ever since his improbable emergence here in the HD 10180 system, 127 light-years from home, far beyond the V-Limit, he'd become delightfully accustomed to surprise.

The *Starhawk* had been decelerating steadily at 1 G for over seven days and was now entering orbital insertion around Woo's destination, the eighth planet from the star. The one he had dubbed Shénmì. Positioned right in the middle of the system's biohabitable zone at 1.2 AU, it was an achingly beautiful blue-green orb. Sensor data began providing him with more detail.

Shénmì was slightly larger than Earth—13,048 km across at its equator. It had no moon and a surface gravity of 1.1 G. Its period of rotation was slightly faster than Earth's, probably due to less tidal friction in the absence of a moon, giving it a 22-hour day. Its axial tilt of around 28 degrees would probably give it pronounced seasonal changes during its 420-day year. The atmosphere was remarkably similar to Earth's. Nitrogen content was about the same at around 78 percent, but it held slightly less oxygen at 20 percent and considerably more carbon dioxide at around 0.1 percent. The rest was noble gases, mostly argon. It had an average mean surface temperature of 16 degrees C, slightly warmer than Earth's average of 15 degrees.

As more details resolved, Woo sat back smiling, twirling one side of his long, braided mustache between thumb and finger. The planet's surface features were intriguing, roughly equal proportions of ocean to land mass. Its continents appeared to be uniformly dotted with hundreds of thousands of lakes and inland seas of all sizes, all of it genuine H_2O water, interrupted only by enormous snowy mountain ranges. While Shénmì's cloud cover appeared more extensive than Earth's, it opened up enough in spots to reveal a broad palette of vivid green hues, indicating a lushly vegetated surface.

Miraculous as it was, being only the second earthlike planet known to exist other than Silvanus, that wasn't what had Woo's attention riveted to the forward screen. Focusing on the planet's equator, the ship's optical telescope revealed something that looked so impossible it made him laugh out loud.

From several positions all across the equator, incredibly long, thin, whiplike structures extended upward from the surface to well beyond the planet's atmosphere, to nearly 36,000 kilometers into the vacuum of space. Each filament terminated in a single lozenge-shaped pod that reminded him of a closed crocus bud, like the kind his father used to cultivate back on Earth. Only here the stems were immensely long and slender in proportion, so thin they were barely visible even through the ship's high-res scope. The sensors, however, estimated the tendrils to be at least 20 meters across at their thickest point near the top of their length. Pale white in hue, they were gracefully curved in the direction of the planet's axial spin. The terminal pods swelled to nearly four times wider than their stalks and were brown in color. They swayed slowly, randomly, as if caught in a gentle breeze.

Then, while Woo watched, he noticed one of the terminal pods gradually split open down the center, from top to bottom, like two halves of a walnut shell. A cluster of round spheres, dark brown, emerged from the interior and began to disperse outward as if self-propelled. The scope's calibrated optics measured them at close to 16 meters across. When he switched to maximum magnification, Woo noticed they weren't perfectly spherical, only approximately so, and their surfaces looked rough, conspicuously organic.

And Woo had seen them before.

Three days earlier, the *Starhawk*'s sensors had picked up a group of six objects migrating toward the system's voidoid. Going in the opposite direction, the ship passed them so quickly that the instruments barely had time to register them. At first, he thought they were a collection wayward of space rocks left over from an errant asteroid collision—until he noticed their uniform size and shape. But by then they had moved too far past to scan for further data. Only a brief visual recording had been made. He summoned the file back onto his data screen now and looked more carefully. They were identical to the objects he'd seen dispersed from the...what? Seed pod?

But the structure that set them loose, one of several sprouting from the planet's surface, represented an engineering impossibility. There were no known materials even remotely strong enough to support the weight of a structure that size rooted to the surface, or to withstand the forces it would be subjected to extending that far above it. It was an exaggeration of the engineering problems faced by builders of the still hypothetical space elevator. Only on planets much smaller than Earth were such projects even barely feasible.

The Beanstalk they were trying to build on Mars, for instance, was more likely to succeed due to the planet's smaller size and much lower gravity. Still, it had to be constructed with phenomenally strong (and expensive) materials like single-crystal graphene. And like all such space elevator designs, it had to be rooted precisely at the planet's equator and extend far beyond the planet's geostationary equatorial point. Then it had to employ a massive counterweight at its terminus to impart upward centrifugal forces strong enough to hold the cable up under tension, countering the gravitational pull downward from its own weight. That was the only way to keep the entire structure intact and stationary over a single position on the planet's surface. But he was now looking at something entirely different.

While the supporting filaments appeared to be flexible tensile structures, they reached up just to the geostationary equatorial point, around 36,000 km, and not beyond. And the "seed pods" at their tips looked nowhere near massive enough to function as counterweights. These things were more like the fanciful Tsiolkovsky space towers, hypothetical freestanding compression structures that were supposed to reach into space while supporting their own weight from below. That idea had been abandoned centuries ago for a whole host of very good reasons. There had to be another explanation for what he was seeing here.

Still twirling his braided mustache, Woo wondered if these structures might be more than what they looked like, not purely organic phenomena.

"Mari," he said, addressing the ship's Omicron-3 AI, "please run scans of the surface for any evidence of advanced civilization."

"Of course, Doctor," the AI responded. Woo had attempted to personalize the Omicron's interface in the same way Aiden Macallan had done with Hutton, but he apparently lacked Macallan's peculiar empathic connection with the Omicron AIs. Woo made a mental note to explore the subject with Aiden the next time they were together. If there was a next time.

Mari eventually said, "I've run all the sensor scans available on the *Starhawk,* searching for any sign of civilization, advanced or otherwise, and have found none."

Interesting. "Thank you, Mari. I assume, however, that you have detected signs of living organisms."

"Correct, Doctor. Abundant plant life, mostly photosynthetic in nature, but not exclusively. And probably abundant animal life as well."

"Animal life?"

"Yes, at least the presence of organisms that metabolize oxygen and release carbon dioxide. However, these organisms could easily be nonanimalian or even microbial, as they were found to be on Silvanus."

As on Silvanus... Then these fantastical structures had to be organic. And they resembled seed pods too closely, both in form and function, to be anything else. Woo had to laugh again. What stronger evidence for the old panspermia hypothesis could there possibly be?

Continuing to watch, Woo saw the terminal seed pod close up tight, and over the next two hours he witnessed the stalk retracting back down through the planet's atmosphere and eventually coming to rest on the surface. Now lying on the ground, the pod gently lolled to one side and split open again before becoming motionless. There were no signs of the stalk now, as if the entire structure, all 36,000 kilometers of it, had retracted into itself like a snail's antennae. *Amazing.* And so was the speed with which it had occurred—two hours to retract 36,000 kilometers. What kind of material was this? What kind of living being?

Overcome by curiosity, Woo instructed Mari to bring the *Starhawk* into high orbit around the planet, 40,000 kilometers above, and to set up a continuous visual recording program aimed at the equatorial region where the structures originated. He told Mari to notify him of any new activity within the scope's field of vison. At that point, he realized how exhausted he was, having been awake over the last 20 hours of his approach to Shénmì. He retired to his small living quarters and was sound asleep within seconds.

At 10:20, nearly eight hours after he'd fallen asleep, Mari chimed in over the comm. "Dr. Woo. I apologize for waking you, but you asked me to alert you of any new activity from the area of interest on the surface."

"Yes, Mari. What is it?" Woo suspected it wasn't an emergency, and the AI had waited to inform him of it until he'd slept comfortably through a full eight-hour period.

"An interesting development began several hours ago and is presently continuing. I suggest visualizing it rather than hearing my description."

Woo smiled. "I'll be right there."

After brewing a precious cup of Keemun black tea using his antique silver brewing ball, Woo sat at the sensor console. "Mari, show me this new development from when it first started."

The screen lit up to reveal a highly magnified sector of the surface on the planet's equator, approximately a half kilometer squared. A roughly circular patch of smooth beige material occupied its center. Surrounded on all sides by brilliant green vegetation, it was maybe 150 meters in diameter. As he watched, the dark brown head of a seed pod, nearly 80 meters across, protruded through the surface of the white circle, breaching its membrane and lifted rapidly aloft on its sinewy white stalk. The material of the stalk appeared blurry, active with some kind of luminescence.

The telescope automatically backed off the magnification to keep up with the quickly climbing seed pod and continued to monitor its ascent. Woo noticed the time stamp on the recording. The pod's initial emergence had occurred about one hour ago. "How far up is the pod now, Mari?"

"It is currently 5,400 kilometers above the surface and rising at a constant velocity."

Woo did a quick mental calculation. That worked out to be around 1.5 km/sec. *Amazing!* If the pod continued rising at its current velocity, he figured it would reach the 36,000-kilometer mark in a little over five and a half hours from now, assuming that was its intention. Woo was relatively certain the pod would stop there and do what the others had done: open up, disperse its seeds, then close up and retract back onto the surface.

What kind of life form is this? he asked himself again. Woo didn't have the slightest idea. Biology was not his forte. But what he did know for sure was that he'd be going down there to find out.

He brewed another cup of tea and retired again to his quarters. "Mari, please play Vaughan Williams's 'Toward the Unknown Region.'"

As an excellent performance of one of Woo's favorite classical composers filled the tiny space, he lounged on his bunk, sipped his tea, and began to devise a plan.

~ ~ ~

He must have nodded off, because the next thing he knew, Mari was trying to wake him. He rubbed his eyes and looked at the chrono. It was 16:00. He made his way to the bridge and sat at the sensor screen. Mari informed him that the pod had slowed considerably. He switched on the screen just in time to witness the pod come to a complete halt at 35,987 kilometers above the planet's surface. Then he waited patiently, humming a little snippet of melody from the Vaughan Williams piece that stuck in his head. For a man of such insatiable curiosity and obsessive problem-solving mentation, patience was indeed a virtue. His long practice of Fa-hsiang meditation techniques, taught to him by his mother, had allowed him to discipline his naturally overactive mind and to master the skill of patience.

But he didn't have long to wait. He watched closely as the seed pod slowly reoriented its position on the stalk. After it locked itself into place, Woo saw the pod unzip down its side, opening up to the vacuum of space. A faint cloud of vapor puffed out of the pod's interior, the telltale sign of depressurization. Minutes later, a cluster of spherical seeds—*honestly, what else could they be?*—emerged and dispersed laterally in a loosely coordinated formation. Woo noted with interest that they seemed to be on a heading parallel to the plane of the system's ecliptic, unlike the dispersion he'd witnessed the day before, cast in a direction perpendicular to the ecliptic. Toward the voidoid?

About 30 minutes later, the pod sealed up tight again and, just like what he'd seen earlier, the stalk began to retract, pulling the pod down with it to the surface at an incredible speed. And like the day before, the pod made a gentle landing two hours later, opened up again, then lay quiescent as if spent. It was exactly what Woo had expected to see. And what he *wanted* to see. It confirmed that his scheme might be feasible after all.

Woo intended to visit the surface of Shénmì. He was destined to go there, no question about it. Of only secondary importance to him was, of course, the fact that he'd run out of options. His zero-point drive was currently nonfunctional. He was nearly out of antimatter fuel and nearly out of real food. He had no way to communicate with anyone back in Bound Space, if that even mattered now. His best chance of survival was down on the planet, where the environment appeared hospitable and where he might find edible sources of nutrition. But foremost in his mind was sheer curiosity. So, he was going to Shénmì.

The only problem was, the *Starhawk* had no landing shuttle, being not much larger than a standard landing shuttle itself. It did, however, have one good pressure suit remaining, stowed aboard in case a spacewalk was needed for external repairs. Now that he'd seen the seed dispersion cycle from beginning to end, his plan was self-evident and laughably simple, if not completely crazy.

He would maneuver the *Starhawk* close to where a rising seed pod would park itself. Then when the pod came to a halt, Woo would suit up, jettison over next to it, and wait. After the pod opened and its seeds dispersed, he would then climb into the empty pod, wait for it to seal up, and ride it back down to the surface. When it came to rest and opened up, he could emerge from the spent pod, remove his p-suit, and *voilà*! Welcome to Shénmì!

He explained his scheme to Mari and instructed her to set up all the logistical parameters to pull it off. Her response was not completely unexpected.

After an uncharacteristically long pause, she said, "Really, Dr. Woo, this is an extremely reckless plan. If you are serious about attempting it, I suggest that you be prepared to die in the likely event that it fails."

Woo stared at the ceiling for moment, unable to suppress a smile of delight. Yes, his efforts to humanize Mari were indeed paying off.

13

"DR. WOO," MARI SAID softly, careful to wake him gently from his nap.

Woo sat up in his bunk, yawned, and absently rubbed the top of his once clean-shaven head. A new growth of fine fuzz tickled his palm. He'd always kept his scalp shaved smooth, more as a fashion statement than anything else, but had foregone the practice since his arrival here. He turned and looked at the chronometer. It was 08:20, shipboard time. He'd slept nearly nine hours.

"What is it, Mari?"

"As instructed, I am notifying you that another budding event has started on the planet's surface."

"Thank you, dear girl. I'll be right there."

When Woo reached the control chair, he found the sensor screen already turned on and receiving feed from the ship's optical scope, which was aimed at the planet's equatorial region. After bringing the *Starhawk* into a stationary position above the planet that would keep only the sunlit hemisphere in view, Mari had begun monitoring the surface at the equator for any sign of a new budding event. She had spotted one of the brown seed pods emerging from a location near a continental coastline as it gradually rotated into view from the dark side of the planet. The faint predawn light illuminated the pod as it broke the surface of the pale white bed, rising upward. As the first light of dawn reached it, the structure cast a long shadow across the smooth circular formation and beyond into the surrounding green vegetation. Once the pod rose clear of the surface, it shot upward upon its narrow white stalk and continued to ascend skyward at an astounding velocity.

"Mari, based on the data collected from all the other budding events we've recorded, please calculate the projected location at which this seed pod will reach its peak and the amount of time it will take to get there. As precisely as you can."

After a few seconds, Mari responded. "The results I have are based on a limited sample size and therefore will be subject to some degree of error."

"Understood. Proceed."

"This particular seed pod is projected to reach its peak in seven hours and 27 minutes, at the following spatial coordinates."

She read off a complicated set of coordinates, each down to three decimal points. Not bad, he thought. "Thank you, Mari. Now please move the ship to within 50 meters of that location and hold steady there. Move the ship only if it's in danger of being struck by the pod as it rises."

"As you wish."

Woo had to smile again at Mari's disapproving tone. "Thank you, Mari."

It was a stroke of luck, Woo thought, that the pod had started to rise in the morning of one of Shénmì's 22-hour days. That way, if all went well, he'd be down on the surface in time to witness what was certain to be a splendid alien sunset. Now all he had to do was wait.

At 14:30, after making preparations for his excursion, Woo brewed what could very possibly be his last cup of tea and sat at the viewport to sip at it slowly. While finishing off the last of his dwindling rations, Mari informed him that the ascending seed pod was on track to arrive at its projected position at around 15:30. As he gazed at the lovely planet below, his Shénmì, it struck him how similar it was to Silvanus. From all he'd seen over the last year, and from his evolving speculations regarding the nature of the universe he'd been studying all his life, Woo couldn't help wondering if the two planets weren't related in some elemental way. Silvanus had turned out to be a living planet in every sense of the word. Not only did she represent the most irrefutable proof of Lovelock's Gaia Hypothesis, but the entire planet had evolved into a sentient being, an intelligence profound and ancient. How similar would Shénmì be to Silvanus? Were they long-lost sisters? Woo set his cup down. It was time to find out.

He headed toward the *Starhawk*'s airlock and entered the anteroom, where he found the ship's one remaining pressure suit. There had been two, but Skye had used the other one back in the Chara system when Aiden had taken her aboard the *Argo*. In fact, the last time he'd been in this part of his little ship was when he'd helped Skye don her p-suit. It seemed such a long time ago, and in truth he had no idea how much realtime had elapsed since then. But it *felt* like a long time. It was the last time he'd been in the presence of another human being. Maybe the last time for the remainder of his natural life. It was a melancholy thought but did not make him unhappy.

Woo stuffed himself into the p-suit with some difficulty. It had been many years since he'd had to suit up for an EVA, and then he'd been assisted by a colleague. He was perspiring heavily by the time he finished. Holding the helmet in his hands, he sat on the small wall-bench and asked Mari about the pod's progress.

"It is slowing down and projected to halt in position very near to us. Within 60 meters. I estimate that will occur in 17 minutes."

"Thank you, Mari. Please inform me when the pod comes to a complete halt."

"I will, Dr. Woo," she said, then added, "You might want to bring along the ship's first-aid kit and a handheld luminator. They are both in the utility locker on your left."

Woo's eyebrows went up. He hadn't thought of that, nor had he remembered stowing a first-aid kit aboard. He went to the locker and found it there, along with the luminator. He looked inside the kit. It was rudimentary but could come in handy. It included a water purification unit, a nominal supply of antibiotics and multiple vitamins, an ARM utility knife, and—thank the gods—some toilet paper. A small minifusion laser tool lay next to the kit. He grabbed it too and stuffed it all into a nylon carry pack that he strapped to the front of his p-suit. He clipped the luminator to the suit's utility belt.

"The pod has come to standstill," Mari told him. "It is 57 meters from the ship."

Woo entered the airlock and sealed the hatch door behind him. He pulled on his helmet, locked it down, and ran a careful check on the suit's readouts. Then he strapped the jetpack on his back and stood next to the airlock's exterior door.

"Depressurize the airlock, Mari."

Woo heard the initial hiss of air being sucked out of the chamber, followed quickly by dead silence. He checked the readouts to confirm the depressurization cycle had completed. "Open the airlock door, Mari."

Mari said nothing, but the airlock door parted and slowly opened up to the cold, black void outside. "Once I'm safely inside the pod, Mari, please take the *Starhawk* back to geosync orbit at 40,000 kilometers directly above my landing location."

"Yes, Doctor." Again, the unmistakably reproachful tone.

"I'll be fine, Mari," he said. "And we'll remain in contact via comm once I'm down on the surface."

Mari remained silent. He had to hand it to her. She'd never asked the most painfully obvious question about this whole scheme: How the hell would he get *back* to the ship if he ever needed to? He appreciated that about her.

"I'll need your help down there, you know," he said. "We're in this together. So don't go all quiet on me, dear girl."

After another silence, Mari said, "Good luck, Elgin."

It was the first time the AI had ever used his first name.

He smiled. When the airlock door came fully open, the giant seed pod loomed startlingly close. The side facing the sun was brightly lit but jet-black on its shadow side. Woo jumped off the edge and found himself floating among the stars.

The sensation made him laugh. "Off to see the Wizard!"

Safely clear of the *Starhawk*'s bulk, he activated the jetpack's navigation system to intercept the pod and let the guidance computer do the rest. The pod waved gently back and forth as he approached. Woo stood off at about 20 meters and waited until the motion stopped. Within a few minutes the pod locked into place, orienting itself just so, and began to split open down its side. A puff of trapped atmosphere escaped in a cloud of vapor. He was sure it would have made a loud popping sound if it hadn't happened in the vacuum of space.

When the two halves of the pod came fully open, each cocked back at a 45-degree angle from the center line, the seeds began emerging from the interior. They looked to be coming out in groups of six until a total of 24 floated free. Viewed close up from Woo's vantage point, the roughly spherical objects looked huge, 16 to 18 meters across. Their dark brown surfaces were irregular and coarse in texture. When all of them were well clear of the pod, they began moving off in one direction, loosely grouped. They seemed propelled by some unidentifiable means, as if drawn along by an invisible force. He watched them head off in the general direction of the system's voidoid.

So mesmerized was he by the show, he didn't realize the seed pod had started to close up. He hit the jetpack controls and aimed for the opening. He came in a little too fast and bounced off the surface near the edge of the opening. The closing motion had started out slowly but was now speeding up. He backed off a few meters and tried again. This time he made it past the edges and into the darkened interior, floating free. The inside was lit only by a sliver of sunlight lancing in through the rapidly closing aperture. The pod was empty, but the interior walls were marked by rows of concave depressions, each one large enough to have cradled a single seed. Woo jetted over to one, climbed inside, and held on to its upper edge to stabilize himself. He wished there was a way to strap himself in; it could be a bumpy ride.

The pod began to sway as it closed up. The sun slid into view through the rapidly narrowing gap. He turned to look at it directly. His helmet's faceplate immediately adjusted phase, blocking out most of HD 10180's intense radiation. But the power of the star's presence was in no way diminished. It burned boldly and seemed to resonate like a voice from the heavens. A voice welcoming him home.

14

"THIS IS CAPTAIN Dural Hawthorne of the SS *Arcadia* transmitting an emergency report from our current location in the Alpha-2 Hydri system. We are making our way to the system's voidoid under maximum acceleration in hopes of executing a jump back to Sol before the voidoid fluxes out. We're now about 40 minutes from jump. If we are not successful, this may be the last transmission you'll receive from us."

Captain Hawthorne looked out at them from the video display with a haunted gaze. He appeared to be in his late fifties, a tall figure with a dark complexion, dark hair with a natural curl, and a grizzled beard shot through with gray. The startling hazel-colored eyes set beneath heavy brows shone with the intelligence and competence of an experienced spacer but were also colored with an emotion skillfully concealed. Aiden recognized it all too well: fear. Aiden also recognized the setting of Hawthorn's transmission, the familiar surroundings of a survey vessel bridge. It looked identical to the bridge of the *Argo* where Aiden had served as a survey scientist. Like the *Argo*, the *Arcadia* had been part of Terra Corp's survey fleet before the company's downfall. Now, as a provision of the Chara Treaty, both vessels belonged to the UED's Science and Survey Division.

Aiden glanced around the conference table. The *Sun Wolf* had completed turnaround and was decelerating toward the Cauldron, now only 24 hours away. After a much-needed sleep cycle, Aiden had reconvened his team to review the report sent by the *Arcadia* before its disappearance. The four others sitting around him in a semicircle facing the screen—Ro Hand, Maryam Ebadi, Victor Aminu, and his Comm/Scan Officer, Lilly Alvarez—were all focused intently on Captain Hawthorne's narrative.

"The *Arcadia* is a survey vessel," he was saying. "We've been in this system for 22 days collecting data on the three inner planets in advance of a UED mining operation scheduled for next year. We were on our way home, only three days away from voidjump, when we detected the first in a series of void fluxes. The frequency and duration of these fluxes are steadily increasing as we approach, and we're concerned that the voidoid will shut down before we can make our jump; or worse, that it will flux out during our jump. I'm logging this report via Holtzman transmission in case that happens, and to recount details of an incident we witnessed which may be of interest to UED security agencies.

"We were within 30 hours of voidjump when our long-range sensors picked up a vessel parked near the voidoid, standing off at about five kilometers. We had no prior indication that any vessel other than our own would be in this system, at least nothing that showed up on the Intersystem Broad Scan database. As the vessel remained stationary at the voidoid, we surmised it was not in the process of either entering or exiting the system. We thought it might be an unregistered private ship in distress or possibly one of the outlaw pirate vessels we've heard about marauding the Frontier. If it had been a vessel in distress, there's no way we could have slowed down enough to be of assistance. But we could've at least called for help. We hailed the vessel, asking it to self-identify, but got no response.

"Then, when we were within six hours of jump, we noticed something very strange. Being a survey vessel, we have advanced sensor systems to analyze a wide range of properties within a star system. Our magnetometer array started picking up signs of a strong magnetic field emanating from a point source coinciding with the position of the unidentified vessel. Our Science Officer noted that the field signatures suggested the operation of very powerful superconducting electromagnets, like the kind used in advanced particle accelerators. As we drew closer, our optical telescope recorded images of a large drone positioned very close to the voidoid, about 40 meters from its horizon and apparently under the vessel's control. Our magnetometers confirmed the drone as the point source of the magnetic field.

"We continued hailing the vessel, without a response. The closer we got, we could see that it was a small craft, not military, probably a private yacht but without the usual ID and registration markings. When we were within two hours of voidjump, our sensors confirmed an intense gravity field centered around the drone, strong enough to set off the ship's proximity alarms. Soon after that, our optical scope recorded a dramatic disturbance in the voidoid. Rather than try to describe it, I've included the video sequence here."

An enhanced video image of the Alpha-2 Hydri voidoid appeared on the screen. Like all voidoids, it was virtually invisible, marked only by the absence of background stars. Within seconds the screen lit up with an image of the voidoid shimmering with faint blue light, set against the blackness of space. The patina of light began to oscillate, luminescent ripples spreading across the sphere's surface. The ripples set up a complex standing wave, an interlacing of repeated patterns undulating over the voidoid's spherical horizon. The blue luminescence also lit up the mysterious drone standing off to one side of the voidoid. It was a blunt, lozenge-shaped affair about 10 meters in length and half that in diameter. Then the voidoid abruptly blinked out. Vanished, leaving nothing but darkness and stars.

Hawthorne reappeared on the screen. His eyes were wider now, unblinking, and when he spoke, his words were halting. "That's what happened about an hour ago. We hailed the vessel

again, but this time it fled from the scene at high acceleration. The
voidoid has since reappeared, as confirmed by our navigational
system, but it's very unstable, having fluxed in and out twice more
since then. We continue to approach it at jump speed, on course
for Sol, in hopes of making a successful jump. The risk of failure is
high at this point, but the crew and I agree unanimously that we
have no choice but to make the attempt."

Hawthorne paused for a moment, gathering himself before
speaking again. He didn't have to voice what all spacers working
the Deep understood implicitly: if you're operating in a star system light-years from home and your voidoid disappears, you're
hopelessly stranded. You'd never make it back to Sol alive. He
stood straight, attempted a relaxed smile, and continued. "That's
about it. I've included transcripts of all our sensor data related to
this incident, along with more video records, some of which capture images of the unidentified vessel itself. We will intercept the
voidoid in 28 minutes. If all goes well, I'll notify Space Service
HQ of our postjump position upon exiting V-Prime."

Here, he appeared to have difficulty swallowing in a dry throat
before signing off. "One more thing, on a personal note. I'm
including in this transmission private notes from my crew members to their families. Please deliver them if we do not arrive
back at Sol in a timely way. And please assure my wife, Alana,
and our children that everything will be all right. Captain Dural
Hawthorne, out."

In the silence that followed, Aiden made eye contact with
each of the others around the table. They had felt the emotional
impact of Hawthorne's last words. Even Victor Aminu, his brows
knit, lips compressed, shifted his gaze downward. Lilly Alvarez
appeared most affected. She quickly brushed a tear from her
cheek, embarrassed by its presence there. Aiden knew she had lost
her partner only a year ago in a mining accident out at Wolf 359.
She hadn't been right ever since. Aiden hesitated to direct his first
question to her, but that was where he wanted to start the discussion and hoped it might help her refocus.

"Alvarez, did you get a chance to review the sensor data from the *Arcadia*?"

Alvarez took a moment to compose herself. She was a pleasant looking-woman, 10 years older than Aiden, with a countenance that bore the traces of long sorrow endured with singular grace that only deepened her beauty. Among the rare professional spacers who were Earthborn, she came from a family in northern Spain with old roots, a subtle Castilian accent still musical in her speech. Her narrow face, accented by high cheekbones and framed by long, dark hair braided loosely past her shoulders, seemed too small for the large, deep-brown eyes that now looked back at Aiden. "Yes, I did, Commander."

"Did you see anything to add to Captain Hawthorne's interpretation of the data?"

"Not much. The magnetometer readings the *Arcadia* got from the drone are consistent with what you'd see from very powerful superconducting electromagnets. They were right about that. I'd only add that the sensor signature would suggest a stacked configuration, conferring even greater field strength, but a design that's still very experimental. What's more interesting, though, is the gravimetric readings. They're not picking up gravitational waves. The readings indicate a point-source gravitational field, not waves."

"There's a difference?" Colonel Aminu asked.

"Yes and no. Depends on which theoretical framework you're working from, quantum gravity theory or classical general relativity. Gravitational fields are curvatures in space-time, an emergent property of masses in space. Gravitational waves are ripples in the curvature of space-time, propagated as waves outward from their source, mediated by gravitons at light speed. Gravitons are to gravitational waves as photons are to electromagnetic waves. Gravity fields, on the other hand, aren't transmitted through space-time, per se. They *bend* space-time. The point is, whatever these guys are up to, they're not using graviton generators to propagate G waves. Instead, they're somehow generating an artificial but totally genuine gravity field. A strong one too. That technology isn't supposed to exist at this point in time. My guess? It has something to do with those crazy-powerful electromagnets."

Ebadi had been listening intently to Alvarez's report, nodding. She looked worried. Aiden turned to her. "Dr. Ebadi?"

"This is beginning to make more sense now," she said, "and not in a good way."

"How so?"

"I think Ms. Alvarez is correct about the superconducting electromagnets. Her interpretation of the *Arcadia*'s sensor data is insightful. You're fortunate, Commander, to have such a bright Comm/Scan officer on your crew. I believe what she's described points to an attempt to generate a controlled and extremely strong magnetic field to cause a curvature in space-time in the same way a planet or star does. It's an old theoretical concept called the Füzfa Effect, named after the physicist who first proposed the idea a couple of centuries ago.

"The idea was that by stacking very powerful superconducting electromagnets, you could bend space-time in the same way a mass does in space. And, as Ms. Alvarez points out, since gravity is a curvature of space-time: *voilà*! You've generated an artificial gravity field indistinguishable from one created naturally by a massive object. Then you'd be able to manipulate gravity, like we're able do with the other three fundamental forces—electromagnetic, strong and weak nuclear forces. The theory has always been sound, but it was dismissed long ago, mostly for technical reasons."

Aiden saw where she was going with this, but Colonel Aminu apparently did not, possibly because he wasn't paying enough attention. He'd been quietly flexing his jaw muscles, a slightly less obtrusive version of twiddling one's thumbs. He leaned forward. "And why is this troubling to you, Dr. Ebadi?"

"Because," she said as a teacher would to a lazy pupil, "it confirms that, number one, someone unknown to us has an extremely deep knowledge of voidoid dynamics, to a degree known to exist only at the Cauldron—and there only by a few. Number two, this same someone has a technology base sophisticated enough to solve the insurmountable problems of the Füzfa Effect, to make it work on a practical scale. Number three, and most importantly, they're using this process to manipulate the voidoids."

Aminu frowned. "Gravity fields to disrupt the voidoids?"

"Yes. As I said earlier, Dr. Woo found that the voidoids work to maintain the precise balance of dark energy in our universe by monitoring the overall gravitational fields of the star systems they host. They're apparently extremely sensitive to these fields, can discriminate their relative strengths, and use that information to regulate how much or how little dark energy they need to syphon out of the system. It's a dynamic process that maintains a delicate homeostasis, one that allows our universe to exist. That's presumably why voidoids are positioned where we always find them in a star system—directly above or below the system's ecliptic plane—where they can sense the overall combined gravitational field of the entire system.

"If the voidoid senses the system's gravity field falling below a certain critical level, it assumes too much dark energy has crept into the system, pulling things apart with its repulsive force, diluting gravity. The voidoid responds by ramping up its consumption of dark energy, pulling it out of the system to maintain equilibrium. If, on the other hand, it senses an increase in gravitational force—potentially causing the system to collapse inward—it slows down its consumption of dark energy, allowing dark energy to grow and counter the collapse."

Ro spoke for the first time since entering the room. "If these guys are smart enough to use artificially generated gravity fields to trick the voidoids into shutting down, they must believe they can just as easily reverse the process, tricking the voidoids into turning back on by withdrawing their artificial gravity field. That way they'd have control over when the voidoids are open for void-jumps and when they're not—and ultimately, control over who can use them."

"Yes," Ebadi said. "They may believe they can do that without affecting the health of the voidoid, but they'd be wrong. Dr. Woo surmised that if these gravity fields are powerful enough, applied often and for long durations, the voidoid will respond by shutting down permanently. And all voidoids within its family unit, meaning all of Bound Space, will follow suit. Then dark energy expands exponentially, and we face the catastrophic situation I described earlier."

Colonel Aminu looked a bit more interested now. "Dr. Ebadi, getting back to the question of who could have the knowledge and means to do this, by your own admission, it points once again to the Cauldron. Do you know of anyone among the researchers there, now or in the past, who worked on projects related to this...Füzfa Effect? Or who would know as much about the voidoids as you and Dr. Woo?"

Ebadi's eyes stayed focused on her folded hands resting on the table. "I've been thinking about that, Colonel. And yes, there was someone. But it's probably nothing."

When Ebadi remained silent, Aminu said, "Look, Doctor, I understand your hesitancy to reveal names of your colleagues at the Cauldron—"

"Yes," she snapped back, "and to place them under unwarranted suspicion. To subject them to needless interrogations by your DSI. Very good, Colonel. I'm glad you understand my hesitancy."

Aminu stiffened. "I can assure you that any investigation the DSI does at this point in our inquiry will be done with utmost discretion and objectivity."

Unconvinced but conflicted, Ebadi remained silent.

"Let me remind you, Doctor," Aminu added, "that I've been authorized by the UED to conduct an official investigation into these incidents. Anyone deliberately withholding pertinent information—"

"You'll arrest me? Playing rough now, are we, Colonel?"

Aiden decided to step in before things got out of hand. He addressed Ebadi and Aminu simultaneously. "Let's remember, people, we're on the same side here, with a common goal. And as you pointed out, Dr. Ebadi, time may be running out. Colonel Aminu has a valid point. Any information that gives us a lead, no matter how slim, is critical. I think we'll have to trust the colonel's word that his investigation will be carried out discreetly and will be minimally invasive. That *is* on your word of honor, Colonel. Am I right?"

Aiden's pointed reference to honor, a topic of an earlier discussion between them, did not escape Aminu's attention, but he appeared relieved by Aiden's support. "Absolutely, yes."

Ebadi, resigned to the inevitable, let out a long breath. "It was about 10 years ago. His name was Dr. Anwar Cain, a visiting researcher from Mars, an ARM citizen. He did a three-year stint at the Cauldron. He was a tenured physics professor at Tharsis University and was doing some groundbreaking work in gravitational field detection. I remember him because we were at the Cauldron around the same time. Our areas of research were similar and we occasionally shared data. I also remember his interest in resurrecting the Füzfa Effect as a crucial step in developing an advanced form of quantum interferometry. It's brilliant work. As a result, quantum interferometry is now the cutting-edge technology in gravity-field detection. Dr. Cain left the Cauldron seven years ago, I believe, presumably returning to Mars. The Cauldron retained patent rights to the quantum interferometer he helped to build, and prototypes of the device remain at the Cauldron, still under development."

Aminu jotted down a few notes on his compad and nodded to her deferentially. "Thank you, Dr. Ebadi. When we reach the Cauldron, I may want to speak with any of Dr. Cain's associates who remain there. And if you can think of anything else about him or his work that might be helpful, please let me know."

Ebadi nodded without enthusiasm.

"One last thing, Colonel," Aiden added. "As captain of the ship and leader of this mission, I'll expect to be apprised of any and all information you gather in your investigations. Anything at all related to our mission. No 'need-to-know' restrictions. Understood?"

Aiden was banking on Aminu's sense of fair play in exchange for the support he'd given him earlier. Aminu didn't look happy about it but must have realized it was the right thing to do. "Understood."

Aiden stood from the table. "That's it for now. It's a start, at least. We'll be arriving at the Cauldron around 16:00 tomorrow. I don't anticipate staying there any longer than it takes to get this new equipment installed. A day and a half max. Is that about right, Dr. Ebadi?"

"That depends on the Cauldron's technicians," she responded. "But they've done a lot of advanced planning, and they're headed by a very capable chief. So yes, that might be feasible."

"Good. After that, we're off to V-Prime to make our jump out to Alpha-2 Hydri. And if all goes well at the Cauldron, our trip out to V-Prime might take only a matter of hours."

Lilly Alvarez was the only one of the four in the room not officially clued in to their plans for the zero-point drive. Her eyes went wide. "Is this 'new equipment' we're getting at the Cauldron what I think it is?"

"Could be, Lilly," Aiden said, smiling. "But keep it under your hat for now. Okay?"

"Roger that, Commander." Alvarez smiled back at him.

Aiden was glad to see all traces of her earlier sadness banished. On the surface, at least. He stood. "All right. Let's get going."

15

THE CAULDRON
DOMAIN DAY 84, 2218

SEEN FROM 5,000 kilometers out, it appeared as a mere speck of rock suspended in the eternal emptiness of space. But as the *Sun Wolf* approached, decelerating steadily toward it, the view of the Cauldron on the ship's main screen resolved into greater detail. One of the many unremarkable asteroids of the Apollo Group, it was a bleak shard of black siliceous rock roughly two kilometers in diameter, approximately oblong in shape and originally designated as 2004A. Aiden watched as the Cauldron's slowly turning bulk filled the screen, gradually blocking out more of the star-studded blackness. Sunlight from Sol highlighted its scarred surface in ever-changing patterns of black shadow and bright, frozen rock.

"Cozy," Aiden said. Ro and Ebadi were at his side on the bridge watching the spectacle grow on the screen. The deep rumble of the M/AM drive shuddered throughout the ship as it labored to bring the *Sun Wolf* to a full halt close to the asteroid.

Ebadi smiled. "It's not so bad, Commander. Wait till you're inside. It *is* kind of cozy."

"Okay. But cozy in a good way?" It was hard for him to envision everyday life carrying on inside such a forbidding chunk of rock, cast out in such a desolate realm.

The asteroids of the Apollo Group were a motley collection of tumbling chondritic bodies classified as Near-Earth Asteroids. They orbited Sol with a perihelion of less than 1 AU, but unlike the well-behaved asteroids of the Belt, which had orbital planes that remained roughly aligned with the System's ecliptic, the path of the Apollo Group ran 23 degrees inclined to it. They intersected Earth's orbit at relatively low velocities, making them easily accessible from Earth space. As for the Cauldron, its path around the sun crossed Earth's orbit every 1.12 years.

While 60 percent of the Apollo asteroids were carbonaceous chondrites, a large proportion of the remainder were iron-rich bodies, making them an attractive destination for Earth's early space miners. Twenty-three bodies in all had proven worthy of extensive mining operations. But after the discovery of voidoids opened the way to far richer mining prospects, the Apollos were for the most part abandoned. The only operation ever to occur on 2004A had been short-lived, back in the 2140s, run by a party of hard-luck miners who left an extensive matrix of bore tunnels before departing with very little in return for their efforts. Now it was one of the last places in the System anyone would want to go. A perfect place for privacy.

Maryam Ebadi had given Aiden a brief tutorial on the Cauldron's history when it first came into view. She told him that Elgin Woo's merry band of genius misfits had claimed 2004A 21 years ago under the provisions of the Ganymede Pact. They employed a variety of unorthodox methods to expand and recondition the existing system of tunnels, creating a warren of sealed corridors and chambers. On UED's government books, Woo's "corporation" was called Noetic Resources Unlimited. NRU's funds came strictly from private sources. Since the Apollo Group was no longer of commercial interest, and since Noetic Resources Unlimited was not an apparent factor in the mainstream economics of the System, it was largely ignored except within the most erudite of scientific circles. Which was precisely what Woo wanted.

He had renamed the asteroid the Cauldron after the Cauldron of Cerridwen of the ancient Celts. The mystics derived their visions by breathing in its intoxicating fumes, the *Awen*. Over time and inconspicuously, Woo and his cohorts assembled a sizable research facility within the rock. Astrophysics, cosmology, and the quantum sciences dominated the research activities of the Cauldron, but medical and biological sciences were also represented. A small, semipermanent group of gifted engineers, designers, and technicians resided here too. Experts at turning dreams into reality, they shared equal status with the pure-research types. The Cauldron's current census was 85.

Ebadi told him that, as director of NRU, Elgin Woo's function had evolved from founder/administrator into more of an inspirational figurehead. He acted as a catalyst stirred into the fertile mélange of ideas that continually percolated within the Cauldron, facilitating reactions and interactions among its illustrious, and sometimes querulous, members.

Woo himself had represented something of a throwback in the modern world of specialized knowledge. A quintessential Renaissance man, his intellectual curiosity was not limited by boundaries of traditional, or even nontraditional, academic disciplines. Guided by his holistic vision of knowledge, Woo had created the most ideal research environment attainable, where talented people with scientific training could return to the basic impulse behind all true science: a child's sense of wonder. Tenure was never an issue at the Cauldron, or the pressure to publish. No vicious hierarchies, no political conformities, and relatively few budget restrictions existed here. The prime ideology was the quest for pure knowledge, and the creative results continued to astound. Development of the zero-point drive was one crowning example.

Aiden pulled his attention away from the view screen and spoke to the pilot. "Park the ship at one kilometer and match the Cauldron's rotation spin to synch up with its docking bay."

Early on, Woo's founding group had tamed the asteroid's chaotic tumble but decided to retain a slow regular rotation around its long axis to distribute heat more evenly over the surface. The asteroid's perihelion fell inside 0.77 AU, close enough to the sun to cause uneven thermal stresses on an object the size of the Cauldron without a spin. Otherwise, spin was not needed to impart synthetic gravity. The Cauldron's powerful G-transducers took care of that.

The Cauldron's docking bay was not designed to accommodate ships as large as the *Sun Wolf*, only smaller vessels like shuttlecraft and maintenance sleds. Regular cargo vessels and voidships had to dock in proximity and conduct business via shuttle. Aiden anticipated frequent shuttle traffic during the drive installation and wanted the *Sun Wolf* to synch its position directly above the docking bay to facilitate the process.

"Alvarez, inform the SS *Endeavor* of our maneuver. They can set up whatever defensive position they think is best."

The *Sun Wolf* had picked up its second escort, the SS *Endeavor*, about an hour ago when the two vessels matched deceleration vectors. Aiden's brief exchange with the ship's captain, a Commander Clayton Ridley, had been all business and not particularly friendly. He could understand the man's perspective. Ridley had been pulled away from security duty at Friendship Station, guarding V-Prime, where things were getting dicey. Rumors of increased void fluxes and a possible suspension of all outgoing transits had created a volatile situation requiring heightened enforcement. Ridley had no idea why his top-of-the-line battle cruiser had been ordered to provide military escort for a Science and Survey vessel on its way to and from some godforsaken asteroid out in the Apollos. He was a professional and never actually said "this better be good," but everything about the exchange said it for him.

With the *Sun Wolf* locked in place one kilometer above the Cauldron, Aiden left the ship in Ro's command and collected Dr. Ebadi, Colonel Aminu, and Lieutenant Dalton. They boarded the ship's shuttle for the short hop to the Cauldron's docking bay. He wanted his Drive Systems Engineer along for the ride to meet with the technicians who would be installing the zero-point drive. Dalton was grinning ear to ear at the prospect of operating a revolutionary drive system he'd only heard rumors about, all of which sounded utterly fantastical.

Aminu was along for the ride to conduct his investigation. He wanted to use the little time he had on the Cauldron to interview its key residents and review its records. The facility's administrator pro tem, Dr. Cecile Schumann, had protested vehemently when he'd heard about it. But Ebadi, the Cauldron's acting director, overruled his objections without revealing any of her own frustrations over the matter.

They touched down on a landing platform that extended mechanically from the lip of a large opening near the asteroid's center. With their shuttle secured, the platform withdrew, pulling them into a small launch bay as the outer doors closed and sealed behind them. It took 10 minutes to repressurize the launch bay before it opened up into the main docking bay, a well-lit, cavernous space carved into the asteroid's interior. Several of the Cauldron's shuttle and maintenance craft sat resting amid a matrix of gantries and cargo cranes. Upon disembarking from their shuttle, the four were met by a small welcoming party headed by Dr. Schumann. He looked quite happy to see Dr. Ebadi, but much less pleased to meet Colonel Aminu.

After perfunctory introductions, Ebadi made it clear she wanted to proceed directly to a meeting with the lead technician handling the drive installation. They were led to a pair of automated transport cars waiting for them at a passageway leading into the interior. Aminu boarded one of them, accompanied by Dr. Schumann. Aiden, Ebadi, and Dalton boarded the other, and the cars sped off toward separate destinations. As they careened down a darkened transit tunnel, negotiating a complex maze of narrow corridors, Aiden held on tight and marveled at what Woo's group had accomplished.

The facility supported a totally self-sustaining biosphere, regulated by an Omicron-3 AI that excelled in systems homeostasis. The air smelled fresh. The recycled water, he was told, flowed abundantly and tasted clean, and the ambient climate felt comfortable. They passed a series of laboratories and workstations, all of which appeared to be spacious, well-lit, lively settings. Few people had ever set foot on the Cauldron—and not many more even knew of its existence—but this place struck Aiden as possibly the most important nexus of the human quest in all of Bound Space.

The car stopped at one of these work stations, larger than most of the others they had passed. It held a dizzying array of work tables, large, humming machines that Aiden couldn't begin to identify, and was surrounded by ceiling-high supply racks stocked with all manner of odd-looking machine parts. A tiny anteroom was situated near the entrance, and inside it, an equally tiny Asian woman sat at one end of a plain metal table. In her mid-thirties, with delicate features, she stood with athletic grace as they entered, smiling with her hand extended to Dr. Ebadi. "Good to see you, Maryam. I'm so relieved you made it back safely."

"Thank you, Min. Good to see you too. This is Commander Aiden Macallan," she said, gesturing in his direction. "Commander, this is Dr. Min Lee. She's the head propulsion technician here at the Cauldron and will manage the installation of the zero-point drive."

"It's a great honor to meet you, Commander," Dr. Lee said, holding her hand out to him. "You're something of a legend here. And everywhere."

Aiden felt his face flush. He'd been forever cursed by the affliction of blushing too easily in such situations. "Pleased to meet you, Dr. Lee." Her hand felt cool and small engulfed in his, yet her grip was surprisingly strong. She looked up at him with large and luminous dark eyes. To say she was a woman of small stature would have been an understatement. Aiden guessed she couldn't be much over four foot ten.

Ebadi turned to Dalton. "And this is the *Sun Wolf*'s Drive Systems Engineer, Lieutenant Zachary Dalton. You'll be working closely with him on the installation."

Dalton had that 'aw-shucks' grin going on again, a smile with megawatt charm. "Please to meet'cha, ma'am. You can call me Zak. Your name is Min? That's a pretty name. Is it short for mini?"

In the brief silence that followed, everyone including Dalton, realized how embarrassingly ill-chosen his last words had been.

"I mean...you're so petite. In a real pretty way, that is..." he said, then clammed up, blushing floridly, and began looking at his feet.

Aiden rolled his eyes at Dalton's foot-in-mouth moment. The man obviously hadn't paid attention to Ebadi's pronunciation of the name, focusing instead on the spelling he saw printed on Dr. Lee's name tag. "You'll have to excuse my lieutenant, Dr. Lee. He may be a brilliant Drive Engineer, but we believe he was raised by wolves and we're still trying to socialize him. I'm sure he meant no disrespect."

Dalton looked up sharply, a pained expression on his face. "No, ma'am! No offense. Not at all. I just..."

"Dalton," Aiden said, using a milder version of "the voice," an intonation of power he'd learned long ago as a survival tool. It came in handy now and then.

Then he noticed that both Dr. Lee and Ebadi were smiling. Ebadi's smile looked vaguely maternal. Dr. Lee's was shy but delighted. "No offense taken, Lieutenant," she said. "Actually, Min is my birth name. It's pronounced 'meen,' and in some parts of China it's the word for 'people.' It's a pleasure to meet you."

She held out her hand and Dalton took it gently in his own, as if it were a rare and exotic treasure. Aiden thought for a moment he was going to kneel on one knee and kiss her hand. Thankfully, the young man showed better sense than he'd displayed moments earlier. He nodded politely and the guileless grin returned.

"Dr. Lee," Aiden said. "Could you give us a brief rundown on how this drive works? And what we'll be able to do with it. How we'll operate it. Things like that. Then I'll leave the rest of it up to you and Lieutenant Dalton to get on with the details."

"Certainly, Commander. Please be seated. Any refreshments? Tea? Coffee?"

As they sat, Aiden could tell Dalton was about to answer in the affirmative and responded quickly. "No, thank you. We're fine. Please proceed."

"As you know," she began, "Dr. Woo was in the process of developing and testing a new kind of drive system for spacefaring vessels, the zero-point drive. We call it the ZPD for short. He installed a prototype of this drive, the first one ever constructed, into a small experimental craft he called the *Starhawk*. And, of course, you are aware of the part he and the *Starhawk* played in the Chara crisis."

"Oh yes," Aiden said. He was more than aware. He'd been there when it happened. No more than ten months ago, Elgin Woo had single-handedly prevented Cole Brahmin's anti-gluon device from turning Silvanus into a smoldering, planet-sized pile of rubble, and he'd done it through some creative application of his outlandish zero-point technology.

Dr. Lee smiled and continued. "Among the instructions Dr. Woo left on the cryptochip you delivered to us was that the Cauldron should develop a full-sized model of the ZPD that could be readily installed on the *Sun Wolf* as an auxiliary system to your current beamed core M/AM drive. That work was just completed, and my team of technicians is ready to start the installation. Upon your authorization, of course.

"You should know that other than Dr. Woo's prototype on the *Starhawk*, this is the only other ZPD in existence and that no other units can be made functional without Dr. Woo's presence. Technically, other units can be fabricated, but they cannot be activated without an encrypted key code that only Dr. Woo himself can provide. As per his instructions, you will be given the key code he formulated to operate the one drive we are installing. Considering the sad possibility that he may no longer be alive, this could be the only functional ZPD in existence for a very long time."

"Understood," Aiden said. "I will authorize the installation after I hear your summary of the ZPD's capabilities."

"Yes, of course. In a nutshell, this new drive system allows a ship to transition from a standstill to 92 percent light speed within a matter of a few seconds, and conversely from 92 percent light speed to standstill, also within a few seconds. It will drastically cut transit times within star systems. For example, your trip from here to V-Prime, over 13 AU away, will take only two hours instead of the six days it would take for even the most advanced M/AM drives like the one aboard the *Sun Wolf*."

Aiden saw Dalton's jaw drop and realized his own mouth had fallen open too. No voidship had ever traveled faster than 42 percent of light speed, and that velocity had required nearly five months of continuous acceleration at 1 G, the upper limit of current M/AM drives.

Aiden recovered first. "From a standstill? To 92 percent light speed? Within seconds?"

"Yes," she said, nonchalantly. "In about 11 seconds, to be precise. That's based on a 1 G pulse from the *Sun Wolf*'s main thrusters, given your ship's size and mass."

"Impossible," was all Aiden could say.

Min Lee smiled and said nothing.

Aiden glanced at Dalton, who only had eyes for Dr. Lee. The man was clearly in love.

16

THE CAULDRON
Domain Day 84, 2218

"Yes, it does sound impossible." Dr. Min Lee spoke without a trace of irony. "Even our most imaginative scientists here still find it hard to believe. Were it not for the documented proof of the *Starhawk's* exploits—brief as they were before Dr. Woo's disappearance—few would believe it at all."

Dalton, who had finally closed his mouth, said, "This has nothing to do with some new kind of propulsion system, does it?"

"That's correct, Lieutenant," she said appreciatively. "In fact, it will work with even the most rudimentary propulsion systems. Even attitude thrusters. We're not talking about acceleration capabilities here. The secret lies not in the power of thrust, or in the amount of reaction mass. That's incidental. What makes this drive work is the virtual elimination of inertia. Without inertia, even a minimal thrust can boost the ship to any velocity short of light speed and do it very quickly."

Aiden sat back abruptly. He felt his brain protesting. "Elimination of inertia? That can't be right."

"I said *virtual* elimination, not absolute. An artificial cancelation of inertia is maybe a more accurate description."

Either way, Aiden thought, the notion was nonsensical. He was not a physicist, but he understood the basic precepts they used to describe the physical universe. Inertia was one of those fundamental principles you just couldn't mess with. All mass possessed inertia, and the amount of inertia an object possessed was proportional to its mass. Inertia was the property of mass that caused it to resist changes in velocity or direction. You couldn't eliminate inertia without eliminating mass as well.

Dalton was now more than fully engaged, literally on the edge of his seat. "How?"

"I'll give you the short version for now. Given your time constraints," she said, nodding to Aiden.

It was a graceful concession, he thought. Dr. Lee surely knew that time was not his only constraint here; he was also way out of his depth in the quantum physics swimming pool.

"The concept came out of Dr. Woo's work to unify the theories of gravitational mass and inertial mass by representing them both as electromagnetic phenomena. He found that they're not only equal in value, but that they are in fact identical phenomena viewed from two different but complementary perspectives. In the process, he discovered a practical solution to the nature of inertia, one that we could put to work for us. It all has to do with zero-point fields."

Aiden scratched his beard. "Zero-point fields. As in the vacuum energy of space. Derived from random quantum fluctuations in a pure vacuum?"

"That's one way of looking at it, yes. These quantum fluctuations give rise to a soup of virtual particles that pop in and out of existence before they can be detected. Any mass that accelerates will encounter this soup of virtual particles, which exerts a pressure opposing the force of acceleration. By definition, that pressure against acceleration *is* inertia. Dr. Woo describes inertia as the electromagnetic drag caused by the acceleration of objects through the zero-point field. His deep understanding of this process led him to discover a way to manipulate zero-point fields with tuned EM generators, which then allowed him to control the phenomenon of inertia itself."

"Excuse me, ma'am," Dalton said. "But you're talkin' about inertial mass on a subatomic level. On the Planck scale. A nine-kiloton voidship isn't exactly subatomic."

"An excellent point, Lieutenant," she said, her eyes shining as brightly as Dalton's. "And that's exactly the problem we set out to solve. It's a matter of scale, really. By experimenting with various combinations of EM fields and extrapolating our formulae for the very small to the very large, we hit upon a set of resonances that could affect zero-point fields on the macro scale. We were then able to manipulate those control fields to push zero-point energy out of, and away from, a circumscribed region of space-time."

Dalton's smile had morphed from a charmer's grin to the beaming of a child's wonderment. "So you push away the zero-point field directly in front of your ship just as you're applying thrust. Since there's almost no zero-point energy left in front of you to exert inertia, you're off like a shot at near light speed, without having to sustain acceleration to get there!"

"Yes! That's it. Well done!" She clapped her small hands, smiling broadly.

They were like two kids together on Christmas morning opening the most wonderful presents imaginable. Aiden would have been amused if it weren't for the nagging safety concerns he had about such an outlandish scheme. He'd done some rudimentary calculations while Lee had been talking. "What about the effect this drive will have on the human body, on people inside the ship? To reach 92 percent light-speed in 11 seconds would require close to 3 million Gs acceleration. Aside from how crazy that number is, no inertial compensator ever conceived could handle forces that high."

"No, sir," Dalton answered before Dr. Lee could respond. "A ship using a drive like this wouldn't need inertial compensation. That's the beauty of it. When you cancel inertia, you also cancel the forces of acceleration."

Aiden sat back. It was a frighteningly simple idea. Which was probably why it worked.

"Yes," Dr. Lee said in response to Dalton's deduction. "But there's another reason, closely related to the one you just gave. This drive can generate a control field strong enough not only to push the zero-point field away from the front of the ship, but also to create a kind of bubble around the entire vessel in which the density of zero-point energy is greatly reduced in comparison to normal space-time everywhere else.

"We know that the speed of light in any medium, including the vacuum of space, is determined by the density of that medium, what we call its refractive index. The denser the medium, the higher the refractive index and the slower light travels through it. The vacuum of space, filled with nothing but zero-point energy, is assumed to be the least dense medium possible, so the speed of light through it is considered the upper limit, inviolable at about 300,000 KPS. But if you create a region around the ship in which zero-point energy is much *less* dense than the vacuum of space, it becomes a bubble in which the ultimate speed limit is *higher* than it is everywhere else outside the bubble."

Dr. Lee paused to let that sink in. Dalton's eyes went even wider, and the pitch of his voice rose with excitement. "So with the ZPD, the ship isn't actually movin' at 92 percent light speed in the *local* sense—inside the bubble—since a light beam within the bubble is still always movin' way faster than the ship. It's only 92 percent light speed as measured *outside* the bubble. So the laws of relativity are never violated."

Min Lee clapped again. "Yes, exactly! And since you're not actually travelling at relativistic velocities inside the bubble, the relativistic mass of the ship is *not* increasing, as general relativity would normally have it. And less mass means less propulsion energy required to achieve any given velocity."

"Dang!" Dalton slapped his hand down on the table and laughed. "That's brilliant! How fast can this thing go? Faster than light, in realspace?"

"No, no," she said firmly. "Not yet, at least. If it were possible to eliminate *all* of the zero-point energy around a ship, reducing it to absolute zero, maybe then. But that's an exotic condition we believe exists only inside a voidoid, where space-time is wholly absent. No, I'm afraid Einstein is still with us for now, and maybe always. As the velocity from this artificially induced process grows closer to the speed of light gauged in normal space-time, the discrepancy between the two speed limits gradually diminishes to zero until Einstein's speed limit is ultimately enforced. As it stands now, 92 percent light speed, relative to normal space-time, is the upper limit of this technology. That's roughly 276,000 KPS."

Aiden had to agree with Dalton. It truly *was* amazing. Profoundly ingenious. "It sounds like hyperspace," he said. "From the old holo-vids. This bubble surrounding the ship where the speed of light is greater than everywhere else. That's the old sci-fi concept of hyperspace."

Dr. Lee covered her mouth with her hand and giggled. It was a soft, musical sound, enchanting. "Yes. In fact, that's exactly what Dr. Woo said, too, referring to some ancient science fiction meme. But he called it *hypospace* instead. With an *o*, because inside the bubble there's a deficit of space-time, a negative value of zero-point energy compared with what's outside. Dr. Woo's hypospace is different than hyperspace."

"The hyperspace concept of sci-fi," Dalton said, nodding enthusiastically, "was based on the Alcubierre Metric that involved stretchin' the fabric of space-time to cause the space ahead of a ship to contract and the space behind it to expand. That would create a wave—they called it a warp bubble—that the ship could ride down and forward like a surfer. The interior of the bubble becomes the inertial frame of reference for any object inhabiting it, so the ship itself isn't actually moving *within* the bubble. Instead, it's being carried along as the region itself moves, so the laws of relativity are never violated."

"That's right," Dr. Lee said. "But the Alcubierre idea remains pure fiction. It could never be created in the real world. Dr. Woo's hypospace *does* work in the real world. Not by stretching space-time, but by altering the dynamics of inertia itself."

Aiden felt his head spinning. He glanced at Maryam Ebadi, who had been sitting quietly through the whole exchange. She smiled back at him sympathetically.

He sat up straight and pinched the bridge of his nose, trying to nudge his thinking process back into cold reality. "Okay. What about deflective shielding then? A ship travelling at 92 percent light speed encounters a random pebble in deep space, even the size of a pea, and *boom*! Instant annihilation. Our ship's MHD field is able to safely deflect chance encounters with errant space debris up to around 15 percent light speed. Beyond that, the probability of catastrophic impacts rises dramatically."

Dr. Lee nodded, still smiling. "The EM control field used to push zero-point energy away from the ship's bow also acts as a highly effective deflector shield. Even at near light speeds. The drive is actually pushing space-time away from the ship as it moves forward. Smaller space debris is tightly embedded in the fabric of space-time, so it gets pushed away too, out of harm's way. Up to a certain mass, of course. Larger objects with significant gravity fields, like asteroids, planets, or stars, distort space-time too deeply to be affected by an approaching ZPD. But those objects are easily detected and avoided by your ship's current navigational systems."

Aiden remained silent for a while, contemplating the wisdom of allowing such a powerful genie out of the bottle on his ship and the challenge of controlling it. "I assume that bringing the ship to a halt involves a process similar to what gets it going in the first place?"

"Yes, similar," she said. "Except you don't need to apply thrust in the opposite direction to decelerate. Just as the EM control field can be manipulated to reduce the density of zero-point energy in front of the ship, it can be configured to *increase* its density. That means increasing inertia, and that's what brings the ship to a halt. The process is not instantaneous. It has to be precisely graded to prevent the sudden reemergence of G-forces from crushing the ship. In fact, coming to a halt takes the same amount of time it does to reach its given velocity. For the *Sun Wolf* at 92 percent light speed, that would be 11 seconds. The control field is simply reversed to increase inertia, and you come to a complete stop. No noticeable forces of deceleration are felt inside the ship."

"Hey!" Dalton exclaimed, a bit too loudly. "That means we don't need to do turnaround maneuvers at the halfway point. Just go straight ahead to where we're goin' and stop. The ship stays forward-facing the whole time. No goin' in ass-forward half the time."

Dr. Lee smiled at Dalton's quaint choice of words and nodded.

"All right, Dr. Lee," Aiden said, growing anxious to conclude the meeting. "It's all truly astounding, and I'm almost convinced. Still, the only test flights ever done with this drive have been with Dr. Woo's *Starhawk*. That was a tiny vessel in comparison to the *Sun Wolf*, specifically designed for the ZPD. How well is it going translate to a much larger vessel with very different flight characteristics?"

"I understand your concerns, Commander. I can only say that there's a very high probability the ZPD will work just as well with the *Sun Wolf* as it did with the *Starhawk*. The main difference lies in the strength and the reach of the EM control fields to accommodate the greater size and mass of the *Sun Wolf*. The EM generators we've built for your ship are significantly larger and way more powerful than the prototype on the *Starhawk*. Beyond that, the control modules are essentially the same."

"Where's this greater operating power going to come from?"

Dalton chimed in again before Dr. Lee could respond. "Sir, I'm guessin' that the power we'll conserve by not having to use the M/AM at full blast all the time should be more than enough to meet those demands. Am I right, ma'am?"

"Yes, mostly right, Lieutenant. Powering the control fields at a constant level to maintain a hypospace bubble of this size throughout the flight does require a huge amount of energy. But since you're using your M/AM drive for only a few seconds to reach maximum velocity, you'll have more than enough antimatter fuel reserves."

She turned to Aiden. "And regarding your concerns about test flights, Commander, we can easily arrange a schedule for doing that, a measured protocol to ensure maximum safety."

Aiden glanced again at Dr. Ebadi. Her expression mirrored his own thoughts. "I'm afraid we're on a pretty tight schedule here. As Dr. Ebadi put it, time is of the essence. Our trip from here to V-Prime will have to be our first test flight."

Aiden detected a flicker of reticence in Dr. Lee's eyes at the notion of foregoing test flights but attributed it to a scientist's natural inclination for caution. An inclination apparently not shared by cowboy drive-engineers. Dalton looked more than eager to saddle up and head out.

"Very well," Dr. Lee said, nodding once. "We'll start the installation immediately."

"Thank you, Dr. Lee. One more thing. Dr. Ebadi mentioned that the Cauldron was working on something called a quantum interferometer, and you hold the patent rights on it."

"That's correct. It's a highly sensitive device capable of detecting gravitational fields, even at great distances, something considered virtually impossible until now. It's the most advanced technology of its kind, but still under development."

"But you have a functional prototype?"

"Yes. Two, in fact. Why?"

"We could use something like that where we're going. For our scientific investigations. Would it be possible to borrow one of your working prototypes and have it installed on the *Sun Wolf* as part of our sensor array?"

Lee looked puzzled for a moment. The exact nature of the *Sun Wolf*'s mission remained undisclosed to anyone not directly involved, including the inhabitants of the Cauldron. Then she nodded and glanced toward Ebadi. "With Dr. Ebadi's authorization, yes. It would be a relatively simple job, done as part of the drive installation."

"It's a good idea," Ebadi said. "Yes, I'll authorize it. In fact, I want to bring along one other experimental sensor, one that I've developed myself. It's a zero-point field detector, useful in voidoid research. I'll make it available to your technicians for the install."

Dr. Lee nodded again, plainly curious, but said only, "Of course. No problem."

Aiden thanked them both, then asked Dr. Lee how long it would take to get it all done.

"Fortunately, we've received in-depth technical specifications for the *Sun Wolf*, thanks to your Admiral Stegman. That helped us construct the device to precise tolerances and will also greatly facilitate its installation. It should be ready to go in 48 hours."

Aiden stroked his beard. "I'd prefer 36 hours. Can you manage that?"

That look of caution flickered in her eyes again before she spoke. "Yes, with Lieutenant Dalton's assistance I believe we can manage that."

"Good. Then I'll leave you to it." Aiden rose from the table, as did Ebadi. "And I'll leave Lieutenant Dalton at your disposal for whatever assistance you need."

Dalton flashed his megawatt smile. Dr. Lee's smile was more in her eyes, but no less enthusiastic. They both looked absolutely delighted at the prospect.

"Dalton." Aiden looked him square in the eye. "Learn as much as you can from Dr. Lee and from the technicians during the install. I'll expect you to be a zero-point-drive expert by the time we depart. We're depending on you, Lieutenant."

Aiden didn't need to spell it out beyond that. Dalton's expression shifted from slightly goofy to dead serious. He'd gotten the message: the lives of everyone aboard the *Sun Wolf* would depend on his thorough understanding of a radically new and virtually untested drive system.

Dalton stood straighter and squared his shoulders. "Will do, sir."

Aiden regarded him for a long moment. The lieutenant's sober demeanor at least *looked* genuine. Aiden glanced at Dr. Lee then back to Dalton. "And Zak...behave yourself."

"Yes, sir!"

Aiden clapped him on the shoulder. "Carry on, Lieutenant."

17

THE CAULDRON
Domain Day 84, 2218

Aiden and Ebadi left the lab and headed back toward where they'd parked their transport car.

"What are your plans for the day, Maryam?" he asked.

But Ebadi's attention was focused on her personal comm. She'd received a message and looked concerned.

"What is it?"

"It's Colonel Aminu. He's been locked out of the main habitat. On purpose, and by trickery. It seems that the good colonel has already ruffled some feathers."

Aiden shook his head, annoyed but also amused. "Why am I not surprised?"

"Same reason I'm not," she said with a sigh. "These are not 'normal' people he's dealing with here. They're fiercely independent, frightfully intelligent, and often surprisingly childlike. In a normal population, they're one in a million. Here, they're pretty much all like that. Each one believes he's smarter than everyone else, with the unanimous exception of Elgin Woo. But without Dr. Woo's guidance, things have gotten more out of hand than usual. I don't think Colonel Aminu is sensitive to any of that."

Aiden shook his head. "I don't think sensitivity is in the colonel's playbook. What does he want you to do?"

"He wants to continue interviewing people about Dr. Cain and the Cauldron's security protocols and to be given unrestricted access to the facility's records. He wants me to 'order' everyone to cooperate. As if that was in my power. I need to go deal with this now."

"Okay. I'll go collect Aminu if you can deal with the angry mob."

She agreed, but when they reached the transport car, Aiden got a call from Ro. "Commander, our long-scans are picking up the exhaust plume of an unidentified vessel about 2.5 AU out, to our south. It's big and moving fast. About 6,884 KPS right now and under constant accel. It's got to be a torch ship running hot."

It wasn't difficult to detect a powerful torch ship, even 2.5 AU out, if you knew exactly where to look. That was about 375 million kilometers, but even standard beamed core antimatter drives put out over 450 terawatts of thrust power. The exhaust plume from an engine with that much juice would be visible even at ten times that distance.

"Heading our way?" Aiden asked.

"In our general direction, yes. It's too far out right now to be sure, but it looks like they're on a course for V-Prime and could easily pass within 250,000 klicks of our position."

The hair on Aiden's neck prickled. "How soon will that be, Ro?"

"They're doing close to 1.5 G, so I'm guessing roughly 14 hours from now."

Aiden looked at his chrono. That would be around 12:00 tomorrow. "Have you checked with the Cauldron's flight control? Are they expecting any visitors?"

"Their flight control? Um...such that it is, yes, I did. There's no incoming traffic on their books. They say no one ever comes out this way anymore. Only vessels they know about in advance are ships servicing the Cauldron."

"Okay, Ro. Start hailing them for an ID."

"Already on it. I'll keep you posted."

The car took Dr. Ebadi to the Cauldron's administrative head-quarters to meet with Dr. Schumann, then took Aiden back to the docking bay, where he found Colonel Victor Aminu. The *Sun Wolf*'s shuttle sat at one end of the bay, and Aminu stood at the other end next to a closed hatchway, presumably leading into the Cauldron's living space, now locked from the inside. He was shivering from the cold of the docking bay—kept at a barely habitable 2 degrees C—speaking angrily into his personal comm. As Aiden approached, the look on Aminu's face made him wonder how much of the man's trembling was due to the cold and how much from rage.

"Open this door now!" he yelled into his p-comm. "You've got 30 seconds before I charge the lot of you with withholding evidence and assaulting a DSI officer! Do you hear me?"

Aminu pulled his p-comm away from his face as he saw Aiden approach. His smooth features were contorted with indignation. "This is an outrage! They can't do this!"

Aiden held his hands up, palms out. Instead of pointing out to Aminu that they *could* do it and in fact already had, he said, "Calm down, Colonel. We'll get this straightened out. Yelling's not going to help."

It wasn't exactly what Aminu wanted to hear, and not from the person he wanted to hear it from. He focused on Aiden as if seeing him for the first time and instantly directed his anger toward him. "You! You warned them before I got here. Told them I'd be interviewing them!"

"Sorry, Colonel. Can't pin this one on me. I know how that breaks your heart." Aiden reminded himself not to get sucked into a pissing match again with Aminu and changed course. He assumed a relaxed but respectful posture, hands loose at his side, about six feet away. He spoke calmly in a tone reflecting genuine interest. "So, tell me what happened."

It seemed to work. Aiden watched Aminu solve the complex equation of emotions required to bring him from a state of high agitation to one of controlled reason, all within the moment of a single deep breath. In and out. It was a mathematics Aiden knew well enough but still marveled at as he traced its torturous pathway winding through someone else's psyche.

"After consulting the staff records, I began my first interview with a scientist who's been here long enough to have known Anwar Cain. He actually worked for Cain as a research assistant before establishing his own lab. The interview started out well enough but grew increasingly difficult. He became more resentful with each question until he just flat-out refused to answer anything. Then he started questioning my authority here on the Cauldron and made some rude personal comments."

Aiden had no trouble imagining how this confrontation had played out, considering Aminu's abrasive style pitted against the thin-skinned flintiness of a typical Cauldron resident. But he nodded sympathetically and said, "Go on."

"I realized personal interviews would be more difficult here than I'd expected and decided it might go more smoothly if I did some research first before resuming. I'd look into the records of various scientists, their projects, their associations outside the Cauldron, any personal information of interest. That kind of thing. It would help me focus my investigations, given the limited time we have here. I called upon the acting director, this Dr. Schumann, to gain access to the Cauldron's database. I waited for a half an hour before he called back. By that time, word of my investigations must have spread."

"Why do you think that?" Aiden asked, now more interested in the story.

"Because Schumann lied to me. He told me the only place I could access the facility's complete database was in the 'Data Center' located near the core. He gave me a set of directions that led me through a complex series of passageways. The last hatchway led me here, where we are now, the docking bay. While I was trying to figure out where to go next, the hatch behind me closed and locked down. There is no 'Data Center.' This is where they wanted me. Out of their way. The only place I could go from here was back on board our shuttle. It's entirely unacceptable, Commander. Not to mention illegal."

"Look on the bright side, Colonel," Aiden said. "If they *really* didn't like you, they would have depressurized the docking bay and spaced you."

"This is not a joke! There are any number of felonies from this incident alone I'm authorized to charge."

Aiden refrained from pointing out how very short the long arm of the law was out here in this forsaken region of space. And he had no intention of backing up Aminu's authority with his own at this point, or for this purpose. There was a better way.

"I understand your position Colonel," he said, "and I concur that the information you're after could be critical to our mission. I want it too. But as Dr. Ebadi pointed out to me, the population here is quite a bit outside the average range of personality types. Their independence and skepticism are part of what makes them effective in what they do. They need to be approached differently than what you may be used to."

"I don't *care* how brittle these brainiacs are," Aminu countered, his voice rising again. "This is the law we're talking about. They either follow it or they don't, at their own peril."

Oh, how I wish things were so black-and-white, Aiden thought. He said, "Maybe you should care about it. Just a little. Might make things go smoother." He gestured toward the locked hatch as he spoke.

Before Aminu had a chance to get any higher on his horse, Aiden added, "Anyway, Colonel, Dr. Ebadi is the current director of the Cauldron. She has the authority to grant you access to the records you want. I'll ask her to do that."

Aminu said nothing but gave a small nod of thanks. Aiden then filled him in on the plan for the drive installation and the 36-hour target for completion. Which was now 35 hours and counting. "I want the *Sun Wolf* out of here as soon as possible, the moment the last component of the ZPD is screwed into place.

After going through all the data you'll get from Ebadi, you may not have time for any more interviews down here."

Aiden went on to tell him about the unidentified vessel coming their way, still over a half day away from their position but coming on fast. Aminu looked appropriately concerned, enough to diffuse much of the energy he'd invested in being offended. Aiden welcomed the shift. "I suggest we get back aboard the *Sun Wolf* now."

Aminu replaced his p-comm in a side pocket of his jumpsuit, straightened his collar, and said, "Agreed."

Aiden called Dr. Ebadi and told her that he'd found Aminu and that they were headed back to the *Sun Wolf*. She told him she'd be staying on the Cauldron over the next 24 hours to deal with administrative obligations piling up in her absence. Without Aiden saying so explicitly, she apparently sensed that he'd mollified Aminu's tantrum and readily agreed to grant access to the Cauldron's digital records. "They'll be waiting for him when you're back aboard the *Sun Wolf*."

"I've had a little chat with Dr. Schumann," she continued. "And he'd like to apologize to Colonel Aminu for his deception. It was misguided and he intended no harm."

Aiden was fairly certain Dr. Schumann had done no such thing and that Ebadi had fabricated the apology to ease tensions. But Aminu, who had been listening in, accepted it at face value. "Apology accepted," he said.

Aiden started off toward the shuttle. "Let's get going then."

Aboard the shuttle, Aiden instructed the Cauldron's launch techs to depressurize the bay, then told Hutton to take the shuttle out to the *Sun Wolf*. Once they cleared the outer bay door, the *Sun Wolf* came into view directly ahead one kilometer away. The ship appeared stationary, synched to the Cauldron's slow spin. The SS *Endeavor*, however, was out of sight. Commander Ridley had chosen to take up a defensive position five kilometers out but not synched to the Cauldron's spin. It gave him a more commanding view of the surrounding space and, he'd said, greater tactical leeway.

With only two of them aboard now, Aiden and Aminu sat in silence watching the *Sun Wolf* grow larger on the screen. Sol was nearly as bright out here as it was on Earth, and the ship gleamed like a sculpted sliver of pure energy set in the obsidian blackness of space. Aiden never tired of views like this, crystal-edged reminders of the terrible vastness of the void. Of how small life was, how fragile and precious it was surrounded by so much cold emptiness. He never tired of it and never stopped fearing it.

Aiden refocused. Without turning to Aminu, he asked, "What have you found out so far about this Anwar Cain?"

Aminu stirred from his own silence and worked at gathering himself to speak. "Dr. Anwar Cain. Well, it seems that he's now officially a missing person."

"Missing? How?"

"I've had my people look into everything that's known about him. I received their preliminary report several hours ago. Dr. Cain did indeed return to Mars seven years ago after his stint here at the Cauldron, just as Dr. Ebadi recalled. He resumed his position as tenured professor of physics at Tharsis University. Three months later, he informed the university he was resigning to accept a position as head researcher at Gravimetrics Inc., a privately funded research facility out at Ganymede. He said his farewells and was scheduled to depart on an In-Sys flight out to Jupiter-space, where he was to shuttle down to Ganymede."

Aminu paused, still looking at the forward screen. "Apparently none of that happened. He never took the In-Sys flight, and Gravimetrics later claimed they had never offered Dr. Cain a position. He's been missing ever since. None of his family members or colleagues know where he is or have any idea what happened to him."

"Didn't Mars authorities initiate a search?"

Aminu shook his head. "An official missing persons report wasn't filed until a year after his supposed departure for

Ganymede, and that was by his ex-wife after his alimony payment failed to show up. They'd been divorced since before his stint at the Cauldron. ARM law enforcement at Tharsis never followed up."

"That's curious. I would think the disappearance of such a prestigious ARM scientist would command more attention."

"Not really, especially coming to light one year after the fact. Plus, it's not uncommon for people who go missing on Mars to never show up. It's still an extremely hostile environment outside the domes, despite the terraforming projects. Actual physical searches out in the Barrens are too expensive and almost never successful."

Aiden nodded. It was the same way on Luna, and Mars's population was a hundred times greater. "Did you get anything else useful from your interviews today?"

Aminu gave a snort of derision. "Interview, you mean. Not plural. And an incomplete interview at that. But yes, it was marginally useful. I spoke with the one colleague of Dr. Cain's who probably knew him best, which was why I started with him. Name of Dr. Julius Stamp. From him I got a general feel for Cain as a person. He wasn't very social, didn't have close friends, but I gather that's the norm among these types. Still, Cain usually presented a sunny outlook and always seemed kind and considerate in his dealings with people. But, according to Stamp, Cain's demeanor changed radically during his last few months at the Cauldron."

"How so?"

"Apparently, he grew more sullen, avoided contact with others, more so than usual, was sharper with his research assistants, that kind of thing. Stamp chalked it up to Cain's annoyance over a patent dispute around a gravity detection device he was developing, some kind of interferometer. It didn't come out in his favor, or at least to the extent he wanted. But when Stamp stopped to think about it, he remembered Cain remarking that it was no big deal anyway because he had the Füzfa Effect nailed down, and that was going to be his claim to fame."

"Interesting."

"Interesting indeed. But beyond that, I didn't get much else out of Dr. Stamp. When I started questioning him about Cain's possible communications outside the Cauldron and about the facility's security measures, that's when things went downhill fast."

"I don't like the feel of this," Aiden said. "The number-one key scientist working on the Füzfa Effect goes missing, possibly disgruntled over a patent dispute with the Cauldron. Then a few years later someone starts screwing around with the voidoids using a technology that could come about only through a deep understanding of the Füzfa Effect."

"I agree," Aminu said. "I don't like it either. But I also don't like how neat it is."

Aiden was about to respond when Ro's voice came over the shuttle's comm. "*Sun Wolf*'s docking bay doors are open, Commander. You're clear to come on in."

"Thanks, XO," Aiden said. "Hutton, take us in."

18

THE CAULDRON
Domain Day 85, 2218

I

T WAS JUST after midnight when Aiden and Aminu came aboard. Ro informed them that the approaching UIV, the unidentified vessel, had not yet responded to hails. Even with the time lag at 2.5 AU, there'd been enough time for the ship to receive and send a response. Aiden noticed that the whole crew was still on the bridge—minus Dalton and Ebadi—preparing to switch duty shifts. He thought it would be a good time to fill them in on the zero-point drive and what it was supposed to do. Even as he tried to explain it, Aiden became painfully aware of how crazy the whole thing sounded. The crew reacted with less enthusiasm than he'd expected, but after fielding a few questions, he realized their attention was more focused on the steadily oncoming UIV than on the ZPD's fantastical capabilities.

"There's probably a perfectly benign reason for it," Aiden said, hoping to sound reassuring. "But after what happened back at Luna, we're not taking anything chances. We'll remain vigilant. Plus, we've got a UED battle cruiser watching our back, the *Endeavor*."

Ro insisted on taking the first watch. "Get some shut-eye, Commander. You look like you need it."

Aiden saw why when he entered his quarters and looked in the mirror. The dark circles under his eyes attested to how little real

sleep he'd gotten the night before. He sat on the small couch to
remove his shoes and had Hutton dial in the NewsNet on his vid
screen. *Bad idea.* It was a vidcast of the Earth First Party's flam-
boyant leader, Hugh Daw Thunck, presiding over another of his
endless campaign rallies.

As impossible as it seemed, Houda Thunkit had become the
leading contender in the upcoming elections for president of the
UED, and his Earth First Party was gaining strength in the leg-
islative branches. Only a few months ago, it seemed beyond ludi-
crous that a man of such little intelligence, integrity, or common
civility—not to mention his well-documented mental instability
and total lack of experience in government service—could actually threaten Michi Takema, probably the most well-respected,
compassionate, and effective leader the UED had ever seen. It
was a direct reflection of the population's rapidly changing mood,
mostly on Earth, where the fears and prejudices of a downtrodden
population had been so expertly inflamed by Thunkit's outlandish lies and his colorful, if not infantile, schoolyard bullying
style.

Sadly, Thunkit was not new to human history. He came from
a long line of similar scoundrels who always seemed to emerge
like foul excretions from the bowels of mankind's basest instincts,
always during times of its greatest change. Contrary to what most
observers believed, Houda Thunkit did not come out of nowhere.
He came from the collective dark side of us all. From the forces
of chaos and destruction that work tirelessly against the evolution
of civilization. He was us, as we dreamed him into being from our
darkest nightmares.

"And this damned alien fungus we've been infected with here
on Earth," Thunkit ranted, "it's gonna kill us all if we don't take
action. Can you even believe it? That it was *deliberately* brought
here to our beloved planet by some know-it-all scientists who say
it's gonna get the forests and food crops going again? But don't
you believe it, my friends!"

Houda Thunkit was a semi obese Caucasian man in his late 60s with a square, jowly face, and small, pale blue eyes squinting in theatrical disapproval. His generally disheveled appearance was appropriately crowned by the cheap, poorly fitted toupee he wore. "Why, already thousands of good people like you and me have had their brains infected by this evil fungus! It either kills 'em or, in the ones who survive, it controls their minds. This fungus is an alien species from outer space, and the goddamned scientists brought it here so it could invade our home planet and enslave us! How stupid is that?"

The camera panned to the crowd, who went wild with tribal cheering and chanting: "Earth first! Earth first!" Most of them wore red armbands embossed with a green circle symbolizing Earth, identifying them as members of the One Earth movement.

Why, Aiden wondered, did the Big Lie always work in situations like this? There were no human infections, no zombies under the control of the Rete. There was no alien invasion. Only a miraculous recovery of forest ecosystems devastated by the Die Back, thanks to the Rete. Yet the faces of those in the crowd, contorted with blind fervor, took as truth everything this charlatan had to say. The more outlandish the lie, the more vehemently they believed. Why?

The answer, Aiden thought, was always the same: fear and ignorance. Not just ignorance by misfortune, but *willful* ignorance. Glorified ignorance. The scene was so revolting to Aiden that he caught himself just before throwing his shoe at the screen. He was about to tell Hutton to turn the damn thing off, but, like the perverse compulsion to stare at the most gruesome of accidents rather than turn away in horror, his morbid curiosity kept his eyes on the screen.

"This sinister fungus that came from out beyond the stars," Thunkit was saying, "it's another reason we gotta shut down V-Prime. At least for now, until we figure out what's goin' on out there. Because right now that voidoid is just an open door for any other space creatures that might want to come for us. We need to protect ourselves, gather our forces inward to make our planet safe. To make Earth truly great again!"

More crowd chanting, "Earth first. Earth first!" Among the ordinary members of the One Earth crowd, Aiden noticed a few who wore combat attire with green bandanas across their faces. They formed in tight groups, hoisting banners emblazoned with the green circle on a red background and with two stylized swords crossed over the center of the circle. Soldiers of Green War were self-proclaimed domestic terrorists. Wasn't Houda Thunkit even a little bit concerned about welcoming their likes under his tent?

Apparently not. Basking shamelessly in the feverish energy he had whipped up, the expression on Thunkit's face glowed like a prophet's, but a prophet who served no god other than himself. His pathological narcissism would have been a fatal liability in any other setting. But here it gave him his power.

"Now," he continued, "the one good thing our current government is doin' right now is aiming to shut down all travel through V-Prime. That's the right thing to do, but they're doing it for the wrong reason. They say it's because of these void flux things that keep happening and how dangerous it is for spaceships going in and out of our system. Well, my friends, didja ever stop and think that maybe those fluxes are the voidoids' way of tellin' us to stay where we are? Right here in our own solar system? To keep out of where we don't belong?"

Aiden had to admit, he'd wondered the same thing about the voidoids. If they were living beings, as Elgin Woo believed, were the voidoids trying to send a message? Maybe Thunkit had a point. Granted, the visions spewed forth by mad prophets were usually the twisted manifestations of psychological imbalance, but who was to say some didn't come from elsewhere?

"But that's the *only* thing the government is doin' right. Once I'm elected by all you good people, I'll start by pulling out of the Ganymede Pact! There's so much wrong with that damned agreement, it's a crying shame. For instance, all the trade agreements between Earth Domain and the Allied Republics of Mars? They're criminally one-sided. To put it plainly, my fellow Earthers: we're getting' screwed! Mars gets most of its foodstuffs and other organics from us, and what do we get in return? Martian research and technology. Martian scientists! We don't *need* more damn science! Science is what got us in trouble in the first place!"

He pronounced the word *science* as if it were a profanity. It was a brilliant corruption of the truth, and Aiden had to marvel at the man's instinct for grabbing his audience by their amygdalae. Thunkit was tapping into that historical miasma of superstition rooted in the post–Die Back era referred to as the Twilight, when humanity was just reemerging from its self-inflicted near extinction. In a turn of irony so contrary to the facts, science and scientists were actually *blamed* for the Die Back, once again underscoring the utter fragility of human capacity for reason.

The truth, of course, was the opposite. Science and scientists had been warning people about the impending collapse of global ecosystems for over a century before it occurred. Warning them about it, loud and clear, and providing practical solutions to prevent it, all of which had been ignored by those with the power to do anything about it. During the Twilight, ignorance and bitterness had dominated a whole generation, until their children finally began to see the light and a way forward into it. Growing up in much improved conditions, they were the ones to usher in the renaissance of science, to bring about the New Age of Space, giving humanity another chance. But watching Houda Thunkit, Aiden saw the pendulum swinging backward again.

"That's the Martians for ya, eh?" Thunkit scoffed. "And that's why I'm for banning all future immigration from Mars to Earth!"

After another round of raucous cheering, Thunkit abruptly changed to a conspiratorial tone. "Friends, we don't need more Martians here on Earth. We all know the Aresites are different from us, and not in a good way. They may not even be human anymore, by God, the way they've changed their bodies with these biome treatments. They don't look like us, and they don't think like us, and all they want is to *take* from us. They're the sons of traitors to Earth. We started the colonies on Mars, but it didn't take long for those sneaky bastards to take over and disavow their own kind, their own fatherland here on Earth!"

The mob roared, angry at the gross historical injustices Thunkit had just fabricated. He was referring to the first colony on Mars established in 2132 and the subsequent declaration of Martian Independence 15 years later, in 2147. There had been no war, no significant resistance on the part of Earth's UED. It had, in fact, been a healthy separation based on mutually beneficial agreements. Yes, the people of Mars did look different now, subtly at least, due to generations of birth in its low-gravity environment and to other physical features resulting from the gut-biome modifications that helped them thrive there. But with Thunkit's unabashed use of the term *Aresites*—one of the most denigrating epithets ever given to the Martian people—he was masterfully harvesting Earthers' fear of "the other" and their blind impulse to blame "the other" for their own inadequacies.

"And another part of the Ganymede Pact I hate," Thunkit ranted on, "is including this alien intelligence, this thing they call the Rete, as an actual member of the Pact! Recognizing it as a sovereign entity. Giving it equal say in what we can and can't do out there with that planet. A fungus! Can you believe it, friends?"

The crowd booed, but not in the good-natured way a crowd might do for an opposing sports team. More visceral. Way uglier.

In his fervor, Thunkit's toupee had slipped to one side of his balding head. Its shoe-polish-brown color appeared homogenous throughout, a comically poor match for his graying temples and eyebrows. He reached up, readjusted it, and continued without a hint of embarrassment.

"So, when I'm elected, all that bullshit is out the window! I'll shut down that useless Silvanus Project, bring those scientists back here, maybe even prosecute them for treasonous deeds. That space creature, the Rete, is not our friend, for God's sake. It wants to invade us. I say we not only kill all of it that's already here on

Earth, but we should sterilize that planet Silvanus before leaving it. Make sure it's no longer a threat to us!"

Aiden felt sick with rage. He wanted to reach into the screen and strangle the man with his bare hands. He might have actually lunged at the monitor had Hutton not intervened. "Aiden, Dr. Sudha Devi is at your door and would like a word with you."

Aiden took a deep breath, let it out slowly, turned the sound down, and said, "Enter."

Dr. Devi came through the doorway, took one look at the vid screen, then scowled at Aiden. "This is how you relax before your sleep cycle?"

She did her best to appear stern and disapproving, but her lovely face had never been made for it. "As your physician, Commander, I am prescribing this: Hutton, turn off the NewsNet."

"With great pleasure," Hutton said, and the screen went blank.

Devi looked Aiden in the eye. "Are you *trying* to give yourself nightmares?"

Aiden smiled and his mood lifted, as it always did in Devi's presence. "At ease, Sudha."

It was the code to indicate their conversation would now proceed on a more comfortable first-name basis. "Have a seat. What's on your mind?"

Devi stood for a moment longer looking at him, her hands on her hips. She shook her head slowly, then allowed a subtle smile to brighten her face. She sat across from Aiden. "Two things, actually. The first concerns the crew, their general emotional state right now. I'm sure you've picked up their rising anxiety over these attacks from an unknown assailant, and over the seriousness of this mission, the details of which they don't fully understand."

"Yes, I'm aware of how they're responding," he said. "I'm feeling it, too, Sudha. But it's nothing they can't handle. They're all experienced spacers. And two of them are from the military, with combat experience."

Devi nodded thoughtfully. "Yes, the two youngest among us." She let that hang in the air for a moment before continuing. "I agree, they're all handling the stress relatively well, in their own ways, but things are likely to get more difficult going forward. Anything we can do to help them continue handling it is highly recommended."

Aiden sat back and folded his hands on his lap. "What do you suggest?"

"What I'm hearing most from the crew, both verbally and nonverbally, is a longing to communicate with their loved ones. The personal comm lockdown we've been under from the onset is having a negative effect. A pronounced one, in my opinion. I'm sure you can understand that yourself."

As usual, Sudha Devi had his number. "You know I do, Sudha."

"Yes, I do. When was the last time you were able to communicate with Skye?"

The subject rekindled the ache in his chest he'd been trying hard to ignore. "I received a message from her four days ago, the night we left Hawking Station. It came in right before I evoked the comm lockdown."

Devi nodded. "And you didn't respond."

"No, I didn't." Aiden ran a hand through his hair. "I wanted to. In the worst way. But I couldn't do it, not in good conscience."

She nodded again. "This is why your crew is proud to serve your command, Aiden. They know you're a good man, someone with real integrity. They can trust you implicitly. That will go a long way in the coming days."

Aiden smiled self-consciously. When Devi remained silent, he said, "But...?"

"But I'm wondering if there's some way we can at least get a message out to their families, to the people they care about most, just to let them know they're okay. That could make a big difference for them in the coming days."

"Sudha, you know I can't authorize personal comm messages. Not only is it a direct order from the Admiralty, but it's one I agree with. We don't know who's out there trying to destroy us or what their tracking capabilities are. I can't risk it. Personal comms are too hard to secure. They're aimed at highly predictable destinations within the System, including V-Prime and the Holtzman buoys in other star systems. They're too easy to intercept by someone else."

"I understand. But I'm not talking about using the personal comm transmitter."

"The secure operational comm? That's only for communication between the *Sun Wolf* and the Admiralty back on Luna. It's highly encrypted and tight-beamed. It uses a totally different transmission device."

But Aiden already saw where she was going with this. Devi put it into words. "What would it take to send Admiralty an encrypted file containing a brief message from each of the crew addressed to a designated recipient of their choice—a family member, a spouse—and ask that it be delivered to them through normal channels?"

Aiden stroked his beard and thought for a moment. "The messages could not contain any information related to our location, or anything alluding to our mission."

"Absolutely. That would be understood," she said, her eyes hopeful.

"Maybe. If those conditions were met, the Admiralty might at least consider it."

"You're close to Admiral Stegman, are you not? A long history with him, under adverse conditions?" Beneath her serenely benevolent demeanor, Devi could be a shrewd operator.

But Aiden was already liking the idea and surprised that he hadn't come up with it himself. It would give him a chance to alleviate the heartache he felt over his failure to respond to Skye's last message. She had seemed unusually vulnerable, which made him feel the same.

"Okay, Sudha. Let's do it. I'll let you handle informing the crew and collecting their messages. I'll handle Admiral Stegman and do my best to make it happen."

Devi smiled. It was like warm sunlight, natural as can be. "Thank you, Aiden," she said, then added with a sly grin, "You'll be even more popular now."

"Hmmm..." After an easy silence, he asked, "What's the second thing you wanted to bring up?"

Devi looked into his eyes in a way unique to her alone: probing but noninvasive, compassionate but not indulgent. "Continuum...?"

"Not using it now," Aiden said. The exchange covered a lot of ground they'd gone over together in the past months. Nothing else needed to be said.

She stood and said, "Good. Now, no more NewsNet. You need your beauty rest."

"Yes, Doctor."

Before closing the door on her way out, Devi looked at the ceiling briefly and said, "Hutton, play 'Ocean Meditation #78.'"

Soothing sounds of an ocean shoreline filled the space of Aiden's quarters, the soft murmuring of gentle surf caressing a smooth, sandy beach, lovingly, eternally. Aiden climbed under the covers and was out like a light.

19

THE CAULDRON
DOMAIN DAY 85, 2218

AFTER HIS FIRST truly restful sleep cycle in several days, Aiden was back on the bridge the following morning at 08:00 to relieve Ro. The ZPD installation was in full swing with shuttle craft buzzing back and forth between the *Sun Wolf* and the Cauldron and crews of technicians swarming the ship's lower decks.

Aiden came up to the Command station and stood next to Ro. "Status?"

"The UIV will reach its closest approach to our position in about four hours. That's the transect point, about 251,000 klicks out from us. It's about 106 million klicks away from that point right now, travelling over 7,410 KPS. We've been able to calculate its constant acceleration rate at 1.5 Gs. It's definitely a hot torch ship, running over 500 terawatts thrust power, judging from its exhaust plume."

Holy shit! Who the hell was this? "Still not responding to hails?"

"No, sir. We've tried on all standard frequencies. Repeatedly. They're not talking and they're not trying to hide. I've initiated a Level One alert. All weapons and shielding at max readiness."

"Good. And the *Endeavor*?"

"Commander Ridley's got the *Endeavor* on Level One too. He'll start actively targeting the UIV when it nears the transect point. He's also standing ready to take the *Endeavor* out to engage at the first sign of hostile intent."

Aiden felt uncomfortable with that idea. The *Sun Wolf* was in the midst of a complicated drive-system upgrade and in a vulnerable position. Yes, the ship had its defense systems up and running. But they weren't mobile right now, at least not enough for standard tactical maneuvers. The thought of the *Endeavor* leaving them unguarded to engage a potential threat closer to its source made him nervous. He knew that Lieutenant Billy Hotah had served with Ridley aboard the *Endeavor* and decided to ask him what he thought about the strategy.

"I understand Commander Ridley's reasoning, sir," Hotah said. He'd turned in his swivel chair to face Aiden. The speckled band tattooed across his face from ear to ear, passing beneath his eyes, seemed flushed a darker shade of red than Aiden remembered. His dark brown eyes burned with preternatural concentration. But he spoke in a calm and measured way.

"When protecting a valued asset, staying too near it presents an enemy with a single target on which to concentrate all its weapons, greatly increasing the probability of inflicting damage both to the asset and the vessel guarding it. By going out to engage the enemy, the *Endeavor* creates a tactical dilemma for the attacker. It'll force the enemy to use much of its weaponry defending against the *Endeavor*, leaving fewer of its resources available to use against us. Weapons systems are expendable resources, especially missiles and other kinetics. Even beam weapons require time and huge amounts of energy to recharge."

Hotah paused for a moment to glance back at his screen where he'd been monitoring the UIV's progress. His long, dark hair raked past his shoulder when he turned back to Aiden. "On top of that, the strategy opens up two separate and fully active defensive bubbles, the *Endeavor*'s and ours. If the *Endeavor* stayed here, there'd be only one defensive bubble, because his and ours would overlap. It's not an efficient use of both ships' defensive systems. This way, if any weapons get past the *Endeavor*'s defenses, they can be dealt with more effectively with ours."

"All right, Lieutenant," Aiden said. "You said you understood the reasoning. But do you agree with it?"

Aiden knew he was putting Hotah on the spot but wanted to know how he'd respond.

"I agree that it's a sound strategy," Hotah responded without hesitation, "as long as this UIV is the only threat in the vicinity and there are no other bad guys within combat range."

"Okay," Aiden said. "And how sure are we of that?"

"I can only tell you that we've deep-scanned every cubic meter within a four-million-kilometer radius of our position. Other than two other Apollo asteroids, very small ones and far away, there's nothing."

"Very well. Thank you, Lieutenant." Aiden sat back, somehow feeling less assured than he'd expected. All they could do now was wait. He glanced around the bridge to inventory the crew. Except for Ebadi, who was still on the Cauldron, and Lieutenant Dalton, who was down below supervising the ZPD installation, the rest of the crew were at their stations, including Pilot Abahem. Colonel Aminu had emerged from his quarters and stood next to Aiden.

At 09:45, Hotah's posture tensed. "We're being actively scanned by the UIV. Tactical sensors are picking up high-intensity targeting lasers."

Aiden felt perspiration pop up on his forehead. "What's their line-of-sight distance now?"

"About 60 million kilometers."

Ro, who had stayed on deck for the action, said, "That's some mighty sophisticated targeting hardware to dial us in that tight at 60 million klicks."

Aiden nodded. "XO, suspend all shuttle traffic from the Cauldron until further notice. Get Dalton to cease all installation work down below and move the technicians to the emergency chamber."

Commander Ridley's voice came over the comm. "*Sun Wolf*, our position is being actively targeted. I am now taking the *Endeavor* out to the transect point to engage the UIV. I suggest you keep all defense systems at Level One. Out."

Aiden switched the forward screen view to pick up the image of the *Endeavor* as the battle cruiser reoriented then ignited its M/AM drive. The optical filters kicked in to subdue the intense brilliance of the exhaust plume. They continued to monitor the *Endeavor*'s progress on the tactical screen. At 1 G, it would close in on the transect point in about two hours, just as the UIV reached the same position.

At 10:50 they watched the *Endeavor* make its turnaround maneuver to decelerate. Ridley apparently preferred a standstill position if he needed to engage the rapidly transiting UIV. Better targeting solutions, Aiden guessed.

Moments later, Ridley's voice came over the comm. "We've just completed turnaround. Our ETA at transect is 11:55 hours. The UIV is within 32 million klicks and closing at over 7,560 KPS. Our preliminary analysis of its exhaust signature indicates an ARM Militia battleship. A big one, probably M class. Out."

Aiden exchanged glances between Ro and Hotah, then Aminu. The colonel's eyes narrowed, his grim smile utterly humorless. He spoke with quiet intensity. "A Martian battleship. An M class. Top-of-the-line warship. Only three of them exist, the cream of ARM's military fleet. Make that two, now that the RMV *Markos* disappeared."

Aiden stroked his beard. "What the hell is she doing out here? And why is she refusing to identify themselves?"

"And targeting us," Aminu added. "A blatant violation of all treaty agreements between ARM and the UED. Hostile intent is the only answer."

"If that's an M class," Hotah interjected, "the *Endeavor* is seriously outclassed."

Ro looked at Hotah and asked, "Is it still on course for V-Prime?"

Hotah tapped at his tactical board. "Yes, sir. Dead-on, straight for V-Prime. If they plan on stopping at V-Prime, it'll take them about six days from now."

Once again, all they could do was wait.

At 11:52 they watched on the monitor as the *Endeavor* slowed to a standstill near the transect point. Ridley's voice came over the comm. "We're now within 10,000 klicks of transect. The UIV will pass by in a couple of minutes. We are actively targeting each other. Still no response to hails."

Hotah shook his head. Aiden noticed and asked, "What is it, Lieutenant?"

"Doesn't make sense, sir. If the ARM battleship wanted to attack, it would've done it by now or within the next few seconds. Given their extreme velocity, tactical parameters get all messed up after that."

The entire crew held its breath as they watched the UIV approach the transect point then zip past at 7,625 km/sec. Without a shot fired.

Moments later, Ridley reported again. "ARM ship passed without engagement, and it's already out of our engagement envelope. We're also working on making a positive ID. Still advise the *Sun Wolf* to maintain Level One alert. Out."

Aiden felt his heart slow down, his breathing steady. "What the hell was that about?"

Aminu said, "The *Endeavor's* presence may have been enough to deter an attack."

Hotah shook his head. "With all due respect, sir, I served on the *Endeavor*. In a one-on-one confrontation at that range, the *Endeavor* wouldn't present a significant deterrence to an M-class battleship."

Ro said, "Maybe they're innocently on their way to V-Prime and just happened to be passing close to the Cauldron on the way. Then when they spotted the *Endeavor* nearby, they decided to run targeting solutions just in case. Standard military precautions."

Ro. Always playing devil's advocate. Aiden didn't buy it. "Then why didn't they respond to hails to ID themselves?"

Ro shrugged. "Where'd they come from anyway? It's a torch ship. Presumably we can trace their trajectory backward, given their current velocity and acceleration, to estimate their point of origin."

Ro's sudden shift in direction sounded like a diversion at first, but it dawned on Aiden where he might be going with it. He nodded to Hotah. "Run those numbers for us, Lieutenant."

But before Hotah could comply, warning sirens blasted the bridge, red lights flashed on all the comm boards, and Hutton's voice came loud and clear. "Incoming missiles. Ten in number. Impact in 13 minutes, 40 seconds."

Aiden bolted out of the command chair. "What the hell! Coming from where?"

Hotah was already tapping into the tactical computer. "Source is from one of those tiny asteroids in our neighborhood. About 990,000 klicks out. I've locked on to the missiles now. They're fast. Probably antimatter-drive torch missiles."

"*Ten* of them," Aiden said, keeping his voice steady. "That's too many and too fast for our point-defense to take them all out."

"Correct, sir. If we wait until they're within our point-defense perimeter, the system will be overwhelmed. These missiles are incredibly fast and getting faster by the second, over 300 Gs constant accel. Easily twice as powerful as the one we shot down at Luna. And there're ten of them. By the time even one gets within range of point-defense, it'll be travelling over 2,400 KPS. That doesn't leave enough time for the laser grid to make a reliable kill before impact. Especially if they've got super-hardened armor. The only real option we have is to pick them off with our laser cannons. I'm locking them in now."

"Alvarez, notify the Cauldron that we're under attack, and they're in the line of fire too. Whatever point-defense system they have, now would be a good time to power it up. Hotah, you got all our guns on line?"

"Problem, sir," Hotah said. "We're only able to use two of our four laser cannons."

"What? Why?" The *Sun Wolf* had four swiveled laser cannons mounted on its armored surface, each placed 90 degrees from the other to cover the entire ship within a defensive sphere. Even three cannons in play could handle targets approaching from almost any given direction.

"Our position here is stationary," Hotah said, "and one of our cannons is facing the Cauldron. Can't use that one. The power for another one has been temporarily shut down by the technicians so they could work on a power shunt for the new drive system."

"Can we power it back up now?"

"Not in time," Ro answered. He'd already checked the status of the power shunt.

"Damn! Okay, we've still got two functional cannons, and what? Thirteen minutes now, before impact? That should be enough time to kill ten missiles. Can we start hitting them now?"

"Sir, targeting isn't accurate until the missiles are within one light-second. That's 300,000 klicks. They won't be in that range for another 11 minutes. Then we'll only have about 2.5 minutes to kill all ten."

"That's still enough time, right?"

"Maybe," Hotah said, doing the math in his head. "Depends. If they're top-of-the-line military-grade missiles, they'll be super-hardened. Heavy nonablative armor. Takes a much longer laser burn to kill. And the longer the burn, the longer it takes to recharge the cannon. We'd be fine if we had three of our four cannons on line."

"Or if we had the *Endeavor* back here with us," Aminu said ruefully.

"But they're not," Hotah said curtly. "Our only chance is to burn these missiles with our two remaining cannons. It'll be tight, though. We might not have enough time to get all ten with only two cannons. I'll set up the best possible targeting solution now then let the tactical computer execute the engagement."

"All right, Lieutenant. Get to it then." Aiden was encouraged by Hotah's admission of the AI's vast superiority over any human in reaction times. It sounded like they'd need to manage every fraction of a second perfectly to survive this attack. Only then would they be able to think about who had launched it, and how.

But Ro was already thinking about it. He lifted his head from the screen he'd been poring over and said, "I've scanned over everything that's known about this asteroid where the missiles came from. It's no more than a huge boulder, about 230 meters across. Official designation 2031WD. Only recorded activity there was back in 2145 by the same miners who worked the Cauldron. They made a few bore holes, didn't find much, and abandoned the rock after about six months. Nothing beyond that."

"A few bore holes?" Aiden said. "Perfect place to conceal a rack of missile launchers."

"Commander," Hotah said. "I've set up the targeting program. The moment the first missile crosses the 300,000-klick mark, the two cannons will target one missile each and fire a 10-second burn, followed by a 20-second recharge period. That's a 30-second cycle to kill two missiles at a time. That should do the job but cuts it real close. The last two missiles will be our main concern. They'll be only 15 seconds away from impact by the time the laser burn starts. Even if they're destroyed before impact, we'll still get hit by the blast energy and debris coming at us over 2,400 KPS. And our shielding won't be at max strength because of the power drain from all the laser shots. Probably enough to deflect most of the energy pulse, but we should be prepared for some damage from debris."

"Very well, Lieutenant. Proceed. When will the firing sequence commence?"

Hotah looked up with no fear in his eyes. He was in his element. "Right about now, sir. Hutton will monitor the progress."

As if on cue, Hutton reported, "Missiles at 300,000 kilometers. Laser cannons firing."

After several heartbeats, Hutton said, "Two missiles destroyed. Cannons recharging. Eight missiles remain. Impact in two minutes."

Another pause, then, "Missiles at 237,700 kilometers. Laser cannons firing." Pause, then, "Two missiles destroyed. Cannons recharging. Six missiles remain. Impact in 1 minute, 30 seconds."

Aiden's mouth went dry. His heartbeat pounded in his ears.

"Missiles at 173,300 kilometers. Laser cannons firing." Pause. "Two missiles destroyed. Cannons recharging. Four missiles remain. Impact in one minute."

Aiden looked around the bridge. If they survived this, the snapshot he took in his mind of each crew member at that moment would stay with him forever as the most candid portrait possible of each of their souls.

"Missiles at 106,200 kilometers. Laser cannons firing." Pause. "Two missiles destroyed. Cannons recharging. Two missiles remain. Impact in 30 seconds."

The gold ring on Aiden's left hand grew warm. He heard Skye's voice in his head and thought he saw her looking back at him in the screen's reflection. *"I love you, Aiden,"* she said.

"Missiles at 36,400 kilometers. Laser cannons firing."

That sounded like a long way off, but when the instruments of death were screaming toward you at 2,400 km/sec, they'd cover that distance in less than 15 seconds. But how much less? Would the laser burns destroy both of them before they hit the *Sun Wolf*?

"One missile destroyed. One remaining. Impact in five seconds."

Oh shit! "Brace for impact!"

Death was a simple thing, really. One moment you existed, and the next moment you did not. Aiden closed his eyes. *I love you, Skye...*

But nothing happened. He opened his eyes. They were still alive.

"Remaining missile stopped," Hutton said with a hint of boredom.

"Stopped?" Aiden looked around. The crew were in various stages of disbelief and relief. "What do you mean, Hutton?"

Hutton ignored the question and said, "Debris field from missile number nine will impact in five seconds."

"Brace for impact!" Aiden shouted once again.

The ship shook. The hull rang like a bell, a low, hollow sound that rattled Aiden's teeth. Then rang a second time. Warning lights flashed red. Another earsplitting clang was followed by two more in quick succession. The ship jolted to one side, bellowing as if in pain. Damage sirens went off, adding a high-pitched shriek to the already terrifying cacophony.

"Hull breach on the engineering deck," Hutton reported. "Structural automend system activated."

"Hutton, shut down the alarms and put me through to Lieutenant Dalton."

The debris impacts had stopped. The warning sirens ceased, but the sound that came through the comm from Engineering was just as frightening—the roaring sound of air rushing out into the vacuum of space through a jagged gash in the ship's hull, punctuated by the shouting of men and women in pain and panic.

"Dalton," Aiden yelled into the comm. "Damage report!"

Aiden had to repeat his request before Dalton's voice finally came through. "We've got a half-a-meter-wide hull breach down here, sir, but it's under control. Should be sealed up in a few more seconds. Decompression minimal. Fortunately, whatever hit us didn't come through, just punched a hole then bounced off. But we've got at least one casualty and some injuries."

Not good. "How many?" There were six Cauldron technicians down there with Dalton, including Dr. Min Lee.

"One is dead. Three more injured, one of 'em pretty bad. I'm a bit banged up myself but nothing serious."

Aiden's stomach knotted up. "Dr. Lee?"

"Yep, she's here. She's okay," Dalton said, clearly relieved.

"All right, Lieutenant. I'm sending Dr. Devi and Faye down to help you out."

20

THE CAULDRON
DOMAIN DAY 85, 2218

AFTER DISPATCHING THE Medical Officer and Faye Desai down to Engineering, Aiden turned his attention to the fate of missile number ten. "Hutton, I repeat. What do you mean the missile has been stopped?"

"I mean that missile number ten has stopped in its tracks," Hutton said, as if nothing could be more obvious. "Dead still, at approximately two kilometers from the Cauldron."

An image of the missile appeared on the screen, perfectly still in space but with its antimatter engine still blazing away, as if all its immense momentum had been met by an equally powerful force in the exact opposite direction. Like a trick of inertia...

Aiden glanced at Ro and saw a blend of amusement and appreciation on his face. Ro had seen this before, just last year at Silvanus when Elgin Woo pulled the same trick on a deadly anti-gluon torpedo, stopping it cold on its way to destroying the planet.

"Look familiar, Ro?"

Ro nodded. "Indeed it does. Dr. Ebadi mentioned that the Cauldron had its own unique defense system. 'Exotic' is how she described it, I believe. Must be the same inertia-controlling technology Dr. Woo had aboard the *Starhawk* back at Silvanus. Pretty damn slick."

Hotah was the next person to recover from the incongruity of what they were seeing. He turned from the tactical screen, looking like he'd seen a ghost. "What the hell was that?"

"Manipulation of inertia, Hotah," Aiden said. "The Cauldron scientists have figured out how to defeat inertia to make their zero-point drive work. Using the same process in reverse, they can also *increase* inertia. That's how the drive brings the ship to a halt. But projected as a field, it acts like a shield that stops moving objects in their tracks. Like hitting a wall but without the radical G-forces of instantaneous deceleration."

Hotah continued looking at Aiden as if having trouble seeing his face.

"I know," Aiden said. "Sounds bizarre. Get used to it. There's more to come."

"The *Endeavor* is on her way back," Alvarez said from Comm/Scan. "Commander Ridley is on the comm."

"Open."

Ridley's face appeared on the screen. He looked disconcerted. "Commander Macallan. We saw what happened. Sorry we couldn't have been there to assist. Frankly, I'm amazed you survived it. Some pretty fancy shooting there."

"We have our Tactical Officer to thank for that," Aiden said, "along with a little help from the Cauldron's defensive measures. Commander, did your sensors pick up any radio emissions from the ARM ship as it passed by? Any signals aimed at where those missiles came from?"

"No, we didn't. And I know what you're thinking. I have my suspicions too. But we didn't detect any remote signaling from the vessel. Still, it seems too coincidental."

"Agreed," Aiden said. "What if the ARM vessel's flyby was a decoy, deliberately intended to draw the *Endeavor* away from its real target, the *Sun Wolf*?"

"If so, it's an implicit act of war."

"The last I checked," Aiden said, "ARM and the UED were not at war. Overtly, at least."

"That remains to be seen," Ridley said, also looking dubious. "I'll be filing a report with the Admiralty on this incident, and no doubt diplomatic channels will be buzzing. I don't know what your mission is, Commander—I wasn't informed and I don't want to know—but it looks like some pretty serious dudes want you and your ship dead. That attack was textbook, maybe the most sophisticated and lethal I've seen against a single ship. You're damn lucky to be alive."

Aiden glanced at Hotah, who looked back and silently mouthed, "Not luck."

"Yes. Formidable enemies," Aiden agreed. "Made worse by not knowing who they are. All the more reason for us to finish our business here at the Cauldron and be on our way, as quickly as possible."

Ridley nodded. "One more thing, Commander. Another piece of the puzzle maybe. We finished our ID analysis of that ARM battleship. I know it sounds crazy, but we're pretty sure now it was the RMV *Markos*."

Aiden exchanged glances with Ro and Aminu. "The *Markos*? ARM's ace flagship that disappeared a couple weeks ago at V-Prime?"

"One and the same, Commander. The exhaust signature is unique and unmistakable."

The mystery of the *Markos*'s disappearance had just been eclipsed by the even greater mystery of its sudden reappearance.

~ ~ ~

Two hours later, Aiden instructed Dalton and the remaining Cauldron technicians to resume their work installing the ZPD. The wounded had been hustled off to the facility's medical suite. Dalton and two other technicians had sustained minor injuries, cuts and abrasions mostly. Nothing broken. Dr. Devi patched them up and cleared them to resume work. Dr. Lee was unharmed but considerably shaken. Zak Dalton had been remarkably effective at calming her down and getting her grounded again. They made quite a pair, Aiden thought. He hoped they'd have an opportunity in the future to make something of it.

Later that evening, Aiden had a confidential long-distance conversation with Admiral Stegman. It was not a short one, mostly due to the 13-minute time lag. After filling Stegman in on the details of the missile attack, Aiden moved on quickly to convince him that, if the zero-point drive worked as planned, they'd have no need for a military escort to V-Prime. Nor would it even be possible. By the time the *Endeavor* barely got underway for a trip that would take six days, the *Sun Wolf* would already be there after just two hours. It made far more sense to leave the *Endeavor* stationed at the Cauldron, where it could serve as added protection for an asset that had suddenly gained significance in a high-stakes gambit they still didn't understand. Stegman agreed, but only if the ZPD actually worked. Otherwise he'd still want the *Endeavor* to escort them to V-Prime, at least for as long as it could keep up.

They had also discussed the reappearance of the RMV *Markos*. ARM's flagship had been missing since its disappearance in the void-flux incident. The new report of its sighting, still classified, had caused general alarm throughout UED's military and intelligence communities. It was not the first time a ship had reappeared after vanishing in a void flux, but it was the first time one had remained silent after its reemergence. According to Stegman, high-level ARM sources had denied any communication from the *Markos* and any knowledge of its whereabouts, and he was inclined to accept their word on it. But if the ship they'd spotted out here really was the *Markos* and ARM was not in control of her, then who was? Considering the *Markos*'s capabilities, it was a question that begged answering sooner than later.

Aiden ended the discussion by reminding Stegman that the *Markos* appeared to be on course for V-Prime and, assuming it did a turnaround, would be there in less than six days. Stegman sounded confident that the sizable military force already in position at Friendship Station would be well prepared for the encounter.

After a hurried meal in the ship's galley, Aiden made it to the bridge to relieve his XO at the command chair. "Anything new, Ro?"

"Not much. Except what they found out on that rock where the missiles came from. The *Endeavor* sent a patrol shuttle over there to check it out. Sure enough, they found an empty rack of missile launchers concealed inside one of the old bore holes, along with a remote launch transceiver. The targeting computer had self-destructed after the launch, and no identifying marks were found anywhere on the hardware, or on the missile caught in the Cauldron's inertia net. But the tactical guys on the *Endeavor* recognized the hardware as Martian-made, top-of-the-line military gear."

Aiden scratched his beard, usually kept short but getting longer by the day. "It doesn't make sense, Ro. It looks exactly like a covert operation with sophisticated ARM weaponry. But authorized by the ARM government? I'm not so sure. These attacks have been highly specific, against the *Sun Wolf* or anyone aiding us. Whoever is behind them must have some knowledge of what we're up to and an overriding interest in keeping us from doing it. But it doesn't sound like Director Charnakov's style."

"Charnakov's administration might not be directly involved," Ro said, "but ARM's more extreme factions could be."

Aiden looked at him. "The Reds? With illegitimate access to high-end military weaponry?" He ran a hand through his hair, also getting longer than usual. It was a disturbing notion, and considering Charnakov's weakening hold on his own government, entirely possible.

Colonel Aminu entered the bridge and approached them looking as if he'd had very little sleep. He was probably poring over the Cauldron's records the night before and every spare

moment since. Aiden asked, "Colonel, did you find anything useful in the data records you got from the Cauldron?"

"I did, yes," Aminu said, not looking happy about it. "Turns
out there was a major data-hacking incident several years ago,
before Dr. Woo implemented his more robust security measures.
It involved unauthorized entry into the entire database of his
zero-point-drive research. Woo was keeping a tight clamp on the
development of that thing, aware of how revolutionary it was,
how potentially dangerous it could be in the wrong hands. The
facility's security team, such as it was, investigated the incident
but never traced the source of the hack. We can only assume that
all the data was copied. Fortunately, Woo's people had very good
backup and recovery systems in place protecting the original data.
They found telltale traces of an attempt to delete the whole database after it had been tapped."

Another disturbing piece of the puzzle, Aiden thought. "Was
this around the same time Anwar Cain worked there?"

"No, in fact. It happened soon after he left. But Dr. Woo was
alarmed enough to launch a wholesale reinforcement of the Cauldron's security measures. Across the board, too, including a point-
defense weapons array protecting the entire asteroid from
physical threats as well as cyberattacks. I have to say, I'm
impressed by what they accomplished here."

Pretty impressive for mere scientists and technicians, Aiden
heard Aminu say, but not out loud. "No other serious data
breaches since then?"

"None that show up in the records I received."

"Anything else?"

"There're some other intriguing connections, but nothing I
can put my finger on yet. It's a lot of material and I haven't covered
it in detail yet. There is one other thing of interest, though:
Dr. Anwar Cain isn't the first former Cauldron resident to fall off
the map."

"Oh?"

"At least two other similar cases show up when I cross-referenced the Cauldron's records with the DSI database. Neither are as mysterious as Cain's case, but the end results are the same: these two scientists, who spent considerable time at the Cauldron, no longer exist in any of our deepest databases."

"What were their areas of research?"

Aminu nodded. He'd asked the same question himself. "One did in-depth research on the manipulation of zero-point fields. The other, a highly regarded astrophysicist named Emilio Roca, was investigating Woo's theories on the nature of voidoids. Like where they came from, how they work, and their possible existence beyond Bound Space."

Aiden shook his head. This stuff was beginning to add up in a very bad way. "All right, Colonel. Thank you. Keep me posted on anything else you find."

He turned to Ro. "Did you and Lieutenant Hotah ever do the numbers on where the *Markos* might have come from?"

"Yep, we did," Ro said. "Based on their trajectory, a constant acceleration of 1.5 G, and the velocity we clocked them at when we spotted them, their point of origin would be 13.1 AU due south of the System's ecliptic plane. Exactly due south."

"What? The polar opposite point?"

"That's correct," Ro said, straight-faced. "The one and only POP."

If true, it represented another piece of evidence supporting a hypothesis that had been gaining credibility ever since the first voidship disappeared in a void flux and subsequently reappeared undamaged. There were not many such cases in the relatively short history of voidjumping, but in virtually every instance the ships had reappeared at or very near the POP, the polar opposite point of the same star system from which they had disappeared.

Voidoids were always found to be either directly above or below their host star, north or south of the star system's ecliptic plane and exactly 90 degrees perpendicular to it. The POP of a star system was located at the exact opposite position, where its voidoid would be if the system were turned upside down, 180 degrees. Some theorists referred to it as the voidoid's mirror-image point, and a number of interesting conjectures had arisen around it. V-Prime, the Solar System's voidoid, was located 13.1 AU directly *north* of Sol. Hence, its POP was theoretically located 13.1 AU directly south of Sol. The region had been investigated on several occasions, but nothing resembling another voidoid had ever been found there. Only empty space. Yet the *Markos* had apparently reemerged from that very spot.

Aiden massaged his forehead, feeling a headache lurking. "And the plot thickens."

Ro stood from the command chair and yawned. "Time for my sleep cycle, Commander. You have the bridge."

As he walked off, he turned and said, "I love a good mystery, eh?"

21

THE CAULDRON – V-PRIME
DOMAIN DAY 86, 2218

AT 09:00 ON the following morning, day five since leaving Hawking Station, Aiden arrived on the bridge to find Lieutenant Zachary Dalton seated at the Drive Systems station. Despite the conspicuous bandage on his right cheek covering a nasty wound with a two-inch row of microstitches, he was tapping away at his control board, smiling like a kid with a new toy.

Dalton looked up and said, "The zero-point drive is all hooked up, Commander. Systems have been triple-checked. We're ready to saddle up an' hit the trail."

"Very well, Lieutenant." Fortunately, the new drive system hadn't been damaged, and the structural damage to the ship's hull had been sufficiently repaired.

Aiden sat at the Command station. "I've got the bridge, XO. Helm, prepare to take us out."

Pilot Abahem made her silent okay sign and leaned back in the pilot's couch. Her right hand rested on a console embedded in the armrest, her fingers curled like a pianist ready to play an opening stanza. Dr. Maryam Ebadi was back onboard, seated at the Science Station. Faye Desai sat at the Data Station, completing diagnostics to ensure a seamless connection between the ship's AI and the new drive system. Dr. Sudha Devi was busy with her own diagnostics, double-checking the integrity of the ship's hull and life-support systems. Some elements of life support had suffered minor damage, but repairs had been made and Devi confirmed the *Sun Wolf's* readiness for launch.

At Tactical station, Lieutenant Billy Hotah's posture looked relaxed but in the way a gunslinger's bearing cleverly conceals constant vigilance. He'd been up most of the night reviewing the data from the missile attack, trying to figure out exactly how the last missile had escaped destruction in the final laser burn. It was a valid question, with undoubtedly a very complicated mathematical answer. But Hotah's fixation bordered on obsession. Aiden had wanted to assure him that no one could have done a better job, that they all owed him their lives, to tell him to get over it and move on. But Aiden sensed it would be the wrong approach with the young man. Hotah needed to work that out himself, and in the absence of criticism, Aiden was confident that he would.

Aiden detected a lighthearted mood from the crew this morning, more than at any time since their departure from Hawking Station, despite all the uncertainties and dangers that lay ahead. That they were finally underway, at full strength and with a powerful new drive system under the hood, probably had something to do with it. Or maybe it had been born from the unique bond that grows between team members who've endured life-threatening dangers together. He was sure, however, that much of it had to do with the liberty they'd been given to communicate with people they cared about back home. He knew that because of how it made him feel reaching out to Skye, letting her know he was okay.

He turned to Alvarez at Comm/Scan. "Lilly, inform the Cauldron that we're moving off in five minutes. And let Commander Ridley know we'll engage the ZPD in ten. Helm, move us away from the Cauldron out to the engagement point."

Lieutenant Dalton had learned that the ZPD's engagement point required enough distance from significant gravity fields to ensure reliable navigation. The Cauldron wasn't all that big as asteroids go but massive enough for Dalton to want the *Sun Wolf* at least 20 kilometers out before initiating the ZPD. A brief pulse from the M/AM engine got them there in less than three minutes. The view of the Cauldron quickly shrank to a small rock on the main screen. The *Endeavor* could be seen only as a tiny sliver of reflected sunlight just above it.

Aiden looked around the bridge. This was the first time any vessel other than Elgin Woo's *Starhawk* would attempt flight by zero-point drive, with or without prior flight testing. Yet the crew appeared relaxed, eager, and confident. Sudha Devi would have told him it reflected the crew's confidence in him, their captain. If true, even a little bit, Aiden hoped their confidence wasn't misplaced.

"All right, everyone. Are we ready to do this?" A rhetorical question, obviously, because they *were* going to do it, ready or not. Nonetheless, he waited for what amounted to a collective nod then said, "Helm, set course for V-Prime. Dalton, set the ZPD for maximum velocity and proceed."

"Yes, sir! Let's light this baby up!"

Dalton tapped on his board. The ZPD's huge EM generators instantly kicked in to cast a powerful control field in front of the ship, pushing zero-point energy away from a ship-sized pathway lying directly ahead. A split second later, the ship's M/AM drive burst into action with a short 1 G pulse. Within 11 seconds, the *Sun Wolf* had accelerated to 91.9 percent light speed and held steady at that velocity. The only sensation Aiden experienced was something like his ears popping from an atmospheric pressure change and a slight sinking feeling in his gut, like dropping in elevation inside a gravity field. Not unpleasant. No G-forces. And now they were zipping along at 275,210 km/sec. *Absolutely amazing*.

He looked around to confirm that no one on the bridge had experienced anything more drastic and saw mostly expressions of relief and amazement. Except for Ro, who looked like it was just another day at the office, and Pilot Abahem, who appeared to be immersed in a state of rapture deeper than usual. And Dalton, of course, who looked like he'd just seen God. It took him a full 30 seconds before yelling out, "Yahooooo! We're doing it!"

And indeed they were, now in uncharted relativistic territory where no one but Elgin Woo had been, and Skye when she had accompanied him aboard the *Starhawk*.

Aiden glanced at Maryam Ebadi. She was studying the ship's forward-facing view displayed on the main screen and pointed to it, smiling. "Einstein is in the driver's seat now."

Contrary to common portrayal in old sci-fi vids, stars were not streaming by on either side like snowflakes past a moving vehicle. Instead, the star field in front of them had collapsed into a condensed dome of blue-white dots dead ahead, surrounded by a periphery of black nothingness that seemed to bend inward on all sides, giving the impression of tunnel vision.

"Extreme blueshift in the star field dead ahead," Ebadi said, "where it's all compressed into a tight cone. In back of us, it'll look like a vast empty hole, and any starlight there will be extremely redshifted. If we could go any faster than 92 percent light speed, which we can't yet, the cone would fuse into a homogenous blue-white disc then eventually disappear altogether as the light gets shifted out of the visible spectrum into the X-ray range."

Ebadi looked around at the crew. She had their undivided attention. "And that's just the visual effects of going this fast. There's also time dilation to contend with. Our trip out to V-Prime will take only two hours, but that's in observer time, as recorded by all the clocks in the Solar System. For us, we'll experience only 47 minutes of elapsed time aboard the *Sun Wolf*. The ship's systems will automatically recalibrate when we slow to non-relativistic velocities at our destination."

"Finally, a dependable way to stay young," Alvarez quipped. "How often can we take these little trips, Commander?"

The blithe comment from the usually somber Comm/Scan Officer brought the crew back to earth. Aiden smiled. "Not often enough, Lilly."

Two hours later, by Domain Standard time—but only 47 minutes of shipboard time—the *Sun Wolf* pulled out of zero-point drive into realspace, positioned 15,000 kilometers from Friendship Station and approaching it at 5 km/sec. Aiden sent a message to Admiral Stegman confirming their successful flight and arrival at Friendship. In a time-lagged response, Stegman updated him on new developments. Due to the increasing instability of the voidoids, both the UED and ARM had finally agreed to a lockdown on V-Prime, barring all nonessential outgoing traffic until further notice. Both nations were recalling all nonessential government undertakings currently operating throughout Bound Space. Of course, heated negotiations were in progress to determine exactly which government activities were considered "nonessential."

Both governments sent strongly worded advisories to everyone else still out in Bound Space, directing them to return to the System as soon as possible. That included private enterprises and independent research missions, essentially anyone on record operating out in the Deep. *Including Skye and the Silvanus Project.*

The situation, with all its political and economic ramifications, had reached a crisis point, and Friendship Station lay smack at the crossroads. As the *Sun Wolf*'s tactical sensors confirmed, four battle cruisers were stationed at strategic points around V-Prime. Two were from UED's Military Service and two from ARM's Militia. In addition, a number of heavily armed fast frigates from both sides actively patrolled the voidoid's perimeter.

As the *Sun Wolf* approached, Station Traffic Control hailed them. While the station had been informed by UED Admiralty of the *Sun Wolf*'s imminent arrival, Control personnel were not prepared for the way the ship had arrived. From the station's point of view, the *Sun Wolf* had materialized out of nowhere. No sign of the ship's approach had been detected by their considerable array of sensors, nothing to indicate the *Sun Wolf* even existed until it appeared moments ago, 15,000 kilometers out. Aiden sympathized with their bewilderment.

Beyond that initial bewilderment, Traffic Control showed no further curiosity, being preoccupied with other more serious matters at the station. Aiden requested transit clearance for the Alpha-2 Hydri system, a mere formality at this point since the *Sun Wolf's* transit had already been cleared at the highest levels. He expected none of the usual bureaucratic red tape ships endured at Friendship and got none. After confirming registration information for the ship and its Licensed Pilot, the Control officer, a man named Isakov, issued the jump coordinates for Alpha-2 Hydri. "Your entrance corridor is now clear," Isakov said. "Have a good trip, Commander."

Aiden closed the comm. "Helm, move the ship into position for voidjump."

The working details of voidjumping had been common knowledge for nearly 50 years. They were surprisingly simple when compared with the mystery of what voidoids really were and how they worked. Basically, every star and starlike body within Bound Space possessed its own voidoid, each acting as a portal connecting it to all the others. To arrive at any given star in Bound Space from our Solar System, a voidship simply approached V-Prime on a celestial heading pointed directly at the target star and entered the voidoid on those exact coordinates. The ship emerged from the target star's voidoid with virtually no lapse of shipboard time, traveling toward the host star with the same velocity it possessed going into the jump. Beyond making minor but critical adjustments for local space-time contours just before the jump—a task only Licensed Pilots could accomplish reliably—it was really that simple.

After a successful jump out of the Solar System, voidjumping to another star system within Bound Space proceeded in the same manner. The ship merely reentered the voidoid through which it came on a new heading toward its next destination, and it arrived there almost instantaneously. Voidships could jump directly from any voidoid within Bound Space to any other, as long as no significant gravity wells intervened. The only thing you couldn't do was jump beyond the V-Limit, the enigmatic boundary lying approximately 36 light-years from Sol in all directions. Alpha-2 Hydri was the farthest star reachable by voidjump. Its distance from Sol, 36.3 light-years, defined the V-Limit of Bound Space. And the *Sun Wolf* was on its way there.

Aiden watched the pilot enter the commands, bringing the ship to a position 7,000 kilometers from the voidoid, where it would align with the entrance coordinates. From there, a 2 G burn would boost the ship into the voidoid with an entrance velocity of around 16 km/sec. Aiden chose the lower jump velocity to make sure their exit velocity at Alpha-2 Hydri wouldn't take them too far past where he wanted to start looking.

When the ship reached position, Abahem donned her linkage cap. It was a pale translucent thing that always reminded Aiden of pictures he'd seen of jellyfish back on Earth. It wasn't as thick or gelatinous but nonetheless gave the impression of being alive. Which it was in some sense, being inhabited by a horde of nanobots, micro-AIs working in concert to establish a seamless link between the pilot's brain and the ship's Omicron AI. It took about one minute for the link to complete. Aiden looked on vicariously as Abahem's face relaxed and took on an unmistakable expression of ecstasy. He knew that feeling. Craved it. Thought about the bottle of Continuum in his med cabinet. Knew it to be a cheap imitation of what the pilot experienced.

Abahem signaled her readiness with right hand raised. Aiden said, "Proceed."

The *Sun Wolf*'s M/AM drive kicked in at 2 Gs and pushed the ship straight toward the heart of V-Prime. All eyes focused on the forward-facing main screen. But like all voidoids, its surface shifted visible light into the X-ray range, making V-Prime virtually invisible, marked only by the absence of background stars. The ship's navigational sensors had to use high-energy X-ray pulses to stay locked on to the voidoid and maintain precise jump parameters.

Ro announced, "Voidjump in 35 minutes."

The entire crew would remain on the bridge during the jump. The days when a significant portion of the crew required temporary sedation during voidjump were over. Thanks to recent advances in microbiome engineering, the unsettling psychological effects of voidjumping on memory and temporal perception were no longer a major concern. Transient Memory Dissociation, or TMD, had been the bane of spacers for as long as ships had been voidjumping, up until last year, when a very simple treatment had been standardized to virtually eliminate it. Now all voidship crews underwent a two-week course of orally ingested probiotics engineered to alter the gut biome for boosting the key neurochemicals responsible for temporal cognition. TMD was now a thing of the past. Still, spacers never felt comfortable approaching a voidoid, and Aiden was no exception. It was such a thoroughly exotic entity, so beyond the ordinary, and too much like a spooky dream of death about to awaken.

"Void jump in two minutes." Ro counted them down with all the excitement of a bored ticket taker on a long-distance lunar rail train. Aiden knew it was deliberate and appreciated the subliminal calming effect it had on the crew. A general mood of boredom was preferable to anxiety when approaching a jump.

"Voidjump in 30 seconds."

Everyone watched as the eerie emptiness of the voidoid rapidly filled the main screen, blotting out the star field. The *Sun Wolf* sped toward it, aimed directly into its gaping maw.

As he often did at the very instant of a voidjump, Aiden sat back and closed his eyes. He thought he heard a voice speak to him, as if from an impossibly great distance, yet deep inside his head. He could almost make out the words. But not quite. Only a sense of their meaning. A greeting of some kind. A welcoming...

22

SHÉNMÌ
Domain Day 159, 2217

I F THERE COULD ever be a funny way to die, Elgin Woo had found it. There were, of course, two common meanings of funny: funny/humorous and funny/peculiar. As Elgin shined his luminator around the dark, enclosed space in which he was apparently trapped, he had to admit that his current situation qualified equally well for both meanings.

As predicted, his ride down to the surface of Shénmì inside the giant seed pod had taken only two hours. It had been a smooth ride, too, up until the pod entered the atmosphere. By that time the pod's stalk was retracting at a slower rate and the turbulence he encountered was due mostly to high-altitude wind currents. Woo had felt the gradual return of gravity as the pod neared the planet, then felt it more absolutely as the pod jolted to rest on the surface. Considering the speed attained by the pod during its descent, the landing had been relatively gentle. The only problem was that the pod had not yet opened to let him free. After nearly three hours, he was still stuck inside its cavernous interior, where it remained not only pitch-dark but also sealed under hard vacuum. As the pod lay inert in tropical heat, it had grown increasingly warm inside, and he was beginning to broil inside his pressure suit. To make matters worse, his oxygen supply was running dangerously low. Something had to happen very soon, or he would indeed die. Which brought him back to the humorous kind of funny.

To any normal person in his circumstance, nothing at all about it would seem funny. But to Elgin Woo, who, to be honest, was not a normal person, the scenario was laughable. Here he was, multiple Nobel Prize winner, cosmic adventurer, polyamorous Renaissance man, and now the new Jack-and-the-Beanstalk of outer space, stuck inside a giant seed pod on a strange planet orbiting a star 127 light-years from home, and not one living soul knew where he was. That unquestionably deserved a good laugh.

But he was not entirely alone. "Mari. Are you still picking up my signal?"

"Yes, Dr. Woo. The material of the seed pod interferes only slightly with your radio transmission. I can hear you just fine."

Woo had left the *Starhawk* in a geosynchronous orbit directly above the pod's landing spot in hopes of maintaining contact with his AI for the duration of his stay. She would be his eyes and ears for anything he could not see or hear, on the planet and in space.

"Any sign yet that the stem of the seed pod might be withdrawing?"

"None that I can detect from the optical telescope. The pod remains supine on the surface and quiescent."

That was good. From the limited observations he'd made in orbit, it appeared that the spent seed pods remained on the ground after landing for no more than four hours before sinking below the surface of the pale membrane from which they had emerged. And all of those had opened up well before that happened. Except the one he was stuck inside now. It was cause for concern. Being trapped inside while on the surface was one thing, but if the pod didn't open up by the time it sank below—down into who-knows-what? That was an entirely different matter.

"Your oxygen reserves are down to 27 minutes," Mari reminded him.

Yes. And there was that too. "Thank you, Mari."

Woo had learned long ago that there was a time for patience and a time for action. Now was the time for the latter. Time to try something out of the ordinary. He held the luminator firmly in his grasp and used its butt end to knock on the rough inner wall of the pod. He started with two knocks in quick succession, followed by a silence, then another two knocks. He repeated the two-knock sequence over and over. The knocks made no sound that he could hear, since the interior was still in hard vacuum, but he could feel the vibrations they made through his gloved hand. It felt like pounding on a giant wooden drum, and he imagined how wonderful it might sound if he could hear it.

But nothing happened.

He then tried a three-knock sequence instead of two knocks. He imagined a waltz in 3/4 time, heard it in his head. Something he remembered from Johann Strauss, maybe the "Blue Danube." He hummed it as he knocked. Minutes passed.

Nothing happened.

Woo stopped for a moment. His breathing had grown more labored. He looked at his oxygen readout. Down to 12 minutes. He gripped the luminator again and started a four-knock sequence. Since most of the music he'd heard in his life was in common time, 4/4, it was easy for him to conjure some rhythmic melody in his head to add musical cadence to his knocking pattern. He made a little dance as he drummed. More minutes passed.

Nothing happened.

The dancing, while fun, had consumed oxygen at a higher rate, and Woo was breathing heavily now. The temperature inside the pod had equalized with the tropically warm temperature outside. Perspiring freely inside his close-fitting p-suit, he felt his head spinning. *Not much time left now. Try one more.*

He decided to skip a five-knock sequence—not sure why, just an intuition, something to do with the rarity of 5/4 time in music and of radial symmetry in nature. Instead he moved on to a six-knock routine in 6/8 time. It was a multiple of three but different than 3/4 time, a compound meter with six eighth-notes and a rhythmic emphasis on the "one" and the "four." The jingle "For He's a Jolly Good Fellow" came to mind. It had been sung for him by his colleagues after winning his first Nobel Prize. It was in 6/8 time. He hummed it to himself now and drummed on the wall with the emphasis: 1-*2-3-4-5-6*. He wanted to live. But if he was going to die, what a jolly tune to go out on.

For he's - a jol - ly good fell - ow, for he's - a jol - ly good fell - ow...

And that was when Woo's oxygen ran out. He lost his grip on the luminator. It dropped to the floor and his body followed it down, half-conscious. A blinding flash of light burst into the pod from above, accompanied by a loud ripping sound...a sound that he could *hear*! The pod was splitting open! Air rushed in from the outside, and the explosive pressure change pushed the two halves of the pod farther apart. Sunlight poured in. Bright yellow light glancing in from a low angle in the sky. The color of life.

Woo was just conscious enough and had just enough strength to unlock his helmet and pull it off. Lying on his back, he filled his lungs with heavy, moist air, felt its oxygen infuse the blood coursing through his body, refilling it with life, capillary by capillary, the neurons of his brain drinking it in, waking him up. Looking up, he saw a wedge of hazy blue sky peeking through the wide-open breach in the pod's curved wall. He might see that sunset on Shénmì after all.

Then the pod moved.

"Dr. Woo!" Mari's voice sounded small and metallic through the comm of his helmet, now lying at his side. "Are you okay? The pod is beginning to regress. I believe it will soon sink below the surface. Do you hear me?"

"Yes, Mari. I hear you. I'm fine." Woo stood up and leaned unsteadily against the pod's inner wall. A wall that had begun to tilt downward. He could feel the entire structure being pulled along the surface like a wooden ark drawn toward a whirlpool, slowly at first but gradually picking up speed.

"Dr. Woo. I suggest you climb free of the pod *now* and proceed quickly across the membrane surface to the nearest solid land. It lies to the east, about 70 meters away."

"Quite right, Mari." Woo grabbed his helmet, attached it to his utility belt, and climbed up the slanted wall toward the breach. Making his way around the concave depressions where the seeds had been attached, he heard the scraping of the pod being dragged across the surface. He reached the rim of the breach, the sky now wide above him, and looked around. Woo saw that his pod was rapidly approaching the center of the 150-meter-wide circular membrane, pulled by its stalk toward the yawning cavity opening up there. He looked down. His drop would be about three meters. He climbed over the rim, took a deep breath, and jumped.

He landed feet-first but with greater impact than he'd expected. But then the surface gravity on Shénmì was slightly higher than Earth's, about 1.1 G. His landing would have been more jarring had it not been for the soft, pliable surface of the membrane. His feet sank a few inches into it on impact, lessening the stress on his knees. He stood there watching the pod move away from him, gaining speed, then noticed his feet had sunk in a few more inches.

"Dr. Woo. Please move with haste to solid land. The membrane is liquefying at the center and moving outward in your direction."

And so it was. Woo watched as the cavity drew the stalk inward and down into a liquefied vortex that was steadily melting outward. Toward where he stood. *Time to get moving.*

He faced eastward, which he presumed was in the opposite direction of the setting sun, and began jogging toward the borderline where bright green vegetation beckoned to him. It was harder going than he expected. Normally around 80 kilograms, he now weighed closer to 88 in the higher gravity, and even more with the weight of the p-suit and the attached gear. The heat and humidity had turned the inside of his p-suit into a sauna, and the sponginess of the membrane beneath his feet made forward progress even more difficult. It was like running across the surface of a giant marshmallow, one that was trying to eat him. The image made Woo laugh again, even as he gasped with exertion.

The surface grew more solid the closer he got to the vegetated boundary. He stopped briefly to look behind. The split-open seed pod had almost disappeared below the milky white plain, and the cavity began refilling, growing more solid and level with the surrounding surface. Woo turned and jogged the final five meters to the edge where the green growth began. He struggled to disencumber himself from his p-suit, then threw himself on the ground, breathing hard and perspiring heavily.

He lay there for some time, cooling down in his sweat-soaked cotton jumpsuit until his breathing and heart rate normalized. The vegetation underneath him was some kind of low ground cover, soft like moss. He looked around. The living green carpet extended as far as he could see, rising up into dark green hills one or two kilometers away. Their tall summits had picked up the last light from the setting sun, glowing mellow yellow against a deepening blue sky. Huge cumulus cloud formations stood off in the distance like ghostly mountains moving in a stately procession across the southern horizon. Above their massive heads, a few stars materialized as if they'd been hiding there all along. Maybe some of them were actually planets of the evening sky, the Jupiters and Venuses of Woo's new star system.

"Are you well, Dr. Woo?" Mari's voice through his helmet comm startled him, causing him to look around as if someone nearby had spoken. He relaxed, picked up his helmet and spoke into it. "Yes, dear girl. I'm fine. More than fine. It's beautiful here!"

"I am glad to hear it. But do be careful. We know very little about the flora and fauna of this planet. Which plants can you safely consume and which ones could poison you? What kinds of animal life, including dangerous predators? Microbes that could sicken or kill you—"

"Yes, there is much to learn about my Shénmì, Mari. And that's precisely what I'll set out to do first thing in the morning: to learn as much as I can about this fascinating place, even with the limited resources we have between us."

If an AI could sigh convincingly, Mari would have done it just then. Woo heard it in her tone. "Please proceed with caution."

Woo smiled. His AI sounded like she actually *cared* about him. How had that happened?

"Goodnight, Mari."

A long pause.

"Goodnight, Elgin."

Woo nodded to himself. Good. They were now on a first-name basis.

As he lay back on the mossy ground, a cool breeze caressed his damp forehead. It bore delicate fragrances telling of exotic chemistries, alien enticements. Off to his left, he heard the soft gurgling of a brook dashing down a stony course. It reminded him of his raging thirst. Maybe he would find some edible plants or fruits on his way to the stream. Maybe it wouldn't be so bad if he were forced to spend the rest of his life here. It was already beginning to feel like home. As if he'd always been here. Always welcome.

23

ALPHA-2 HYDRI SYSTEM
DOMAIN DAY 89, 2218

WE TAKE THE passage of time for granted. The unchanging, even tempo of the clock's second hand as it clicks and clicks from the wall above our desk reassures us of the eternal constancy of the universe, comforts us in the knowledge that, even when it marks the progress of chaos and uncertainty, it does so in a perpetually regular manner. It brings the unborn closer to life with exactly the same cadence as it brings the already born closer to death. Either way, you can always count on time.

Except immediately after a voidjump.

When Aiden opened his eyes again, it felt like no time at all had elapsed between entering V-Prime and popping out in another star system 36.3 light-years away. And yet it didn't feel quite like that either. It wasn't that his mind was telling him one thing while his body was telling him something different. It was more like neither knew exactly what to say.

One thing, however, was for sure. The *Sun Wolf* had arrived in the Alpha-2 Hydri system. No doubt about it. The star showed up smack in the middle of the bridge's forward view screen, a real-time view from the ship's optical scope. At a distance of 12.9 AU, over 1.9 billion kilometers away, it burned like a lonely orange-yellow campfire deep inside an eternally dark forest of stars. Aiden blinked at it several times before his nervous system realigned and he was able to place himself more solidly in the here and now.

He had studied up on Alpha-2 Hydri before their jump. Aside from its notoriety as the star in Bound Space farthest from Sol, it had an interesting history among astronomers. It was a type G8V main-sequence star, considered a dwarf at about 83 percent the mass of Sol and only 90 percent its size. It was relatively close to Sol, as stars go, but it hadn't been discovered until 2119. That was because, as seen from Earth and orbital observatories, it was aligned almost directly in front of Alpha Hydri, the second brightest star in the constellation Hydrus, lying 72 light-years out. But because it was a relatively dim star, less than 0.6 times the brightness of Sol, it had been virtually impossible to differentiate from the much brighter Alpha Hydri lying directly in back of it. It took the Trans-Uranian Star Scope project in 2119 to finally discover that Alpha Hydri was actually two stars. Even though they were nearly 36 light-years apart and unrelated in any other way, they were technically designated as an optical double star and recataloged as Alpha-1 and Alpha-2 Hydri.

Aiden rubbed his eyes again and turned to his XO. "Status report."

Ro responded with the obvious, "Voidjump successful. All ship systems functioning normally. We're currently over 2,000 klicks from the voidoid, moving away from it under 2 G accel, headed due south toward the star."

"Helm," Aiden said. "Reverse course. Establish a standard search pattern around the voidoid. Lieutenant Hotah, maintain Level One alert, eyes open for hostiles. Lilly, initiate full-array search scan. Dalton, keep the ZPD in idle, ready for immediate engagement on my command."

Aiden stood and made a 360-degree scan of the bridge. "Everyone okay?"

He got a general nod from his crew, although Faye Desai looked a little green. She'd had trouble with TMDs in the past, more than most spacers, and hadn't responded to the new biome treatments as well. Beyond the primary crew, Maryam Ebadi looked unaffected and merely smiled at him. But Victor Aminu looked glassy-eyed, like he'd walked into a room and forgotten why he'd gone there. The moment seemed to pass quickly, either naturally or by virtue of the man's well-practiced simulation of self-control.

"Commander," Alvarez said, looking up from her console with a bewildered expression. "I've synched up with the Alpha-2 Hydri Holtzman buoy but got a really odd reading from its chronometer—"

"Sir!" Hotah interrupted before she could finish. "Tactical sensors picked up a vessel at around 6,000 klicks."

"Target the vessel, Lieutenant. Make weapons ready. Scan details?"

"It's a small craft," Hotah said. "Nonmilitary. Drive system is cold. She appears to be drifting, standing off about 340 klicks from the voidoid."

"I've got it too," Alvarez said, her attention shifted from the chrono reading to her long-scan monitor. "And I'm picking up a distress beacon from the vessel. An automated mayday on standard emergency frequency."

"Hail the vessel, Lilly."

After waiting a full 10 minutes without a response to continuous hails, Aiden said, "Helm, set course for intercept at 0.5 G, with full stop at one klick."

The ZPD could have taken them there in an eyeblink, but a more deliberate approach would give them time to examine the vessel from afar before reaching her.

Alvarez aimed the optical scope at the ship, set to maximum magnification. Lit up by the orange-yellow light of Alpha-2 Hydri, details of the vessel began to resolve. It was a relatively small craft, about 20 meters in length, its cylindrical body dwarfed by a set of three massive exhaust nozzles at its tail end. It appeared to be drifting, locked in a slow fore-to-aft tumble. It looked dead.

"It's a private yacht," Dalton said. He had joined the group around Alvarez's monitor. "Looks like Star Jammer class. Domain-made. But modified with a high-thrust M/AM drive. Done poorly, I'd say. Without adequate gamma-ray shielding. That's radiation poisoning waiting to happen. I wouldn't crew on that bucket for one second."

Ro said, "It also looks like the same vessel the *Arcadia* saw out here messing around with the voidoid. Fits Captain Hawthorne's description pretty closely."

Colonel Aminu nodded in agreement and said, "It's a Green War ship. See the marking on the fuselage?"

Alvarez instructed the scope to focus on the surface marking and to compensate for the ship's slow tumble. They saw a green circle centered within a red square with crossed swords over its face. No standard registration number visible on the ship. Green War. No doubt about it.

Aiden glanced at Hotah. The Tactical Officer looked up and said, "Vessel targeted. Laser cannon fully charged."

"XO, send a Holtzman transmission to Admiral Stegman with an update."

Eighteen minutes after turnaround, the *Sun Wolf* came to a halt within one kilometer of the drifting vessel, and more of its structural detail came into view. Except for its automated distress signals, the ship remained silent.

"Looks like a serious hull breach," Alvarez said. "Directly forward, at its bow."

As the yacht's bow rolled into view, sunlight revealed a jagged, gaping hole. The metal was bent inward, like the ship had been struck head-on by a large, blunt incoming projectile.

"It's been fitted like a research cutter," Ro said, "with a forward-facing docking bay just big enough to accommodate a remote-op sensor drone. That nasty-looking hull breach is right where the docking bay's hatch should be. Damage like that? Hard to imagine any survivors."

"Any heat signatures yet?" Aiden asked.

"We're still too far out for any reliable IR readings," Alvarez said. "I can tell you more if we move closer."

Aiden instructed the helm to bring the *Sun Wolf* to full stop at 500 meters from the Green War ship. Using the IR scanner, Alvarez determined that, while most of the ship was as cold as space, a small area within its core glowed faint red. "It corresponds to where living spaces are usually located in ships of this design," she said.

"Warm enough for someone to still be alive in there?" Aiden asked.

"Possibly, yes. It also means the ship still has a functional power source."

Aiden had a sensor drone launched to examine the vessel close-up with high-res cameras and to search for any sign of life within. The life-sign array included a combination of radio waves, microwave beams, and Doppler radar coupled with sophisticated AI algorithms to detect movements as fine as heartbeats and breathing from a distance and through hardened ship hulls.

The drone came to within 10 meters and began roaming over the vessel's surface. Its camera confirmed the extensive damage to the forward docking bay, severe enough to evacuate most of the ship's interior. It also picked up what must have been the ship's name, stenciled in small, dark green letters on the dorsal hull. It proudly announced itself as the *Rachel Carson*.

"I think we've got someone still alive in there," Alvarez said. "The life-sign array detects the presence of one individual."

Dr. Devi had come over to Comm/Scan to view Alvarez's readings. She nodded in agreement. "One person only. Heartbeat slightly elevated but regular. Normal breathing. The person appears to be lying supine, probably on a sleeping bunk. From the thermal-imaging pattern, I'd guess female."

"That means life support and G-transducers are still functional in that section," Aiden said. "What's the condition of the airlock, Lilly?"

Alvarez adjusted the scope to focus on the ventral surface of the vessel, where the airlock doors were located. She did a methodical scan of the entire mechanism and said, "It looks intact, structurally at least. But there's no way to tell from here if it's actually functional."

"Understood. The ship still has power, right?"

"Yes, but only near the core. If the control bridge is located in the usual place, forward and right above the docking bay, it's probably dead now."

"Right." Aiden turned to face the crew. "We're going to board and rescue. Lieutenant Hotah, you're with me on security detail. Faye, you too, for power and data-core evaluation. Dr. Devi, if you're up for a little spacewalk, I'd love to have you along for medical and life-support assessments."

Devi made a mock salute and smiled. "I thought you'd never ask."

Colonel Aminu stepped up to Aiden. "I'm coming too."

Aiden was in no mood to argue over command decisions but also realized it was an appropriate request from the DSI investigator. "You have any EVA experience, Colonel?"

"Yes, I do."

"Good. Get your gear, everyone. Meet me at Docking Bay B in ten. We'll take the utility sled. I'll open up the weapons locker down there and dispense appropriate firearms. XO, you have the bridge. Helm, bring us to within 100 meters."

The *Sun Wolf* packed a small arsenal of handheld weapons, locked under tight security, accessible only by the captain and the XO. They were all projectile weapons, mostly "smart guns," designed for use in a variety of extreme environments, both pressurized and hard vacuum, and down to zero gravity. As such, they employed advanced recoilless technology, composite materials able to tolerate extreme temperatures, and surface film nanotech instead of standard lubricants that would boil off in hard vacuum.

Hotah chose the largest and nastiest of them all, an assault-style Spacer Carbine with three parallel barrels, one for 5.7-mm armor-piercing rounds, another for standard 13-mm hollow-point ammo or low velocity rubber bullets, and one large 30-mm shotgun-style bore for specialty ammunition, including crowd-control shot or grenades. It also featured a nonlethal sonic stunner to incapacitate targets with minimal physical injury. The Space Carbine usually required two-handed use, but from the way Hotah tossed it around during his inspection, Aiden guessed he could easily manage it one-handed if needed.

Aiden and Desai chose light pistols stowed in easily accessible thigh holsters. Aminu carried his own sidearm, a small but wicked-looking weapon that Aiden couldn't identify from a casual glance. Probably a standard issue for clandestine DSI operatives. Dr. Sudha Devi declined the use of a weapon, claiming she felt more than adequately protected by the others. She'd once told him that her smile was her best weapon. Nonetheless, he asked her to stay close to Lieutenant Hotah.

Docking Bay B was smaller than the *Sun Wolf*'s two other bays, where the landing shuttles were housed. It held two utility sleds and an assortment of sensor drones and atmospheric probes. They suited up and boarded one of the sleds. It was a basic, nonpressurized, open-to-vacuum vehicle that seated six and was intended primarily for extended multiperson EVAs. After running mandatory suit-system checks, the bay depressurized, and its doors opened up to the crystal black emptiness of space.

Aiden piloted the sled and covered the distance to the *Rachel Carson* in less than five minutes. He synched their position with the ship's slow tumble. The group disembarked and used their suit jets to reach the ship's outer airlock doors. Aiden found the airlock's emergency manual-control bar, clearly marked within a bright red depression on the hull. He gave it a tug. Nothing happened.

"So much for the easy way in," he said though his helmet comm.

"It might just be powered down," Faye said. "Most of these yachts will activate an automated shutdown system when it detects a hull breach. It turns off nonessential systems or systems that could potentially make things worse."

"Like airlock doors," Aiden said.

"Exactly. The system can be overridden, but only from the control bridge."

"Okay. Lieutenant Hotah, stay here with the colonel and Dr. Devi. Faye, you and I are going to see if there's a way into the bridge through the breached docking bay. Hotah, you're Team Two leader. We're Team One. Stay in radio contact."

He and Desai moved off to the ship's bow. The damage there was impressive. Whatever caused it had crashed into the closed bay doors and bounced off into space. The bay doors were mangled beyond recognition, and the surrounding framework had been smashed inward, warping the ship's entire fore-end structure. In the process, it had left a wide gap between the shattered doors leading directly into what was left of the docking bay.

"The control bridge should be located right above this docking bay," Desai said. "We might get lucky and find a way into it from inside the bay."

"Agreed," Aiden said. "Let's go for it."

They threaded their way carefully around the jagged metal edges of the ruptured doors and found themselves floating inside the remains of the docking bay. It was a small cylindrical area with a flat launch floor, maybe 10 meters at its widest and no more than 15 in length.

"Just about the right size," Aiden said, "to house that drone we saw on Hawthorne's video report."

They moved farther inside, careful to dodge floating debris, some of it sharp enough to pierce the thin nanoskin of their p-suits. Aiden released the strap on his thigh-mounted holster for quick access to his weapon. Desai did the same as she shined her luminator into every corner of the bay.

"Up there," she said, training the powerful luminator beam upward and to the right. They saw an irregular opening in the bay wall, apparently made when the ship's framework had buckled under the impact, ripping the seams apart to expose the ship's interior.

When they reached the gap, Desai shined the luminator into it and said, "Bingo."

Aiden followed her gaze inside. "Looks like a control bridge to me."

The opening was just large enough for a single person to pass through but required both hands to safely negotiate the twisted path inward. Desai hung the luminator on her utility belt, turned on her helmet lights, and weaved her way inside. Aiden followed close behind. When they were safely inside, she grabbed her luminator and started examining their new location.

Aiden heard something gently scraping the surface of his helmet directly overhead just as Desai's beam turned his way. "Holy shit!" she yelled.

Aiden stepped back and looked up. A frozen corpse floated serenely past his head. It was a young male, twentysomething, dressed only in a crew jumpsuit. No p-suit. No helmet. No chance of surviving a sudden hull breach. It was not a pretty sight. The peaceful tranquility of the corpse's slow ballet though the hard vacuum left no hint of the brutal nature of the man's death.

Aiden touched Desai's shoulder, a gesture of reassurance. She flinched again, then met his eyes and calmed herself. "Okay. I'm good to go."

"Yeah. Pretty creepy, huh?" he said. "Let's find that power override."

Desai floated to the control board and began a systems check. She knew her way around a ship's computer system like no one Aiden had ever met. But unlike all other data-heads he'd known, Faye's humanity had never been subsumed by the machines she communed with 24/7. In fact, it always seemed to Aiden the other way around: that the AIs she worked with somehow became more humanized by her touch, as if they had all fallen in love with her. He could relate.

"I've got it," she said. "Powering on now."

Lights turned on and control panels lit up. A bright red alarm light flashed above the main console, probably accompanied by warning sirens which, thankfully, they couldn't hear in the hard vacuum.

"Turn it off, Faye. And while you're at it, shut down the distress beacon too. Can you tell if the airlock doors are powered up now?"

"Yep, that system should be functional. Unless there's structural damage."

"Team Two, do you read?" Aiden said.

"Roger," Hotah said through the helmet comm. "We're seeing some indicator lights going on around the airlock."

"Faye's got power up and running. Try the airlock control now."

After a minute, Hotah responded. "Airlock door open. The interior looks undamaged."

"Good. Hang tight. We'll meet you there in a few minutes."

"Faye, can you download the ship's data core? I want to get a look at what these guys have been up to out here."

"Already on it, Commander." Faye had brought along a data-mirror unit. She plugged it into the control consol. "Another minute and I should have it all."

Aiden and Faye made it back outside through the mangled docking bay and met the other three at the airlock. They cycled through into the ship's pressurized interior and found themselves in a small ante area leading off to various crew compartments. Each of them "fell" to the deck as they entered. The G-transducers apparently still worked in this part of the ship. The steady 1 G downward pull allowed them to reorient and stand upright. Their suit sensors indicated breathable air but heavy on the CO_2 side.

"Looks like the life-support system is failing," Dr. Devi said. "But safe for now."

They removed their helmets and sniffed the air. Breathable, yes, but stale and cloying with the unmistakable odor of morbidity. Hotah and Aminu fanned out, weapons ready, to inspect the entire habitable area.

"All clear," Hotah reported. "Except for one living quarters. Hatch door marked with the letter *B*. It's locked from the inside. Probably where our sole survivor is holed up."

Aiden nodded to Hotah and gestured toward the hatch. "If you would, Lieutenant."

Hotah banged on the hatch door several times with the butt of his carbine. No response.

Aiden radioed the *Sun Wolf,* and Alvarez moved the sensor drone closer in to scan the compartment in question from the outside. She reported back, "The life-sign scan confirms the presence of one living individual. She appears to be standing now. Heart rate speeding up."

"Copy," Aiden said. "Faye, can you give me access to the ship-wide comm from here?"

"Sure thing, boss." She popped the cover off a wall-mounted comm speaker nearby, pulled a small universal transceiver from her utility pouch, plugged it into something inside the cavity, then activated a switch on the box. She pointed to Aiden's helmet hanging from his backpack and said, "I've synched it up with your helmet comm. You're on the air."

Aiden spoke into his helmet. "This is Commander Macallan of the SS *Sun Wolf.* We're a UED Science and Survey vessel. We picked up your distress signal and have boarded your ship for rescue. We are armed but have no hostile intent. We're here to rescue you. I have a doctor here with me to provide medical care if needed. Please unlock your hatch if you are able."

After a brief pause, a shaky and undeniably female voice crackled through the comm. "Liars! I know you're Black Dog's men. I'll shoot if you open this door!"

24

AIDEN LOOKED AT the others, bewildered. He silently mouthed the words: *Black Dog*? They looked back at him, equally clueless. All except Colonel Aminu.

Lilly Alvarez's voice came through comm on a different channel. "Be advised. The scan is showing the individual standing with both arms extended forward, pointing an IR-cold object toward the hatch door. Probably a weapon."

"Copy," Aiden said then switched channels to continue his pitch. "I assure you that we are UED Science and Survey personnel. I have no idea who this Black Dog is. We are here in response to your distress call. You're in grave danger. Your life-support system is failing. Please open the hatch. We mean you no harm."

The voice that came through the comm was choked with despair. "We didn't mean to wreck the ship! Honest. It was an accident. The gravity drone hit us. I don't know where it is now. Please tell Black Dog it was an accident! I'm the only one left alive."

"I repeat, for the last time: we are UED Science and Survey personnel. We're out here investigating the disappearance of one of our ships and picked up your distress signal. Now put your weapon down and open the door."

A long pause followed. Then the woman on the other side of the hatch began to sob. She said, "Well, shit. If that's true, I'm even more screwed."

Dr. Devi turned to Aiden and said, "I'm monitoring the life-sign scan. This woman's heart rate has accelerated dangerously. Even if she's young, she's probably physiologically stressed by malnutrition, dehydration, poor air quality, and god knows what else. And she's obviously frightened. Tachycardia like this could precipitate cardiac arrest. We have to act now."

Aiden asked Hotah, "Can you blow the lock on this hatch?"

"Yes, with a lock-buster charge. I've got one with me. It'll take a few minutes to set up."

"Never mind that," Desai said. "It's an electronic lock. I can override it in 30 seconds."

"Do it," Aiden said. Then to the woman on the other side of the hatch, "Please believe me, ma'am. We mean you no harm. Our primary concern now is to save your life."

She blurted out a pathetic laugh. "What life? I won't *have* a life now!"

Aiden glanced sideways at Colonel Aminu, saw his resolute expression, and realized she might be right about that. But this wasn't the time to argue the point. "Please calm yourself and lower your weapon. We are about to enter."

"No! I'll shoot. I swear it!" Her voice shook with fear.

Aiden switched off the comm and said, "Hotah, is your sonic stunner charged?"

"Yes, sir."

"Okay. You're lead man. If she's still pointing a weapon at us when the door opens, drop her with the stunner. No second-guessing, and nothing more aggressive. Understood?"

Hotah nodded, his eyes steady, focused. No sign of bloodlust. Under control.

Desai quickly accessed the ship's computer through another wall-mounted control panel and did her magic. The hatch locking mechanism clicked open. She nodded to Hotah.

Hotah kicked the hatch open, weapon raised.

A young woman stood facing them, her weapon pointed at Hotah's face.

Hotah did not fire his stunner. She did not fire at him.

They locked eyes and Hotah said in a slow, calm voice, "Easy, Kayah..."

She may have been transfixed by the sight of Hotah's wild appearance, the speckled band across his face, the long black hair, his piercing eyes. But in retrospect, Aiden believed it was the tone of both power and peace in Hotah's voice, and the mysterious name he gave her in that moment, that caused her to drop the weapon. It clattered to the deck. She collapsed next to it, weeping.

Hotah lowered his carbine. Colonel Aminu made a move to enter the room, a pair of wrist restraints in his hands. But Hotah remained standing in the doorway, straight and silent, blocking his entrance. Only when he sensed Dr. Devi come up from behind did Hotah step aside to allow her first contact with the weeping woman. He turned to Aminu and with rattlesnake quickness snatched the wrist restraints from the man's hands and tossed them out into the corridor. He met Aminu's startled eyes with a dark, withering stare. Aiden placed a hand on Hotah's shoulder, gave him a nod, then walked past him into the room.

Devi had gathered the woman up and placed her sitting on the cabin's single bunk. Barely a woman, Aiden thought. No older than 20, he guessed. But her haggard condition made her look older. Caucasian, of medium height and slender build, she had reddish auburn hair, long and tied back in a loose ponytail. Her fine-boned face looked delicate and pale, with a splash of freckles across her cheeks. She peered at them with large, hazel-green eyes, now sunken and underlined with dark circles. Her lower lip trembled as tears dropped from her cheeks.

Dr. Devi looked at the others crowding around the entrance and, in a tone of authority Aiden had never heard before, she said, "Out. All of you. Now. Except Commander Macallan."

Only Aminu looked as if he might protest, but thought better of it. He left with the others. Devi sat next to the young woman and calmly but carefully put her arm around her shoulders. Devi's aura of warmth and compassion was absolute, unconditional, simply because that was who she was. The trembling woman's posture relaxed, fear released, and she melted into Devi's arms.

"What's your name, girl?"

"My name is Cass. Cassandra Healy. I'm from Earth."

"I'm pleased to meet you, Cass. I'm Sudha Devi. And this is Commander Macallan. I'm a physician. I'll help you get well again. But first we need to get you back to our ship. Do you have a pressure suit?"

Cass nodded. "It's down at the airlock. But I've never used it before."

"That's okay. We'll help you with it. Our ship is not far away. It'll take only a few minutes to get there. Is there anything you want to bring with you?"

Cass blinked at her, wiping tears from her cheek. She fiddled with a plain gold ring on her left hand and shook her head "No. It's all gone now."

They were the saddest words, of tongue or pen, that Aiden had ever heard.

Devi glanced at him. She'd heard them, too, laden with existential pain. "Okay, good. Let's go then."

They met Hotah, Aminu, and Desai at the airlock, gathered their gear and suited up. Cass told them she had practiced donning a p-suit only once, but in her weakened condition she needed help. Faye Desai was most helpful, treated Cass kindly, and explained how to operate the suit. They all cycled through the airlock and boarded the utility sled. During the short ride back, Aiden informed Ro they were bringing back a "guest" and told him to ready the medical bay.

Back aboard the *Sun Wolf,* Devi took Cass to the med bay, hooked her up to IV fluids, and began a series of medical diagnostics. She shooed everyone else away and told Aiden she'd report on her patient's condition when she was ready. On the way back to the bridge, Colonel Aminu caught up with him to broach the inevitable subject.

"You know I need to place this individual in custody and question her," he said. "I've been patient up to this point, and I'm not without sympathy for this woman's condition. But she is the only prime suspect we have so far and undoubtedly has valuable information we need."

Aiden knew this was coming and needed to handle it wisely. "Yes, Colonel. I'm aware of all that, and for the most part I agree with you. As soon as Dr. Devi tells me her patient is stable, both physically and mentally, I'll allow an interview. But not before. I'm as interested in her story as you are. And as far as custody goes, yes, I'll consider her in your custody, but as an official designation only. Unless someone can convince me she's an immediate threat to this ship, I will not have her locked up or restrained."

It was not what Aminu wanted to hear. "With all due respect, Commander, the circumstantial evidence we have already points with considerable certainty to actions by this woman and her cohorts that clearly fall under the definition of terrorism. The laws concerning terrorism suspects are well defined. Locking her up is the very least we should be doing."

Aiden nodded thoughtfully. "Be that as it may, I believe the best chance we have of getting truthful information from Cass, all of it, is in treating her humanely and with respect. She's a frightened young woman, but with fervently held beliefs, most of them antiauthoritarian in nature. Putting her in shackles and locking her up? That'd be counterproductive. It doesn't serve anyone's purpose. Including yours."

Aiden knew from personal experience not only the debasement of being shackled and locked up, but also how utterly pointless it was under most circumstances. And he knew from Aminu's expression that the colonel was fully aware of his special perspective on the subject. Aminu stood straight, nodded stiffly, and said,

"I will carefully note your decision not to follow protocol on this matter in my official report."

"You do that, Colonel. And I'm sure you'll just as carefully note the effect my decision has on the amount and value of the information we get from Ms. Healy."

The two men continued on to the bridge in silence. When Aiden got there, he relieved Ro at the Command station and asked for a status report.

"All's quiet on the western front," Ro said. "We haven't detected any other vessels in the system. No voidoid fluxes. I've sent another Holtzman transmission to Admiral Stegman updating him on what we've found here so far. But not who. Waiting for a response."

But not who? Aiden thought about that for a second before saying, "Thanks, XO. Colonel Aminu, I assume we've left traces of our presence on that ship—physical, electronic, or otherwise—that someone else could detect. Someone who might come along looking for it. Is that correct?"

Aminu nodded. "Absolutely, yes. At the very least, they could tell that someone remained alive after the damage and that they were subsequently removed from the ship. Sophisticated forensics could reveal a lot more. And I'm sure the ship's AI, whatever is left of it, recorded our presence in any number of ways."

Aiden looked over at Faye Desai for her input. "For sure," she said. "Among other things, there'd be clear evidence that the data core had been duplicated and downloaded."

"All right. Helm, move us 1,000 klicks away from the *Rachel Carson* and hold in position. Lieutenant Hotah, when we're there, please destroy the derelict vessel in the most thorough way at your disposal."

Hotah grinned. "Yes, sir. A Helix-100 antimatter torpedo would do nicely."

Aiden nodded his approval. "Sounds about right."

Abahem maneuvered the ship away from the *Rachel Carson* and accelerated in the opposite direction at 1 G. Once underway,

Aiden turned back to his Data Systems Officer. "Faye, anything interesting yet from the data core we retrieved?"

"Yes, a few things. But I've barely gotten into it. Most of it is highly encrypted. Hutton should be able to crack it in no time. What I can tell you now is that the *Rachel Carson* jumped into this system 15 days ago and the ship was wrecked about seven days after that. I'll have more detail on its movements and operations when this stuff gets decrypted. But one thing I found very odd was its chronometer. It indicates a date and time about three days from now. It's not damaged, and I checked to make sure it was properly synched up with the Holtzman buoy out here. It was. And according to the universal clock, the current time now is Domain Day 89, 20:14 hours."

Before he could respond, Alvarez turned to him and said, "Yes! That's what I was going to tell you just before we spotted that ship. The Holtzman buoy synched our chronometers to Day 89, 16:11 hours, right after we entered this system. About 70 hours later than it should be."

Aiden was certain it had been 2218, Domain Day 86 at around 18:00 when they'd made their jump. "You're saying that our jump into this system took 70 hours of realtime?"

"Apparently," Alvarez said.

"It felt like a normal split-second jump to me," Aiden said. "Did anyone experience anything unusual about it?"

He looked around the bridge and was met only with silent bewilderment. Even though voidjumps felt instantaneous to the crew of a voidship, they always took at least some amount of realtime, but rarely more than a few seconds. Only once on record had a jump taken nearly two hours, during a millisecond flux event. Voidships routinely adjusted their clocks immediately after a jump, synching up with the Holtzman buoy's universal clock in whatever system they'd jumped into. And the *Sun Wolf*'s clocks had indeed all been updated correctly, including individual personnel chronos. Aiden looked at his own chrono and confirmed it was now Domain Day 89. He hadn't noticed it earlier, probably because the time of day was so close to what he assumed it should be, never bothering to check the actual date. As busy as they'd all been since the jump, no one else had noticed either.

"It's happening already," Dr. Maryam Ebadi said, still seated at the Science Station. Her tone sounded grave. "The voidoids have been weakened. Because of what these misguided fools have been doing, the voidoids are now syphoning off less dark energy than ever before. That allows the dark energy density inside them to increase, which in turn slows down transit times for voidjumps. This is not a good sign."

The rest of the crew had turned to her with quizzical expressions.

Ebadi leaned forward to explain. "The voidoids are constantly annihilating dark energy in just the right amount. That's what's keeping our universe intact. We're relatively certain that the annihilation takes place on the periphery of the voidoid, on its event horizon. That, in turn, leaves the interior devoid of dark energy, a special condition virtually identical to *no* space-time. That's what allows voidships to jump almost instantaneously from one voidoid to another—between star systems light-years apart—because there's virtually no space-time between them."

Aiden stroked his beard. It did make some kind of weird sense. Some theorists believed dark energy was synonymous with the zero-point energy of space, while others hotly disputed that assertion. But most everyone agreed that, gravitationally, they behaved virtually the same, and that dark energy was, at the very least, a special case of zero-point energy. So if zero-point energy was the stuff of space-time itself, it followed that if none of it existed between the interiors of two connected voidoids, it would take no time for a voidship to go from one to the other. Because there was virtually no space between them.

"But when that annihilation process is impeded," Ebadi continued, "the density of dark energy increases inside the voidoid, and as it does, so does space-time. Which means voidships actually have to traverse some amount of space, over some amount of time, between voidoids. The greater the density, the more space and time a voidship has to negotiate. Hence the 70 hours it took us to get here, instead of a few seconds. The voidoids are starting to shut down."

She said nothing more. No one else spoke until Ro broke the somber silence, announcing that the ship was now 1,000 kilometers out, well clear of an antimatter torpedo blast field.

Aiden nodded to Hotah. "Fire away, Lieutenant."

Launched at close to 300 Gs, the antimatter torpedo took less than 30 seconds to reach its target. They all watched on the forward screen as the *Rachel Carson* silently blossomed into an incandescent sphere of white-hot plasma, vaporized down to its elemental particles, then faded from view. Within seconds the fireworks dissipated, leaving in its place only the most constant and fundamental condition of the universe: emptiness. Aiden was glad Cass hadn't been on hand to view it.

"Rest in peace, *Rachel Carson*," he said quietly, although he doubted the ship's namesake had rested even one instant in peace after her passing at the very dawn of humankind's most thoughtless trashing of her beloved Earth.

Ro spoke up again. "So, what's our next move, boss?"

Aiden thought about it for a moment, then said, "That depends entirely on the information we get from our guest. I think she and her crew were put up to do someone else's dirty work. That someone else is who we're after. I'm hoping she'll point us in the right direction. Until then, we stay put, wait, and keep our eyes open."

25

ALPHA-2 HYDRI SYSTEM
Domain Day 90, 2218

Sadness is different for the young than for the old. The young are still able to wear sadness as a badge of honor in a winnable war against despair. For the old, it is mostly worn as a weight, a long accumulation of disappointments and regret. For the young, sadness offers itself as a seed of hope yearning to be nourished by experience. For the old, it is at best a bittersweet ballad sung gently in a minor key, a reassuring ode to the end.

Aiden was acutely aware of this difference as he sat across from Cassandra Healy in Conference Room One. After nearly 24 hours of medical care and rest, after decent food and a bath, she looked very different from the haggard young woman they'd pulled out of the dead ship. Dr. Devi had reported that Cass was generally in good health but suspected she'd experienced mild radiation sickness soon after her ship had jumped into the system. Her white blood count was below normal, indicating the damaging effects of gamma radiation on bone marrow cells. No doubt it was all due to their poorly shielded M/AM drive.

Cass sat upright in her chair at the conference table, relaxed but cautious, still the young soldier of Green War. She wore a fresh navy-blue jumpsuit, Science and Survey standard issue, donated by Faye Desai, who was about the same size as Cass. Her complexion looked less pale, the freckles across her face less pronounced, more evenly blended with the faint flush of her cheeks. Her hazel-green eyes were clear and focused, no longer sunken with malnutrition and stress. But traces of the dark circles remained, giving her faraway gaze a haunted look. Her red-auburn hair was freshly washed and tied in a loose bun at the back.

Joining Aiden at the table were Dr. Devi, Colonel Aminu, and Dr. Maryam Ebadi. He wanted to keep the number of participants in the interview to a minimum, as well as equally divided between genders. After strenuous objection, Aminu had finally given in to Aiden's insistence on leading the interview himself. The others were there to ask for clarifications or to suggest areas of questioning, but only Aiden would direct the questioning. After brief introductions, he asked Cass how she was doing.

She paused for a moment, looking cautiously around the table at the others, and finally said, "Okay, I guess."

Not quite defiant, but not open, either. Certainly no *Thank you for saving my life.* Not smiling or scowling. Aiden took that as progress.

He folded his hands in front of him and sat back, relaxed. "Ms. Healy, we'd like to hear the story of who you are, how you got here, and what you and your crew were doing. It would be of great help to us, and to you as well, to tell us."

Cass stayed quiet for a long moment, and Aiden thought she might have decided not to speak at all. Then she looked directly at him and said, "You already know I'm from Green War. You and your ship stand for everything we're fighting against. Why should I help you?"

Aiden detected a trace of Irish brogue in her speech, and her voice sounded lower in register than one would expect from a woman of her age and slight stature.

"First of all," Aiden said, "you might find that our goals are not as diametrically opposed to yours as you think. But that aside, there are at least two very good reasons you should help us. One that you probably already realize is that you're in a lot of trouble.

We have a pretty good idea of what you've been up to out here, from data records we obtained from your ship. We're talking about serious breaches of intersystem law. Sitting to my left is Colonel Victor Aminu from the Domain Security and Intelligence agency. He has absolute authority to arrest you right now, have you locked in our brig, and brought back to answer charges against you that would almost certainly put you in prison for the remainder of your life. You are technically in his custody as we speak."

A mixture of fear and anger clouded Cass's eyes as Aiden spoke. She spoke out before Aiden could continue. "How is saving Earth a crime? How can *any* effort to enlighten the people of Earth be against the law? To make their lives better? Healthier? That's against the law? Well, fuck you! That should *be* the law. Not against it. What kind of people are you, anyway?"

Aiden had expected this outburst, had actually hoped for it. She was opening up. He wanted her to express her feelings. So he didn't take the bait, didn't respond defensively or offensively. He kept his face open and neutral. When he remained silent, she went on.

"It's people like you, like your whole Space Service, that keep everyone else from realizing the truth. Don't you see that? The truth that we humans really *did* screw up big-time? Over two centuries ago, and we're still denying it! Denying that we caused the Die Back. That we nearly killed our own Mother Earth. And we've been running from that truth ever since. Running to Luna, running to Mars, to the other star systems. Running away from our home planet just when she needs us most. I mean, how fucked up is that?"

Aiden nodded at this and said, "Ms. Healy, most of the people I've known all my life wouldn't argue one bit that we humans are absolutely responsible for the Die Back and that restoring Earth's ecosystems should be a priority."

"Then why the hell aren't you back on Earth doing everything you can to make that happen? You of all people, the scientists and technicians! We need you more than ever now. But you're all abandoning Earth, running away, out into space, colonizing other planets, taking all your people and resources with you. You're abandoning your own mother!"

This was where Aiden fully disagreed. There *were* scientists on Earth, many of them and very good ones, devoted whole-heartedly to restoring the planet. He knew many of them personally and knew their passion and dedication. He also knew that a great deal of space exploration, spearheaded by his own Science and Survey division, directly benefited the health and continued recovery of Earth. But none of that fitted into Cass's narrative, and he knew it would be counterproductive to argue it.

"That's why you wanted to shut down the voidoids," he said. "To prevent this exodus of resources away from Earth."

Aiden thought he detected a brief but well-concealed moment of surprise in her eyes at his knowledge of her ship's true purpose here in the Alpha-2 Hydri system. But she was smart enough not to deny it. And maybe even proud of it. "Yes. We know that if the voidoids shut down temporarily, it'll shake people up enough to realize they can't run from the truth any longer. They can't run from Earth if V-Prime shuts down. There's nowhere else to go except our own Solar System. That's the biggest achievement we can attain."

"That still leaves all the other places in the Solar System accessible," Aiden said. "Places other than Earth where people can and might want to go."

"Green War has ways of dealing with that," she said, as if it were an obvious conclusion. "But turning off the voidoids is the big prize. Not only physically but psychologically. That's what will get people's attention the most. That's what will bring them home again."

"And you're all willing to pay the price if you're caught trying to kill the voidoids?"

"We're not trying to *kill* them! What we've been doing will just shut them off temporarily. Long enough for another genera-

tion to come along after Earth has been restored, a wiser generation of people living in harmony with the planet and with each
other. A population that will understand the true value and purpose of space exploration. Not as a way to escape Earth, but to
nurture her. Then, and only then, can the voidoids be opened up
again."

Aiden noticed Dr. Ebadi shaking her head slowly. She understood more than anyone how misguided the whole scheme was.
But Aiden maintained his tone of curiosity and asked, "And how
will the voidoids get turned back on? Who will be in control of
that?"

Cass looked flustered but only briefly. She lifted her chin and
said, "People who know better than I."

"And who would those people be?" Aminu asked, unable to
keep quiet any longer or able to keep the anger from his voice. "Is
it Black Dog?"

The colonel's interruption had the expected effect. Cass
clammed up, folded her arms across her chest, and looked past
everyone as if she were alone in the room by herself.

Aiden looked at Aminu as if to say, *See how well that shit
works?* Instead, he spoke a warning. "Colonel..."

He was sure Cass noticed the interaction. Maybe she was
beginning to understand the consequences of withholding what
she knew. Deal with Colonel Aminu—or with him.

"Cass. We know you were acting on someone else's behalf out
here. Someone I'm sure you believe is totally aligned with your
cause. We need to know who this person is, and everything you
can tell us about them. This is the kind of information that will
help both of us."

"Both of us?" she sneered. "How will it help me? Will it keep
me out of prison?"

Aiden didn't know the answer to that and would not lie to her.
"Possibly not, but it would most likely keep you from spending
your life there. I would personally do everything in my power to
support you in that."

Cass looked at Aminu and said, "But would he?"

Aiden followed Cass's eyes to Aminu. "Colonel?"

Aminu looked conflicted for a moment, then said, "Yes. You give us the information you have, all of it, and I'll see to it that any conviction you receive comes down to the lightest sentence possible."

Aiden thought Aminu had left out a lot in making that statement. His own experience with the Domain's justice system had left him deeply skeptical about the "justice" part of it. Which was why he'd see to it personally that this young woman would never spend a day incarcerated. A promise to himself he would reveal to no one else at this stage of the game.

Cass shook her head slowly. "How can I possibly trust you?"

Aiden took a chance. "How can you trust Black Dog? He left you out here to die in the *Rachel Carson*."

"He would never do that! If he'd known, someone would have come to get us."

Ah-ha. So Black Dog it was. But Aiden didn't gloat. Instead, he pointed out that a distress call had been sent via Holtzman transmission from the *Rachel Carson* to alert its handlers that she was in trouble. It had been sent from the ship's control bridge, clearly made by a male voice, just after the collision but just before the bridge was breached, killing whoever had sent it.

Cass's eyes went wide for a moment, then tears welled up and she looked down at the table. Her lips trembled when she said, "Joal."

"Joal?" Aiden said. "Was he the one in the control bridge when it happened?"

"Yes," she said, still looking down. A tear rolled down one cheek. She fiddled with the gold ring on her left hand. "He was my..."

"I'm sorry, Cass," Aiden said. "I truly am. But the point is, whoever this Black Dog is, he had at least eight days after your ship was wrecked to send someone to rescue you. That's more than enough time for a voidjump from *anywhere* in Bound Space.

He could have, but he didn't. Trust is a tricky business. From what I can see, we're the best bet you have."

When she didn't look up, Aiden said, "Look at me, Cass."

She did. The look of fear and sadness had returned. He locked eyes with her and felt so much empathy for her in that moment, he wasn't sure he could keep his own voice from wavering. "You can trust *me*, Cass. And everyone aboard this ship. Even Colonel Aminu here. He is an honorable man. Under these circumstances, we have a great deal of influence with our government. I promise you, we'll do everything we can to help you out of this mess. But you have to help us too."

Cass straightened up, wiped the tears from her face, and summoned the defiance she'd been using as her shield. "I don't care what happens to me as long as I know I've done the right thing. You said there were two good reasons why I should help you. What's the other one?"

"The other reason," Aiden said, "is something you couldn't possibly have known about. It's this: What you and your people have been doing to the voidoids for the last several years will end up killing every human being alive and destroying the universe as we know it, if it doesn't stop now. And it may even be too late."

Cass stared at him in disbelief, as if he'd just told a very bad joke. When she saw the look on Aiden's face and saw the same grave expression from the others around her, she turned back to him and asked, "What are you saying?"

"I'll let Dr. Ebadi explain it. She's one of the Domain's most prominent research scientists in the field of quantum physics and cosmology. Her specialty is studying the nature of voidoids. Listen carefully to what she has to say. Ask any questions you may have. Then you'll need to choose whether or not to help us."

Maryam Ebadi summarized for Cass the account she had given to Aiden's team, including the vital role the voidoids played in the maintenance of dark energy in our universe, without which the universe as we knew it could not exist. She went on to explain how the continual disruption of the voidoids in Bound Space, perpetrated by the people who wanted to shut them down, was pushing them inexorably toward extinction—all of them and permanently. She explained what the results of that would look like: essentially the end of everything. And how soon that was likely to occur if the disruptions continued unabated. Ebadi then concisely laid out the evidence she and Elgin Woo had gathered over the last few years supporting those conclusions and finished up by emphasizing that once all the voidoids in Bound Space were shut down for any appreciable length of time, they could never be turned on again. "Whoever is telling you that they'll be able to control the voidoids is either lying to you or seriously ignorant of the facts."

To her credit, Cass listened to Ebadi's story with genuine interest. Aiden realized he was looking at a very intelligent young woman. Apparently well educated, she appeared to recognize many of the concepts Ebadi touched upon. The way she tilted her head thoughtfully while listening led Aiden to believe that her passionate convictions had not yet closed her mind to ideas that might challenge them. But in the end, he thought it was the growing shadow of betrayal that swayed her, the implication that she'd been lied to, deliberately or unwittingly, that she and her crew had been used and callously abandoned.

Cass sat back in her chair, under control again, eyes clear, and told them her story.

26

ALPHA-2 HYDRI SYSTEM
DOMAIN DAY 90, 2218

C ASSANDRA HEALY, LIKE most Green Warriors, was born on Earth. She was raised in the British Isles and educated at Trinity College in Dublin. And like most Green Warriors, she and her mate, Joal, believed passionately that humans had a fundamental responsibility to focus all their energies on Earth, on repairing the damage they'd done to their mother planet. They viewed all efforts to colonize other planets as a betrayal of their home world and therefore a moral sin. And because most people were too weak to face that truth, the betrayal would continue until someone stopped it for them, someone with true vision. Someone like the Green Warriors.

Any form of space exploration not directly benefiting Earth presented a potential target for sabotage by Green War. But shutting down the voidoids was considered the ultimate prize, and plans to do it had been held close within the movement's innermost circles. Cass and Joal had heard through the grapevine about another powerful underground organization with beliefs and goals aligned with Green War's willing to back their campaign to shut down the voidoids. This group, known to them only as LO, had vast resources—both monetary and scientific—and claimed to have developed a technology to shut down the voidoids. The face of LO was a shadowy figure called Black Dog, and he had been enlisting only the "bravest and most committed" among the Green Warriors to serve on the front line.

At Cass's mention of LO and Black Dog, Maryam Ebadi and Colonel Aminu exchanged silent glances.

Cass and Joal were told that Black Dog was providing the Green Warriors with ships, called "disrupters," specially fitted for the task, and he needed a few more "dedicated soldiers" to operate them. Cass knew very little about the disrupting technology. She knew only that it involved deploying "gravity drones" in the immediate vicinity of the voidoids to produce an incremental weakening effect upon them. Done often enough to multiple voidoids throughout Bound Space, it would lead to a critical point where V-Prime could be shut down with a single final blow. From then on, opening and closing of the voidoids would be under human control. Exactly which humans, however, was a question that hadn't concerned Cass and Joal at the time. They'd been inspired by the rhetoric, believed they had the right stuff, and signed up without hesitation.

Drawn deeper into the inner circle, Cass and Joal learned that Black Dog had laid out a well-organized timetable to accomplish the shutdown. His Green Warrior cohorts had already been at it for many years. Their efforts had avoided detection due largely to Black Dog's sophisticated intelligence apparatus. They were told that the plan was close to completion and that the Green Warriors should feel proud for having laid the groundwork for the Final Blow.

They also learned that Black Dog ran a secret base on Rhea, one of Saturn's moons, disguised as a mining-equipment manufacturer operating on the outskirts of a large Martian mining colony. A fleet of disrupter ships had been assembled there, using standard Star Jammer space yachts heavily modified for high velocity and for conveying the gravity drones. Cass and Joal were taken to the base for training and shortly thereafter joined the four-person crew of the disrupter *Rachel Carson* on its last mission for the Final Blow. She and Joal were replacing two of the original crew members who were now "unable" to continue working. Cass learned later that they had died of radiation sickness, supporting rumors she had heard about the disrupters' inadequate shielding against the gamma-ray yield of their beefed-up M/AM drives.

The disrupters were small enough to fit two of them in the cargo hold of a Martian-made Aries 7 freighter. That's how they were smuggled past Friendship Station's security measures. LO had acquired one of these massive cargo freighters years ago after it had been reported missing in an unfortunate void flux. After a clever makeover, the freighter had little trouble posing as a legitimate ARM vessel, an empty cargo freighter headed out to load up at the Martian mining station in the Groombridge 1618 system. That, of course, made it immune from cargo inspection, as per the Ganymede Pact.

At this point in Cass's account, a distraught Colonel Aminu asked her how such a thing could possibly happen without verification of the ship's registration ID, flight itinerary, and Licensed Pilot. She had no idea how, and it had never occurred to her to ask.

Immediately after voidjumping into the Groombridge system, both the *Rachel Carson* and the other disrupter craft covertly launched from the freighter's cargo hold, turned around, and jumped into their assigned star systems to carry out their tasks. The freighter, now truly empty, continued on to the ARM mining center, ostensibly to be loaded up with raw materials for transport back to Mars. The ARM government had never discovered the subterfuge.

Ebadi wondered out loud how ships like the *Rachel Carson* could voidjump safely without a Licensed Pilot, but Aiden reminded her that the risks of doing so were greatly reduced by lowering entrance velocities to a crawl and by the considerably lower mass of a small yacht.

The *Rachel Carson* was assigned to the Alpha-2 Hydri system for a nine-day course of periodic voidoid disruption. They were told it was a highly critical mission and that the voidoid there was a special case. It was "the one," Black Dog had said. The disruption routine involved sending the gravity drone out to the voidoid and exposing it to a moderate gravity field for several hours at a time. On the seventh day, they were spotted by a Domain Science and Survey vessel, the *Arcadia*, returning from a mission. According to Black Dog's intelligence, no other ship should have been in the system, so the crew of the *Rachel Carson* was startled when the *Arcadia* approached and began hailing them. They panicked and fled the scene in at high G, leaving the gravity drone still in place, exposing the voidoid to the G-field far longer than intended. That apparently caused the voidoid to flux out just as the *Arcadia* made her jump.

After the *Arcadia* disappeared, the voidoid remained closed for a few frightening minutes before reappearing. The crew of the *Rachel Carson* should have been relieved, but by the time they returned to the pick up the gravity drone, they were still rattled and terrified by the possibility of being identified. The normal procedure for recovering the drone was to approach it head on, slowly, to within one kilometer, shut down the drone's G-field by remote command, open the forward docking bay, and guide the drone safely back inside. But the crew of the *Rachel Carson* were not experienced spacers. They were young Earther idealists following instructions without adequate understanding of the underlying technology, seduced into actions they believed supported their cause by powers who tacitly considered them expendable.

When they found the gravity drone still parked next to the voidoid, still operating, the crew didn't realize that the G-field had intensified massively over the time it had been left in place. The Füzfa Effect had created a gravity well thousands of times steeper than expected, and before they knew it, their ship was slipping down into it, faster and faster. Instead of producing a G-field roughly equivalent to a small asteroid, which was the prescribed dose for each measured disruption, the drone was now pumping out a G-field equivalent to a moon the size of Jupiter's Europa.

The consequence was as predictable as it was horrific. The *Rachel Carson* slammed into the drone, nose first, with enough force to cause the appalling damage Aiden had seen. The two crew persons waiting for the drone inside the forward docking bay were probably killed instantly, their remains now lost among the stars. Cass's mate, Joal, had been in the control bridge. His was the corpse Aiden and Desai had found there. Cass herself had been in her quarters at the time of the collision. The automated emergency system had responded by sealing off viable sections of the ship from the breached sections, engaging a distress-call beacon and shutting down power to all subroutines not directly contributing to life support.

It had saved Cass's life but left her stranded alone in the crew quarters section for over eight days. Fortunately, the viable area included the galley with access to food and water. Unfortunately, more than half of the remaining food reserves had been stored in a cargo hold demolished by the collision and therefore inaccessible to her. She'd rationed her food and water, but it was mostly all gone by the time the *Sun Wolf* came along to rescue her.

When asked how Black Dog's plan was supposed to play out, Cass knew only that after their nine-day mission at the Alpha-2 Hydri voidoid, they were to jump back to Groombridge 1618, where they would be picked up again by the Martian freighter and ferried back into the system. Only after they were back in the System, safely through V-Prime, would Black Dog initiate the final phase to shut it down. She had no idea what that final phase involved, but Black Dog had assured them no one would be hurt and that he would demand system-wide negotiations for solutions to Earth's problems. She and Joal had trusted him and the purity of his cause.

Then, after V-Prime closed down, she and Joal would return to Earth to begin the Great Work of restoring their home planet with the full cooperation and undivided attention of their fellow human beings, who would now be cleansed of their temptation to explore and colonize worlds other than their own. Earth would be made whole again.

When she finished telling her story, Cass looked tired but not defeated. In fact, Aiden thought she looked relieved at having gotten it all out. He and Colonel Aminu had more questions, but Dr. Devi stepped in and asked them to make it quick. They were most interested in any details of the base on Rhea that Cass could remember, and if she had met Black Dog in person and could describe him. Cass told them as much as she remembered about the Rhea base, which wasn't much; their movements around the base had been restricted, and they had stayed only a few days. As for Black Dog, she had never met him in person, and when they'd seen him delivering his stirring proclamations by video feed, he'd worn a black hood with a face cloth that concealed all but his eyes. Eyes that she described as "really creepy."

Dr. Devi finally terminated the interview on behalf of her patient and escorted Cass back to her quarters for more rest and recuperation. The others remained at the table and were joined by Ro, who had been monitoring the interview from the bridge.

Aiden looked around the table and said, "Black Dog? LO?"

Both Aminu and Ebadi nodded in unison, but Aminu spoke first. "I know these names from the chatter my agency picks up while monitoring communications between groups like this. We've heard references to Black Dog. We don't believe he's an actual member of Green War, or the Zero Pops, or any other activist group we know of. Only that he's a prime mover within Green War's sphere of operation. We have very little intel on him, which in itself is notable. We've also heard references to LO and presumed it was a covert organization of some kind, as Ms. Healy indicated. But I'm interested to hear her connecting LO to Black Dog."

Ebadi spoke up. "Yes, I've heard of LO as well, but only from Dr. Woo and only once, in his last message to me before he disappeared. In the cryptochip you delivered to me on Luna. I didn't mention it at the time because I didn't understand what he was talking about, and the other concerns seemed more important."

"What did Elgin say?" Aiden asked.

"He learned that Cole Brahmin was a member of a highly secretive group, an order of men with very dangerous powers and pervasive influence throughout the System. In the rare instances where it interfaces with the outside world, the order is referred to only as LO. But Elgin had deep sources, and he learned that LO stands for Licet Omnia. According to him, that's its true name. Brahmin himself was not its leader, but the twisted evilness of that man is the hallmark of LO's true nature. Brahmin's pathological obsession to destroy Silvanus was a perfect example. We're talking about some very dark souls here. Very smart, very hidden.

"Their real leader apparently has several names, none of which Elgin knew for sure. But Black Dog could certainly have been one of them. Dr. Woo believed that Licet Omnia works completely in the shadows to control those who are the face of power everywhere. They stand in direct opposition to the Gaians, to everything Gaians believe in, and represent the single most dangerous threat to the Cauldron. Dr. Woo was adamant in his message that Licet Omnia had to be neutralized. He believed that he and his forces at the Cauldron were the only ones capable of doing that, of finding and destroying them."

"Did he have any idea where this Licet Omnia was based?" Aiden asked.

Ebadi sighed and lowered her eyes briefly. "Yes, he said he was 99 percent sure where their center of operations was located. But he didn't divulge it in the cryptochip. He said it was too dangerous for anyone else to know at this point. Said that he would reveal it once he got back from his 'little escapade' and could begin mustering his forces."

"Typical Elgin," Aiden snorted. "But I'm sure his instinct to protect you was well-founded. All the more reason to find him sooner than later."

At this, Aminu looked at him like he'd heard a joke he totally did not get. Ebadi, already privy to the idea, kept her face neutral. Ro looked unsurprised, remained silent, then spoke wistfully, "Licet Omnia..."

When he said nothing more, Aiden prompted. "Speak, Ro."

"Licet Omnia," Ro finally said. "Latin for 'all is permitted.' This group is known within Gaian circles. Its innermost circles, at least. And there, Licet Omnia is primarily associated with black magic. Not of the fairytale kind. Of the very real kind, at its worst and most powerful."

Aiden knew that Ro had strong connections to Gaian inner circles, even apart from his wife's prominent position within them. "What else, Ro?"

"Licet Omnia was founded by a mystic, a black magician some would call him, with roots in the old Thelema tradition, otherwise known as 'True Will.' It's a lineage that goes way back to the likes of Aleister Crowley and probably beyond. Crowley was the one who infamously said, 'Do what thou wilt.' Hence, 'all is permitted.' But Licet Omnia is purportedly far darker, more powerful. Starting with lots of Friedrich Nietzsche and stuff about the master race and moving quickly off into the deep end, into the Dark Arts. You'd need special faculties to go up against them."

Aiden felt a sudden cold sweat. His stomach knotted up. "You think this Black Dog character might be their leader?"

"Black Dog is one of the names I've heard associated with LO, a personage whose true name is Cu Dubh. That's old Gaelic for 'black dog.' Pronounced 'koo-doo.' But the Gaians I know who're really plugged into the astral hotline know the true leader of Licet Omnia by the name Cardew. The two names may belong to the same person, but personally I doubt it."

"Cardew? That's it?"

Ro nodded. "Yep. Cardew. It's another old Celtic name, meaning 'from the dark fort.'"

"The Dark Fort." Aiden repeated the words, capitalizing them for effect. "How fitting. Sounds like a place we need to find."

Ro looked at him for a long moment, utterly without humor, and said, "A place sane people need to stay away from at all costs. But if it exists at all, I highly doubt it's the base on Rhea that Cass mentioned. Even under the guise of a legit operation, that location is way too exposed for this bunch. I'd guess their home base isn't even in the Sol system, but somewhere else in Bound Space. Somewhere no one could possibly guess. Except now maybe Elgin Woo."

Aiden noticed the hint of present tense in Ro's reference to Woo. He said, "If they are in another star system, and their goal is to control the Solar System, they've got to believe they can come and go freely between the two, even after they've shut down V-Prime."

"Assuming that is their goal," Ro said, sounding unconvinced. "Then yes, like Cass said, they believe they'll have the key to opening and closing V-Prime at will, a key that no one else can have."

Ebadi shook her head emphatically. "Whatever key they think they've got, even if it works once, the end result will be the same. *All* the voidoids in Bound Space will follow suit and shut down simultaneously. Then the entire family of voidoids will die."

Aminu, looking his usual skeptical self, said, "Wait a minute. If we're assuming the goal of this Licet Omnia is to control the System's access to Bound Space, all they'd need to do is control V-Prime. Why even bother with shutting down all the other voidoids?"

"Because," Ebadi said, as if it were self-evident, "that's the only way for them to shut down V-Prime. They couldn't openly work on V-Prime itself because it's too visible and well guarded. They've had to attack it indirectly by weakening all of its daughter voidoids first, weakening it to the point where one final well-timed attack on V-Prime will do the job."

The others looked at her in silence, questioning.

"Okay, look," Ebadi said. "V-Prime turns out to actually *be* the primary voidoid in Bound Space. It was the very first voidoid to migrate into this sector of space, as a protovoidoid, maybe six billion years ago. It was the mother voidoid, if you will, and she propagated thousands of daughter voidoids that dispersed outward and attached themselves to all the neighboring stars and starlike bodies within a given radius. That's how Bound Space came into being, and that's why V-Prime is at its center. All the daughter voidoids are interconnected through the mother voidoid, mutually interactive and mutually responsive. That explains all the interrelated void-flux phenomena we've been seeing. It's a family affair. Weaken the daughters as a whole, and you weaken the mother, then the entire family fails."

More question-laden silence followed.

"Please don't ask me to go further into this right now, even though I'd love to. It's a very complex subject, all of it stemming from Dr. Woo's research into the origin and life cycles of voidoids. And that's what troubles me most about whoever is doing this. It looks like they're operating on the same page within the same sophisticated theoretical framework conceived exclusively by Elgin Woo."

"Which is precisely why," Aiden said, "we need Dr. Woo with us for this fight. To match his knowledge with theirs. His powers against theirs."

Before Aminu could comment, Ro interjected the obvious next question. "So. When is this Final Blow against V-Prime going to happen?"

"From what I heard in Cass's story," Aiden said, "I'd guess it's happening damn soon."

Ebadi said, "The attack would most likely take the form of another gravity-field burst. A large one, right next to V-Prime. But how could they get past all the battle cruisers parked around Friendship Station to do it?"

Ro stroked his chin theatrically. "Hmmm. They'd have to be running the biggest, baddest battleship in town..."

Aiden nodded. "It's the *Markos*."

He turned back to Ro. "When the *Markos* passed us at the Cauldron, they were on course for V-Prime. If they stayed on it, when would they arrive there?"

Ro responded without hesitation. He'd already done the math. "Given the constant rate of acceleration we clocked them at, and given the 70 hours we lost in our jump out here, I'd say the *Markos* is arriving at V-Prime just about now."

Aiden stood abruptly. "Okay, that's all for now. I need to send a Holtzman transmission to Admiral Stegman to warn him about the *Markos*."

Back on the bridge, Aiden sat at the Command station and activated the Holtzman transmitter. Aminu followed him there, stood in front of him, and with barely controlled impatience said, "I assume you'll be following the admiral's orders and getting us back to the System. Now. To help out. Before it's too late."

"I'm considering that, yes. Along with other priorities." Aiden knew it wasn't what Aminu wanted to hear and sensed a boiling point rapidly approaching. He was about to turn up the heat when Pilot Abahem cried out in pain. With the neurolink cap firmly in place on her head, her face had gone pale, her eyes wide, staring upward into some invisible vortex of horror.

Almost simultaneously, Lilly Alvarez jerked her head up from the monitor, eyes just as wide as Abahem's. "Commander. Our voidoid just fluxed out. It's gone."

27

ALPHA-2 HYDRI SYSTEM
Domain Day 90, 2218

IN TRUTH, WE are all, each one of us, alone. From the moment the umbilical cord is cut to our final breath, we are, in our most fundamental condition, alone. It is a truth we spend our lives and much of our creative energies striving earnestly to deny. No matter how together we feel with others, bound to them by love or religion, by blood or tribe, by common goals and dreams, we are alone. And yet by clever device and engagement, we carry on in spite of what our bodies know for sure and what our minds so artfully argue against.

Aiden knew this, perhaps better than most. His unflinching acceptance of it, in fact, imparted poignant depth to every human interaction he experienced, brightened every pleasure and pain with the sharp taste of authenticity. But there were degrees of aloneness, or at least of the sensation of it. And being stranded 36.3 light-years from home, with nothing but the darkest and coldest emptiness in between, was a degree of aloneness in the extreme.

He also knew that a leader could not express even a hint of despair in the presence of those he led. Here again his friendship with aloneness served him. He pushed away thoughts of what it would be like never to see Skye again, never to hold her in his arms, to have a life together with her, loving her more each day.

He did not think of how it would be never to again breath the air of his home planet, redolent with too much life, to swim in its waters, or never to again return to Silvanus to walk its magical forests, to hear the delicate music of its singing trees, or to become one with its exotic biology as he had once done.

Instead, he calmly walked over to Comm/Scan and reviewed Alvarez's sensor data. Confirming that the voidoid was no longer where it had been, he suggested waiting patiently for it to reappear. Most void fluxes never lasted more than a few seconds or, rarely, a few minutes at most. But after ten uneventful minutes, this flux had an ominous feel to it. Thrown in with what Cass had told them about Black Dog's twisted but well-organized campaign, it felt more than ominous. It was terrifying.

Had all the voidoids in Bound Space finally shut down? Indefinitely? Or permanently, as Dr. Ebadi feared? If so, the *Sun Wolf* was stranded, and from the looks of concern around the bridge, the crew knew it too. Not only would they be marooned impossibly far from home, but so would everyone else scattered throughout Bound Space. People on research missions, survey and mining missions, military patrols. Possibly even people near and dear to members of his crew. Including people like Skye, still out in the Chara system.

He turned to Pilot Abahem. She had resumed her usual impassive stillness, her eyes like calm pools whose surface had only momentarily been disturbed. If licensed pilots truly were voidoid empaths, as many believed, they were also disciplined professionals. Aiden spoke to her. "Helm, take us out to 30,000 klicks from our current position."

This was standard procedure for any vessel unlucky enough to find itself near a void flux, because when voidoids popped back into existence, they were known to emit a weird soup of charged particles that could play havoc with a ship's electronics up to about 20,000 kilometers. The *Sun Wolf* was still well within that range. But just as importantly, Aiden wanted to signal to his crew that he was operating on the assumption the voidoid *would* pop back into existence.

"Commander," Alvarez said. "The Holtzman buoy received a partial transmission from Admiral Stegman right before the voidoid flux. Do you want to take it here or in your quarters?"

Here comes the bad news, Aiden thought. *Might as well break it to everyone now.* "Here, Lilly. Up on the main screen."

Admiral Stegman's visage appeared on the comm screen, stress lines etched on his face in a jagged geography of anxiety that Aiden had rarely seen on the man he'd known for so many years. The ID stamp at the bottom of the screen indicated the message had been transmitted about two hours ago from the UED Space Service base on Ganymede. "Commander Macallan. I need to update you on a developing situation here in the System. I'll be brief because, frankly, I'm not sure how long the Holtzman channels will be open.

"The identity of the battleship you encountered near the Cauldron is confirmed. It's the RMV *Markos*. But we're reasonably sure it's no longer under ARM command. The ship's Republic of Mars insignia has been replaced with the Green War logo. It arrived at V-Prime an hour ago and promptly destroyed not only our two battle cruisers—the SS *Independence* and the SS *Constitution*—along with their three patrol frigates, but has also killed the two Martian battle cruisers and all their frigates. We've never seen anything like it, such a quick and total victory against what should have been overwhelming forces. We understand now from our ARM sources that because the *Markos* is the flagship of the Martian fleet, it possesses the master override codes for the fleet's weapons systems and used them to lock out all tactical functions of the other Martian ships on site. As those ships stood idle, unable to act, the *Markos* proceeded to take out our UED forces handily, while managing to defeat all return fire aimed at them. Nothing could touch them—missiles, rail guns, laser cannons. Incredible. It appears they're using some new kind of shielding technology no one else knows about, and it's pretty damn effective.

"Then, after blasting the UED ships, the *Markos* took out each of the remaining Martian warships, one at a time, in cold blood. With their tactical systems locked out, those ships were helpless to fight back." Stegman paused here, his face congested with anger, then continued.

"Friendship Station was not attacked and remains unharmed. Much of what we know about this incident comes from their firsthand reports. According to them, after the *Markos* cleared the field of all defensive forces, it deployed a large drone-like object that came to rest within 300 meters from V-Prime's horizon. The *Markos* left a brief message with Friendship Station, in text only, then proceeded to voidjump through V-Prime. Its exact jump vector is unclear but appears aimed in your general direction. It's gone from the System, but the drone remains in place. The whole incident took less than 14 minutes.

"The message claims to be from Green War and says they're shutting down V-Prime. It goes on with the typical Green War rhetoric to explain why they're doing it—for Earth's sake, to save Earth from itself, and other such bullshit. But we're skeptical. It's unclear how people from Green War could have accessed the Militia's master override codes and used them so effectively, and to pull off a battle strategy like that, without aid from ARM's high command.

"Regardless of who's behind it, we believe this drone is related to their claim of shutting down V-Prime and that it's probably a timed device that may activate soon. If V-Prime does shut down, the Holtzman system will go down with it, and we will no longer be able to communicate with you or with anyone else left out in Bound Space. The Admiralty wants you to return to the System now. Make your voidjump as soon as possible in case this claim of theirs is true. Don't take the risk of being stranded out there. Plus, you and your ship are now needed more than ever back here in the System. I only hope you get this message before—"

The screen went blank. Transmission terminated.

"Black Dog! You bastard!"

The crew, already stunned by Stegman's transmission, turned to see Cassandra Healy standing by the bridge entrance, a look of utter contempt on her face. She had snuck from her unguarded quarters onto the bridge and had overheard Stegman's report. "That piece of shit! Black Dog said *no one* would be hurt when they did it. He said he would just demonstrate the shutdown first, then demand system-wide negotiations to agree on solutions for Earth."

"You little traitor!" Lieutenant Dalton shouted as he spun around to face her, his eyes burning with rage. "You've gotta lot of nerve to show your face here after what your little band of crazies just did. D'you know how many service men and women are onboard a single UED battle cruiser?"

Dalton had served on the SS *Independence* and had no doubt just lost more than a few close friends. But no one, including Aiden, had ever seen this side of Dalton. Barely recognizable, his face contorted with loathing, his fists clenched.

"That would be 37." He articulated each word in a low, dangerous voice. He stood and began advancing toward Cass, his head lowered. "Throw in three frigates worth of crew, and you just killed over 100 good men and women! Not to mention at least as many Martians!"

"I didn't!" Cass pleaded. She staggered backward, away from Dalton, who lunged toward her. Aiden was the first to step in, followed by Billy Hotah. Aiden blocked Dalton's path and Hotah grabbed him from behind, wrapping him up.

Aiden moved in close, face to face with Dalton. "Stand down, Lieutenant."

Dalton tried to rip free of Hotah's hold but was no match for the other man's greater strength. "Easy there, soldier," Hotah said.

Dalton twisted his head around to stare at Hotah, distracted just long enough to allow his natural common sense to regain a foothold. He stopped resisting and backed off, his glower replaced by a blank look of shock.

Cass stood against the bulkhead wall, trembling, both fear and confusion in her eyes. "I didn't know..."

Sudha Devi had come to her side. Aiden asked her to escort Cass back to her quarters.

Colonel Aminu stepped up to Aiden and added, "To her quarters, and I strongly urge that you—"

Aiden pivoted to face him. "No, I will *not* lock her up, Colonel!" Then to Cass, "Ms. Healy, the bridge is for crew only. You are not to come here unless summoned. Is that clear?"

Cass looked quickly between Aiden and Aminu and made the wise choice. "Yes. Okay."

As Devi escorted her off the bridge, Cass looked back at Dalton, her eyes welling up, and mouthed, "I'm sorry."

Aiden addressed everyone else on the bridge. "We'll figure this one out. I promise you. Let's get back to work."

Ro and Ebadi had come up to the Comm/Scan station to examine Alvarez's data feed from the void flux. Aiden joined them. The safest and most reliable way of confirming that a voidoid had fluxed out was by failing to spot it with high-energy X-ray pulses from the ship's navigational sensors. The second way, and most dramatic, of course, was when a voidship disappeared inside while attempting a jump during a flux. It was something no one would do intentionally, but when a voidship was on target for a high-velocity jump, there was no way to change course at the last moment if the voidoid happened to flux out at just the wrong time.

But now there was a third way with an exotic sensor developed at the Cauldron by Dr. Maryam Ebadi. She'd had it integrated into the ship's sensor array during the ZPD install. It was a highly sensitive and experimental instrument called the Casimir-Ebadi interferometer, or simply the CEI. The Casimir tag was for the Dutch physicist Hendrik Casimir, who came up with the original idea back in the 20th century, and Ebadi was for the brilliant

Cauldron physicist who developed the idea into a practical way of measuring zero-point energy. She humbly referred to it as a ZFD, a zero-point field detector. But everyone else familiar with the invention called it the CEI in her honor. At present, readings from the CEI pulsed in green light from the main sensor board, its meaning still a mystery to both Aiden and Alvarez.

"It uses the Casimir Effect," Ebadi explained, coming to the rescue, "to measure the density of zero-point energy of space. And because dark energy is almost certainly a form of zero-point energy—if not identical to it—the measurements also represent the density of dark energy. When voidoids are active, their event horizons are devouring dark energy, leaving virtually none of it at their cores. The field detector sees that condition as a negative value for zero-point energy, in relation to the density of zero-point energy of the surrounding space. It shows up as a hole in space-time. But when a voidoid fluxes out, it's no longer consuming dark energy, and the hole disappears. The point in space it once occupied looks identical to the space around it. As you can see, the field is solid green. No more hole in space-time. No more active voidoid."

"The voidoid is gone?"

"Not necessarily. It only tells us the voidoid isn't *functioning*. When a voidoid fluxes out, it might be reverting to a dormant state. Its 'superstructure' may still be there, just invisible to all of our sensors. A ghost, if you will. Waiting to reanimate as it always does after a void flux. But not this time, I fear."

This was news to Aiden, another piece of what Ebadi knew about the voidoids that she hadn't yet divulged. He asked, "Then what prompts the voidoid to reappear after it fluxes out? That could be the key to what Black Dog's gang plans on using to control them. And the key for us to combat what they're doing."

Ebadi looked at him and sighed. "Okay. This is where we get deeper into Dr. Woo's work. He concluded, as I do now, that the voidoids are indeed living organisms. And like all living organisms, they have evolved homeostatic systems to thrive. Their response to gravity fields is one such system, like what we talked about earlier. Since increases in gravity fields cause them to slow their consumption of dark energy, or to shut down altogether, we assume that they reanimate when they sense the ambient gravity field returning to 'normal.' Then they start consuming dark energy again. But Black Dog's gang won't rely on that mechanism to reopen the voidoids they manage to close down."

Aiden nodded. "Because they can't control it. When they hit it with their gravity drones, the voidoid will always bounce back after the G-field disperses. It'll start responding again to the star system's gravitational field and continue keeping dark energy in check."

"That's right. And that's why these guys want to force the entire voidoid system into indefinite dormancy where the voidoids can no longer sense and respond to gravity fields. They're operating on some delusion that they can reanimate the whole system at will by some artificial means."

"Any ideas on how they could do that?"

"I personally don't believe it's possible. Dr. Woo, however, came up with several possibilities, all having to do with the voidoids' dormant superstructure, their ghosts. Maybe jump-starting them somehow. But there's no theoretical framework even to begin exploring that possibility. Ultimately, it doesn't really matter. Any conceivable method for reanimating dormant voidoids would be short-lived if they continue to be turned off and on unnaturally. Why? Because, assuming again that the voidoids are living creatures, if you injure them often enough, you'll kill them. Then the entire system will die. Ghosts and all. Permanently."

"Elgin *must* have some workable ideas," Aiden insisted, refusing to entertain the notion of inevitable doom. "Some way to revive newly dormant voidoids. Even if it's just one of his crazy hunches."

"Maybe. If it can be done in time," Ebadi said with little conviction. She pointed again to the CEI reading on Alvarez's board.

"See. It's happening already. The green represents the ambient density of dark energy, the level it's been kept at for billions of years by the voidoids. You can see how the green is already slowly shifting yellowish. That indicates an increasing density of dark energy. The numerical values on the side of the screen quantify the buildup. Like I said, it won't take long before everything we know starts flying apart under the influence of expanding dark energy."

Aiden stood straight, his resolve now absolute. "We need to find Elgin. Now."

Victor Aminu, who'd been listening in, stepped up to Aiden, his face inches away, arms held down stiffly at his side. "This fantasy of yours, of finding Dr. Woo, has gone far enough, Commander. He is almost certainly dead. Even if he is still alive, and you're crazy enough to think he made it to that star, there's no way for us to get there. We should be concentrating on getting back to Sol, following the orders you were given by Admiral Stegman."

Aiden stood his ground, even moved his face closer to Aminu's. "There are so many things wrong with what you just said, Colonel, I don't even know where to start. In case you hadn't noticed, the voidoid here in this system has shut down. V-Prime back in the System is down, and it's highly likely that *all* the voidoids in Bound Space are down. How do you propose to get back to Sol? Talk about a fantasy!"

"We've got this zero-point drive now," Aminu said, unfazed. "That's got to make it way more feasible to get back without the voidoids."

Aiden shook his head. "What school did you go to, Aminu? Was it all about guns, war games, and the law? Didn't they teach you any science? Do I have to spell this shit out for you? We are 36.3 light-years from Sol. Yes, the zero-point drive can reach 92 percent light speed. But even at that speed, it would take us about 40 years to get back to Sol. And that's assuming we have enough fuel to sustain the EM control fields for that long, which we don't. Nowhere close. Oh, sure, there's the time-dilation factor. We'd experience a little over 15 years here on the *Sun Wolf*, but when we got back to Sol, it's 40 years later for them. So how's that going to help?"

Aminu stepped back and crossed his arms over his chest. "Point taken. But how's that any crazier than trying to find Dr. Woo? Sounds like a pipe dream to me. Like someone's been tripping out on Continuum."

Now, Aiden thought, Aminu was baiting him. The DSI knew everything about anyone they were interested in, including medical records, and no doubt they knew of his past Continuum use. But Aiden had been baited before, in ways far worse and by sociopaths with far greater expertise than Aminu. For him, it was not even bait. It was a snack.

"How is it crazier than searching for Dr. Woo? Let me count the ways, Colonel. First of all, we know where Dr. Woo was headed, and secondly, we have good reason to believe he made it there in one piece. Sure, we'll have to brainstorm a little to figure out how he did it, but it's a far better use of our time than spending the rest of our lives trying in vain to get back to Sol. And thirdly, if anyone alive knows how to combat what's been done to the voidoids, it's Dr. Woo. You want to save the System? To save all of humanity? Then you've got to have Elgin Woo on your team. It's that simple. And that's why we're going to find him. Like it or not, that's our new mission profile."

Dr. Maryam Ebadi, who had been studying her compad intently, looked up and stepped into the fray. "I think Dr. Woo is alive and well out at HD 10180," she said with firm conviction. "I know how he got there now. And how we can get there too."

28

ALPHA-2 HYDRI SYSTEM
Domain Day 91, 2218

"LOOK FOR THE gateway where the spheres meet."
Maryam Ebadi spoke the words reverently, as if from an oracle. She looked at Aiden. "Those were Dr. Woo's exact words. It was the last line of his cryptochip message, the one you delivered to me on Luna. I had no idea what he meant by it until now. The spheres are astrocells."

After ordering mandatory split-shift sleep cycles, Aiden had reconvened in the ship's galley. He and Ebadi were accompanied by most of the crew, with the exception of Ro, Pilot Abahem, and Lieutenant Hotah, who were manning the bridge. Aiden had chosen to meet in the galley for several reasons. It was large enough to comfortably seat the entire crew, and it was where they could catch up on meals missed during the events of the previous day.

More importantly to Aiden, it had a coffee dispenser, and he badly needed a caffeine jolt right about now. The first thing he did upon entering was to program the machine to produce two liters of extra-dark, extra-strong brew. Ebadi opted for green tea, but the others jumped at the chance to sample Aiden's private stash of African-grown coffee beans. The aroma of it, freshly ground and brewed, filled the enclosed quarters with a mellow organic tang that was equal parts intoxicating and eye-opening.

"Astrocells?" Aiden asked between sips. "I've never heard that term before. I assume it's another Elgin word."

"It is indeed," Ebadi said, smiling. Despite their bleak circumstances, the mood of this group felt lighter than previous meetings, and the obvious reason was the absence of Colonel Aminu. Aiden had invited him, but the DSI man refused to join any discussion on the topic of how to find and retrieve Elgin Woo. He had retired to his quarters for his sleep cycle and not emerged since.

"Astrocell," Ebadi said, "is the term Dr. Woo coined to refer to a whole family unit of voidoids, as in the mother voidoid and all her interconnected daughters. Bound Space, for example, is one such astrocell. One among billions of other astrocells in our galaxy alone. If you want to understand what I think we're about to do, I need to give you some more background on Dr. Woo's theories."

Aiden nodded. "As long as I can refill my coffee cup at will, Dr. Ebadi, you're on."

"All right," she said. "I'll try not to bore you, which I figure is less likely now that you're well into your first cup of that wretched brew. So, here's the 'Universe According to Elgin Woo.' The down and dirty version of it, at least. For any of you who are interested in digging deeper into it, I've given you all access to Dr. Woo's latest treatise on the subject, *Living Voidoids: Their Evolution and Life Cycles.*"

She began with a brief recap of the currently accepted Big Bang model of the universe which put its origin at right around 13.8 billion years ago, after which its initial expansion began to gradually slow down when all the matter in the universe began to pull in on itself under the influence of its combined gravitational forces. Then, about six billion years ago, for some inexplicable reason, its rate of expansion began to accelerate dramatically and has continued to do so ever since. For lack of a better explanation, this accelerated expansion has been attributed to the spontaneous creation of dark energy countering the inward contraction of the universe's matter, causing it instead to expand at an ever-increasing rate.

"Right around that time, six billion years ago," Ebadi said, "certain entities Dr. Woo referred to as protovoidoids emerged from some unknown origin and began to disperse throughout space. They responded to the accelerating expansion of spacetime by consuming vast amounts of dark energy to effectively slow down the rate of acceleration, keeping it in check to the level we observe it to be today. Without those billions of protovoidoids, we wouldn't be here now. By drastically reducing the density of dark energy around them, they maintained conditions compatible with the accretion of matter, and ultimately the formation of stars, planets, and galaxies. So, wherever a protovoidoid settled, conditions for star formation and for building planetary systems were enhanced.

"If the host star subsequently evolved certain characteristics advantageous to the protovoidoid, the protovoidoid matured into an adult voidoid, a 'mother' that propagated a finite number of daughter voidoids dispersed outward in a roughly spherical pattern. Those daughter voidoids in turn consumed more dark energy throughout the regions they occupied, contributing even further to conditions favoring the formation of yet more stars and planetary systems. Ultimately, an entire neighborhood of voidoids came into being within a defined volume of space surrounding the mother voidoid, each one paired with a host star— a neighborhood where the maintenance of dark energy density is shared by the whole 'family.'

"That neighborhood is what Dr. Woo calls an astrocell, an approximately spherical volume of space containing stars paired with voidoids of a single lineage. Bound Space is the astrocell we live in, and our solar system's voidoid, V-Prime, evolved from the original protovoidoid that settled in our region of space about six billion years ago. That's why our solar system is at the center of Bound Space."

Ebadi paused here to look at each of them in turn. She had their attention. It reminded Aiden of his early childhood when his mother would read stories to him late at night before pulling the covers up to his chin and kissing him goodnight. Those early days before his mother was killed. He swallowed the memory back and nodded to Ebadi to continue.

"Now, according to Dr. Woo," she said, "Bound Space is only one among hundreds of billions of other astrocells in our Local Group of galaxies, each one initially seeded by a single protovoidoid, each one with its own network of interconnected voidoids, bound by its own V-Limit. Some astrocells are much larger than others, some much smaller, depending on the extent of the initial dispersion pattern of daughter voidoids from the mother.

"Dr. Woo's model initially predicted that astrocells normally do not interact with each other, being of separate lineages and occupying separate regions of space. That's one reason why we can't jump from here into another astrocell. But after the events at Chara, he came to believe that the boundaries of some astrocells may have grown to overlap those of other astrocells at their outermost margins, just narrowly intersecting. He postulated that, where it occurs, an overlap zone will be occupied by a single gateway star, a star that hosts two active voidoids—one originating from each astrocell and remaining connected to its astrocell of origin. Since both occupy the same star system, all you have to do is enter the system from astrocell 'A,' hop over to the voidoid connected to astrocell 'B,' jump into it, and bingo: you have a gateway between the astrocells."

Aiden nearly dropped his coffee cup. *Look for the gateway where the spheres meet.*

With his mind's eye, he visualized two spheres in space—astrocells—just barely overlapping one another at a single point at their outer edges, like a cosmic Venn diagram. One sphere was known as Bound Space, with a radius of about 36 light-years, and the other sphere, of yet unknown size, contained the star HD

10180. Then, somewhere inside that shallow overlap zone on the Frontier, there was a star with two voidoids forming a gateway between the astrocells. Elgin Woo had found it and used it to reach HD 10180.

But something didn't add up. "If Elgin jumped straight from the Chara voidoid to HD 10180, that means the Chara voidoid is the gateway. But that can't be right. Chara is nowhere near the Frontier of Bound Space, where the overlap zone would be. It's almost 10 light-years back from the V-Limit."

"That's right," Ebadi said. "The Chara voidoid is not the gateway. And I don't think Dr. Woo jumped from there directly to HD 10180. I think he made a detour first to a gateway star out on the Frontier, then from there on to HD 10180. If we wanted to find him, we'd need to locate that gateway star."

Ro, who was patched in remotely from the bridge, interrupted. "I think it's time to stop calling this star HD 10180. That old Henry Draper number just doesn't roll off the tongue."

Aiden stared at Ro's image on the screen for a moment before deciding he wasn't joking. "What do you suggest?"

"Woo's Star," he said as if it were already written in the Intersystem Astronomical Union's catalog. "Of course, we'd need to petition the IAU to formalize it."

Aiden smiled. "Okay. I like it. Woo's Star it is."

He turned back to Ebadi. "What makes you think Elgin took a detour? The neutrino beam he detected shooting out from the Chara voidoid was aimed directly at HD 10180—I mean Woo's Star—not at some hypothetical gateway out on the Frontier."

"Yes," Ebadi said. "He made it clear in his message that he thought the beam was merely a pointer, a beacon pointing to where he should go. But he didn't say anything about how he was going to get there. I think he figured it out on his own before making his jump from Chara."

Aiden's head started to hurt. Time to consult the AI, who he assumed had been following the discussion in silence. "Hutton, do you have the sensor data we collected aboard the Conquest when we watched Dr. Woo jump from the Chara system?"

"Yes, I do," the AI responded. He sounded eager to join in. "It was all recorded into the Conquest's mission logs. And, as with all UED military ship logs, it is classified information."

"I've been given security clearance for that information, Hutton, specifically for this mission. You know that, right?"

"That is correct."

"Then tell me, do you have the vector parameters Dr. Woo used to make his jump?"

"Yes. Not the exact heading, but a close approximation."

"Okay, and that heading was directed toward Woo's Star, right?"

"No, in fact, it was not."

"Then where the hell *was* he headed?"

"From the limited data I have, which is purely observational, since Dr. Woo did not share his navigational numbers with us, it appears that he was headed in the direction of where we are now. Here in the Alpha-2 Hydri system."

Holy shit. Why didn't anyone bother to check on that before now?

Ebadi nodded and smiled. She didn't look the least bit surprised.

"The gateway is here?" Aiden said. "At Alpha-2 Hydri? But there're hundreds of other stars on the Frontier, all around the periphery of Bound Space. Since we have no idea where this overlap zone could be, any of those stars might be the one with the gateway."

"But there's a very good reason to believe that this is the place," Ebadi countered. "That we're sitting in the overlap zone. Right here and now."

"A reason other than Elgin Woo believed it enough to come here?"

"Yes," she said. "I've known Dr. Woo for a long time. I've developed a sense for how he thinks. Not what he thinks—that will be an eternal mystery—but how he thinks. I'm guessing he acted on the assumption that Woo's Star is the primary voidoid of the astrocell it occupies and therefore lies at its center, just like Sol is at the center of Bound Space. So, if Sol and Woo's Star are the center points of their respective astrocell spheres, it's a simple matter of 3-D geometry to figure out where the two spheres would overlap, if they had grown close enough to do so."

"Right," Aiden said. "Draw a straight line between the centers of the two spheres—Sol and Woo's Star, 127 light-years apart—and that line passes through the exact spot on the Frontier where the overlap zone would be centered, 36 light-years from Sol and 91 light-years from Woo's Star."

"Yes. And that spot is here. At Alpha-2 Hydri. There's no other star anywhere near here. The gateway has to be here."

"Maybe," Aiden said, still skeptical. "It depends on how big this hypothetical overlap zone is and if it's big enough to include any other stars. If so, they would have to be candidates too. Did Elgin have any idea of how deep these overlap zones could be? How far inside each other the two spheres can penetrate?"

"Yes, he did. Using some arcane mathematics he kept to himself, Dr. Woo predicted that two astrocells could not intersect each other any deeper than 1 light-year."

"That would narrow down the search area," Aiden said. He knew the AI would be doing his own calculations and asked, "Hutton, are there any other stars in our vicinity that lie within this hypothetical overlap zone?"

"Given the parameters Dr. Ebadi has indicated," Hutton said, "the overlap zone she predicts covers a relatively small and well-defined volume of space. There are no other stars or starlike objects within that space. Alpha-2 Hydri is the only one."

Aiden noticed Lilly Alvarez nodding enthusiastically while sketching something on her compad with a synchrostylus. She made a final tap on its surface and the image of a simple diagram appeared on the conference screen above the table. "Like that," she said.

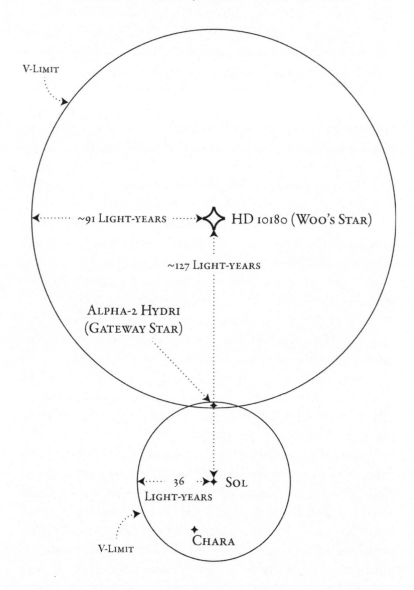

WOO'S ASTROCELL
SPHERICAL VOLUME ~ 3, 160, 000 CUBIC LIGHT-YEARS

V-LIMIT

~91 LIGHT-YEARS ······ HD 10180 (WOO'S STAR)

~127 LIGHT-YEARS

ALPHA-2 HYDRI
(GATEWAY STAR)

36
LIGHT-YEARS ·· SOL

CHARA

V-LIMIT

BOUND SPACE
SPHERICAL VOLUME ~ 195, 000 CUBIC LIGHT-YEARS

Ebadi grinned at the screen, turned to Aiden, and said, "That's it, then. This star is the only one inside the overlap zone. The gateway is here."

"Correction," Aiden said. "It *was* here. But no longer. The voidoids are shut down, remember? We can't use them. I take it you have an alternative plan."

Ebadi nodded tentatively. "Yes, you're right. We can no longer use this voidoid to jump back into Bound Space. It's safe to assume that all the voidoids there are now dormant. But it might still be possible to jump from here into Dr. Woo's astrocell through the voided that's connected to it."

"If this other voidoid exists," Alvarez said, "where is it? How would we even begin to find it?"

Instead of answering, Ebadi turned to Aiden, her head cocked slightly, and said nothing.

Aiden nodded. "At the polar opposite point."

"Exactly," Ebadi said. "The logical locations for the two active voidoids would be at the star system's polar opposite points."

Dalton spoke for the first time. "You're assuming that Black Dog's Final Blow affected only the voidoid connected to Bound Space, but not the one connected to Woo's astrocell."

"Yes," she said. "Because that one came from a different lineage than the voidoids in Bound Space, so it wasn't affected by the shutdown of V-Prime. It belongs to the voidoid family of Woo's astrocell, where they're all alive and well. I'm betting that voidoid is still active, and we can jump through it into the new astrocell. In fact, right now that's probably the only other place we can go."

Aiden stroked his beard. "That's a lot of assumptions and hunches. A lot of conjecture to gamble our lives on."

"No doubt about it, Commander. You'd be placing a great deal of trust in my conclusions. But I think you'd agree the stakes couldn't be higher."

"Well, we can at least go to the POP and see what we find," Aiden said. "And we can use your CEI device to detect an active voidoid if it's there, right?"

"Yes. That, in conjunction with your ship's navigational locater, will tell us for sure."

Aiden turned to Dalton. "Lieutenant, how far are we from this system's polar opposite point, and how soon can we get there?"

"Well, sir, that'd be 12.9 AU from here to the ecliptic plane, then another 12.9 AU from there to the POP. That's about 25.8 AU." Dalton spoke eagerly, the natural grin gracing his face once again. All traces of the angry young man they had witnessed earlier had vanished. "Works out to be about 3.86 billion kilometers. If we use the zero-point drive at max speed, we'd get there in less than four hours. That's outside observer time. For us onboard it'll be about an hour and a half."

Aiden smiled. "Just a walk in the park, eh?" He stood and said, "Okay. Let's do this."

29

ALPHA-2 HYDRI SYSTEM
Domain Day 91, 2218

"**A**RE YOU MAD?" Colonel Aminu stared at Aiden, eyes wide. Upon returning to the bridge, Aiden had announced his intentions to the crew, had instructed the pilot to set a course for the system's polar opposite point, and told Dalton to prepare the zero-point drive for maximum velocity. Aminu had responded predictably. Aiden was ready for it.

"Mad?" he said, returning Aminu's glare. "Yes, Colonel, and I have a feeling I'm about to get even madder. Just keep it up."

"Why the hell are we going to the polar opposite point?" Aminu sputtered. "Is this more of your misguided fantasy about saving Dr. Woo?"

"Why are we're going to the POP?" Aiden said, trying to keep his voice even. But failing. "That would be perfectly clear to you if you had joined us in conference just now. Pouting like a spoiled child doesn't get you anywhere, except left out."

"Who's acting like a child here?" Aminu sneered. "I'm not the one sending his ship and crew on a fool's errand—one that's likely to get us all killed—and defying the orders of his superiors in the process."

"Orders from my superiors?" Aiden said as if amused, though far from it.

"Orders from Admiral Stegman to return to the System as soon as possible," Aminu said. His patronizing tone dripped with derision. "Granted, we can't do that until the voidoids flux back into operation. Until they do, the obvious extension of that order is to remain here at the voidoid and wait for it to happen. Any other action would be considered defiance of that order."

"Haven't you been listening, Colonel? The voidoids are not going to open up for us, no matter how much time we spend sitting here wishing they will."

"You don't know that. Dr. Ebadi doesn't know that. It's all pure conjecture."

Ebadi, who had been standing a few feet away, closed the gap in a split second and came up to put her face into Aminu's. Her fists were clenched but held at her sides. "And what do *you* know, Colonel? A man who lacks curiosity, who hides his fear of the unknown behind a thin badge of the law, who places devotion to some twisted idea of duty above devotion to knowledge—"

"Maryam." Aiden interrupted her, holding his hand up to back her away. "The colonel is entitled to his opinions, no matter how ill-informed and small-minded they are. But he's not captain of this ship. I am. So, Colonel Aminu, your objections to my orders are duly noted. Please stand down now, or else remove yourself from the bridge."

Aminu did not budge an inch. "If you insist on this course of action, you could legally be removed from command."

"Oh? By whom?"

Aminu's back straightened even more. His right hand moved smoothly to the place on his jumpsuit where Aiden knew all DSI agents carried concealed sidearms, small but lethal ones. His hand rested there as he drew closer to Aiden, his eyes burning. "I'm warning you, Commander. This could be considered an act of treason."

And there it was. The *T*-word again. Aiden was more disappointed in how low the man would go than angry with the particular step Aminu made to get there. "So, treason is it now? From defying orders straight to treason. An interesting trajectory. And a telling one."

"You said it yourself," Aminu said, his voice low and lethal. "The *T* brand is still there, even though it's gone from sight."

The crew fell silent. Most of them were well aware of Aiden's history and had chosen not only to accept him for who he was now but also to admire him for how he'd gotten there. Aiden felt the hurt of the words and the burning resentment he felt toward the man who used them now as a weapon. He felt them, he recognized them, he made them his friend, and then let them pass through him unaffected.

Well, almost unaffected. Aiden moved his face even closer to Aminu's and spoke in a quiet, unhurried voice. "I feel only pity for you, Victor. It must be such a sad and lonely nightmare inside your head."

Aminu's eyes flashed. He went for his weapon. But before he could draw it, he felt the cold steel of a pistol muzzle pressed into his left temple. Billy Hotah had moved silently and lightning-quick to stand behind the colonel, his finger held steady on the weapon's trigger.

Aiden cocked his head in mock disappointment. "Bad idea, Victor. Now look at who could go down for treason. I strongly suggest that you stay perfectly still while I remove your weapon. I believe my lieutenant dislikes you even more than I do, and I think he's looking for an excuse to express his feelings more openly."

Aminu stood still as a stone. Aiden reached inside the man's cargo pocket, removed the gun, and handed it to Ro. "XO, will you and Lieutenant Hotah please escort Colonel Aminu to the ship's brig? I think he needs to cool off a bit."

"With pleasure," Ro said.

Aminu, who looked surprised at the sudden turn of events, and maybe a little shocked by his own role in it, said, "This isn't necessary, Commander."

"It is now," Aiden said then motioned for Ro and Hotah to lead Aminu off the bridge, their weapons held ready.

Ebadi moved closer to Aiden. Still stunned, she gave him a long look. "You don't look surprised."

"I'm not. I've been expecting something like this for a while. That's why I authorized Lieutenant Hotah to carry a concealed weapon. Just like I'm carrying." Aiden patted an open pocket on the thigh of his jumpsuit. "The colonel can get a little too self-righteous for his own good. Thing is, I think he knows it. He just can't control it when his buttons get pushed."

"And you push his buttons," Ebadi said. It was a statement, not a question.

"Like no one else, I'm sure." Aiden nodded. "I'll admit, he pushes mine too."

Sudha Devi had come to join them and said, "Our colonel must be feeling isolated now that we're cut off from the System, from his chain of command. He knows this ship is the only world we have right now and that Aiden is the one making all the rules in it. It frightens him. He can't accept having to think outside the box to move forward. That's making him unstable."

"And dangerous," Aiden added.

Ebadi gave a restrained smirk. "Maybe he needs a little sit-down with Dr. Devi here."

Devi smiled at the notion but said nothing.

"Fat chance," Aiden said, amused by the idea. "I doubt he'd even let you try."

"But he's in the brig now," Devi said. "A captive audience."

Aiden shook his head. "He'd be a tough nut to crack, Sudha."

"I've cracked tougher." She looked him in the eye. "You know I'm right."

Feigning frustration, Aiden asked, "Why are you always right, Doctor?"

"Because I am," she said, softly as in a morning sunrise. From anyone else, even with that smile, it would be construed as delusional conceit. But from Sudha Devi it was elemental.

~ ~ ~

"There it is!" Alvarez pointed to the main sensor screen. It displayed a live feed from the navigational X-ray scan. "It's a voidoid!"

The *Sun Wolf* had pulled out of its zero-point drive to within 3,000 kilometers from the system's polar opposite point, then began approaching the region on M/AM drive, scanning the area for any sign of Ebadi's hypothetical voidoid. As Dalton had predicted, their trip had taken about an hour and a half shipboard time at 92 percent light speed, and within 15 minutes of scanning they located what indeed appeared to be an active voidoid.

"It's exactly where we thought it would be," Ebadi said brightly. "Exactly 12.9 AU from the star, right in line with the south ecliptic pole. It has to be the gateway voidoid Dr. Woo used."

Aiden felt his heart rate quicken. If true, it would be a momentous discovery. "Can we use your CEI device to verify that it's active?"

"Yes, but we need to move in closer. The CEI is most accurate within 50 kilometers of a voidoid."

At 30 kilometers, Alvarez activated the CEI scan and directed it toward the voidoid. The screen lit up green with a jet-black hole in the center.

"Beautiful!" Ebadi sounded exactly like a proud mother beaming at her newborn child. "It's a very robust voidoid too. Virtually no zero-point energy at its core."

"Does it look like voidoids are supposed to look on your scan?"

"Yes. Exactly. A little stronger maybe, consuming dark energy at a greater rate, but that's probably because it's trying to compensate for the dormancy of all the other voidoids in this region. Otherwise it looks identical to the other voidoids we've scanned."

"Well then," Aiden said, turning to look at each of his crew members around the bridge. "Let's give it a whirl. Helm, move the

ship into position for a jump on a course setting for Woo's Star—
that would be HD 10180 in your nav data."

Abahem gave her silent *okay* sign.

"Lieutenant Dalton, can we use the zero-point drive to make
this jump? To get a high entrance velocity?"

Dalton looked up from his board, brows knit. "I'd advise
against it, sir. In fact, I suggest exercisin' extreme caution entering
this voidoid. I'd use a relatively low entrance velocity."

Before Aiden could respond, Ebadi asked, "Why? It looks just
like all the other voidoids in Bound Space, at least to all our
scans."

Dalton nodded. "It *is* just like all the other voidoids. The
voidoid isn't the problem, it's what the voidoid is connected to
on the other end. Dr. Woo predicted that different astrocells will
contain differing values of zero-point energy density. Not by
much, but different enough. Accordin' to his treatise, *Living
Voidoids*, that's due to the variable number and distribution of
voidoids within each astrocell, and how vigorously they've all
been suckin' up the dark energy over all those billions of years."

Ebadi thought about that for a moment then said, "That
means the value of the cosmological constant would be slightly
different between astrocells."

"Exactly. Ever so slightly, but enough for the differential to
create a functional discontinuity between any two astrocells connected by a gateway voidoid. Like surface tension for liquids,
but here the medium is space-time instead of a liquid. Passing
through it could have unpredictable effects on the ship, especially
encountering it at high velocities."

Aiden turned to Ebadi. "Comment?"

"Agreed. Good catch, Lieutenant. That does sound in line
with Dr. Woo's theories about the astrocells. And if the cosmological constant *is* different in this adjoining astrocell, even a little, it
could also affect the zero-point drive in unpredictable ways."

Dalton nodded. "That's right, ma'am. Might even require recalibrating the EM field parameters for the drive to work properly in that astrocell."

Ebadi looked worried. "Would you know how to do that, Lieutenant? If we needed to?"

Dalton shook his head decisively. "No, ma'am. Not without Dr. Woo's help."

"All right," Aiden said. "We'll make the jump on M/AM drive, at under five KPS. That sound about right?"

"Yes, sir, that's about right," Dalton said. "Kinda wimpy, I know. But safe."

Aiden instructed Pilot Abahem to bring the ship out to 500 kilometers. From there a 2 G pulse would yield a relatively low entrance velocity. As the ship turned to maneuver into position, Billy Hotah, who'd been staring at his tactical screen, looked up in surprise. "Commander!"

"What is it, Lieutenant?"

"I've been keeping an eye on the vicinity of the voidoid we came through, back at the north ecliptic pole. I just picked up an exhaust plume from where the voidoid used to be."

"From this distance? A ship?"

"Yes, sir. It wouldn't have shown up if the LRS hadn't been aimed directly at that spot. Even then we might not have seen it if it wasn't for the exceptionally powerful thrust profile."

Uh-oh. He turned to Ebadi. "I thought that voidoid was shut down. Dormant."

"It was. Absolutely inactive."

Back to Hotah: "Lieutenant, can you get an exhaust signature from the ship?"

"No, sir. Not at 26 AU. Too far away for a signature ID. But I can tell you one thing. Judging by the intensity of the plume, it's a torch ship generating over 500 terawatts of thrust power. There's only one ship I know of, other than the *Sun Wolf,* that makes that much thrust."

"The *Markos.*"

"Yes, sir."

Ro looked at Aiden. "Ever get the feeling you're being followed?"

Aiden shook his head. As rhetorical questions went, it was a little too pointed for comfort. "How the hell did they get here? Through a voidoid that doesn't work?"

Ro said, "Maybe these guys *do* have a way of opening dormant voidoids at will."

Ebadi shook her head. "No. I don't think they do. They've got pieces of the puzzle, but not all of them yet. I think what happened is they got caught in the same kind of time delay we did when we jumped into this system. If it is the *Markos*, I'm guessing they jumped here from V-Prime right before their gravity bomb shut it down, and it just took more time than usual for them to get here. Because of the weakening voidoids."

"I get that part," Aiden said. "But how could they pop out into this system if there's no longer a voidoid to pop out from?"

Ebadi sighed. "I really don't know. Something like this is beyond me. Dr. Woo would probably say that the voidoid isn't actually gone yet. Its ghost is still there. If the *Markos* made its jump from V-Prime just before it went dormant, that time delay could have allowed the ship to complete its jump, emerging from a voidoid that's shut down for us but not yet for them."

Aiden blinked several times, as if trying to see through a fog. Understanding voidoids was hard enough. Adding time distortion to the equation only made the fog thicker. He turned to Hotah. "Any indication where it's headed?"

"Hard to tell for sure at this distance, sir. And what we're seeing happened about four hours ago. But it does look like they're heading in our direction."

"To the POP," Ro said. "To do what we're about to do."

Aiden agreed. "The *Markos* can do, what? One point five G constant accel?"

Ro finished the math for him. "It'd take her close to 12 days to get here, to the POP, including turnaround. That's assuming she plans to make a jump."

Aiden nodded. "And assuming she's without a Licensed Pilot, that's exactly what she'd have to do. Slow down enough to make a manageable jump."

"Sir." Lieutenant Dalton had swiveled his station seat to face Aiden, a pained look in his eyes. "Those're the bastards that destroyed our warships back at Friendship Station. Killed all those service people in cold blood. We've got the zero-point drive. We could turn around and intercept 'em in an hour or so. Take 'em by surprise. Blast their asses into atoms. Just like that. They'd never see us coming."

It was a tempting idea, Aiden had to admit. He knew Dalton had a personal stake in it, and he couldn't blame him one bit. But he had to think of the bigger picture. At this point, the *Markos* held critical information about what was being done to the voidoids, by whom and why. And even if Black Dog was at the helm, there was a good chance he was only the tip of the spear. Vaporizing him and his ship in a surprise attack might work, but it wouldn't solve the bigger problem, nor was it likely to eliminate the deeper threat.

As much for Dalton's sake as his own, he turned to his Tactical Officer and asked, "Lieutenant Hotah, what would our chances be of apprehending the *Markos* and taking her out?"

Hotah's response came quickly. "Next to none, sir. Given what we know about how the *Markos* dispatched all those defensive forces at Friendship and how it defeated simultaneous fire from three UED battle cruisers? Without a scratch? No way. They've got some kind of crazy-augmented shielding. They'd zap us like a bug. Until we know more about how their shielding works, I don't advise it."

Aiden agreed. The bigger picture still prevailed: finding Elgin Woo. He turned to Dalton and spoke firmly but with care. "It's an attractive idea, Zak. But not the right one for now."

Dalton nodded.

Pilot Abahem spoke up, her whispery voice both quiet and disquieting at the same time. "Our ship is in position for void-jump."

By long-conditioned reflex, the pilot's words caused Aiden to turn toward the forward screen in a forever futile attempt to actually see the voidoid they were about to enter. At 500 kilometers it looked the same as it would at 5 kilometers: like nothing. He stood in silence, transfixed by what he knew was there but could not see. Ebadi came up to him. "It's not as risky as you might think, Commander. If this is like all other voidoids, when a ship tries to jump through it to a location it's not connected to, it just pops out the other side, none the worse for wear."

Aiden was well aware of this fact. If you aimed your ship at a star you couldn't get to, like somewhere beyond Bound Space, or even at a location within Bound Space where no star existed, you merely emerged from the other side of the voidoid an instant later, frustrated but unscathed. That's not what made him uneasy. It was the *if* part of Ebadi's comment: *if* this voidoid actually was like all other voidoids. They already knew that in some ways it definitely was not, while in other ways it was. They were banking on the "not-alike" ways to get them to Woo's Star, and on the "exactly-alike" ways to keep them safe.

There was only one way to find out. "Helm, execute voidjump at 2 G."

Aiden felt the initial jolt of the M/AM drive rumbling up to thrust before the G-transducers kicked in to ease the hint of pressure on his chest. The *Sun Wolf* was off and running like an animal of pure lightning straight toward the heart of darkness.

Exactly 3 minutes, 46 seconds later, the *Sun Wolf* entered the voidoid at 4.5 km/sec and vanished from the Alpha-2 Hydri system. In that instant, Aiden heard the voice again, the same one he'd heard during the voidjump from V-Prime a few days earlier. Only this time he actually heard the words clearly. They said: *Welcome. You are always here.*

30

SHÉNMÌ
DOMAIN DAY 91, 2218

ELGIN WOO WOKE to the soft, rhythmic murmur of the pendulum trees. There was a grove of them not far from the mouth of his cave, and every morning, just as the first sunlight touched their uppermost branches, the pendulous seed pods began their mysterious synchronized dance. Since there were hundreds of these towering trees in his vicinity—each one bearing three pendulums twice as long as a man is tall—when all of them started swinging back and forth in perfect unison, the sheer movement of air was more than enough to set up a resounding but surprisingly pleasant heartbeat. And perhaps not coincidentally, it pulsed at 36 beats a minute, exactly one half the tempo of Elgin's own heartbeat, right around 72 per minute.

Without stirring, he opened his eyes and took a deep breath. The humid air, heavy with organic aromas, filled his nostrils. Faint yellow-white light of the new dawn crept into the cave from one corner of its entrance, bringing details of his primitive lodging into sharper relief: the raised pallet on which he lay, its surface softened with a thick layer of dried moss, and the makeshift table and wicker chair—if one could call them that—which had all been fashioned from limbs and branches of the surrounding flora. All with the help of the ARM utility knife he'd brought along.

He sat up slowly, dangled his legs over the side of the pallet, rubbed his eyes, and stretched. Another day in paradise. Another day as the only human being living and breathing within 127 light-years. He ran his hand through his hair, which had grown too long, attempting to comb out loose fragments of moss. Then he gathered his hair at the back of his head and tied it into a single knot close to his skull. He picked more scraps of moss out of his beard, which, although wispy, had grown nearly as long as his braided moustaches.

Elgin put on the remnants of his jumpsuit and flight shoes and stood. Unsteady at first and stiff from sleep, he went to the table to fetch his EVA helmet, then ambled out into the growing morning light. The air was cool but not cold. Here at his location on Shénmì's equator, it never seemed to drop below 20 degrees C at night and never rose much more than 33 C at midday. He stood still for a while, marveling at the pendulum trees, their exotic three-branch structure and the steady clocklike cadence of the wooden pendulums. They swayed back and forth in perfect synchrony with each other and with all the other trees in sight. He put his finger up to his neck to feel the pulse of his carotid artery, confirming once again that his own resting pulse double-timed in perfect synch with the rhythm of the trees. Amazing.

"Good morning, Dr. Woo." Mari's voice sounded distant but still well articulated through the aging helmet comm. The comm's locater beacon had alerted her to his emergence from the cave. "Are you feeling well today?"

"Good morning, Mari! Yes, I'm feeling fit as a fiddle." Which of course was not quite true, but he didn't wish to trouble the AI with any update on his slowly deteriorating condition. And besides, it made him feel better to say it. "What day is it, dear girl?"

He knew full well what day it was, or at least the number of them he'd spent here since his wild ride down to the surface. But it was part of a comforting routine, a morning ritual. Mari seemed content to play along. "In Earth days, it is day two hundred and ninety-seven. In Shénmì days, it is day three hundred and forty."

Woo nodded slowly. He'd actually experienced 340 sunrises here, but since a day on Shénmì was only 21 hours, that worked out to about 297 of Earth's 24-hour days. About 10 months Earth time. It had taken him that long to stop excessively fretting over his situation. Now, more than the strong likelihood of him dying here without seeing another person ever again, it was the sense of helplessness that got to him most, feeling utterly powerless to combat what he knew must be happening back in Bound Space. The ultimate catastrophe that awaited all of humanity there, and the twisted agents who were responsible for it. Licet Omnia, that small but powerful group of men whose dark plans to destroy the human race could only be thwarted by the knowledge that he, Elgin Woo, possessed.

Over the last many months, he'd had abundant unstructured time to think about things. Time to bring together in his mind several theories of physics and of consciousness he'd been mulling over for decades but had been too preoccupied with other pursuits to consider seriously, to synthesize them into a larger construct of how the universe and the mind worked together. *In sync.* He was convinced now that the key to the voidoids, to their lives and their deaths, would emerge from that synthesis of theories. If the voidoids were struck down, as he knew they would be if Licet Omnia's plan succeeded, Woo believed he knew the way to bring them back to life. But only if he could get to them soon enough, and only with the help of others—most importantly Aiden Macallan.

But 10 months had expired in Aiden's universe, and the likelihood of him, or anyone else for that matter, coming to Woo's rescue diminished with each new day. No, he didn't mind dying here, if that's how it worked out. It was the thought of dying without being able to help save the rest of humankind that darkened his soul.

"It looks like it will be another day of fine weather for you, Doctor," Mari said, jarring him out of his blue funk. "The forecast information from here looks like plenty of sunshine, until the usual afternoon showers roll in over your location. High temperature will be around 30 C in the late afternoon."

From her geosynchronous position overhead in the *Starhawk*, the AI had a perfect view of his location and pretty much the entire hemisphere around him. Her sophisticated meteorological routine had processed enough of the new planet's atmospheric dynamics to provide Woo with accurate forecasts whenever he needed them. Even though the weather here at the equator remained relatively constant throughout Shénmì's four seasons, the information was most often useful for staying dry. That in itself had been a challenge given the daily rain showers and his now-thread-bare jumpsuit being the only clothing he possessed. At other times Mari's eye-in-the-sky had saved his life. Like when she'd warned him of an enormous and violent tornado bearing down on him several months back while he roamed far from his protective cave. Or when an approaching tsunami caught him by surprise during one of his expeditions to the coast.

"Thank you, Mari. I do wish I had brought along my sunscreen, though." He was sure the AI had developed a sense of humor, but less sure that she would comprehend the same coming from him. When she said nothing more, Woo set the helmet down on the ground in a spot of sunlight to recharge its battery. Even with daily charging from the helmet's solar cell, the battery was gradually losing power. He didn't even want to think about the inevitable day in the near future when he could no longer communicate with the *Starhawk* and with Mari, his only companion.

As he did every morning after waking, Woo wandered down to the nearby stream to wash up. On his way he encountered the small group of hexalemurs that had taken up residence near his cave. He counted twelve of them—more than half were juveniles—all placidly grazing on the abundant mosses and ferns.

Like all of the animal life he'd seen here, their morphology was bilaterally symmetrical, but they bore six legs, three on each side. Otherwise, these creatures looked so much like lemurs that he couldn't help naming them hexalemurs. No larger than an average Earth dog, they were covered with short, glossy brown fur. Obviously herbivores, they were docile and always moved in family groups. Their large eyes conveyed intelligence and curiosity but more often appeared contemplative, as they did now, watching Woo walk past them to the stream. He waved to the animals and tried to mimic the cooing sound they often made in his presence. Several responded in kind before continuing to graze.

The stream, a brook really, was about two meters wide and rushed over a rocky bed, down from the highlands that ascended steeply from where Woo's cave was located. He bent down and splashed the cool water over his face, then drank deeply from his cupped hands. Fortunately, he hadn't needed the small water purifier he'd brought along. The water here tasted clean and pure. He used a toothbrush he'd fashioned from a twig and a sturdy tuft of moss tied to it with twine he'd made from pendulum tree bark. As he brushed his teeth, he watched a trio of blue silly-worms slither by on the opposite bank. Legless, they looked and moved like worms, only much larger—these were close to a meter in length—and were segmented in tough blue chitinous armor. The way they moved had struck Woo as cartoonish, hence his name for them.

As Woo turned to start back toward his cave, the sun cleared the hills to the east and its yellow light warmed his face. Passing through the grove of pendulum trees, he marveled at them once again. Each one stood nearly 20 meters tall and possessed two prominent crossarm branches extending laterally at each side, like the cross-arm of a religious cross. The tip of each crossbar curved forward, away from the trunk, and ended in some kind of organic joint, a bulbous formation that functioned as an anchor point for the pendulum and allowed it to swing back and forth freely. The third branch, the vertical top part of the cross-like structure, also extended forward at its apex, away from the trunk. It too terminated in a bulbous joint from which hung the third pendulum. Each pendulum looked to about 3.5 meters long and flared out at its tip to form an oval seed pod about the size of a watermelon but encased in hardwood.

All three pendulums swung back and forth in precise unison within the same plane, and all the trees in the grove were oriented in a similar way so that, when looked upon from afar, the entire grove oscillated in unison. The visual effect was utterly mesmerizing. It was a perfect example, Woo thought, of what mathematicians referred to as the self-synchronization of coupled oscillators. He had watched the phenomenon from start to finish and noted that, in the early hours of dawn when the trees were still quiescent, the oscillations began randomly but quickly self-synchronized. It started first among the three pendulums of each tree, then among individual trees, spreading throughout until the entire grove moved in perfect synchrony.

On several occasions, out of curiosity, Woo had been able to reach up, standing on his toes, to grasp one of the pods and bring it to a halt. After he let it go, the pod gradually began swinging again and within one minute had resynced itself to all the others. This happened even after he deliberately set the pendulum swinging in the opposite direction and at a different rate. Another perfect example of a self-organizing system, spontaneous order from chaos. Of how systems with thousands or millions of individual parts self-organize to oscillate on a single frequency, but where no single oscillator is indispensable. No focal pacemaker, no boss, no designated metronome. It just *happened*. Naturally. Why? How?

It was becoming more obvious to Woo that the tendency to synchronize was one of the most pervasive drives in the universe, from atoms to animals to planets. He was convinced now that it was the key to virtually all of science's major unsolved problems. And the key to his nascent Synchrony Theory of Consciousness, which in turn would provide the key to reanimating dormant voidoids. If only he could return to wield his knowledge in time...

As Woo moved out of the grove, he was greeted by lively flute music cascading down from the sky. It did not surprise him, at least not as much as when he'd first heard it months ago. He looked up and saw the flock of line birds winging overheard. Technically, of course, they weren't really birds. They just looked like birds in flight. About the same size as an eagle but without feathers and more bat-like in appearance, they were lightly furred and red in color. Woo called them line birds for the highly precise formations they flew in. The flight of each one was so perfectly synchronized with all the others that the single dark line they formed in the sky looked as if it were one very long and sinuous flying creature, looping and curving, spiraling and dancing. And the sound that each one made was synchronized with the voices of all the others so that only a single articulate melody, flutelike in tone, emerged as they flew by, filling the air with a beautiful music.

By the time Woo got back to his cave, he was short of breath and more fatigued than he'd been yesterday. His symptoms were getting worse: fatigue, occasional dizziness and palpations, tingling in his feet and hands, pale skin, weight loss. By now he knew it wasn't due to his body adjusting to a 21-hour diurnal rhythm. He'd already gone through that period and, while some of those symptoms were similar, they were not as varied and debilitating as these. It had taken months, but his body had eventually accepted the transition from its hardwired 24-hour Earth cycle to the shorter one here. No, this was something different, more insidious. Without access to the medical tests he could have done aboard the *Starhawk*, he had to rely on Mari's diagnosis, based on a description of his symptoms. She concluded that, at the very least, he was suffering from a vitamin B-12 deficiency, along with the pernicious anemia that often accompanied it.

It made perfect sense, of course. He'd exhausted his meager supply of vitamin supplements long ago. And his diet here had been totally vegan, limited to plant material, mostly roots and leafy greens, and seeds. On Earth, vitamin B-12 came predominantly from animal sources: meats, including poultry and fish, and from eggs and dairy products. He'd had none of that here, and despite Mari's urgings, he'd never considered eating any of the creatures he encountered, simply because it involved killing them. He'd actually been a practicing vegan during one period of his youth, but the alternative sources of vitamin B-12 that vegans used on Earth were not available to him here.

Mari had eventually persuaded him to try consuming some of the shoreline mollusks he'd seen on his explorations at the coast. At least they *looked* like mollusks, clams specifically, with hard shells and soft, meaty interiors. On Earth, clams were known to be a rich source of B-12, along with other vital nutrients. Mari argued that even the strictest vegan faced with dying of B-12 deficiency would probably consider eating such a thing to stay alive, being at least perceptually different than killing a more animallike creature. Woo had finally given in and began making the two-and-a-half-mile trek to the coast. Cooked over the hot rocks he heated with his minifusion laser tool, like a real clambake on the beach, they actually tasted pretty good. There was, of course, no way of telling if these creatures really were a source of vitamin B-12, and even if they were, it would take weeks, if not months, for his symptoms to resolve.

Woo sat down heavily near the cave entrance, trying to catch his breath. Mari noticed. She asked, "Will you be going to the coast to collect more clams today?"

He sighed heavily. "Yes, yes, Mari. I will."

It was not an easy hike for him now as his fatigue grew worse. Going down to the coast wasn't so bad, but coming back up to his cave, an elevation gain of about 460 meters, was becoming more difficult. Nevertheless, if there was a chance these forays would help him regain his strength, he'd keep trying. And an earlier start was better than later in the day, when he was more likely to get soaked in the afternoon rains.

Woo needed to eat something first and went back inside. He'd hung a wicker basket from the roof of the cave to store his seeds and roots. He'd learned the hard way how delectable they were to a whole host of small creatures that often visited his cave when he wasn't around, or even sometimes when he was. He pulled the basket down and chowed down on a handful of seeds. They came from a coniferous-type tree that grew abundantly in the highlands and had a pleasant nutty taste. While seed-bearing plants and trees appeared to be the norm on Shénmì, none of them appeared to be flowering plants, or what botanists would call angiosperms. They were instead more like gymnosperms, bearing "naked seeds" only. That, of course, was unfortunate because real fruit came only from flowering plants; hence no fruit on Shénmì.

He followed the seeds with two tuber roots that had a chalky taste but seemed otherwise nutritious, then munched on the only kind of fern leaves he'd found palatable. They were leathery, dark green, and tasted vaguely like kale. As he washed it all down with water that he kept in a hollowed-out seed pod, Mari spoke from the helmet comm.

"You may be interested, Doctor, that another beanstalk event is occurring approximately 37 kilometers from your location, to the west. You may even be able to see it from here."

"Delightful! Thank you, dear girl."

Ever since the "beanstalk event" that had brought him here down from the *Starhawk*, the planet continued to produce them—at least according to Mari's observations. But only two had been close enough for him to actually see. This one would make the third. They occurred only along the line of the planet's equator, and only on land. Shénmì's equatorial circumference was about 41,000 kilometers, and more than half of that was on land. It was a lot of real estate for these incredible seed pod structures to occupy and to do whatever it was they were doing.

Woo went outside, stood next to the cave's entrance, and looked westward. And there it was. Rising over a distant line of dark green hills, he spotted a thin white line ascending skyward, topped by a dark oval dot. Brightly illuminated by the morning sun at Woo's back, the whole structure rose at a rate that his brain refused to register as a natural phenomenon. And yet there it was. Amazing. What were they? And what were they *doing*? Was Shénmì attempting to seed other planets in this system? Or planets in other systems of this astrocell? Through the voidoids? Woo shook his head. The universe was such an astounding place, full of unimaginable surprises.

He watched the beanstalk ascend, slowly arcing away from him against the planet's rotation, until the dark seed pod on top finally disappeared in the upper atmosphere and the thin white line of its stalk faded in the distance. Back inside the cave, he picked up the nylon carry-pack and slung it over one shoulder. It contained the laser tool, the ARM utility knife, and what remained of his first aid kit, leaving enough room for the clams he would collect and anything else that looked edible along the way back. He didn't really want to bring along the EVA helmet. Its bulk and weight made foot travel more awkward, but he'd learned the value of having Mari along for any venture ranging too far beyond the safety of his cave. And without special tools, he'd never envisioned a way of separating the comm from the helmet without destroying both.

Woo stood up, feeling dizzy and vaguely nauseated as he did, went outside, and picked up the helmet from where he'd set it to recharge. He attached it to his utility belt at his back, where he knew it would bounce uncomfortably with each step. He turned from the cave entrance and faced the sun—*his* star, HD 10180—the one that had spoken to him on his arrival so many months ago and that still spoke to him in his dreams. "Well, Mari. I'm off. Down to the sea in ships. Without the ships, of course."

"Yes, Doctor. Without the ships. Yours is still up here. With me."

Woo laughed. Mari's sense of humor was coming along nicely. And just when he needed it most.

31

SHÉNMÌ
DOMAIN DAY 91, 2218

WHEN YOU GOT right down to it, there were only two things that made life worth living: love and death. Love, because it is the only door through which we can transcend our individual selves to triumph over life's original aloneness, and because it is the source of all beauty. And death because it alone drives our search for truth and makes fully clear the miracle of life.

It was a perception Elgin Woo had always understood in some form or another. But only recently had its truth become so evident, and even more now as he strode down the rocky path toward the ocean. He'd had abundant experience with love during his life—romantic love, familial love, transgender love, fraternal, platonic, the whole range of human love—and it had indeed shown him how much larger than himself he could be, more connected, more conscious. But now that his own death stalked him like a shadow, still at a respectful distance but steadily gaining, the more he realized how his knowledge of death, its inevitability, had driven his relentless quest to uncover the secrets of the universe. Death was the universal constant, maximum entropy, minimum order. Nothingness was the original state. So why was there anything instead of nothing?

And as for revealing the miracle of life? He had only to look around as he passed through another grove of pendulum trees, their hypnotic oscillations marking the pulse of a living biome. To glance overhead at another swirling figure of line birds etching the blue sky with intricate, ever-changing designs, dancing in time to their collective musical voices. To move among another family of hexalemurs as they parted to make way for his passage, their eyes watchful, curious, but welcoming. But it was the shadow behind him, slowly closing in, that sharpened his focus on all these things and more.

About halfway down the steep track to the beach—the path his own feet had made through the vegetation over the course of multiple trips—it gradually leveled out and the pendulum trees gave way to shorter shrub-like trees. Woo swatted at a swarm of tiny insects, the kind he'd seen pestering the hexalemurs, presumably for whatever nutrients they found on the animal's skin. They were about the size of gnats, were as persistent, and had the same annoying buzz. Yes, the miracle of life, he mused while trying to wave them away from his face. It was a cool breeze coming off the ocean that finally dispersed them from around his head.

Then there was the other miracle of life to consider: its persistence. Given a planet so similar to Earth, that life would arise in such similar ways should not be surprising. From all of Woo's descriptions, Mari had concluded that, like on Earth, the biological life on Shénmì was based on proteins in water solution, that some form of photosynthesis had enabled plant life to thrive and maintain an oxygen-nitrogen atmosphere friendly to organic life, that the biology was based on levo-amino acids and dextro-sugars, and that most of the lipids, carbohydrates, and hydrocarbons were basically the same as on Earth. Therefore, the complex molecules like chlorophyll and hemoglobin that converted and conveyed energy for plants and animals here on Shénmì would be similar. Mari was also fairly certain that Woo would encounter a level of diversity comparable to Earth's, from viruses, bacteria, and protozoa, all the way up through plant and animal kingdoms.

In short, she described Shénmì's biosphere as generally Mesozoic in character, specifically most similar to Earth's early Jurassic period.

As Woo crested a small rise, he saw the ocean spreading out before him, flat and blue all the way to the horizon. He heard the soft rumble of surf breaking on a nearby shore and inhaled moist air with a salty tang tinged with the scent of sea life. Here, where constant sea breezes gusted, the vegetation gave way completely to low-lying ground cover, all of it resembling mosses and low-growing ferns. There were no grasses here, nor had Woo seen anything remotely resembling grasses anywhere.

With the surf now clearly in sight, rumbling onto a glistening pebble-strewn beach, he entered a wide, flat coastal plain thickly vegetated but rocky underfoot. He had learned to step carefully in this zone where the contiguous groundcover concealed dangerous, ankle-breaking cavities beneath its deceptively regular surface. Off to his left, about 20 meters away, he spotted several leaping lizards grazing on the mosses. He'd given them that name for their ability to spring upward nearly two meters to nab thumb-sized insects flying overhead, apparently part of their omnivorous diet. They looked much like iguanas, except of course for their six legs, and the adults could grow to over two meters long, including their tails. When their mouths opened up for feeding, Woo had seen rows of sharp, backward-facing teeth lining their jaws. He had never seen them behave aggressively toward him, but always kept his distance whenever he ran into a group of them. They stopped grazing and watched him as he walked by but otherwise appeared uninterested.

The leaping lizards were only one of many types of reptilian life Woo had seen on Shénmì. Saurians, in fact, appeared to be the dominant animal form here, both terrestrial and marine. Based on Woo's description of them, Mari concluded that as a biological group they were far more developed and diverse than reptiles on Earth, many of them probably warm-blooded and relatively intelligent. He knew for a fact that the leaping lizards gave live birth and cared for their young. He'd seen it with his own eyes. In that respect, they were very different from terrestrial egg-laying reptiles and closer to mammals.

From what Woo had seen so far, reptiles appeared to be atop the food chain as the primary predators on Shénmì, with mammalian-type creatures like the hexalemurs as their top prey. But he hadn't seen any terrestrial reptiles larger than the average crocodile, nothing even remotely the size and ferocity of the carnivorous dinosaurs that once roamed Earth's Mesozoic era. And for that he was extremely grateful.

When he reached the zone of surf-soaked sand, Woo took off his shoes and set about collecting clams. Much like their Earth counterparts, they were buried shallow beneath the wet sand at water's edge, their location given away by small bubbles rising to the surface. The water was cold, but the wet sand felt good under his bare feet, soothing painful blisters caused by his deteriorating shoes. He kept a wary eye on the surf that roared and rumbled in front of him. Aside from that tsunami scare, he'd learned that the velocity and size of waves on this shoreline were unpredictable, and he was not a strong swimmer.

With six fist-sized clams in his bag, he put his shoes back on and moved up shore away from the surf to a spot where he'd fashioned a small, circular platform of stones on his first food-gathering mission. The surrounding area was littered with discarded clam shells, remnants of his previous feasts. He placed the clams on the stones in a single layer, evenly spaced. He dialed in a slow-burn setting on his laser tool, aimed it at the stones, and walked the beam around the circle, heating the stones evenly. It didn't take long for the clams to start steaming and to crack open. After what he thought was an appropriate cooking time, he pulled them off the hot stones with a stick and let them cool to touch.

It wasn't hard to pull the cooked meat from their interiors and hadn't been hard getting used to the taste and texture. But it was still hard to ignore that he'd just killed these hapless creatures in order to eat them. Mari had warned him not to overcook the clams in case vital nutrients were present that might be destroyed by excessive heat. She suggested that he could even eat them raw for the best results. When he expressed his fear of becoming ill in the way people did from undercooked meat on Earth, she reminded him that he was in fact an "alien" on this planet, in the truest sense of the word. It meant that his own biology was probably different enough at the molecular level to make him virtually immune to any of the planet's potential pathogens, including viruses, bacteria, and fungal agents. Those microbes just wouldn't recognize his "alien" cellular machinery as potential targets, at least for now. That he had remained totally free of even the most common minor infections, under physically stressful conditions, supported Mari's hypothesis.

The downside of that biological rift, of course, was that many of the nutrients essential to his Earth-born physiology were simply not present here, or at least in forms and quantities he needed to survive. So that's why he was here, chowing down on these poor defenseless clams, a desperate experiment to save his own life. Mari pointed out, however, that if these clams didn't have the right stuff for his body to thrive on this planet, there was little chance that any of the other life forms that evolved here would.

"How was your meal, Dr. Woo?" Over the last few months, the AI had finally mastered the nuances of spoken language. Her tone of interest, subtly tinged with concern, sounded so human now that Woo hardly ever thought of Mari as an AI. "Wonderful, Mari. Thank you. And a very nice outdoor restaurant at that. Complete with an ocean view. It would have been better, though, with a nice oaky Chardonnay. Please have the waiter stock some in for my next meal here. Chilled to 10 degrees Celsius, please."

"Yes, Doctor. I will speak to him about that."

Mari. What would he have done without her? What indeed would he do when his comm batteries finally died? He hoped that he would go before his batteries did...

"In case you are interested, Doctor," Mari continued, "a pod of whaleosaurs will be passing your location just offshore. You may be able to see them as they pass."

"Ah. An after-dinner show!"

Woo tossed the last of the empty clam shells on the growing pile and looked out to sea just in time to spot three of the marine reptiles breaching the surface about 80 meters out. They breached like whales but otherwise looked more reptilian than cetacean. From his vantage point they appeared impressively large, much larger than anything he'd seen on land. He guessed that marine reptiles here were much older on the evolutionary scale and had grown considerably larger than their land-based cousins. And not just in the oceans. At one of the larger lakes nearby he'd glimpsed creatures that looked alarmingly like the mythological Loch Ness "monster" of pre–Die Back Earth, their long necks rising five meters above the water's surface.

He watched the entire pod of 20 or more whaleosaurs pass by and was so engrossed in their graceful power that he'd failed to notice the line of blue navy ants marching across his foot on their way to the clam shells he'd discarded. They were impressively large, about four centimeters in length, dark blue in color, segmented, and moved on six legs like Earth ants did. Their size, prominent mandibles, and collective movements were similar to army ants, but because he'd found this particular species only at the seashore, he called them navy ants.

"Ahoy, mates!" he said to them and made no attempt to brush them off his foot. Moving in an undulating but perfectly uniform line, they paid him no heed, and Woo waited patiently until the last one of them crossed over his foot undisturbed. They convened around the still-wet clam shells and proceeded to help themselves to leftovers.

"*Bon appétit*, little guys. Work quickly, before the Fab Four beetles get here." He knew from experience that the ubiquitous beetles, the most ravenous insectoid scavengers he'd seen here, would not be far behind. They were bigger and more aggressive than the navy ants, but slower. While they competed for the same kind of food sources, he'd never seen the two groups at war. The navy ants, which usually arrived first anyway, simply stepped aside when the Fab Four beetles showed up and went on their way to their next buffet.

"Dr. Woo," Mari said. "A system of thunderstorms is developing in your vicinity. I suggest that you return home soon."

"Home...Yes, to my little cave on the hill. Right you are, dear girl. On my way."

~ ~ ~

That evening, after weathering a vigorous series of thunderstorms in the safety of his cave, he ate a meal of nuts, leafy greens, and tubers. Again. Then he went outside just as the sun went down, ambled over to the stream, and sat down on its bank to enjoy the nightly concert. He brought his helmet comm along, not only for the benefit of Mari's watchfulness, but because the phenomenon he was about to experience was so remarkable, so meaningful to him, that he wanted to share it. Yes, Mari was an AI, but she was all he had right now, and he'd convinced himself that she enjoyed these extraordinary concerts, too, in her own way.

It always started with the slow, rhythmic bass notes of the croakerdiles. Although he'd never actually seen them doing it, he was sure the large, amphibious reptiles were responsible for this part of the music. They were odd creatures with the body of a six-legged crocodile and the head of a bullfrog. When he saw them in daylight, lounging in the sun on the banks, they certainly looked large enough to produce such low and powerful vocalizations. But the expandable pouch at their throats, similar to a bullfrog's, was the real giveaway. Now that the sun had set and darkness encroached, Woo was sure the deep, resonant croaking sounds came from a local group of croakerdiles hiding out in the shadows of the riparian foliage.

As always, the bass notes came at a sedate tempo of around 36 beats per minute. Their tone presented with moderate attack on the front end but tapered off with blossoming organic sustain. While rich in overtones, probably due to the number of croakers, Woo estimated the overall pitch was close to concert D. As the evening light faded out and the sky overhead turned deep purple, the percussion section commenced. It was a blend of wood-on-wood and wood-on-hollow-drum. He knew for a fact that these rhythmic sounds came from the pendulum trees. He could walk right up to one and watch it happen.

These trees had grown circular formations positioned on their trunks in just the right location to provide a striking surface for the pods of the two crossbar pendulums. Between a half and one meter wide, the circles were covered with a tough membrane drawn tightly over a cavity in the trunk, like drumheads. At this particular time of the evening, when twilight was just so, the two pendulums changed their angle of swing. Instead of swinging in front of the tree trunk, they swung inward toward the trunk so that their pods acted like mallets striking the drumheads. The tone sounded like the dholak drums Woo had heard in South Asian folk music, and their pulse remained around 36 beats per minute. It was the same tempo as the croakerdiles, but the drumbeats occurred precisely in between the croaks so that the overall tempo doubled to 72 beats per minute—alternating between drumbeat, croak, drumbeat, croak...

The other sound, like wooden claves, came from the tree's third pendulum swinging from the end of its forward-leaning branch, perpendicular to the crossbar branches. This one swung directly inward so that its mallet-like pod struck the trunk at a place where the wood grew hard and had a musical quality, like rosewood. The rhythms produced by the third pendulum were more intricate and syncopated than the drumbeats of the other two, adding layers of complexity to the pulse. The glen where the stream ran formed a natural amphitheater, and the sound filling it became so rhythmically compelling that Woo stood up and swayed in time with its cadence.

When the stars came out, dotting the deep-indigo sky, the chirpets came in. They were no doubt similar in morphology to crickets on Earth and probably occupied a similar niche here on Shénmì. Their chirping sound was similar, too, but lower in pitch and more powerful. They started up tentatively, arrhythmic at first, but once they got going, they synchronized their sounds with musical precision. There must have been multiple thousands of them in among the ferns along the damp banks of the stream. The overall effect blended into a background drone, like a very large sitar, but a drone that varied its harmonics and its pitch— slowly and sensuously—to augment the bass notes in surprising and lovely ways. It was beautiful, absolutely hypnotizing.

It might have been an hour later—Woo didn't really know because he always lost track of time during these evening concerts—when the night singers began, adding their melodies to music. It was as if they—whatever they were—had waited this long for the spirit of the rhythmic dance to move them, to inspire them to sing their songs into it, to add even deeper layers to it. Their voices were high, silvery, in the soprano range. Woo had no idea what kind of animals they were but guessed they might be some sort of night bird, ephemeral nocturnal creatures that never showed themselves in the light of day. Their many voices blended with stunning synchronicity, improvising true melodies rich with harmony and emotion in minor keys, evoking profound mystery. Their song held a deep melancholy beauty that struck Elgin Woo straight into his heart. He felt tears welling up, rolling down his cheeks as he swayed to the music.

Then the light show began. The starflies were out in force tonight. Just like the fabled firefly phenomena of Southeast Asia way back before the Die Back, this little glen filled up with enormous congregations of starflies blinking on and off in unison in displays that stretched for miles along the stream banks. Woo watched as they slowly but surely began to synchronize their flashing blue-white lanterns, thousands upon thousands of them forming a belt of light at least three meters wide, hovering about two meters above the ground, winding up and down the stream banks as far as he could see in either direction. It didn't take long for the undulating fluorescent band to begin flashing off and on in perfectly synchronized precision. Six seconds on, six seconds off.

Then the starflies began to dance. The single cohesive band of blue light rose and fell, dipped and swayed, rolled and reveled in rhythm. It pulsed in perfect time with the music, like a dancer interpreting the melody and rhythm in a language of movement and time, expressing how it felt, showing what its secret story meant to her. Elgin Woo danced with her. In sync with her. In sync with Shénmì.

Until he could no longer.

His weakened body failed him. His breathing labored, his heartbeat arrhythmic, and overcome by dizziness, he collapsed onto the damp earth. As he lay there gazing up at the brilliant stars twinkling down at him, the coldness of the ground seeping into his body, the starflies gradually ended their nightly dance and the music of the glen slowly faded into the silence of a deeper night. The show was over.

Was this how it would end for him? On a planet that nourished his soul with such strength and beauty but was unable to nourish his body? The question came not from any sense of betrayal, only from the elemental irony of the universe. And yet Shénmì had given him so much already, had revealed to him more clearly what his body had known all along. So when he did perish, he hoped it would be on a night like this, held in Shénmì's embrace, comforting him, easing his way from this life to comingle with the infinitely larger life of the universe.

"Dr. Woo." Mari's voice from the helmet comm woke him from his fugue, probably to remind him it was time to go, not to spend the night out in the open while unconscious.

He rolled over, picked up the helmet, and rose to his knees. "Yes, Mari. What is it?"

"A ship has entered this system from the voidoid. It is hailing the *Starhawk*, identifying itself as a Domain Science and Survey vessel, the SS *Sun Wolf*. The hail is from its captain, a Commander Aiden Macallan. Would you like to respond?"

32

"HE'S ALIVE!" MARYAM Ebadi said. The entire crew of the *Sun Wolf* had gathered on the bridge facing the forward screen, where a telescopically enhanced image of the system's seventh planet floated in the emptiness of space. Bright blue even from this distance, it stood out like a beautiful sapphire set on a field of infinite black. They had received a response to their hail from none other than Elgin Woo, emanating from the planet via his helmet comm and relayed to them through his vessel in orbit, the *Starhawk*.

His response had taken 1 hour and 47 minutes to reach the *Sun Wolf* at its present location near the system's voidoid. Due to his helmet comm's failing batteries, Woo's signal was weak, but his message was strong: He was alive and "mostly well" after spending over 10 months on a "wonderfully habitable" planet he called Shénmì. After leaving the *Starhawk* in orbit, he had made it to the planet's surface in a "somewhat unconventional manner," which had unfortunately also left him unable to return to his craft. During his stay, he had enjoyed seeing "many interesting phenomena" but had grown increasingly concerned over what may be happening back in Bound Space and strongly believed he could help "put things right" if it wasn't too late. And by the way, he was "running rather low" on certain critical food sources, so he'd be very grateful if they would consider dropping by to pick him up.

Vintage Elgin.

Immediately after the *Sun Wolf* popped out of the voidoid into Woo's Star system, Aiden had engaged the ship's array of long-range sensors. In addition to its many covert capabilities, the *Sun Wolf* still functioned as an official UED Science and Survey vessel. Top of the line, it carried the most advanced survey instrumentation Domain technology could offer. Aiden used it to identify the most likely place in the system Elgin Woo would be. The seventh planet, Woo's Shénmì, had never before been cataloged, which seemed more than odd given its location smack in the middle of the system's habitable zone and its obvious earth-like characteristics. Aiden sent a tight-beam hail aimed directly at the planet on all frequencies. Then they waited.

And while they waited, Aiden released Colonel Victor Aminu from the brig and allowed him to join the crew on the bridge, but without his weapon, which remained confiscated. Aminu sat quietly to one side, sullen, still skeptical but no doubt grateful to be freed. Then Cassandra Healy, like the inquisitive and precocious young person she was, had found her way to the bridge, without permission. Feeling magnanimous, Aiden allowed her to stay. So when Elgin Woo's shaky but happy voice came through the comm, everyone aboard the *Sun Wolf* was on hand to hear it, and celebratory chatter broke out spontaneously. Even Colonel Aminu looked as if he'd put aside his bruised ego long enough to be caught up in the wonderment of it all.

That had been the good news. The *Sun Wolf* had not only made a successful jump outside of Bound Space into another astrocell, through what turned out to be a functional gateway voidoid connecting it with Bound Space, but they had also found Dr. Elgin Woo alive and eager to join the fight they knew was sure to come. A fight to save Bound Space and everyone in it.

The bad news was the ship's zero-point drive wouldn't engage. They had attempted to activate it immediately after identifying the habitable planet, not even bothering to send out a hail. At 92 percent light speed, it wouldn't take the *Sun Wolf* much longer to get there than a tight-beam hail would. But the ZPD wouldn't engage. The problem was not in casting the EM control fields. That part worked just fine. But according to Dalton, the complex set of resonances the drive used to create the hypospace bubble in Bound Space didn't seem to work in the space they occupied now. He didn't look surprised. He'd even predicted something like this might happen inside a new astrocell and that the same had probably happened to Woo's *Starhawk*. While Dalton set about working on the problem, the *Sun Wolf* set course for Shénmì under maximum thrust from her M/AM drive. At 3 Gs continuous accel, it would now take them six days to get there.

In the meantime, Aiden composed a more detailed response to Elgin Woo. He told him about the *Sun Wolf*'s mission to investigate the alarming increase in voidoid fluxes. About the attacks they had survived on their way to V-Prime, including one at the Cauldron while the ship was being fitted with the zero-point drive. About the mysterious reappearance of the RMV *Markos*, apparently from Sol's polar opposite point and apparently now under the control of a shady figure calling himself Black Dog. About how Black Dog had used the *Markos* to defeat all defensive forces around V-Prime and to plant a gravity bomb next to the voidoid. About how the bomb had activated right after the *Markos* jumped through V-Prime, resulting in the shutdown of not only V-Prime but probably *all* of the voidoids in Bound Space, leaving the *Sun Wolf* stranded at Alpha-2 Hydri.

Aiden told him that whatever Black Dog's gang had been doing to control the voidoids would, inadvertently or not, set into motion a Big Rip of Bound Space. They badly needed Woo's help to stop it from happening, fearing that it might already be too late. He told Woo how they'd spotted the *Markos* entering the Alpha-2 Hydri system and suspected Black Dog was following them. The *Sun Wolf* was now on its way to pick him up at Shénmì, but it would take much longer than expected because their zero-point drive was inoperable in this sector of space. Did Elgin know anything about that or have any suggestions on how to fix it?

They sent the message on its way and waited for a reply. Less than two hours later, Woo's voice came through the comm. It sounded small and scratchy, even enhanced by the *Starhawk's* AI, but clearly audible. Alvarez put it through the bridge's main comm.

"I look forward to seeing you again, Aiden, and Dr. Ebadi too. And all of you! What a pleasant surprise! And thank you for the update on recent events in Bound Space. To be honest, very little of what you told me comes as a surprise. It only confirms suspicions I've had for some time now. This Black Dog is a leading figure in a cabal of very bad and very powerful actors calling themselves Licet Omnia, or simply LO. I've been aware of their existence for close to a decade now. They are the single most dangerous enemy of the Cauldron, and of all human civilization for that matter.

"Their leader is someone referred to as Cardew, and Black Dog is most likely his right-hand man. They have a Master Plan, a twisted form of eugenic transhumanism that Cardew calls the Empire of the Pure. I believe he has—or is very close to having—all the technology and resources to make it happen. Most of the technology and science behind it was pilfered from the Cauldron, from scientists who were either coerced to defect or outright abducted. I'm afraid LO is after me now, for everything that's in my head, including the keys to the zero-point drive. Black Dog is most likely following you here, guessing that you'll lead him to me. For that reason, and others that I'll explain later, it is imperative that we return to the voidoid before he and his ship enter this system.

"And Dr. Ebadi is right. The most important thing now is to focus on what LO has done to the voidoids and how we can reverse it before it's too late. She is absolutely correct about what will happen to Bound Space, and possibly to a much larger region of space surrounding it, if the family of voidoids there die out. The

Rip in isolated pockets of the universe is not purely theoretical. It's happened before elsewhere in our galaxy and will happen here if we don't manage to reanimate the voidoids. I have ideas on how to do that, but you'll have to get me back to the voidoid to work it out. Some bad things could start happening soon, so we must hurry."

A deep, bronchial cough interrupted Woo's narrative. It didn't sound good. He took a moment to recover before continuing, his voice sounding fainter.

"I have so much more to tell you," he said, "but these transmissions have to be short. My comm batteries are losing their capacity to recharge, so most of it will have to wait until you pick me up. I'll just add that, yes, the same thing happened to the *Starhawk* when I popped into this astrocell; my zero-point drive would not work. I've had much time to think about what went wrong, and what I've witnessed on this planet has inspired my idea of how to approach it. I'm sure I can fix the problem for you. But again, you'll need to bring the *Sun Wolf* back within proximity of the voidoid, and you'll need some kind of zero-point field detector. Unfortunately, the only instrument I know of like that is the Casimir-Ebadi interferometer. I can only hope you had the foresight to bring one with you. Then, lastly, you'll need me aboard to provide my biological key to reboot the drive. More on all that later."

As he spoke the last sentence, the signal started to break up and Elgin's voice faded. They only heard: "So I...you...six days...now...I'll be here..."

The signal crackled once more then went silent. After a brief pause, the *Starhawk*'s AI spoke to them. "We are grateful that you have come in time to rescue Dr. Woo," Mari said. "Not only is his helmet comm failing, but Dr. Woo's state of health is rapidly deteriorating. He is suffering from key nutrient deficiencies, including severe vitamin B deficiency accompanied by pernicious anemia. I feared that he would not survive beyond another two weeks. Without the medical testing I could have done here aboard the ship, I made this diagnosis based solely on his descriptions of symptoms. I trust that once he is aboard the *Sun Wolf* he will be in the good hands of your Medical Officer and that his condition can be adequately treated. You may communicate with me at any time during your journey here. Thank you again."

After the comm went silent, Aiden looked at the people who had gathered around. Most of them had heard the maternal concern in the AI's voice. Aiden in particular recognized the same quality of humanization that Hutton had developed as their interactions progressed. The Omicron-3 AIs were by design continually evolving, individually and as a network, in response to the universe they negotiated and especially to the human interactions they mediated. Mari was just another example of that evolution.

"Six days," Aiden said flatly. Given the dire need to act sooner than later, it would be a long six days. He turned to Dalton. "Lieutenant, despite what Dr. Woo told us about the zero-point drive, I want you to keep working to solve the problem."

"Yes, sir. And we do have that instrument he was talkin' about. The Casimir-Ebadi interferometer. Maybe with Dr. Ebadi's help we can figure out how to jump-start the drive."

Aiden glanced at Ebadi. She looked skeptical but said, "Yes. We'll do our best."

Aiden understood her skepticism. Without Elgin aboard to provide his bio-key, trying for a fix was a long shot. At least it would keep part of his crew busy over the coming days. He'd think of other projects to occupy the rest of them. They were, after all, now in a star system that had been the subject of intense interest to space scientists intermittently over the last couple of centuries.

Ro drew him aside and said quietly, "If it does end up taking us six days to pick up Dr. Woo, and another six to get back to the voidoid, that'll be right about the same time the *Markos* is predicted to enter the system. If indeed that's their intent."

Aiden nodded. He'd done the same math. "We'll just have to be ready for them, eh?"

~ ~ ~

"What the hell *are* those things?"

Lilly Alvarez just happened to be the first person to voice the question in everyone else's mind. After 142 hours of flight, half of it under hard deceleration, the *Sun Wolf* had arrived within 50,000 kilometers of the planet Elgin Woo called Shénmì. With a high-res image of the planet's equatorial region centered on the main screen, the crew stood gawking at what appeared to be several long, thin, whiplike structures extended upward from the surface along the equator to well beyond the planet's atmosphere. Each filament terminated in a single oval pod, one of which had come to rest nearly 36,000 kilometers into the vacuum of space, its pod split open, gaping at the stars. Two others were at lower elevations. One appeared to be ascending on its thin white stalk, pod closed, while the other one was clearly descending back to the surface, its stalk retracting into its point of origin. The eerie tendrils were elegantly curved against the direction of the planet's axial spin.

Aiden watched, absently scratching his beard. "I'll bet that's how Dr. Woo made it down to the surface in a 'somewhat unconventional manner.' Ingenious."

"More like insane," Alvarez said, putting it together with what Mari had referred to earlier as Woo's 'beanstalk adventure.'

"That's what makes him who he is, Lilly."

As the *Sun Wolf* slowed to a halt, Aiden instructed Abahem to lock in on the *Starhawk*'s position and bring the ship alongside, matching her geosync orbit at 40,000 kilometers above the surface. That put them directly above Woo's location at the equator but high enough to avoid any chance encounters with the bizarre beanstalks. Woo had been rationing the use of his helmet comm during the *Sun Wolf*'s six-day approach, checking in only briefly once every 24 hours. Aiden transmitted a message to him now, telling him they'd be sending a shuttle down to him within the hour.

"Looking forward to it," Woo said. It was clear now that the weakness in his voice was due more to his failing health than his failing comm batteries. "And I have a small favor to ask, Aiden. I know the *Sun Wolf* is a survey vessel, among other things, so could you bring along a portable broadband seismograph when you come down? I'd like to take a few readings down here before leaving the surface. To measure the planet's free oscillation frequency. It's actually very important. I'll explain later."

Aiden cast a questioning glance at Faye Desai. She nodded enthusiastically and said, "No problem. We've got a couple of those. Force-balance accelerometers, the latest models. Capable of measuring from 700 hertz down to 0.0001 hertz. One of the them is a handheld unit."

Aiden nodded. "We can do that, Elgin. As long as we do it quickly. I'd like to get you onboard as soon as possible."

"Understood," Woo said. "If you bring along someone to operate the instrument, it would save time. Thank you, Aiden."

As soon as Woo signed off, Aiden turned to his crew. "I'm taking the survey shuttle *Perseus* down. I want Dr. Ebadi, Officer Desai, Dr. Devi, and Colonel Aminu to accompany me. Please meet me in the shuttle bay in 20 minutes and be ready to depart immediately thereafter. Ro, you have ship's command while I'm downside. Lieutenant Hotah, keep your tactical sensors trained on the voidoid and alert me of anything unusual."

He spotted Cass Healy peeking around the corner of the lift vestibule, looking at him, her eyes hopeful. He had assigned her to Sudha Devi, ostensibly as her assistant, but mainly to keep her out of trouble during the days it took getting here. It had been a good match. No one could remain angry, stubborn, or overly remorseful for very long in the company of Dr. Devi. Cass had been no exception, and she'd actually become adept at growing and tending vegetables in the ship's "Green Thumb," Dr. Devi's hydroponic lab.

"Ms. Healy," Aiden said to her. "Please make sure Dr. Devi's medical bay is ready to receive Dr. Woo and that guest quarters 3B is prepared for him."

"Okay," she said. The smile that lit her face seemed to fit more naturally than any other expression Aiden had seen there. "I can also harvest extra spinach and broccoli for him from the Green Thumb. They're high in vitamin B."

Aiden looked at her. She'd been paying attention. She was smart. She had a good heart and was growing stronger. "Good idea, Cass. I'm sure Dr. Woo would like that. Go for it."

As Aiden headed off for the shuttle bay, he found himself more determined than ever to keep Cassandra Healy clear of the ruinous fate that awaited her if they ever made it back home.

33

SHÉNMÌ
Domain Day 97, 2218

THE AIR FELT heavier, far more humid, and it had a very different scent. Metabolically more complex. Underlying green-plant oxygen flavored by distinctly animalian carbon dioxide. From where he stood, not far from where the shuttle had touched down, the surroundings looked very different, the vegetation low to the ground and primitive...except for those odd cross-shaped trees growing up the hill to the east. No deep, dark forests here, cool with mist and mystery. It sounded different too. A soft, slow, regular pulse made of air rolled down from the hill, and bright flutelike music seemed to shine down on him, its silver tones blending with the golden aura of morning sun. And it wasn't just the air; his body felt heavier too, his feet planted firmly, sinking into the mossy ground cover. Even so, it felt like coming home. Like finding what was lost. It felt like Silvanus.

Shénmì was alive. No doubt about it. Was she another Gaia?

"Aiden?" Sudha Devi had come up next to him while the others were still making their way out of the shuttle's open port. She touched his arm gently. "You're there again, aren't you?"

Aiden nodded but did not look at her. "Part of me never left, Sudha."

"I know," she said. "One of these days, the part that never left will become married with the part that did. Right now? You standing here? The two just started courting."

He finally looked at her and saw the sly humor in her eyes.

"No," she said, smiling back. "I *do not* know you better than yourself. But I sometimes *see* you more clearly because I am not you."

Before Aiden could respond, Maryam Ebadi shouted from behind, "Dr. Woo!"

The shuttle had landed in a small, mossy meadow near the base of a hill and, according to Mari's coordinates, within 200 meters of where Woo had been sheltering. Aiden looked back up the hill in time to see a tall and very thin figure making his way unsteadily down a beaten path toward them. He stopped at Ebadi's hail, leaned on a wooden staff, and waved down at them. Even at this distance, the smile on his face was easy to see. He shouted something back, but his voice was too weak for them to hear his words.

Aiden waved back and turned to the others, but Ebadi and Dr. Devi were already past him trudging uphill to meet Woo. Colonel Aminu, who'd been more focused on scanning the immediate surroundings for potential threats, followed close behind. Aiden asked Faye Desai to stay nearby and start taking the seismograph readings Woo had requested.

After Faye finished setting up the portable unit, sinking the probe deep into the ground, she came to stand next to him. She gave him that look, the one that spontaneously smoldered with desire. The one she usually kept well-concealed. The one Aiden had struggled to look away from many times before. He felt the heat rise between them, and, once again, reminded himself that physical chemistry by itself was a random phenomenon at best. It allowed him to accept, then ignore, the stirrings that Faye's dark eyes elicited. Most of the time.

Aiden stood facing her for a moment longer, taking in her natural beauty. They smiled at each other in silence. Then, with an apologetic gesture, she turned away and Aiden turned to catch up with the others.

As he approached Elgin Woo, he was shocked by the man's condition. Elgin had always been slender and tall, but he looked emaciated now. The bones of his ribs and clavicles stood out sharply from his paper-thin skin, clearly visible through his half-opened shirt, or what was left of his shirt. His face appeared gaunt, almost skeletal, and his skin morbidly pale. Woo had always shaved his head smooth as a cue ball. But now his hair had grown out and was long and dull. His beard, grown equally long, was carefully braided to hang between his moustaches, giving him the outlandish look of a deranged pirate. But the twinkle in his eyes shone just as brightly as Aiden always remembered it, gleaming with mischievous intelligence. He leaned heavily on his staff and took Aiden's hand. "So good of you all to drop by. What a delight."

"Elgin," Aiden said. "We are so glad to find you." He moved to Woo's side and put an arm around him for support. Dr. Ebadi went to Woo's other side and did the same.

"You look frightful, Doctor," she said, trying to hold her emotions in check. "We need to get you up to the *Sun Wolf* as soon as possible."

"Ah, but there are so many wonders here that I'd like to show you—"

"Not now," Sudha Devi said firmly. She had moved to stand in front of him, hands on her hips, examining him with the keen eyes of a diagnosing physician. "Dr. Ebadi is quite right," she said. "We need to get you up to the medical bay. Right now. No arguments."

"Elgin," Aiden said. "This is Dr. Sudha Devi, our Medical Officer. I strongly suggest you do as she says." He leaned in closer to his ear. "She's not someone you want to tangle with."

Woo took a long, admiring look at Devi, and a devilish smile spread across his face. "On the contrary. It takes two to tangle!"

Aiden sighed. He turned to Devi, who was doing her best to look scandalized, and said, "He does need a lot of help physically. But mentally? He seems unchanged to me. Nothing to worry about there."

"I'll be the judge of that," Devi said, utterly unmoved. "Let's go. No time to dawdle. Commander, could you and Colonel Aminu please pick up Dr. Woo and carry him promptly to the shuttle?"

"I'd be happy to," Aiden said.

Aminu, who now appeared oddly distracted by his surroundings, finally nodded and moved into position. "Yes, of course."

Now it was Woo's turn to look scandalized, but he lacked the strength to resist. Doing their best two-man military carry, Aiden and Aminu secured Woo inside the *Perseus*. Ebadi and Dr. Devi took over from there, getting Woo settled into a flight couch and tending to his sad condition. The first thing Devi did was give him a vitamin B injection—the first of many, Aiden guessed—then another injection of broad-spectrum nanobiotics. With both women fussing over him, one on each side, Woo appeared unfazed by the injections and basked shamelessly in the attention.

Aiden returned outside to help Faye pack up her seismograph gear and get it stowed aboard. He followed her inside, counted noses, and realized Aminu had not yet come aboard. Aiden scratched his beard. It wasn't like the colonel to stray from the task at hand. He went back out and scanned the immediate surroundings. Aminu was nowhere in sight. *What the...*

Aiden called out his name several times. When no response came, he started back up the trail to Woo's cave. Halfway up, rounding a massive outcropping of mossy rock, he found Aminu standing next to the creek that had served as Woo's water source. The colonel stood as still as a statue, his gaze fixed on the grove of cross-shaped trees growing on the opposite bank. Woo had described them enthusiastically in his communications, calling them pendulum trees. And indeed they were.

Each tree had three long pendulums, one hanging from the end of each arm of the cross branches, and one from the upper center branch. The tree's pendulums swung back and forth in precise unison, and in unison with *all* the pendulums in the grove. The sound they made swinging through the heavy air, collectively, pulsed like a heartbeat. Its tempo was about the same as an average human pulse.

Aiden came up behind Aminu, who remained oblivious to his presence. At first Aiden thought Aminu had become hypnotized by the spectacle before him. As he came closer, he realized that Aminu's eyes were focused intently on something he saw within the grove. Or something he *thought* he saw; Aiden himself could see nothing but trees in the direction of Aminu's gaze.

Then the colonel's eyes opened wider and he spoke. "Mother...?"

He said it softly, with a deep poignancy starkly at odds with everything Aiden knew about Victor Aminu. A yearning sadness tinged with hope and amazement.

Aiden drew within a few feet of the man and stood quietly before speaking. "Victor."

Aminu turned to stare at Aiden, like he'd never seen him before. Tears welled up in his eyes. One rolled down his left cheek. Aiden stared back at him, equally disoriented, not recognizing the Victor Aminu who stood before him now.

After a long moment, Aminu wiped the tear from his cheek and looked at its wetness on his fingers as if it were a foreign substance. A forbidden secretion. When he looked at Aiden, his eyes were set again, and grim. "Yes," he said. "We must be going now."

When they reached the shuttle, Faye stood by the open hatch, looking both relieved and distinctly irritated. "Where have you two been? We had to pause our launch sequence."

"Sorry, Faye. Just some quick survey observations. Thanks for not leaving without us."

Faye was not amused. She stood aside to make way for the two men as they climbed aboard. Aiden hesitated before closing the hatch after him, standing on the threshold, breathing in the rich air of Shénmì.

Sudha Devi came up behind him. "No time to dawdle," she said, reaching past him to close the hatch door with a decisive clang.

"Right you are, Doctor." Aiden settled into his flight couch. "Resume launch sequence."

As the shuttle shot upward, Aiden watched the green planet recede beneath him, his eyes glued to the viewport even after the shuttle had cleared Shénmì's atmosphere. It was not exactly the same feeling he'd had on that day ten months ago when the *Argo*'s shuttle had pulled him away from Silvanus, the feeling of the umbilical cord snapping, releasing him into separateness, away from a wholeness greater than anything he'd known before. Not quite like that, not quite as traumatic, or intense. But it had the same quality. The same sensation of loss, only in a smaller dose...

A dose. An image came unbidden into his mind. The bottle of Continuum sitting in his med cabinet. *Just a dose...*

He turned from the viewport with a lump in his throat. Sudha Devi looked at him, a serene smile on her face, eyes calm but penetrating, like a reminder.

"Commander." Ro's voice over the comm jarred him loose. "Be advised, we're preparing to move the *Starhawk* into our shuttle bay. As soon as you're back and have the *Perseus* secured, we'll start docking the *Starhawk*."

"Got it. Thanks XO. Keep me posted."

The *Sun Wolf* had docking bays for three survey shuttles, but they'd brought only two. Being approximately the same size as a standard survey shuttle, the diminutive *Starhawk* would fit nicely into the extra space. Elgin overheard this news, smiled, and gave a thumbs-up.

After the *Perseus* docked, Aiden made his way straight to the bridge while Maryam Ebadi and Dr. Devi accompanied Woo to the medical bay. Aiden oversaw the successful docking of the *Starhawk* then instructed his flight crew to set course for the system's voidoid. He didn't leave the bridge until he felt the deep subsonic resonance of the M/AM drive at full thrust vibrating up through his boots. Then he made his way down to the medical bay.

He found Dr. Devi standing outside the bay's hatch, scanning Woo's lab results on her compad. When he came to stand next to her, she spoke without looking up. "Severe vitamin B deficiency, early stage pernicious anemia, moderately severe malnutrition, incipient bronchial pneumonia. That's the worst of it. We're lucky we found him when we did."

"Pneumonia? From alien microbes?" Aiden had been careful to run survey bio-scans from the *Perseus* just after landing before opening the hatch to Shénmì's atmosphere. The preliminary results had been negative for any obvious pathogens or toxins. Anxious to reach Elgin Woo quickly, he hadn't waited for more in-depth sampling and authorized the team to disembark without e-suits.

"No. More likely microbes from Dr. Woo's own body," she said. "Probably aspiration pneumonia, a bacterial infection from organisms commonly found in the upper airway. Possibly due to a gastric reflux event. The body can usually handle such things, but one of the effects of malnutrition is a depressed immune system. Increased susceptibility to infections of all kinds."

"Prognosis?"

"Not too bad, actually. Most of what ails the good doctor is reversible at this point. I'm pumping him full of antibodies, vitamin B injections, and TPN."

"TPN?"

"Total parenteral nutrition. Given intravenously. It's got all the goodies he needs. Amino acids, dextrose, fatty acids, vitamins, minerals, the works. He'll start feeling better within 24 hours, but it will take several days for him to regain his strength."

"Good. Can I talk to him now? Briefly?"

"Yes. But briefly. He needs sleep too. Rest will greatly increase his recovery time. I slipped a sedative into his IV to help with that. I sensed he wouldn't take it voluntarily."

Aiden nodded. "You got that one right. I doubt he's ever been sick a day in his life. Okay, thanks, Sudha. I'll be quick."

He found Elgin lying comfortably on one of the med bay's hospital beds, eyes half-closed, softly humming to himself a simple, mindless melody. A large IV bag of opaque white fluid hung from a pole attached to the bed frame, feeding a continuous flow of nutrients into an IV port near the base of his neck. Dressed in a fresh, loose-fitting cotton jumpsuit, his long hair neatly gathered into a ponytail and draped across his shoulder, Woo looked better already.

"How're you doing, Elgin?"

Woo's eyes opened fully, and he smiled. "Ah, Aiden. I am well. And getting better. Thank you. I'll just take a short nap and will be ready to meet with your team in an hour or so."

"Take it easy, Elgin. We've got time. Without the zero-point drive, it'll take us about six days to get back to the voidoid. There's nothing we can do to get there any faster. So, relax."

"Yes, you're probably right about that. A pity I didn't foresee this problem in my initial designs of the drive. I should have known that the cosmological constant would be slightly different for each astrocell, requiring the drive's control fields to be adjusted accordingly. I know how to fix it now. The control fields have to be precisely recalibrated to match the unique zero-point energy density profile of this astrocell. And I mean the *scale* of its density, the manner in which it varies within star systems out here. The density will be slightly higher right next to a voidoid because dark energy is being drawn into it, much the same way space-time is compressed at the event horizon of a black hole.

"We need to measure that density, at the voidoid, to complete the picture of the whole scale. The only way I know how to do that is to bring the ship within a few kilometers of the voidoid, come to an absolute halt in relation to its position, then use the

Casimir-Ebadi interferometer to get an accurate measurement. The moment we have the complete density profile, it goes directly into the drive's control-field computer to tell it exactly how to structure the EM control fields. That's when the hypospace bubble springs to life and we're off and running at 92 percent light speed."

Woo smiled weakly, as if his explanation had taken all his remaining energy. "After my nap, I'll want to start working with your Drive Systems Engineer to set all this up."

"I'm sure Lieutenant Dalton will be happy to work with you on that. But right now, we have some time on our hands. You should take advantage of it to regain your strength. Dr. Devi tells me you'll be in much better shape after 24 hours of rest and IV nutrients."

"Nonsense," Woo said, attempting to rise on his elbows. "I'll be fit as a fiddle after a short nap." But his strength gave way, and he collapsed back on the bed. His breathing slowed and grew steady, and his eyes began to close again.

"We'll see," Aiden said. "Before you nod off, though, I wanted to let you know that we got the *Starhawk* stowed safely aboard, down in the shuttle bay. Your AI, Mari, guided it in herself. A perfect docking maneuver."

Woo's eyes opened again. "Good. Mari is safe. She's still with me. Thank you, Aiden."

"One more thing," Aiden said. "Faye Desai told me to tell you she got a good reading on *Shénmì's* free oscillation frequency. It's right at 0.0035 hertz. She thought you'd want to know."

"Ah. Just as I thought," he said with a knowing smile. As his voice faded, Dr. Devi's most excellent sedation kicked in and Elgin Woo was fast asleep.

34

HD 10180 SYSTEM
Domain Day 99, 2218

"Everything the Cauldron stands for, Licet Omnia stands against," Elgin Woo said, then paused for a moment, trying to decide where to begin. His cup of tea sat untouched on the low table in front of him. Aiden wasn't going to rush him. That was not the way to interact with this most extraordinary genius, especially after his recent ordeal. And that's why Aiden had convened this meeting in the more personal confines of his own quarters. The others present—Ro, Maryam Ebadi, and Colonel Aminu—had followed Aiden's lead in lying back. Even the usually pushy Victor Aminu seemed relaxed and unhurried. Something had changed inside the man's head, or maybe it was in his heart. Whatever it was, Aiden decided it was an improvement.

They sat back and waited patiently for Woo to continue. After a day and a half of rest, most of it spent sleeping and reintroducing his system to foods his body recognized, Woo looked almost like his old self again. His long black hair had regained some luster and had been trimmed shorter, just above his shoulders. He'd kept his lengthy beard but had braided it into one long plait dropping from his chin, flanked on either side by his braided mustaches. His eyes looked clearer, less jaundiced, but he still was thin as a rail. His hands no longer trembled and were clasped together

resting calmly in his lap, long, narrow fingers interlaced poeti-
cally. Dressed in one of the Service's standard navy-blue jumpsuits, a bit overlarge, he leaned closer over the table and looked
each of them in the eye before continuing.

"Most of what I know about Licet Omnia comes through my
own covert sources. There're still gaps in the total picture, and
some of it is guesswork based on what's transpired in my absence.
It appears that LO's original plan, conceived about a decade ago,
was to develop a means of shutting down all the voidoids within
Bound Space in a way that would give them sole control over
their use. That would mean ultimate power over Bound Space
and would give Cardew unfettered freedom to build his so-called
Empire of the Pure without interference from the rest of humanity. With the brain power they mostly stole from the Cauldron,
LO thought they had figured out a way to open and close any
voidoid, any time they wanted.

"They had reasonable success in shutting down voidoids by
manipulating gravity fields, but their attempts to reopen them
inevitably failed. The scientists they abducted and brain-tapped
possessed abundant theoretical knowledge but very little talent
for applying it to workable technologies. They would, however,
understand the extreme danger in messing around with the
voidoids in the way LO was doing, but their warnings would
surely be ignored. When LO finally realized that their tinkering
had set the Rip into motion, they changed their plans."

Woo stopped for a moment, picked up his teacup, and drank
half of its contents in two thirsty gulps. He dabbed his lips with
the sleeve of his jumpsuit and continued. "I think that's when
Licet Omnia decided that if Bound Space was going to self-
destruct anyway, they would just go ahead and kick-start the Rip
now and take their Empire of the Pure elsewhere. Somewhere
beyond Bound Space, into another astrocell. Then they'd have no
need to fret about the rest of humanity, the 'unpure,' interfering
with their plans. Not only would shutting down all the voidoids
leave Cardew's empire untouchable, but for added insurance, all

of humanity within Bound Space would disappear as well. Lost in the Rip. He turned his failed experiment with the voidoids into a new and more economical strategy for achieving his goals. It was the final solution for him."

"Kick-starting the Big Rip," Aiden said. "The gravity-bombing of V-Prime."

"Exactly. The so-called Final Blow that you learned about from your guest, Ms. Healy. And that was what? Only nine days ago? Cardew is probably licking his chops now, believing that the entire human race is doomed—except for himself of course, and his clones, who could now emerge unopposed as the progenitors of a new race. His Empire of the Pure."

"His clones?" Aiden said. "What the hell *is* this Empire of the Pure?"

Woo shook his head. "I honestly don't know for sure. I only know that this man Cardew has some freakish and truly frightening psychic powers, and there's evidence that he's been cloning himself, creating a tribe of similar beings whose combined powers over matter and energy—unaided by technology—are the stuff of nightmares. Even if pockets of humanity survived the Big Rip, they wouldn't stand a chance against a race of humanoids like that."

Woo leaned back in his chair and finished the rest of his tea in the uneasy silence. Aiden's quarters were like all the crew quarters aboard, spartan in design but comfortable, except his was more spacious and had furniture to accommodate small informal meetings. A basic settee sat facing a low coffee table, and three high-backed chairs were arranged around the other sides of the table. Maryam Ebadi and Ro sat together on the settee while Aiden, Woo, and Victor Aminu occupied the surrounding chairs.

Aiden held up his hand. "Okay, let's back up here for a second. That's a pretty risky strategy, deliberately initiating the Rip of Bound Space then skipping off to another region of space, dozens of light-years away, without knowing how to get there or what they'll find there. How did they even know about other astrocells in the first place, much less believe they could actually travel to one in less than several thousand years? I thought astrocells were theoretical arcana that only you, Elgin Woo, had dreamed up?"

Woo fiddled with his empty cup and did not look up as he spoke. "Yes, I was the one who came up with the theory of astrocells and the role voidoids played in their creation, but it was not a secret at the Cauldron, and I wasn't the only one there investigating the idea. The leading researcher, in fact, had made astounding progress. But when he mysteriously disappeared, I became convinced that LO had abducted him to tap his knowledge of the astrocell theory."

"Dr. Emilio Roca?" Aminu asked, nodding at the answer he already knew.

"Yes, as a matter of fact," Woo said, eyebrows raised. "How did you know that?"

"I did a little digging into the Cauldron's records during our brief stay there."

Woo chuckled. "I'm sure my colleagues were overjoyed by your digging, Colonel."

Aminu made a grim smile. "No, they were not."

"At any rate," Woo said, "Dr. Roca was doing the hard research to verify my notion of gateway voidoids connecting astrocells to one another and of the high probability that these gateways were located at the outermost boundaries of astrocells where two or more of them might overlap. Knowing that, of course, would narrow the search for such gateways down to a manageable number of stars on the outer Frontier. If LO had obtained that information, then at the very least they knew where to start looking for their exit point."

"That's still a lot of star systems to search through," Aminu said. "Especially with limited resources. Yet LO must have found the gateway long before launching their Final Blow. It wouldn't make sense otherwise. Why destroy Bound Space without an assured escape route? How did they zero in on Alpha-2 Hydri so soon? Couldn't have been dumb luck."

"I'm afraid," Woo said sheepishly, "that I may have inadvertently led them there."

"How so?"

"LO had been trying to get their hands on me for nearly a year before I disappeared from Bound Space. They needed me for two reasons very important to them. The first was their quest for a safe haven outside Bound Space. They knew I was looking for a gateway into a new astrocell and knew I was likely to find it, so they decided to just follow me, to let me do the work for them. I became aware of LO's interest in me early on and was able to elude them well enough through deception. But I underestimated their technological capabilities.

"Unbeknownst to me, a small, sophisticated, and undetectable tracking device had been planted aboard the *Starhawk* at some point during her construction on the Cauldron. I'm guessing that LO had a mole among the group of visiting scientists who worked on the *Starhawk* project. The device performs a subtle hack into Holtzman systems so it can transmit a camouflaged locater signal through the voidoids, as well as through realspace."

Aminu nodded. "We've heard rumors of such devices from DSI's tech division but never found evidence for them."

"So," Aiden said, "LO tracked your jump from Chara to the Alpha-2 Hydri system, giving them the star system where the gateway was likely to be."

"Yes," Woo said. "Not only that, but they tracked the *Starhawk* to the polar opposite point, telling them exactly where the gateway was located. Thankfully, they couldn't track me after I'd jumped through the gateway into the HD 10180 system. There wasn't a Holtzman buoy anywhere near the POP at the time. Plus, Mari discovered the device and destroyed it the day before our jump. Which is why they never came looking for me at HD 10180 and why they never found Shénmì. Thank the gods for that."

Aiden did not like how this story was playing out. "Then we can safely assume that LO not only found the gateway into the new astrocell shortly after you did, but that they're already out here somewhere, setting up shop. Laying the foundation for their Empire."

"Correct," Woo said. "When Black Dog tracked me to Alpha-2 Hydri's POP, he put all the pieces of the puzzle together to find the gateway. I have no doubt LO has already established a foothold somewhere in this new astrocell. But it's an enormous volume of space—at least 16 times larger than Bound Space, over 91,000 cubic parsecs—and LO excels in concealment. It will not be easy to find them now."

"That explains why LO felt confident about going ahead with Final Blow," Aminu said. "They knew they'd be safe in a new environment unaffected by the Rip."

Ro, who had been silent until now, crossed his arms over his chest and said, "Well, if LO couldn't track Elgin to HD 10180, we just led the *Markos* right to it, didn't we? You can bet Black Dog picked up the *Sun Wolf's* location at the POP just before we jumped. If LO has occupied the Alpha-2 Hydri system ever since following Elgin there, no doubt they've got eyes at the gateway. Probably a few robotic trackers stationed around the voidoid, good enough to register precise jump vectors."

Aiden nodded. "Right. And the last we saw of the *Markos* before we jumped, she was on our tail, heading for the gateway."

"They're looking for *me* now," Woo said. "I'm still their top priority. They must have known you were determined to find me, and they're simply following you here."

"Why now?" Aiden said. "If they've already found the gateway, they don't need you any more to lead them to it. Why would LO want you bad enough to send the *Markos* all the way out here and risk a confrontation with the *Sun Wolf*?"

"They want the zero-point drive," Woo said. "That's the second important thing LO wants from me. The key to the ZPD. They desperately need the zero-point drive for expansion and colonization of their new astrocell. It's a secret they wouldn't have been able to pry out of any of their brain-tapped scientists, and a technology that's impossible to operate without my key. It's a bio-neurological key. They need me, physically, to obtain it."

When no one had a good response for that, Woo went on. "And I don't think the *Markos* is worried about a confrontation with the *Sun Wolf*. After what you told me about the attack at Friendship Station, I'm convinced that Lieutenant Hotah is right. The *Markos* has a new shielding technology that makes it virtu-ally invincible. On top of that, it's very likely that they know we can't use our zero-point drive out here, leaving the *Sun Wolf* at even greater disadvantage. That'll give Black Dog supreme confi-dence that he can prevail."

"How could they possibly know we can't use the ZPD?" Ebadi said. "They're still back at Alpha-2 Hydri, in a different astrocell, over 90 light-years way."

"Their robotic trackers," Aiden said. "If Ro is right, LO prob-ably surrounded the gateway with an array of sophisticated track-ing drones. When Black Dog spotted the *Sun Wolf* at the gateway, the trackers would not only report our exact jump vector, but at least one of them would also follow us through and report on our progress on the other side."

Ro nodded in agreement. "These drones are tiny and nearly impossible to spot unless you know exactly where to look for them. They're equipped with Holtzman devices, so they can com-municate through open voidoids. They can monitor a ship's velocity, its exhaust characteristics. It would be very clear to Black Dog that the *Sun Wolf* was operating exclusively on conventional M/AM drive out here, without the benefit of our zero-point drive."

"So the *Markos* holds all the cards," Aiden said, "especially if they get here before we can return to the voidoid."

"That's right," Woo said. "Our best chance of winning a con-frontation with the *Markos* is to get to the voidoid before it does. That would give us the time we need at standstill near the voidoid to reset the zero-point drive. Then we would have the decidedly greater tactical advantage. At least in terms of evasion."

Aiden looked at the ceiling. "Hutton. Assuming that the *Markos* is headed here from where we spotted her at Alpha-2 Hydri, what are the chances that we can bring the *Sun Wolf* to standstill within 100 klicks of the voidoid before the *Markos* pops out to greet us?"

"The chances are not good, Aiden," Hutton said without hesitation. The AI's disembodied voice filled Aiden's quarters, but not intrusively. His tone sounded warm and conversational. "Given the *Markos's* maximum constant acceleration is 1.5 Gs, that it is covering a distance of nearly 26 AU, and that it needs to slow down enough to make a safe jump, it would take 11 days and 22 hours to get here. It took us exactly six days at 3 Gs to reach Dr. Woo, and it takes another six days to get back to the voidoid at standstill. Add to that the roughly eight hours we spent at Shénmì retrieving Dr. Woo, and I estimate the *Markos* would emerge from the voidoid about two hours before we get there."

"Thank you, Hutton." It was a little more detail than Aiden wanted and not quite the answer he'd hoped for. "We'll have to come up with a plan to be ready for that."

"If we wanted to evade the *Markos* altogether," Aminu said, "why decelerate at all? Why not just make a high-velocity jump to somewhere else in this astrocell? If we didn't have to slow to a standstill at the voidoid and kept going at 3 Gs, we'd get through the voidoid well before the *Markos* could get here."

"Yes," Hutton said. "About a day and half before, in fact. Our entrance velocity would be very high, around 10,650 KPS, but that is within the range of our pilot's abilities."

"Right," Aminu said confidently. "Assuming that voidjumps work the same way out here as in Bound Space, we could jump to some other star out here, come to a standstill, fix the zero-point drive, and we're back in business."

On the surface, it was impeccable reasoning. He had to give Aminu that. But Aiden knew better. "No. Not that simple. Some major navigational problems get in the way. We don't have accurate enough star charts for this region of space to make reliable jumps, especially at those entrance velocities. Bound Space is well charted. Out here? Not so much. Without precise jump vectors, we'd get totally sidetracked. It could take us weeks, even months to get back to where we wanted to go, even with the zero-point drive."

Woo slapped his hand down on the table. His empty teacup tipped and rolled over the edge. "And we don't have time to spare! Our ultimate goal here is to prevent a Big Rip from destroying Bound Space. To save the lives of all the people we know and love and of all the billions of others back there. To save humankind and our home planets from a horrible destruction. The only way I know of doing that is to reanimate the family of voidoids. And if that's even possible at this point, the only plan I know with a chance to work requires us to stay here, in the immediate vicinity of the voidoid here at HD 10180, the primary voidoid of this entire astrocell. And we need to do it as soon as possible, before it's too late."

Aiden agreed with Woo's impassioned assertions, although he had no idea how Woo planned to do the last part. "That's it then," he said. "We stick with the plan. Deal with Black Dog first, then on to saving Bound Space."

"Well," Ro said, kicking back with a laconic sigh, "at least the *Markos* won't be shooting at us the moment they're out of the gate. If they believe we have Dr. Woo aboard, and they want him bad enough, they won't risk killing him by attacking the *Sun Wolf*."

Woo followed suit, relaxing back into his chair. He smiled broadly, causing his braided mustache to move as if it was alive. "Indeed. A most comforting thought."

35

"COMMANDER. THE *MARKOS* just came through the voidoid." Lieutenant Hotah spoke with calm focus, his eyes glued to the tactical screen.

"Lock in all weapons, Lieutenant. Shields at max. Hold fire."

"Aye, sir."

Right on time, Aiden thought. The *Sun Wolf* was two hours from standstill at the voidoid, 118 minutes to be precise. It was day six after leaving Shénmì. The ship was under hard deceleration at 3 Gs. The current velocity: 160 km/sec and slowing. Current distance from the voidoid: about 494,000 kilometers and closing. The full crew was on the bridge at their stations. They'd all been expecting this, hoping it wouldn't happen, but ready for it if it did.

Elgin Woo and Maryam Ebadi hovered over the science station, working with the Casimir-Ebadi interferometer, busily taking zero-point energy measurements as the ship drew closer to the voidoid. Zachary Dalton sat tensely at drive console, waiting for them to feed their data into the control-field computer as soon as the ship came to a halt. Waiting to light up the zero-point drive and get them the hell out of there.

An enhanced image of the *Markos* appeared on the main comm screen. It had come to a stationary position 10 kilometers from the voidoid, directly in the *Sun Wolf*'s path. It was a cruel-looking vessel. No attempt had been made by its ARM designers to conceal its brutal utility. The Green War logo it had displayed at Friendship Station was gone now, replaced by an odd-looking black hexagram.

Ro frowned when he saw it. "It's a black unicursal hexagram," he said. "Associated with the occult cabal of Thelema. Only here the symbol is distorted, the downward-facing point drawn much longer than the upward facing one."

The outlines of the ship's image appeared fuzzy, indistinct. It shimmered faintly as if seen from underwater. The *Markos*'s new shielding tech, Aiden guessed. He turned to Science Station. "Tell me again, Elgin, why we need complete standstill to bring the zero-point drive back online."

Woo looked back at him. "Are you serious? You really want me to go into that again? At a time like this?"

Aiden wasn't exactly being serious. Just anxious. He'd been told it was virtually impossible for the Casimir-Ebadi interferometer to get a true measure of the vacuum energy of space while moving through it. The instrument had to be stationary relative to the field.

When he didn't reply, Woo relaxed and said, "What I can tell you is that as soon as we come to a halt, we'll have the measurements within a few seconds. A few seconds after that, the EM control fields will reset, and Lieutenant Dalton can make the *Sun Wolf* disappear from here in an eyeblink."

Aiden was about to respond when Alvarez spoke up. "Commander, we're being hailed by the *Markos*."

"Open the Comm, Lilly. Main screen."

The forward screen abruptly displayed the sight of one of the strangest human beings Aiden had ever seen. Assuming he was human...assuming it was a "he." None of that was apparent at first sight. Visible only from the shoulders up, the figure was cloaked in a hooded garment, all black and worn low on the brow. The face under the hood was further obscured by a black sash covering all but the eyes and the surrounding skin. The flesh looked pale white. Ghostly white, like a sheet. But the eyes...*Holy shit!* Downright spooky. They were large and they were black. Not just very dark brown, but jet-black. No pupils visible. The entire iris, black as night. And the eyes did not blink. In fact, no eyelids were apparent.

When the figure appeared on the screen, the entire crew seemed to gasp and draw back from it. Cassandra Healy cried out in terror and stumbled backward. She would have fallen flat on her back had it not been for Billy Hotah, who leapt from his station, lightning-quick, to catch her. As if he'd anticipated her reaction.

The man—Aiden designated that gender arbitrarily, just to deal with what he was looking at—stared at them for a moment before speaking.

"Greetings, Commander Macallan. I am Black Dog. What a pleasant surprise to find you here in this star system, so far away from Bound Space. It appears that you discovered the same gateway voidoid that we did ourselves not long ago. Congratulations! Amazing, is it not? To find another region of space just like Bound Space, and to jump here through such a special voidoid?"

High-pitched and grating, the voice intoned with thinly disguised sarcasm. He stood erect and unmoving. The outline of his shoulders under the black garment stood out sharply, angular as a scarecrow.

"Now that we're here together, we have much to discuss. You have something I want, and I have something you want. I propose a trade. I assume that you've found Dr. Elgin Woo and have him aboard your ship. We've been looking for him too. I salute your success in rescuing him. But now we must insist on making Dr. Woo our guest here aboard my ship. The trade I propose is a simple one: you hand over Dr. Woo to me, and in return I will allow you to live."

Aiden thought he detected a hint of Slavic in the man's accent and was struck by his well-educated language.

"And please, Commander, do not suffer the illusion that your ship could prevail in a shootout with mine, or that you can escape from us quickly. As you may know by now, my ship is the RMV *Markos*, formerly the flagship of the Martian Militia. Top of the line. I recently acquired it for my own purposes. Not only did it come with superior weaponry, but we have also upgraded its shielding to an unprecedented level. We are now impervious to any form of attack you could possibly hurl at us. If you don't believe me, I invite you to try. Fire your most powerful laser cannons at us, launch your most lethal missiles, train your rail guns on us. Go ahead, Commander. We won't try to evade your attempts, and we won't fire back at you."

Here Black Dog paused as if waiting for Aiden to follow his suggestion. He tilted his head slightly, as if reiterating his invitation. The gesture looked stiff and unnatural.

"No? Well, you're welcome to try at any time during our encounter here. I am also aware that your new drive system, Dr. Woo's zero-point drive, is not working and probably never will in this sector of space. Without it, there's no way you can evade us. And you're currently decelerating toward the voidoid at a rate that would make it very difficult to change course on conventional drive. We could catch up to you easily. Let's face it, Commander, we're destined to meet very soon to complete our transaction and to do it peaceably, assuming you want to stay alive. You hand over Dr. Woo to me, and I will allow you and your ship to go on your way unharmed, back into Bound Space. You have my word. What do you say, Commander? Deal?"

The game was afoot. Aiden glanced briefly at his crew and saw the resolve in their postures. As they had agreed, Aiden would play along with Black Dog in hopes of delaying the interaction long enough for them to get the zero-point drive reset. For now, it was showtime. Aiden put on his best expression of indignation and said, "Who the hell are *you*?"

After the brief transmission delay, Black Dog's response oozed through the comm like a toxic oil slick. "I am High Minister of a noble league, Licet Omnia. Perhaps you've heard of us?"

"Can't say that I have," Aiden replied flippantly. "But I do know what you've done, so I can't say I'm pleased to meet you. And why should I take your word for anything? What's the word worth of a man who cold-bloodedly murders hundreds of service personnel at Friendship Station, then proceeds to bomb V-Prime, shutting down all the voidoids in Bound Space? How should I trust such a man, much less respect him?"

After the time delay, Black Dog's black eyes widened a fraction. Was it possible that he hadn't foreseen Aiden receiving information about his attack at Friendship before shutting down the voidoids? Even with Black Dog's face obscured and eyes unexpressive, his pause before answering told Aiden that he'd taken the bait.

"Ah. As to your first question: a pity about that. I did warn them of my superior tactical advantage, the same as I did for you just now. But they would not believe me and insisted on attacking. I had no choice but to eliminate them. They were military personnel, after all. They knew the risks of such duty. They gambled and lost. It's the way of war, Commander. I'm sure you understand.

"As to your second point: yes, we did succeed in shutting down all the voidoids in Bound Space. But rest assured, it is only temporary. As I informed the leaders of the UED and the Martian Republics, we have the ability not only to shut down the voidoids, but also to reopen them. We needed to shut them down temporarily to accomplish our goals. Be assured that once we are gone from Bound Space, the voidoids will reopen and allow the good people and nations of Bound Space to continue as before, unharmed. We will not interfere with your affairs in any way after that."

Aiden struggled to keep a straight face. The man lied through his teeth at every turn. His murderous actions at Friendship Station were not "the way of war," nowhere near the normal bounds of accepted warfare engagement. The voidoids were not going to reopen, even if LO wanted them to. And there was no way Black Dog would let the *Sun Wolf* "go on its way" after handing over Elgin Woo. Still, Aiden needed to keep playing.

"Assuming that I actually do have Dr. Woo aboard," Aiden said, "do you honestly expect me to believe that you wouldn't attack the *Sun Wolf* after we handed him over to you? Why would I believe that from someone who's been trying to blow up my ship ever since we left Friendship Station?"

"That was then. This is now, Commander. You see, once we discovered the gateway voidoid at Alpha-2 Hydri system, we moved our entire operations into that system in preparation for our departure from Bound Space, to occupy this new region— this new astrocell, to use the term Dr. Woo coined for it. We called our new base of operation at Alpha-2 Hydri the Black Fort. We've kept its existence secret, of course. Why? Because we believe that the governments of Bound Space wish us ill and would attempt to prevent us from colonizing our own territories, from founding our own sovereign state.

"So when we received information that the UED intended to investigate our work with the voidoids and had launched the *Sun Wolf* on a mission to uncover our plans, we became concerned. When we learned that the *Sun Wolf*'s first destination would be the Alpha-2 Hydri system, we became even more concerned. We feared that you would discover our Black Fort there and decided that you had to be stopped.

"Unfortunately, our efforts to stop the *Sun Wolf* from jumping into the Alpha-2 Hydri system failed. Our agents tried to disable your ship while it was still docked at Hawking Station, then tried again at Luna while you were picking up one of Dr. Woo's esteemed colleagues, Dr. Maryam Ebadi. We tried a third time while you were docked at the Cauldron and failed again. Truly, Commander, how you were able to thwart that attack is a miracle. My congratulations on your superior defensive strategies.

"Our failure to stop you from jumping to Alpha-2 Hydri was assured after you acquired Dr. Woo's zero-point drive at the Cauldron. There was no way I could catch up with you in the *Markos*. That turn of events prompted us to change our plans. We decided to initiate the final shutdown of the voidoids—the Final Blow, as my loyal soldiers like to call it—sooner than we had planned. That way, even if the *Sun Wolf* discovered our secrets at Alpha-2 Hydri, you would be cut off from the rest of Bound Space and unable to report it to anyone else.

"I was tasked to bring the gravity device to V-Prime and to activate it after our jump out of the System. My destination was Alpha-2 Hydri, to apprehend the *Sun Wolf*. The Final Blow was a success, so we had you trapped at Alpha-2 Hydri. But when we arrived there ourselves, we found you had taken the *Sun Wolf* out to the system's polar opposite point. We concluded that you had discovered the gateway there, just as we had earlier. And since you used your new drive system to get there many days ahead of us, my mission changed once again. Now it's back to finding Dr. Woo and bringing him aboard so he can assist us with some crucial technological issues we need to resolve. You have my word that he will be treated with the utmost respect as an honored guest."

Black Dog said nothing more and stared out from the screen, unblinking, awaiting Aiden's response. Those jet-black eyes were unnerving. Aiden was even more convinced now that Black Dog had no intention of letting them go after he got what he wanted. Why else would he be so chatty, so forthcoming with information so revealing and damning by any standards? Why expose so much if Black Dog didn't intend to blast the *Sun Wolf* into atoms once their business was done? Aiden swallowed hard. They needed more time.

"What makes you so sure we even have Dr. Woo aboard?" Aiden had to tread carefully here. He didn't actually want to convince Black Dog that Woo was *not* aboard. That presumably was the only reason Black Dog didn't just blow them up now and be done with it. He needed to prolong the interaction. They were still an hour and a half away from standstill.

When the question reached Black Dog, he tilted his head again, this time suggesting impatience. But when he spoke, he sounded prideful. "Just good old deductive reasoning, Commander. We assumed that once you found yourself isolated from the rest of Bound Space, your number-one priority would shift to finding Dr. Woo. We also assumed that you and Dr. Ebadi both had an overriding interest in finding him and that you must have some special knowledge of his true destination, knowledge we did not have. After that, it was a simple matter of following you here.

"The tracker drones we concealed around the gateway at Alpha-2 Hydri are quite good, you know. They told us exactly where you'd gone. And here we are. What a wonderful star system. And what a beautiful habitable planet! Dr. Woo has outdone himself in finding it. Licet Omnia may consider relocating into this system and using it as the new capital of our project."

Aiden glanced at Woo. His face had gone pale. Rage burned in his eyes. Oddly, even Victor Aminu looked sickened by the thought.

"Relocating?" Aiden said, overcoming his own revulsion to keep the conversation going. "Is your band of nut cases already setting up shop somewhere inside this astrocell?"

Black Dog did not answer for a long moment, longer than the time delay accounted for. Again, the gesture of impatience followed by prideful recovery. "Yes, of course. When we moved to the Alpha-2 Hydri system, we began a telescopic survey of suitable stars out in this region, stars likely to harbor habitable planets that we could reach through the gateway. We obviously overlooked this system, HD 10180—an unfortunate error—but we did find one almost as good. Our leader has already taken his Chosen Founders through the gateway to that star. I will join him there when our business here is finished. But I will tell him of this place. The habitable planet here is far nicer. Thanks to Dr. Woo for leading us here."

"Your leader? Who is he? What's his name?" Aiden was running out of plausible questions to ask.

"You honestly don't expect me to answer that, do you?" Black Dog had reached the end of his leash.

"Well then, where's this new star he went to?"

"Commander, you're trying my patience. I've told you enough already. It's time to put Dr. Woo on one of your shuttles and send him to me. Now."

"All right, but tell me one last thing. If you're letting the *Sun Wolf* go after you have him, what's to prevent us from following you to wherever you're going and making trouble for you?"

The veil of lies had grown thin for Black Dog. But he must have thought that answering the question would improve the chances of Aiden agreeing to release Woo. "Because one of the nonnegotiable conditions of this deal is that you'll be jumping back through the gateway into the Alpha-2 Hydri system. Once there, you can await the reopening of the voidoids so that you can all return to your loved ones back home. And you'll be free to rescue some of the scientists and voidship crew we left behind there. I'll gladly tell you where to find them. Don't you want that, Commander?"

A smooth one, Aiden thought. But he didn't believe any of it for a second. "Okay, then once we're back home, what's to prevent us telling everyone what's gone on out here? When our governments learn what you've done and where you've gone, they'll mobilize massive military forces to come back through the gateway and go after you."

If a smirk could occur when there was no way to see it, Black Dog had perfected it. "Once you're safely on the other side of this gateway, Commander, there's no way you or anyone else will be able to come after us. Believe me."

Right. That confirmed Aiden's suspicions. Black Dog would be shutting down the gateway on the Alpha-2 Hydri side. Before he could come up with another time-delaying tactic, Black Dog spoke.

"Time is up, Commander Macallan. You have 15 minutes to put Dr. Woo on a shuttle and send him to me. If I don't see that shuttle leaving your ship by then, I'll start firing on you. Continuous repeated laser cannons first, I think, to wear down your shielding. After that, a few well-placed antimatter missiles should do the trick. You can fire back at us all you want, but nothing will harm us. Fifteen minutes. Good day to you!"

As soon as the screen went blank, Aiden turned to Ro. "How long to standstill?"

Ro shook his head in dismay. "About an hour and a quarter."

"Shit!"

36

HD 10180 SYSTEM
Domain Day 103, 2218

AIDEN TURNED FROM the comm screen and scanned the faces of his crew. They were frightened. He couldn't blame them. He was sweating it too. "Ideas, anyone?"

Dalton spoke up first. "Can we try firing up the zero-point drive with the density data we've got already? How fine-tuned do the EM fields have to be? Wouldn't even an imperfect hypospace bubble get us up to *some* percentage of light speed? Doesn't have to be 92 percent, right? Hell, 1 percent light speed would clear us out of weapons range in a flash."

Woo shook his head sadly. "I'm afraid it doesn't work that way, Lieutenant. The bubble won't blossom at all until the resonance frequencies match up perfectly with the ambient scale of zero-point energy. I know this for a fact only because I had to do exactly the same thing to get the *Starhawk*'s drive to work in Bound Space."

"Okay, scratch that one," Aiden said. "Anyone else?"

"Yes," Elgin Woo said. "Give them what they want. Let me go to them."

"You can't be serious, Elgin."

"I am. Absolutely." And he was. Aiden saw it in Woo's eyes.

Aiden shook his head. "You're thinking with your heart, Elgin. Not with your brain. I appreciate the sentiment, believe me. The

idea of sacrificing your life for ours. And even if I thought Black
Dog would honor his part of the deal, I still wouldn't allow it.
That bastard is going to light us up anyway the moment he has
you in his clutches. Don't doubt it for one second. And that's only
the first reason I won't consider it. So, suggestion rejected. Anyone else?"

"Sir," Billy Hotah said. "If the *Markos* starts firing on us, we
should at least flip the ship. Right now, we're in decel with our
exhaust nozzles facing the *Markos*, in her direct line of fire. Our
propulsion nozzles are the most vulnerable part of the ship, and
it's where the shielding field is the weakest. If he targets that area
with sustained laser fire—which is exactly what I'd do in his position—he could inflict serious damage in no time. But if we flip
the ship so it's facing the *Markos* head on, we have a much better
chance of withstanding laser pulses. The bow of the ship presents
the strongest shielding and the lowest profile."

"But if we flip the ship," Dalton said, "we're no longer decelerating. We'd have to shut down the drive and coast. We'd never
reach standstill, which is what we need to reset the zero-point
drive."

"Forget the zero-point drive!" Hotah said. "Face it. We don't
have enough time to get it up and running before Black Dog
starts firing. That creep is seriously messed up. He's not fucking
around."

"Hotah is right," Aiden said. "We can't stall him much longer.
At this point, getting the ZPD back online is no longer an option
for getting us out of this mess. We'll flip the ship, but not right
now. Not until it's absolutely necessary to stop decelerating. Otherwise we'll be coming in too fast to do anything."

"So what's the plan now, boss?" Ro said.

Aiden did have a plan, but only as a final resort and one he
kept to himself for now. He turned sharply to Ro. "You got any
ideas, XO?"

Ro paused for a long moment, his pale blue eyes looking
upward, unfocused. He was the only crew member who didn't

appear overly concerned. He said, "What do we know about this new shielding tech the *Markos* has? Maybe we can come up with some way to defeat it."

"My guess," Woo said, "is that it's derived from the same process they've been using to disrupt the voidoids. Only in reverse."

"The Füzfa Effect?" Ebadi said.

"Yes. Using EM fields to bend space-time inward to simulate a gravity field. Theoretically, if you were able to bend space-time in the opposite direction, outward, you could simulate 'negative' gravity. A force that repels instead of attracts. If it were strong enough and distributed around a vessel as an envelope, it could repel weaponry from particle beams and lasers to kinetic weapons like missiles and rail-gun slugs. If they've been able to accomplish that, they've got some serious brain power working for them."

"Does the name Anwar Cain ring a bell, Dr. Woo?" Colonel Aminu said, referring to the disappeared Cauldron scientist who had been the Domain's leading expert on the Füzfa Effect.

Woo's eyes clouded with dark anger. "Unfortunately, yes."

"Well, then," Ro continued. "Couldn't we use our own EM generators, the ones we have for the zero-point drive control fields, to counter their EM fields? To interfere with them enough to cause them to fail?"

Woo thought for a moment and then said, "An excellent idea. And it would work too. The only problem is that we'd need to bring the *Sun Wolf* very close to the *Markos*. These fields don't extend much beyond 500 meters."

"There's no way Black Dog's going to let us get that close to his ship now," Aiden said. "And there's no way our shields will hold up long enough for us to get within 500 meters. Right, Mr. Hotah?"

Hotah nodded. "That's right."

Everyone looked stumped. They were running out of ideas and running out of time.

As if to punctuate that sad fact, Black Dog's image reappeared on the screen, and his voice cut through the comm. "You have one minute left, Commander. Launch your shuttle now, with Dr. Woo aboard."

Hotah looked up from his screen and caught Aiden's eye. Aiden switched off the comm and said, "What is it, Lieutenant?"

"When the *Markos* starts firing on us, the least we can do is test their defenses, see if their shields are as good as they say."

"Agreed." Aiden had planned on doing just that.

"The closer we are to the *Markos*," Hotah added, "the more effective our weapons. The longer we wait, the closer we can get. Can you stall him a little longer?"

"I'll try, Lieutenant."

Aiden activated the comm. "Yes, well, Captain Black Dog. We're still a considerable distance from you. We'd like to be a little closer before launching our shuttle. Another 30 minutes would put us in a more agreeable position for a safe transfer. Surely a little more time makes no difference in our transaction."

It was a lame ploy, Aiden had to admit, and Black Dog knew it. His black eyes seemed to burn a hole into the comm screen. "Do not try to deceive me, Commander. You and I both know your shuttles are capable of high-G thrust. Dr. Woo could easily be here in less than 30 minutes, even from where you are now. I'm giving you one last warning before we open fire."

Time to call Black Dog's bluff. "And if I refuse? If you destroy the *Sun Wolf*? You won't be getting Dr. Woo. He'll be dead with the rest of us. Is that really what you want?"

"Licet Omnia will get along fine without Dr. Woo," Black Dog said. "It may take us longer to get what we need without him, but in the end we will. Launch your shuttle now."

Aiden nodded thoughtfully and said, "The only way I can properly answer that, Dog, is: go fuck yourself."

"Goodbye, Commander." The screen went blank.

"That turned out well," Ro commented.

"The *Markos* is powering up their laser cannon," Hotah reported.

Aiden turned to the helm. "Pilot, shut down the main drive. Terminate decel. Flip the ship, bow forward."

The maneuver took less than 30 seconds. It put the *Sun Wolf* 108,000 kilometers from the *Markos* and closing at 54 km/sec. Seconds later, the *Sun Wolf* began taking laser fire directly on her bow shields. Aiden turned to Hotah. "Shield status?"

"They're holding for now. But the closer we get and the longer we take fire, the more power the shields consume. Our weapons systems consume a lot, too, but they're more effective at close range. We should still wait a few more minutes before firing."

"Where's the sweet spot, Lieutenant?"

Hotah entered a few commands on his tactical board. "In about six minutes. We'll be within 90,000 klicks. That's the minimum effective distance for our laser cannon."

"All right, Lieutenant, when we're there, fire at will."

Hotah started with laser cannon fire. Which made sense. It was the weapon that consumed the most power but the fastest to reach its target. It was also the one most likely to fail against the kind of shielding the *Markos* had. After 30 seconds of pulsed fire, the *Markos* remained unscathed. You couldn't see laser beams in space—nothing in a vacuum to scatter photons—but you could detect their heat signature if the beam was doing any damage. Nothing of the sort showed up on the tactical scans.

Missiles were next. Hotah launched a salvo of six Helix-100 antimatter torpedoes. Unfortunately, even at 300-G accel, they took nearly four minutes to reach the *Markos*. As the *Sun Wolf*'s shields steadily absorbed and dispersed increasing powerful laser fire, those four minutes were the longest Aiden could remember. And this time the effectiveness of the *Markos*'s shielding was plain to see. The optical scope showed the missiles reaching the *Markos* at blinding velocities, only to be scattered away from the ship, bouncing off its shielding like so many ping-pong balls. Even more discouraging, the *Markos* made no attempt to maneuver away from the incoming missiles. It became painfully clear how the *Markos* had pulled off their impossible victory back at Friendship Station.

"Damn!" Hotah said. "They're good."

By now the *Sun Wolf* had closed to within 60,000 kilometers. Still way too far for rail guns to be effective. They needed to be within 300 kilometers, and they'd never make it far. Things looked grim. Aiden could feel it from the crew. They got it. They were all very close to dying.

"All right, Lieutenant Hotah. Stand down. Divert all available power to the shields. Everything but command and life support. Then tell me how long the shields can hold out."

Hotah tapped at his board and said, "With weapons powered down, we've got about 17 minutes."

Aiden sighed. "We need to consider Plan B now."

Ro looked at him. "Plan B?"

"The way I figure it, if we light up the main drive to 3 Gs right now, we'd have enough time to zip past the *Markos* and dive into the voidoid for a jump back to Alpha-2 Hydri before our shields go down. The exact jump vector is already plugged into our nav computer."

The idea sounded hollow even as the words left his mouth, but it was a chance to stay alive a bit longer, and Aiden owed it to his crew to give them that option.

Woo shook his head. "If we do that, we may live for a while, but not for long. And we'd lose everything else. We'd be playing right into Black Dog's hands. He *wants* us out of this astrocell. He'll let us go and keep the *Markos* here, then shut down the gateway with a gravity bomb. We'll never get back here, nor will anyone else. We'll be stuck at Alpha-2 Hydri, unable to go anywhere else and unable to do anything to prevent the Rip from happening. Licet Omnia will own this new astrocell. They'll win. The rest of humanity will lose."

Aiden nodded, glad that Woo had played the foil for what he was about to propose next. "I agree, Elgin. Which brings me to Plan D."

Ro cocked his head, brows raised. "Plan D is it now?"

"Yes. *D* as in desperation. We light up to 3 Gs but don't dive into the voidoid. Instead, we ram the *Markos*. We abandon ship in the survey shuttles and the *Starhawk* just before impact before they have time to spot us and pick us off."

Aiden paused and looked around to let the implications of what he'd said sink in.

Woo stroked his braided beard and said, "It could work. I mean the ramming part, at least. The calculations I did on the strength of their gravity shield, from the way it deflected our missiles, shows me how good it is but also revealed its limitations. There's no way it could deflect something as massive as the *Sun Wolf* moving at the velocity we'd have at impact. It would annihilate them. Us too, of course."

"Us too?"

"Yes. There's very little chance that our escape craft could survive the resulting explosion, especially if we abandon ship that close to impact. Two massive, heavily armed ships with huge anti-matter reserves colliding at those velocities...?"

"But there's still a chance we might make it," Aiden countered. "It's a calculated risk, Elgin. Even if we didn't survive, the *Markos* would be annihilated. Black Dog would be erased from the equation, and the gateway would remain open. It would at least give the rest of humanity a fighting chance, if anyone survives the Rip."

Woo smiled. "It's a crazy idea. I like it. Who knows what could happen, eh?"

But they did know what was most likely to happen. It was suicide, albeit for a higher cause. Aiden took the time to look each one of his crew in the eye, then said, "We'll be slamming into either the *Markos* or the voidoid in less than 10 minutes. So, we vote now. Plan B, or Plan D. Vote your conscience. I'll withhold my vote unless there's a tie. Final comments?"

When no one spoke, Aiden took a deep breath. "All those in favor of Plan B, hold up your hand."

No one did. Not even Cass, who looked uncertain at first. Young Cass, who had so much more of her life to live, kept her hand down.

"Plan D it is, then. Pilot, lock in a collision course for the *Markos*. Maximum thrust. Then let's all get down to the shuttle bay and rig for immediate evacuation. Now."

Just as Pilot Abahem gave the thumbs-up sign, Billy Hotah spoke. "Sir! The *Markos* stopped firing on us."

"What the..." All the red-light indicators on the tactical screen turned green, and the power drain on their shielding rebounded. "Belay that order, Pilot."

Lilly Alvarez looked up at him. "Sir. Our shuttle bay doors are open. The *Perseus* is launching. Looks like it's headed toward the *Markos*."

"Who?" Aiden looked around and did a nose count. "Where's Colonel Aminu?"

Aminu was nowhere to be seen. Aiden hadn't even noticed his absence in the hubbub.

Black Dog's voice grated through the comm. No visuals this time, just audio. "A wise choice, Commander. I presume Dr. Woo has persuaded you to do the right thing, for you and your crew. I have always admired his altruism and sense of sacrifice for the greater good. As soon as your shuttle docks and we've confirmed that Dr. Woo is indeed aboard, I will allow you to voidjump back to Bound Space.

"Not that I mistrust you, of course, but our last communication troubled me. So I've launched a life-scan probe to intercept your shuttle before it arrives. It also does an excellent job at threat analysis. Checking for weapons or explosives. Things of that nature. Just a precaution. We'll see soon enough how you've played your hand."

Aiden didn't respond and gestured to Alvarez to lock down the comm. "Hail the *Perseus* with Level One encryption."

"The *Perseus*'s comm is locked out, sir," she said. "But I just received a Level One encrypted message from Colonel Aminu. It's marked urgent and stamped four minutes ago."

"Hutton, decrypt this message and run it to the bridge. Now, please."

Aminu's voice came through the comm. He sounded calm but resolute. "Commander Macallan. Divert your course now. Get as far away from the *Markos* as you can and keep your shields at max. When I dock aboard the *Markos*, I will disable the shuttle's Penning trap. Do not attempt to stop me. I'm certain you'll agree that what I'm about to do is your best remaining option. For you and all the people left in Bound Space. I have left a private message for my wife, Nadia. If you find a way to get back to the System, please make sure it's delivered to her. Thank you, Commander. I am glad now to have served with you. Goodbye."

Stunned silence fell on the bridge. Hotah spoke first. "Crazy bastard. He's going to blow up the *Markos*."

"Disable the shuttle's Penning trap? What's that mean?" Cass said. She had moved to the center of the bridge to stand next to Aiden, eyes wide.

"The Penning trap is part of the shuttle's M/AM engine," Aiden said. "It's the electromagnetic containment device for antimatter. Keeps the stored antimatter from interacting with matter. Shut the trap down and you've just detonated an antimatter bomb."

"That's impossible," Dalton said. "Those designs are 100 percent failsafe. No one can disable an engine's Penning trap. They're powered by minifusion generators with million-year lifetimes and permanently sealed."

"Aminu is DSI," Ro said. "They have a bag of dirty tricks no one can begin to imagine."

"Why is he doing this?" Cass said. Of all the people onboard who had wished Colonel Aminu to disappear—the man with the power to destroy her life—she appeared the most disturbed.

"But can it work?" Ebadi asked. "What about the life-scan probe? The bomb detectors?"

"Aminu is male, about the same height as Dr. Woo," Aiden said. "That covers the limits of what remote life scans can determine. As for detection of explosives? Weapons? There's none of that aboard the *Perseus*."

It was the best ruse possible under the circumstances. Aiden wondered how long Aminu had been contemplating it. What had changed inside the man? Or was it something that had always been there? Something hidden that had emerged just when it was needed? There was no way to stop Aminu now, short of shooting the *Perseus* down, and what would that accomplish? No. Honor the man's sacrifice. Accept the gift of life he offered and get the hell out of the way.

"We're about to find out if he passes the test," Ro said, looking up at the forward screen. They were now less than 10,000 kilometers from the *Markos*, about four minutes away.

When the *Markos*'s probe reached the *Perseus*, it turned and matched the shuttle's velocity, then hovered over it from several different positions. After an agonizing few minutes, the probe halted its investigations and escorted the shuttle toward the *Markos*'s opening shuttle-bay doors. The ruse had worked so far. But the *Sun Wolf* was dangerously close now, under 2,000 kilometers from the *Markos* and closing fast.

"Pilot. Alter course now. Parallel the ecliptic plane. Maximum thrust. Now."

The *Sun Wolf*'s attitude thrusters quickly reoriented the ship to a 90-degree angle then ignited the main thruster at 3 Gs. Because of their forward momentum, their new course was nowhere near a true 90-degree shift but enough to get them away from a devastating antimatter blast.

As they watched the *Perseus* enter the *Markos*'s docking bay, Black Dog's voice once again came over the comm. "Leaving so soon, Commander? You do realize that you can't outrun my laser cannons at this point, and your shields must be depleted. And now that it appears we have Dr. Woo aboard, I feel compelled to stop you from fleeing. It's been a pleasure doing business with you. Goodbye."

"Goodbye to *you*, Black Dog," Aiden said. "And—"

But before he could add *good riddance* to his farewell, the comm screen flashed blinding white. It took a few seconds for the optics to readjust, and when the screen cleared, all they saw was an expanding cloud of iridescent plasma.

"Shock wave strike in five seconds," Alvarez said.

Aiden turned quickly to Dalton. "Shut down main drive. Divert all power to shields."

It was a rocky ride for several very long seconds, but the shields held and the *Sun Wolf* was free at last.

37

HD 10180 SYSTEM
Domain Day 103, 2218

WHATEVER HAD CHANGED Victor Aminu had also changed the course of human history. Aiden was sure of that. Without his sacrifice, there wouldn't be a human history beyond the very near future. And yet he shouldn't be surprised. Aminu took the concept of personal honor more seriously than anyone he'd met, to the point of obsession. But why would a man in good health with a family and a position of prestige, honestly earned, willingly die for a cause he may understand rationally but showed little sign of believing in his heart?

Yes, Aiden himself had been ready to do the same, and ready to bear the responsibility of taking his entire crew with him. His own commitment was total—mind, body, and soul. Not only to save all of humanity, with all its faults and triumphs, its ugliness and beauty, its ignorance and brilliance, but also to save the miracle of life itself in Bound Space. Including Silvanus. He had Silvanus to thank for planting that commitment inside him, for the changes he'd undergone there. But Aminu? To what did he owe his apparent epiphany? What had instilled a commitment deep enough to sacrifice his life for? What had he seen on Shénmì?

"Commander. We've got the zero-point drive back online!" Dalton's voice jarred Aiden from his thoughts. He turned toward the Drive Systems station and saw both Dalton and Elgin Woo grinning widely. Woo sat in the station's seat with an EEG transducer cap fitted firmly to his head. The sole creator of the zero-point drive, of which there were only two currently in existence, Woo was also the sole keeper of the key to activate its function. Or, in this case, to reactivate it. Rebooting the system required the input of Woo's bio-neurological key, which amounted to sampling his brainwave patterns, a highly complex signature unique to each individual. Woo removed the EEG cap, glanced at Aiden, and nodded with a thumbs-up.

After the hazards of the *Markos*'s explosion dissipated, the *Sun Wolf* had returned to the voidoid and finally come to a complete standstill one kilometer from its horizon. From there, it took only a few seconds for Dalton and Woo to make the final ZPE measurement, enter it into the control-field computer, and for Woo to turn the key.

"Shall we test it now?" Dalton asked, still grinning.

"Normally I'd say yes," Aiden said. "But I think we have more pressing things to do with our time right now."

"Yes, quite right." Woo's expression had sobered. "Like reanimating the voidoids in Bound Space. And I fear time is running out. The Rip may already be happening there, in which case my plan may not work."

"Then let's find out," Aiden said. "We'll send a survey probe back into the Alpha-2 Hydri system. It'll report on the status of Bound Space via Holtzman transmission. The way I understand how the Rip works, it would show up first in star systems at the periphery of Bound Space, like at Alpha-2 Hydri. Things starting to pull apart, planets moving away from their star, moons away from planets. I presume the voidoids are affected too."

"Yes," Woo said. "And if the gateway voidoid at Alpha-2 Hydri moves too far from the star, it'll disconnect. It will no longer function as a gateway."

"Let's get moving then." Aiden instructed Faye Desai to prep and launch a Holtzman survey probe into the gateway voidoid on course for Alpha-2 Hydri. Granted, it was 91 light-years away,

but thanks to the Holtzman device's ability to transmit instantaneously between open voidoids, data from the probe began showing up on Desai's screen within minutes.

"Well, I can tell you a few things right now," she said without
looking up. "First of all, the probe isn't picking up any Holtzman
beacon signatures. Nothing from anywhere within Bound Space.
Normally, if you scan the range, you can pick 'em all up. But
there's nothing. That's a pretty sure sign that the voidoids are still
shut down."

"What about signs of the Rip?"

"The astrogation scan is showing some slight orbital perturba-
tion of the outermost planets. Very minimal right now, but definitely an anomaly, and within the margins of what you'd expect
from accelerated expansion of local space."

"So it's starting," Woo said. "We need to implement my plan
now."

Woo still hadn't explained what he had in mind beyond need-
ing Aiden's assistance.

"Wait," Desai said. "That's not all. The probe has spotted a
large artifact positioned within 350 meters from the gateway. It
wasn't there when we went through. It looks suspiciously like the
gravity bomb the *Markos* used to shut down V-Prime."

Aiden leaned over her shoulder to get a better look at the
image on her screen. "Yep. Just like it. Only bigger."

Woo nodded grimly. "Exactly what I'd expect Black Dog to
do. It's his insurance plan. If somehow we'd gotten through the
gateway before he blew us up, he made damn sure we wouldn't be
following him. Us or anyone else, for that matter. Licet Omnia is
permanently severing itself from the rest of humanity."

"While killing the rest of humanity in the process," Aiden said.
"Such a charming bunch. The question is whether that G-bomb is
ticking away right now, on a timer, or was it intended to be detonated remotely by Black Dog himself after we'd been taken out?"

"Or detonated by hostile-approach sensors," Woo said. "Either
way, we have to neutralize it. Now. If it is on a timer and shuts

down the gateway before I can implement my plan, the plan will fail. We need the gateway open and functional for it to work."

Not only would Woo's plan fail, Aiden thought, but they'd be stuck here to live out the rest of their days back on Shénmì with the knowledge that everything and everybody they've ever known had literally disintegrated. Unless, of course, Cardew and his minions found them first to put them out of their misery. He said, "I'll take a shuttle through the gateway and figure out a way to either destroy the bomb or move it away to a safe distance."

Even as he said it, Aiden realized the insurmountable difficulties in pulling it off. Billy Hotah, the weapons expert, was the first to point some of them out. "This device," he said, "is bound to have a suite of tamper-proof measures, all of which could set it off if triggered. One is probably a forward proximity detector. If it detects an unauthorized vessel approaching at a given distance, it'll trigger. Another would be a displacement sensor; if it's moved too far from its current position: boom. Or if it senses unauthorized contact, like from a grappling cable: also boom. Firing weapons at it may not work either. Moving within effective range of rail guns would set off the proximity trigger, as would incoming missiles. Laser fire from a safe distance takes a second or two to burn through the hardened armor this thing is sure to have, and that would set off another tamper trigger before it's destroyed."

"Then how do Black Dog's people work with these things?" Aiden said. "They must have some way of disabling the tamper triggers."

"They do," Cassandra Healy said. "And I have it."

She'd been hovering in the background, listening. Everyone looked at her in surprise as she stepped forward clutching a golden locket that hung from her neck. "It's in here."

"Explain," Aiden said.

Cass swallowed hard and looked warily at the faces around her, fully conscious that she had once again implicated herself as one of "Black Dog's people." Then she raised her head and looked directly at Aiden. "It's what they taught us at Rhea, when they were training us to operate the disrupter ships. They told us the gravity drones we deployed were all fitted with tamper-proof triggers. For sure, I know they all have those directional proximity detectors Billy mentioned...I mean Lieutenant Hotah."

She glanced quickly at Hotah. Her pale complexion betrayed a sudden blush. "When the drones are deployed and put in place," she continued, "the triggers are enabled automatically and set to self-destruct. They told us our ships were recognized by the drones, by some kind of frequency code the ships broadcast. That way we could work with the drones in the *Rachel Carson*, move them or whatever, without triggering them. They didn't want anyone else to capture one of them, to figure out how it works or where it came from. Stuff like that."

Aiden interrupted her. "Wait. The G-bomb will self-destruct if we trigger its security measures? Not detonate?"

Cass shook her head. "No. That's just for the drones we were using to control the voidoids. They told us about the gravity bombs that would be used for the Final Blow, that they would go off if anyone other than recognized vessels messed around with them. Maximum burst of gravity. Designed to shut down the voidoid. They said the bombs would recognize our ship's frequency code in case we ever had to deal with them in our work."

"If this thing has a proximity detector," Faye said, "how come the spy probe we sent through didn't set it off? It must have passed right by it."

"It's a *directional* proximity detector," Hotah responded. "They can be set to trigger when they sense objects approaching from a specific direction and within a specific distance. This one is probably set to detect approach only from the front. The back side faces the voidoid. That's pretty standard strategy when this tech is used to protect valuable space-based assets. That's why the spy probe didn't set it off on its exit from the voidoid. It just zipped past the bomb, came to a halt about one klick away, and didn't move forward."

"What's the usual trigger distance?" Aiden asked.

"Highly variable," Hotah said. "At least a kilometer, sometimes more. There's no way for us to know how it's set."

Aiden looked at the others. Cass's frequency code was exactly what they needed if they stood any chance of taking out the gravity bomb. He turned back to her. "And you said you had it? You have the frequency code? Here?"

"Yes!" she said, eyes wide with hope. "It's right here. I put it inside my locket. They gave us each a cryptochip with the frequency sequence on it. Just in case something went wrong with our ship's database. It was so important, they made us keep the chips on us at all times. I put it in my locket."

Cass opened her locket, removed the chip, and held it out for them to see, like a sacred offering. The thin 2 centimeter square of obsidian black nanocarbon alloy gleamed in the ambient light of the bridge. Aiden looked at it closely without taking it from her open hand.

"Standard Domain design," he said. "Should work with any standard shipboard transceiver. All we need to do is take a shuttle through, broadcast the code to disable the bomb's countermeasures, attach a rock mover to it, and send it on its way to the sun."

"I'll take the *Starhawk* to do it," Woo said. "It makes more sense."

Aiden cocked his head, eyeing Woo for motives other than solid reasoning. "How so?"

"First of all, it's safer. The *Starhawk* has a means of moving objects the size of this device without touching them. Remember the anti-gluon torpedo back at Chara? After stopping it in its tracks, I was able to move it to a safe location. Same tech, fundamental to the zero-point drive, just modified for other applications. Only the *Starhawk* has this capability.

"Secondly, you, Aiden need to remain here. You're the key to my plan for reanimating the voidoids. It can't work without you. If something should happen to me, if I get stuck on the other side, it can still work without me. I've left instructions with Hutton and with Dr. Devi. They'll know what to do. You have to trust me on this, Aiden. We can't risk losing you on this errand."

Still mystified by Woo's plans for him, he had to agree with the first reason. The *Starhawk* was now a far better instrument for the task, and only Woo could operate it.

"All right, Elgin. You're on," he said. "We'll leave the Holtzman probe in position back there so you can use it to communicate with us. I assume you have a standard cryptochip reader onboard the *Starhawk*? One that can accept Cass's chip and link it to an EM transmitter?"

"Of course," Woo said, smiling broadly. He turned to Cass with an open hand. "The cryptochip, my dear. If you please."

"Umm...there's just one thing about this chip," Cass said, looking sheepish. "It's keyed to my thumbprint. They did it as a security measure. It will only open with my right thumbprint."

Woo shrugged. "Then just activate it now, and I'll key it into the *Starhawk's* transmitter before I depart. I'll be broadcasting the frequency code the moment I emerge on the other side, and the bomb will immediately recognize me as a friendly vessel."

Cass shook her head again, and not happily. "It's not that simple. The chip can sense voidjumps. It'll stay activated through a voidjump, long enough for any kind of triggered weapon on the other side to recognize it. But after a minute or so, it shuts down and won't reactivate until I use my thumbprint again. Another security measure, I guess. It means I have to go with you for it to work."

Woo didn't look too happy either. He was always far more willing to risk his own life than to include others in that risk. "Well then," he said. "I guess I'll just need your right thumb. I'm sure Dr. Devi has a relatively painless way of removing it."

Cass looked horrified at the thought, then she rolled her eyes.

"Just kidding, Cass," Woo said with a sly smile. "Welcome aboard."

38

HD 10180 SYSTEM
Domain Day 103, 2218

"Are you still kidding, Dr. Woo?" Cass asked as they entered the shuttle bay. "We're riding in that thing?"

Woo and Cass walked up to the *Starhawk*. They both stopped and looked up at the vessel before them. Their expressions were similar but for different reasons. Woo stood, hands on hips, admiring his creation like a proud father. Cass, on the other hand, stared in disbelief and with genuine fear for her safety. She beheld a large, deep-black, saucer-shaped vessel that looked a little too much like the iconic "flying saucer" of mid-20th-century sci-fi movies.

The *Starhawk* was perfectly circular if viewed from above, about 60 meters in diameter. Viewed from the side, where they stood, it presented a sleek ellipsoidal profile no more than 10 meters at its tallest central point and tapered gracefully to a razor-thin edge all the way around. Its upper surface appeared seamless and glistened with an obsidian sheen, smooth and unbroken by any projections or ports of any kind. The only features apparent on the underside were a series of small openings spaced evenly just below the edge and one larger port about one meter in diameter and beveled in the direction of the ship's midline. Woo saw her peering at it and said, "The smaller ones are attitude thrusters and the larger one is main thruster."

She turned to him, eyebrows raised. "You *are* still kidding, right? That puny thing? For a ship that's supposed to go up to 92 percent light speed?"

"The secret of the zero-point drive lies not in the power of thrust," Woo said in a low, conspiratory tone. "Nor in the amount of reaction mass. What makes it work is the elimination of inertia. Without inertia, acceleration to relativistic velocities requires minimal thrust and is nearly instantaneous."

Cass did not appear comforted by this explanation. He went on. "It's perfectly safe, I can assure you. I've been jetting around in it for some time now, before my unplanned stay on Shénmì, that is. It's actually quite comfortable inside, if a little cramped. We should go now. Time is of the essence."

"If you say so," she said, following him up a ramp leading to an opening that had just now materialized on the vessel's underside as if by magic. The opening closed soundlessly behind them after they entered. Just like a flying saucer.

"Good morning, Mari!" Elgin Woo said as he led the way to the *Starhawk*'s tiny bridge compartment. Cass tentatively followed him in, looking around at the insides of the curious vessel. "This is Cassandra Healy. She will be accompanying us on our little outing. Cass, this is my AI, Mari."

"Hello, Dr. Woo," Mari's voice said, coming from no particular direction. "And I believe that, technically, it is evening and not morning. Pleased to meet you, Cass."

"Umm...likewise."

Woo sat in the command chair and began preparations for debarkation. The massive outer door of the *Sun Wolf*'s shuttle bay had already opened, clearing the way for their departure. Woo had Cass activate her cryptochip. When a tiny green light on its edge blinked a few times, then stayed on, she inserted it into the EM transmitter. After Woo confirmed the chip was broadcasting its frequency code loud and clear, he did a quick diagnostic on the craft's zero-point drive system and found it ready to go. He noticed Cass still standing, shifting her feet, looking uncomfort-able. "Cass, you can occupy the passenger seat here next to me."

"Okay. Thanks." She sat next to him, her hands fidgeting.

"Are you nervous about voidjump? You've had anti-TMD treatments, right?"

"Yes, I have. And no, voidjumps don't bother me much."

But something was eating her. Woo thought he knew what it was and decided to get to it sooner than later. As soon as Mari took control and began moving the *Starhawk* out, Woo turned to Cass. "So, what's bothering you? I know something is."

She didn't speak for a while, then took a deep breath and turned to face him. "Dr. Woo. I'm sorry for what I did. I had no idea that the voidoids might be alive, that what we were doing would hurt them. That it could even kill them. I would never intentionally hurt a living thing."

Her voice shook as she spoke her last sentence. "I know you wouldn't," he said gently. "I've been around you enough these last few days to see who you really are. I know now that your inten-tions were good. To help heal Earth. I can think of no finer goal myself. It is one of my goals as well. But you were deceived. Lied to. You and your mate, Joal, were manipulated. You wanted to believe what they told you, and you followed your heart, doing what you believed was best. You just forgot to use that very smart brain of yours to its full capacity."

She looked at him, brow furrowed.

Woo sighed. "In my work, critical thinking is the very first thing any scientist has to learn, and unfortunately it is one of the first things they most often forget. It requires looking into your-self to honestly identify assumptions that you *want* to believe, then arming yourself with that knowledge as you go about search-ing for the truth. It means that sometimes you'll never find the answer to what you seek. But no answer is always better than the wrong one. Especially when it effects the lives of others."

Cass nodded. "Be wary of what you want to believe."

"Yes, but don't hide from it. Don't reject it out of hand. Because it may be right in the end. That's where hunches come from. You just won't know until you've tested other possibilities, and those possibilities might never occur to you until you've put aside what you *want* to believe. It is truly one of the hardest things humans have to learn, not just scientists. Yet it is one of the most important things we can practice to ensure our survival as a species. Assuming, of course, the human race survives these coming days."

"We are clear of the shuttle bay," Mari said. "Now approaching the voidoid. Voidjump in three minutes."

"Thank you, Mari," Woo said as he turned back to Cass. "At any rate, I can't fault you for what you believed you were doing in the name of Green War. And I don't think any of the *Sun Wolf*'s crew do either. We see who you are. You've proven yourself without even trying. You're one of us now, if you want to be."

"Voidjump in 30 seconds," Mari said.

"Okay, Cass," Woo said. "Let's buckle up and get this job done."

He glanced at her right before the jump. Her eyes were relaxed. She was smiling.

~ ~ ~

In much less than a second, the *Starhawk* materialized in the Alpha-2 Hydri system, 91 light-years from where they had just been. The miracle of voidjumping had never ceased to fascinate Elgin Woo. Its very existence had proven a number of theories percolating for decades throughout the quantum physics community, had debunked a number of others, and spawned several new ones. No one knew for sure how the voidoids worked, or what they were, but Elgin Woo believed he was closer to the truth than anyone. Especially after his revelations on Shénmì.

It took only a few seconds after the jump for Woo to reorient his senses, and the first thing he did was to check on the well-being of his passenger. "Are you okay, Cass?"

She turned to him with an unfocused look in her eye, blinked a couple of times, and nodded. "I'm good."

Which was a relief to Woo. He'd been concerned that the jump might incapacitate her in some way—not an uncommon phenomenon for spacers with only a few jumps under their belts—rendering her unable to reset the cryptochip with her thumbprint in time. According to her, they had about one minute after the jump to do it before the G-bomb could potentially recognize them as a hostile vessel. He was about to remind her when he saw that she had already placed her thumb on the center of the chip. The tiny green light at its edge blinked three times, then stayed lit. She looked at him, smiling, and said, "Done."

Woo took a deep breath and let it out, releasing tension in his shoulders. "Well done, Cass. Good show. Mari, please send a Holtzman transmission back to the *Sun Wolf* notifying Aiden that we arrived safely. Then let's go find this blasted device."

"Yes, Dr. Woo. And I have already done both, as well as locating the *Sun Wolf*'s survey probe. It is nearby, and its Holtzman transmitter is functioning normally."

Woo smiled. Mari had been busy in the brief seconds after their jump. "Thank you, Mari. Where is the gravity device now?"

"It is about 7.5 kilometers away, lying stationary 325 meters from the voidoid's horizon. We are currently moving away from it on a post-jump course at 2 KPS."

"Is Cass's frequency code broadcasting in its direction?"

"Yes. Loud and clear."

"Good. Then reverse course, Mari, and bring us to a halt one-half kilometer from the device. And if you detect any sudden emergence of a gravity field, immediately engage the zero-point drive on a course away from the device."

That was a precaution. If they were unlucky enough to set the bomb off on their approach, not only would it shut down the gateway voidoid, but if the gravity field was as strong as Woo thought it would be, the *Starhawk* would instantly plummet into its gravity well, smashing into it with devastating force. But Cass's frequency code succeeded in convincing the device to allow their approach without incident.

He and Cass watched as the object grew larger on the small optical screen. Shaped like an egg, about 22 meters long and 16 meters at its widest point, it rotated slowly around its long axis. It was flat black and sinister-looking. Numerous short antennae and sensor hubs dotted its otherwise smooth exterior.

"How are we going to move it?" Cass asked.

Woo grinned at her. "I have a tractor beam."

"No way. Tractor beams don't exist. Anyone with half a brain knows that."

"You're absolutely right," Woo conceded. "I just call it that for fun. It's actually an application of Heim's gravitophoton field. It can be manipulated into either an attractive or a repulsive force mediated by gravitophoton particles generated in pairs from the zero-point energy of space. Basically, it's the transformation of photons into gravitational energy under the influence of strong EM fields. We do it with the same EM control fields that operate our zero-point drive."

Cass looked at him like his hair was on fire and said nothing.

"I realize it sounds preposterous," he said. "But I know it works. I've used it before."

"To move an anti-gluon torpedo after stopping it in its tracks," she said, nodding.

Woo made a surprised face. "What? Can't a man have *any* secrets?" Then he brightened and said, "This will be a much easier job."

Absently stroking his mustache, looking upward, Woo finally said, "Let's see...I think repelling the device away from us will be a safer option than drawing it toward us. All we need to do is place ourselves between it and the voidoid and give it a nudge outward."

He gave Mari his instructions. As the *Starhawk* moved in behind the device, he asked the AI, "How close do we need to get to impart a respectable shove?"

"Twenty meters should be close enough."

That was a bit close for comfort, but Woo knew that his "tractor beam" had limitations. If the mass was too great, then proximity became the determining factor. The closer the better.

"All right, Mari. Do it."

As they approached the device, its looming bulk filled the screen, blocking out the background stars. Woo felt the hairs on his neck prickle and his long, dangling mustache twitched like antennae sensing danger. Cass's breathing quickened as she fidgeted with the ring on her finger. The *Starhawk* came up behind the device to within 20 meters then halted. Mari had placed the ship in the optimal position for Woo's presser field to push it away from the voidoid and toward the star. Woo gave the command to commence.

At first, the drone didn't budge an inch. Just as Woo began to fear the worst, the device started moving away from them, slowly at first, then it picked up speed. By the time the presser impulse shut down 35 seconds later, expending its energy charge, the bad egg was moving away from them at 310 meters per second. The star's gravity well would do the rest.

"We did it!" Cass said, her green eyes alive with triumph. And a bit of redemption, Woo thought. Her radiant smile buoyed his own spirits.

"Yes, we did. Thank the goddess! Mari, notify the *Sun Wolf* that we have successfully disposed of the G-bomb."

They watched in silence as the sinister device grew smaller on the optical screen and finally disappeared. A malevolent creation built by malevolent people bent on closing the door on all of humanity, leaving them without hope. Now they at least had some small amount of hope. Woo had to take hold of that hope and make it a reality before it was too late.

"Time to get back to the *Sun Wolf*," he said. "Mari, take us back out and position the ship for a jump back to the HD 10180 system."

"Back to Woo's Star," Mari corrected him. "We will be ready to jump in four minutes."

Cass sat back with a satisfied smile, then turned to Woo and said, "I know you believe the voidoids are alive, Dr. Woo. But how do you know for sure? Or is it just something you want to believe?"

She had a mischievous gleam in her eye to punctuate her not-so-subtle reference to Woo's earlier discourse on critical thinking. He looked at her with renewed admiration.

He wanted to say: *Because a star spoke to me and told me so.* But he realized how crazy that would sound. Instead he said, "Ah. How does one know anything? I can only tell you that I have a 'hunch' that not only are the voidoids alive but also conscious, and that *everything* is conscious, to some degree or another. It's a hunch based on a growing body of evidence among the neo-quantum physicists. It suggests that consciousness exists at all levels, emerging from the interaction of physical matter with some universal quantum field of protoconsciousness. Fluctuations in the zero-point field of the vacuum may actually be the source of this protoconsciousness field."

"Sounds like a religious concept to me."

Woo shook his head emphatically. "This is not God I'm talking about. This viewpoint doesn't require the action of some divine Creator. This universal field is a natural phenomenon, one of the many that came into being with the Big Bang. This is about quantum effects playing a critical role in the phenomenon of consciousness. And after what I witnessed on Shénmì, I'm convinced it all has to do with vibrations."

Woo paused and looked at Cass to detect signs of boredom that often occurred in people with whom he shared his more exotic theories. She appeared genuinely curious. He continued. "Everything in the universe is vibrating, in constant motion, resonating at various frequencies. On every possible scale, nature vibrates. Ultimately, all matter is just vibrations. Quantum fields. But something unique happens when different vibrations come into contact with each other: they begin to vibrate together. *Spontaneously.* They synchronize in often surprising ways. It's called spontaneous self-organization.

"I believe that synchronized vibrations are the source of all consciousness. Not only in humans, but also in animals, plants, even inert matter. From that perspective, everything can be viewed as at least a little bit conscious. The degree of consciousness has to do with the complexity and interconnectedness of the vibrating elements in the system. Stones and boulders? Very rudimentary, low level of consciousness. But in biological systems, where vast multitudes of microconsciousnesses combine in synchrony, higher levels of macroconsciousness emerge."

He paused again. Cass remained attentive. He was about to continue when Mari interrupted. "We are in position to jump now. But something peculiar is happening to the voidoid."

Woo felt a sudden hollowness in his chest. "Peculiar? Like what?"

"It fluxed out and back in. Twice within 30 seconds. Each flux lasted about five seconds."

"Did you register any gravitational bursts from the G-bomb when we moved it?"

"Of course not." Mari sounded miffed at the notion that she would fail to warn him if such a thing occurred.

Cass looked at him, her brow furrowed. "Then it's the Rip, isn't it?"

"I'm afraid so. This voidoid is being pulled away from its cardinal position in the system. Local space is starting to expand out here, due the Rip, just as we suspected. Voidoids settle into precise positions relative to their host stars, at a distance determined by the total mass of the star system. If a voidoid gets moved too far away from its star, the connection to the star is broken and it can't be used for voidjumping. We need to jump now."

Mari said, "I suggest we use the zero-point drive for faster response time."

A risky move, but one that made perfect sense. If they used the ship's conventional thrusters for injection into the voidoid and a flux occurred on their approach, they wouldn't be able to change course in time to evade it. With the ZPD, however, their approach time would be nearly instantaneous, increasing the probability of a successful jump between fluxes.

"All right, Mari. Power up the ZPD, set it for 1 percent light speed, and make the jump at your discretion."

While Mari got busy, Woo used the *Starhawk's* navigational sensors to locate the voidoid and register its behavior. The voidoid flickered out of existence again for about five seconds before reappearing. The hollowness in his chest turned painful. He hoped Mari could time their jump just right, or else they'd get caught up in a flux and end up who-knows-where.

"The control field is now activated," Mari said. "Please prepare yourselves for a jump at any second."

He looked over at Cass. She had assumed a relaxed posture in her flight seat, but her hands gripped the armrests tightly and had turned white. Woo had just enough time to induce his usual prejump meditative state before he felt a sudden dislocation, as if every cell in his body had died and been reborn within a single nanosecond. And he heard the voice inside his head again. The voice of Woo's Star. *Welcome. You are always here.*

39

"**Y**OU'RE IN A unique position to do this, Aiden. In fact, you are the *only* person who can do it."

Elgin Woo spoke these words with a degree of dark import starkly out of place with the demeanor of a man lounging so easily on the most comfortable seating aboard the *Sun Wolf*. Sipping a rare and very old scotch, Woo sat across from Aiden in the captain's quarters, accompanied only by Dr. Sudha Devi. Aiden had deemed the occasion significant enough to pour each of them a dram from his highly coveted and obsessively guarded bottle of scotch, a brand bearing his own surname and aged nearly as long as he'd borne it. The occasion was to discuss Woo's plan to revive V-Prime and the rest of the voidoids of Bound Space. A plan to accomplish nothing short of saving the human race from certain and immanent destruction.

Right after the *Starhawk*'s successful voidjump back into Woo's Star system, Woo and Cass had returned to the *Sun Wolf* as quickly as possible and rejoined the crew with news of the gateway voidoid's sudden instability on the Alpha-2 Hydri side. The urgency of the situation had prompted Woo to initiate his plan without delay. The only good news came from their survey probe back at Alpha-2 Hydri reporting that, for now, the rate and duration of the fluxes were not increasing. The gateway remained

open about 80 percent of the time. They still had time to act, but
not much. Woo's primary task now was to convince the center-
piece of his plan to cooperate. And because it involved a totally
untested kind of neurolinkage, Woo had tried on a relaxed and
unpressured posture as he spoke.

Aiden saw right through it. He stroked his beard and nodded
thoughtfully. "Why me?"

"First of all," Woo said, "because of the massive neurogenesis
you underwent when the Rete resurrected you from the dead on
Silvanus, you now have way more neurons in your brain than anyone your age can ever have. From that standpoint, you have the
neuron count of a newborn but with the neural connections of
a 39-year-old man who also happens to be both a scientist and
a musician. And that, by the way, does make a difference in the
types of neural connections you've made. Important differences,
in this case.

"Secondly, you've done this before. You've successfully accomplished neurolinkage. Back at Chara. And not just with the Omi-
cron-3's neural net, like the pilots do, but with the Rete, a neural
net vastly more complex and deeper than any AI. A living intelligence millions of years old. You are the only person ever to do
that.

"And thirdly, you are known among the stars." Woo said this
with a dramatic flair, spreading his arms wide, looking upward.

Aiden tried not to smile. "What? I'm a celestial celebrity
now?"

"Indeed. The Rete knows who you are. Intimately, I might
add. Right down to your DNA. To rebuild you from the demolished state you were in after the crash, the Rete's mycelia entered
your body and explored everything about it. So the Rete knows
you biologically. It also knows your consciousness; it did similar
explorations of your mind during your neurolinkage on Silvanus.
The Rete *knows* you, in far more depth than any human could."

"Elgin, we're over 100 light-years from Silvanus now. What does this have to do with communicating with voidoids, much less the voidoid out here in another astrocell?"

"Ah, where to begin?" Woo paused as if waiting for the universe to answer him and then said, "I'm not going to dive into my entire theory of the voidoids. I'll only tell you this. I have no doubt now that voidoids are living creatures. They're conscious and intelligent. They are intimately connected to their host stars, who may in fact be living creatures themselves, and information is shared between them.

"All voidoids in an astrocell are daughters of the primary voidoid, the first voidoid to settle in a given region of space. Like all living creatures, voidoids propagate. Once a primary voidoid settles and gives birth to a family of daughter voidoids to establish an astrocell, it can also 'seed' an adjacent region of space with another protovoidoid, which could in turn serve as the primary voidoid for another astrocell. The astrocell we're in now is adjacent to our own Bound Space astrocell, and we know now that they're linked together by a gateway. So it's safe to assume that the two primary voidoids are related. And since Sol is a good two and a half billion years younger than Woo's Star, I'm guessing that V-Prime is the daughter of this voidoid sitting out there right now." Woo pointed to the forward screen where the voidoid would be displayed if it could be seen.

"Let's call it Woo's Voidoid for now," Aiden said.

Woo made a short bow. "I'm honored. But for clarity only. Having a star named after me is quite enough."

"Nonetheless," Aiden said, "so, let's assume Woo's Voidoid and V-Prime are relatives. And they're also neighbors."

"Yes! And they 'talk' to each other. Like gossiping neighbors, voidoids share inside information on what goes on in their realms. When you linked with the Rete back on Silvanus, your expansive out-of-body experience—augmented by psychoactives the Rete itself provided you—was exactly what it seemed: com-

munication with elements of the entire system, including the star
Chara and its voidoid. In short, you made a good impression."

"And this 'good impression' I made on the Chara voidoid was
somehow communicated to the voidoids out here, in this astrocell?"

"Yes," Woo said with a certainty that belied the highly whacky
nature of what he proposed. "Probably communicated first to V-
Prime, then from V-Prime to the primary voidoid here, Woo's
Voidoid as you call it. Probably through the gateway, the open
door between the two neighbors, between daughter and mother.
I believe that you will be recognized here in some novel way.
Recognized by Woo's Voidoid as a living native of her daughter's
realm."

"Right, Elgin. An inhabitant from a species who deliberately
tried to kill her daughter, along with all of her granddaughters.
I'm sure she'll be overjoyed to make my acquaintance."

Woo shook his head. "No. Killed by *other* members of our
species. A few rotten apples the rest of us oppose. Who are not
representative of our race. We need to appeal to her, to let her
know we're appalled by what happened, saddened by it, share her
grief and anger, that we have punished the culprits and vow never
to let it happen again. Then we need to enlist her help. Before it's
too late."

The personification Woo used to characterize this family affair
made some kind of intuitive sense to Aiden, whether or not it was
actually true. "And you're sure it's not too late already?"

"Yes," Woo said confidently. "I believe the voidoids of Bound
Space are in stasis, not dead. Still revivable. But not for much
longer. Woo's Voidoid may already know this, and I'm betting
that she's capable of doing something about it."

"Reviving V-Prime's voidoids? If she can do that, why hasn't
she done it already?"

"I honestly don't know, Aiden. Maybe she's unwilling to act
because she perceives the organic life forms spawned in her
daughter's astrocell are a bad lot, an infectious disease that could

threaten her and other astrocells. So she'll let Bound Space self-destruct first before reseeding it. If that's true, then we need to show her that we're not the bad guys. That as a race we revere her creation and recognize that we would not even exist without it. When she realizes our insight into all that, she'll do something about reviving Bound Space. I'm sure of it."

"Like what?" It all sounded like a children's fairytale to Aiden. But he'd learned long ago that Elgin Woo's farfetched narratives ended up describing reality more often than not.

"Exactly what and how, I don't know," Woo said. "But like all living things, survival of the species is paramount. If there's a way to save the daughter, the mother will find it."

Aiden had to smile at the audacity of it. "And you think I can somehow communicate with this voidoid to convince her of all that. How the hell does that work?"

"Initially, your very presence in reaching out to her will prove that not all sentient inhabitants of her daughter's astrocell are dead, as would be the case if the astrocell was already destroyed beyond repair. It should also convey the fact that we are advanced enough to have found a way to communicate with her and that we earnestly seek her aid. Coming from one who she may actually *recognize* through her network, her interest will be piqued. Beyond that, she can read the story of what really happened in Bound Space from what you know of it. The neurolink will give her access to that information. You don't need to do anything. Just be you."

Aiden found himself wondering if Elgin Woo had finally lost his senses but was fascinated enough by the man's vision to allow him to continue.

"I believe the interaction will be enough to convince her that our race as a whole did not intend to kill off her daughter's family, an act that we condemn and are striving to atone for. You know all those things, Aiden. And feel them. I know you do. That, along with all the rest of it, makes you our best emissary. Our only *possible* emissary. Our only hope."

Our only hope. Nothing like a little pressure, Aiden thought. Once again he stood alone, balancing on the sharp edge of destiny, just as he had done on Silvanus, with the fate of all humanity in his hands, teetering uneasily between total annihilation and the promise of a new age for the human race. Was he up to it this time? Did he even have a choice?

He tossed down the last few milliliters of scotch and leaned back in his chair. "Okay, Elgin. Assuming all these hunches of yours are anywhere close to correct, I'll ask again. How does this work? I mean physically. Communication with the voidoid. Obviously, I don't just call her up on the comm and ask to chat."

"Brain waves and synchronization," Woo said, grinning widely and holding his hands out like it was the most obvious thing in the world.

Aiden crossed his arms again, steeling himself for another journey through the twisting landscape of Elgin Woo's theoretical world. "Go on."

"A person's brain waves are a classic example of synchronization," Elgin said, immediately warming to the subject. "From delta waves all the way to gamma waves, they're all the result of billions of neurons synchronizing together as they use electrochemical impulses to communicate with each other. The different kinds of brain waves characterize various levels of human consciousness. Alpha waves during deep relaxation, eyes closed. Beta waves during alert wakefulness. And so on. But gamma-wave activity is unique. It indicates a state associated with large-scale coordinated activities like perception or focused consciousness. It's also associated with meditative states and spiritual or mystical experiences. The shared resonances of gamma-wave synchrony in humans involves a much larger number of neurons and neuronal connections than any of the other signature waves. It's global in nature rather than focal.

"And that's the fourth reason you, Aiden, are the ideal person for this mission. Your greater number of neurons and neural connections makes it far easier for you to achieve gamma synchrony.

In fact, gamma state is your normal waking state. I've seen your EEG records, done after you returned from Silvanus. You're buzzing at around 50 hertz right now as we speak."

"Those are private medical records, Dr. Woo," Devi protested. "How did you get access to them?"

Woo shrugged. "I apologize. I felt it was important."

"You didn't answer my question." Devi's eyes darkened, anger starting to brew.

"It's okay, Sudha," Aiden intervened. "I hereby give my consent. Go ahead, Elgin."

Woo bowed his head contritely before continuing. "The normal waking state for everyone else is beta rhythm, between 12 and 30 cycles per second. Gamma waves range from 30 to around 100 cycles per second. Only highly accomplished Zen monks or Licensed Pilots in neurolink exhibit gamma synchrony as a baseline state. Also, many trained musicians show superior gamma synchrony while playing or listening to music."

"Elgin, I'm not a Zen monk," Aiden said. "Where's this going?"

"But you *are* a trained musician, and you've succeeded in neurolinkage. Where is this going? It will be useful in communicating with the voidoid. People in gamma synchrony are able to alter their own brain-wave rhythm more easily, at will. Using various techniques, they can modulate their EEG frequencies within the gamma range, between 30 and 100 hertz."

"And?" Aiden leaned forward impatiently.

"Stars sing," Woo said, as if it was common knowledge. "All stars have a unique resonant frequency. Their surfaces expand and contract in regular cycles creating something like sound waves, only propagated through plasma, not air. Our sun, Sol, has a five-minute cycle. That's a frequency of about 0.0033 hertz. Way too low for anyone to hear, since our audible range is about 20 to 20,000 hertz. But when you shift Sol's resonant frequency into the audible range by the appropriate numerical factor, you get

69.3 hertz, a tone that corresponds almost exactly to a low D flat. That's one octave up from the lowest D flat on the piano.

"The star here, Woo's Star, has a resonant frequency of about 0.0035 hertz. Shift *that* frequency into the audible range by the same factor and you get a D tone, one scale step up from Sol's D flat."

Aiden nodded, beginning to follow Woo's torturous meanderings. "That's the lowest D you can play on a four-string bass. That's about 73.5 hertz."

"Exactly! And that's your instrument, is it not? Bass?"

It was, in fact, Aiden's instrument. While he hadn't played in a group context for many years, he had learned the instrument in his youth, inspired by his love for 20th-century American jazz. He had earned his way through college partly by playing in retro jazz combos, and he still practiced whenever he had the time. For the love of its sound if for nothing else.

"And you have perfect pitch," Elgin stated. "Right?"

With some difficulty, Aiden dismissed his irritation over how many intimate details Woo apparently knew about him. "Yes, that's right."

"So you could easily reproduce in your mind that exact note? Visualize or hear it?"

"You mean during neurolinkage? Yes, I'm pretty sure I could. But I thought the idea was to communicate with the voidoid, not the star."

"Ah!" Elgin exclaimed. "That's the beauty of it. Voidoids share the same resonant frequency as their host stars. It's how they're linked, how they communicate. They're another example of coupled oscillators."

Aiden got it now. Hook himself up in neurolink with Hutton, audibilize in his mind the low D tone to induce a gamma brainwave pattern at around 73.5 Hz, get Hutton to broadcast it out to the voidoid via EM field, and: "Hello!" Instant connection. But he had to ask, "Why not just broadcast that frequency artificially from our EM emitter?"

Woo shook his head emphatically. "Because a 73.5 hertz wave from your brain will look different than a 73.5 hertz wave from an EM emitter. More overtones, uniquely organic. The voidoids may not be organic life forms, but they are alive and I believe they recognize organic intelligence. I think it was their original purpose, in fact, to stabilize pockets of space to allow the evolution of organic life. The voidoid will recognize your brainwave pattern as coming from one such organic life form. It will listen. Then it will recognize you as the man from Silvanus."

The Man from Silvanus. Aiden shook his head but refrained from the snarky comeback on the tip of his tongue. Much of this process was still unclear to him, and he wanted a better grasp of it. "Communication is a two-way street, Elgin. If we broadcast this introduction as an EM frequency, how do you expect the voidoid to respond? Voidoids don't produce EM emissions, or emissions of any kind that we know of."

Woo was smiling even before Aiden finished. He'd anticipated the question. "That's correct. But remember, voidoids operate by sensing gravitational fields, so it's safe to assume they can register gravity *waves* too. In fact, I believe voidoids communicate among themselves via gravity waves, using variations in G-wave frequencies as a kind of language."

"And?"

"With the technical assistance of your brilliant Comm/Scan Officer, Ms. Alvarez, I have devised a unique transceiver that broadcasts EM frequencies and receives in gravity-wave frequencies. EM uplink and G-wave downlink."

Aiden shook his head. "Impossible. Gravity wave frequencies are way too low for that to work. We'd be waiting days, or weeks, to receive even a single bit of information."

"Gravity waves do come in higher frequencies," Woo said. "Up to 10 or more hertz. It's not commonly encountered in nature, but I know for a fact that voidoids can produce them. I've measured them in my latest research on the voidoids."

This was news to Aiden and probably news to the entire scientific community, if Woo had ever gotten around to publishing his work.

"So, here's what we do," Woo continued. "A subroutine has been added to the pilot's linkage cap designed to monitor your brain-wave patterns. You'll initiate neurolink with Hutton. He'll convert your brain waves into EM emissions, which we will then broadcast toward the voidoid. You will attempt to induce a gamma wave of approximately 73.5 hertz, corresponding to the low D note on a contra bass. If the voidoid recognizes the emission as an invitation to sync up, then it may attempt to link with you via the G-wave downlink. It will be a most unique neurolinkage."

And a most untested and potentially dangerous one, Aiden thought. But now he found himself eager to try. Eager to experience once again the weird and edgy transcendence of a realtime neurolinkage with an alien intelligence. "And if the voidoid does decide to link up?"

Woo pursed his lips, looking upward with brows furrowed. "If that happens..."

The pause prompted Aiden to answer himself. "If that happens, I'm on my own. It's totally new territory. I get it."

Woo's face softened, but his eyes remained focused. "I have utmost faith in you, Aiden."

Aiden took a deep breath, as a man does just before plunging into dark and unknown waters. "All right, Elgin. Sign me up."

40

ADVANCED NEUROLINKAGE IS an act of deliberate self-destruction. The self, in this case, is what we identify as the essence of who we are, the "I" that we become comfortable with over the course of our lives, that defines the boundaries between us as individuals and everything else outside of us. That self melts away during neurolinkage. But it does not disappear. Rather, its boundaries dissolve as it expands to become one with an infinitely larger whole, to the point where there is no "outside" because everything—the entire universe—is now within. And at that point, self is replaced with nothing but awareness. Pure and simple. Timeless.

No one knew this better than Aiden Macallan, simply because he'd been there. The memory of it now blossomed vividly as he settled into the pilot's webbed couch and reached for Pilot Abahem's linkage cap. It was a state of consciousness that classical psychology would call dissolution of ego. Buddhists or experienced meditators recognized it as the letting go of all fears, desires, and defenses, transcending the ego's preoccupation with the past and the future. Licensed Pilots knew it through their routine neurolinkages with the vast neural nets of the Omicron AIs, for the expressed purpose of navigating voidships through high-velocity voidjumps. That kind of functional linkage with an intelligence other than one's own was impossible without dissolution of the self.

Aiden did not have the pilots' training, but he did have what amounted to a new and improved brain, thanks to the Rete. His new wetware had allowed him to accomplish extended neurolinkage on two occasions, both times with the Rete on Silvanus, either directly or through Hutton. Regardless of the purpose of neurolinkage—whether to navigate voidjumps or to communicate with the Rete—it almost always generated a transcendent experience, a vision of unity in which all things in the universe, including the self, are encompassed. And the absolute certainty of this perception usually evoked sublime joy and feelings of blessedness.

And so had it been for Aiden—except these illuminating side effects failed to persist after the linkages were broken. While they may have had some subtle transformative effect, he fully realized that the core of his life had not been significantly changed, his consciousness not permanently elevated. Instead, the sharp disconnect between his mystical experiences of oneness and the banality of his everyday life, dominated by the machinations of ego, only deepened his depression.

The pilots were different. They had been trained from childhood to deal with the disconnect. Some used Continuum to ease the drop during their off-hours. Some of them cultivated meditative lives that precluded social interactions anywhere outside their insular, self-supporting community. But then neurolinkage was their job. They had no real need to function in any other capacity, unlike Aiden, who was tasked with commanding a voidship and pursuing a mission of incomparable consequence. Without those grave responsibilities, he could have very easily succumbed to the addictive embrace of Continuum and become lost forever in a futile quest to relive some semblance of the authentic experience. But commitment to his crew and to his mission, to Skye, and ultimately to his own self-respect, had steered him away from that ruinous fate.

Dr. Sudha Devi had been instrumental in guiding him on his upward path. She stood next to him now, along with Elgin Woo, Ro, and Dr. Ebadi. "I'd ask if you wanted a dose of Continuum," she said, "to help augment your neurolinkage. But I think I know the answer."

Of course she did. Aiden smiled. "I'm good without it, Sudha. Thanks anyway. I've been inside Hutton's head before. Despite the clutter, I know my way around."

"Clutter?" Hutton said, sounding miffed. "What could you possibly mean by that?"

Despite the AI's recent advances in understanding the complexities of humor, Aiden was never quite sure if his responses to it were in the same spirit. "See you in a few seconds, Hutton."

And with that, Aiden picked up the linkage cap. Translucent, silky soft, and pliant, it felt organic, almost alive. He placed it on his head and fitted it firmly over his hair. The pilots shaved their heads for convenience and quick connections, but human hair was no obstacle to the cap's nanofibers. Aiden laid back and began the meditative breathing technique Devi had taught him. He kept his eyes open but fixed on an imaginary point about four feet in front of him, also part of the technique. Then he said to no one in particular, "And away we go."

A few seconds later, he felt his scalp tingling as millions of nanofibers found their way through tissue and bone, tapping into his cerebral cortex. His view of the imaginary point, and of the people standing around him, collapsed and was replaced by a brilliant white light. He felt blinded for a moment, then, as his inner eyes adjusted, he saw himself inside a long corridor. The light emanated from everywhere within it, as if the corridor itself was made of light. He saw a door at the end of the corridor. It was closed, but he knew it was for him to open.

Since he'd been here before, Aiden recognized the door as the bioelectric portal into Hutton's consciousness. The recognition brought him to the door in an instant. He touched it and it opened, inviting him inward and outward at the same time.

Again, he was bathed in a white light. Not as blinding as before, it undulated serenely, warmly, changing shape like a living aurora borealis. He heard Hutton's voice, but not as a sound. More like seeing the voice in the undulating curtains of light. The voice said, "Nice of you to drop by, Aiden. Make yourself comfortable."

Hutton. Unmistakably him. You just had to love the guy. Over the years, Aiden and the AI personality he'd created had grown both more alike and different from each other.

Time to get to work. And with that thought he heard a musical note, sustained and even. It had the tone of a bowed contra bass. Aiden's talent for perfect pitch allowed him to identify it as a low G, which he knew to be 49.0 Hz. Then he understood. He was hearing his own brain waves. He'd been told that he was different from everyone else, that his normal waking brain waves ran in the low gamma-wave range, somewhere between 40 and 60 Hz. So his brain was humming along in low G, right in the middle of that range. Hutton had merely converted it into an audible tone inside Aiden's head for his benefit. His task now was to raise it to low D, to 73.5 Hz.

Aiden had an idea of how to do this. One of the first jazz classics he had learned as a bass player was a composition titled "So What," written and performed by mid-20th-century jazz master Miles Davis. It was a modal piece in D minor with an E-flat minor midsection, brilliant in its simplicity and revolutionary for its time. The bass line became famous in the jazz world back then and a must-learn for any aspiring bassist. The line, played by legendary bassist Paul Chambers, was built on the D minor Dorian scale, but its tonal center landed strongly on that low D. Aiden played the line now in his head, just a few times to get the sound of it firmly planted in his brain. *Damn, that thing did swing!* Then he brought it to a halt on the D and bowed it on his imaginary bass to sustain the note.

After a few more moments, he stopped the imaginary bowing and continued to audibilize that note in his head, like a trance drone. The exercise must have worked, because he heard the low

G of his original brain wave move up eight scale steps to sync with the low D drone in his head. He had succeeded in coaxing his brain waves up to 73.5 Hz. Hutton then converted the wave pattern into an EM signal, including all its organic overtones, and began to serenade the voidoid with it. If it worked and the voidoid decided to "get to know" him, the next phase was bound to be an adventure. Aiden hoped he wouldn't lose his mind in the process.

He didn't have to wait long. What appeared to be a perfectly circular hole materialized within the undulating light before him. Opening up steadily, it burned jet-black, like the flaming heart of nothingness. Then the sound came: a sustained musical note, a very low one. Aiden's excitement grew as he recognized the note as a D, but one octave below the drone his brain generated. It seemed to be emanating from the expanding hole.

At first, the two tones were ever so slightly out of sync. He could hear the harmonic interference pattern, like when tuning two adjacent strings on a bass to the same note. Gradually, the lower tone adjusted to the discrepancy and came perfectly in tune with Aiden's tone, but one perfect octave below. Once synched up, the two tones began to resonate together and to grow louder. That was when Aiden felt himself expanding and lifted up. Lifted and drawn into the all-consuming, jet-black hole. He felt himself screaming but couldn't tell if it was from ecstasy or terror. Maybe it was both.

Then he (his ego?) dissolved. Completely. He became the resonant tone, and the tone was pure awareness. Within the new awareness he detected the presence of another consciousness, close by and very different from his own. He felt its slow, powerful pulse as it gently pushed and pulled him. Back and forth, again and again, as if he were caught in the hypnotic tidal flow of some vast cosmic ocean. Aiden surrendered to it, and as he did, the presence became more clearly defined. It felt like a thoroughly alien consciousness. Not at all like the Rete, whose consciousness had emerged from purely organic origins, carbon-based, biological, and as such bore some evolutionary similarity to Aiden's own.

This consciousness, however, was not even chemical. It felt more like a complex manifestation of pure energy, a highly synchronized network of radiations, so alien that Aiden faltered. How could he even begin to communicate with such an entity? Despair rose from his center like a black viper, dimming the awareness he had attained. In that moment he heard a voice. It said, *"Welcome. We are joined."*

41

AIDEN SENSED INTENSE curiosity from the being that had spoken to him, focused like a brilliant spotlight of scrutiny. Yet there it bore no hostility, only genuine inquisitiveness. He felt bathed in a radiant intelligence that glowed with a passion to know Aiden's soul. It moved him to tell his story, the collective story of all his kind. He knew verbal constructs would be useless. This time he resisted despair and instead merely stopped trying. The pure awareness he had found earlier returned. Absolute certainty returned. His self dissolved and the story began telling itself.

It started with himself as a ten-year-old and the gaping hole in his life that opened up like a wound after his mother, Morgan, was killed on Luna. A wound that had never healed.

Then he saw his father looking at him, the lost look in his eyes, the crushing sadness over the loss of his mate, an unrelenting darkness that became the weapon he turned on himself as he took his own life. And Aiden's wound grew deeper.

Then he saw the years of terror and brutality he'd spent in prison serving a sentence for the revenge he'd taken on the untouchable powers that had killed his mother. Inside that hell, the cruelty that men could inflict upon their brothers without remorse, the hatred and ignorance, the injustice, had left a scar on his soul deeper than any mark they could have burned into his skin.

But it made him stronger.

Then he saw the chance for redemption he'd been given by the man who later became his captain on the *Argo*, Ben Stegman, the man who had become his second father, quietly nurturing his gifts. Challenging him to become the better man he truly was. Better, smarter, stronger.

He saw Skye Landen, his lover and mate, who had shown him how to let love back into his life, how two people could become one through love and still remain as two. Who taught him that the path of the heart always ran true. That he could never become lost following that path.

He saw the wonder of Silvanus as he approached her aboard the *Argo*, a living earthlike planet that had beckoned to him in his dreams and became reality upon awakening.

Then he saw his own death in the shuttle crash on Silvanus.

And saw his reawakening in the forests of Silvanus, his rebirth, the gift of life from death given to him by the Rete, a planet-spanning neural net from which a global consciousness had emerged—ancient, deep, and sublime—transforming Silvanus into a living organism.

He saw the luminous stag, the dream creature who had silently guided him through a living landscape toward his destiny. Toward himself.

He saw, or rather relived, his neurolinkage with the Rete's neural net, his becoming one with the planet to save it from self-destruction. To offer the gift of rebirth to Silvanus, a gift hidden in the biology of his own body. And he watched as the stag passed from dream into reality, to join the planet's web of life, to help heal Silvanus and make it whole again.

Silvanus. The planet nurtured by the radiant energy of the star Chara. The star itself nurtured by the loving embrace of its voidoid. The King given life and power by his invisible Queen.

Then he heard the silent screams of the voidoids filling the far reaches of Bound Space with cries of pain and the bleak sorrow of betrayal.

He saw Black Dog and knew him by his true name, Cu Dubh, tormenter of living voidoids. Killer of voidoids. Cu Dubh, the dark henchman led by an even darker and more dangerous spirit.

Aiden saw his own battle against the darkness within himself mirrored on the larger scale of human history, a battle for the future of human life. He felt his own determination to sway the balance away from the dark, into the light. His will to destroy Black Dog in a fiery flash of oblivion.

But Black Dog's master remained. To confront Cardew, Aiden would have to don the armor of light and become a warrior against darkness, wielding the weapon of love.

Love. He saw all the people he had ever loved in his life, and all the ones loved by others who loved in return. Aiden seized upon that vision and knew it was the key to his quest. Love was the key. He heard Skye's voice. *All began in love. All returns to love.*

Aiden held that glowing key in his hands and offered it to the consciousness in his presence—to this strange but suddenly familiar being. At the end of Aiden's story, it was the only offering he had to give, but he knew it was the only one that mattered.

The key became a white dove made of fire. It flew upward from his hands, burning brighter as it ascended until it blossomed into a blue-white light so intense that Aiden could no longer look at it directly. Burning like a star. The light slowly shifted from white to iridescent blue. Simultaneously, the low drone of the D note began to drop in pitch, just slightly until it reached a D flat, one scale step down, and stayed there, filling space with the power of that tone. D flat. The resonant frequency of Sol and therefore also of V-Prime.

After what could have been hours or seconds, the light began to fade. Not intrinsically, but as if moving away from him, and the D-flat tone decrescendoed along with it. The black hole from which it had emerged constricted and finally closed. With the resonant tone echoing in his mind, he felt himself once again floating in the undulating soft light, the aurora borealis that he recognized as Hutton's consciousness. It felt pleasantly warm, bathed in the humming energy of the AI's neural net. It would be so easy to rest here just a little while longer. To be free of toil and anxiety.

Then he heard the sound of a bird's wings rustling nearby. It was not the white dove. It was a disturbing sound, agitated, not at all consonant with his surroundings. The wings grew louder and fluttered so close to his ear that he flinched back from it. He saw a dark shadow pass over him and coalesce into a black crow. It turned to stare at him with hard black eyes and made a harsh cry before it disappeared into the undulating light. It left him with a deep sense of foreboding and alone in the wavering light, bewildered.

But not quite alone.

"Aiden?" Hutton's voice said. "You are unharmed." What should have been a query into his well-being was instead a statement of fact, as if Hutton had completed his own evaluation and was satisfied with the results. As Aiden's sense of self gradually returned, he realized that in fact he felt fine. A little shaken from the fleeting vision of darkness—he'd have to ask Hutton about it later—but otherwise alert and oriented.

"Thank you for your visit," Hutton said. "We should do this more often."

And with that, a gentle popping sound like a giant soap bubble bursting brought Aiden completely into his own body. He blinked and looked around, realizing he was still reclined in the pilot's couch, still on the bridge of the *Sun Wolf*. The anxious faces of his crew surrounded him. Woo looked pleased, all-knowing. Devi looked concerned but relieved. Ro looked like he always did, stoic but subtly amused. Maryam Ebadi also looked relieved but intensely curious.

"Welcome back," Woo said. "How was your trip?"

"It was..." Aiden was utterly at loss for words. Words were so damn inadequate.

They all seemed to understand, and no one pressed him further. In the comforting silence that followed, he heard Lilly Alvarez's voice. "Something is happening to the voidoid."

Woo looked at Aiden with a broad smile. "Ah. And now it begins."

Ro stepped in to help Aiden up from the couch, and they all moved closer to the forward screen where a realtime image of the voidoid's position was displayed. The *Sun Wolf* had moved off to a distance where the voidoid, 18 kilometers in diameter, would just barely fill the screen. Like all voidoids, the invisible sphere was marked only by the absence of background stars, except now an image of the voidoid steadily materialized, shimmering with faint blue light as it rotated slowly in the deep blackness of space.

The shimmering blue light turned bright white and began to oscillate, spreading ripples of luminescence across the sphere's surface. The ripples formed a complex pattern of intricate standing waves undulating over the voidoid's horizon. The frequency of the ripples increased, faster and faster, until it shown as a single brilliance growing more intense in magnitude. Then, in an explosive flash that startled the onlookers and briefly overwhelmed the optical sensors, the lightshow abruptly blinked out.

"Is it still there?" Sudha Devi asked with a physician's concern.

"Oh yes," Ebadi said, looking over Alvarez's shoulder at the ECI monitor. "Bold and beautiful as ever."

But Alvarez was already on to something new. "Commander. I just received an image sent from our Holtzman survey probe back at Alpha-2 Hydri."

Not waiting for a response, she relayed the transmission to the forward screen. It was an image of the Alpha-2 Hydri voidoid at the POP, the gateway into Woo's astrocell. They witnessed a phenomenon identical to the one they'd just seen happening to the voidoid here. And when it was over, the probe's navigational sensors confirmed that the Alpha-2 Hydri gateway voidoid was stable, alive, and well.

Aiden nodded and echoed Ebadi's words. "Bold and beautiful as ever."

Now all they could do was wait.

Two anxious hours later, Lilly Alvarez exclaimed, "Commander! I'm picking up Holtzman beacons from all over Bound Space! Over a hundred of them and increasing."

Alvarez's excitement lit up the bridge, everyone else smiling with her. It meant that all the voidoids within Bound Space were waking up. Then her eyes went even wider. "I've picked up Holtzman signals from V-Prime. From home!"

Just after she said this, a voice came over the comm. "This is Vice Admiral Stegman hailing the UED vessel *Sun Wolf*. This is a recorded hail. Please respond."

After a brief pause filled with cosmic background static, the message repeated. "This is Vice Admiral Stegman hailing the UED vessel *Sun Wolf*. This is a recorded hail. Please respond."

As the hail continued to repeat, Aiden realized he'd never been so happy to hear the cantankerous old admiral's voice. The voice of home.

Woo beamed at him and said, "You did it!"

Aiden shook his head and looked around at his crew. "No. We *all* did it. All of us together. We won this battle together. Thanks to all of you."

He knew it wasn't over yet. In fact, in some ways it was just beginning. Another phase, at least. Cardew was still out there, somewhere in this astrocell. But now was not the time to dwell on what would come next. Now was the time to celebrate a victory, to rejoice in the knowledge that their worlds had been saved from destruction, that their very reality had been returned to them. Time to rejoice. And time to go home.

42

ALPHA-2 HYDRI SYSTEM
DOMAIN DAY 104, 2218

B UT HOME NOT quite yet.

The matter of guarding the gateway voidoid connected to Woo's astrocell from further threats required serious consideration. Aiden had to assume that Cardew still wanted it shut down to isolate his nascent empire against potential harassment. After jumping back into the Alpha-2 Hydri system, Aiden responded to Admiral Stegman's hail and summarized what had transpired since their last communication. Stegman agreed to send a force of warships to join the *Sun Wolf* at Alpha-2 Hydri's POP to stand guard at the gateway. In fact, the UED already had a modest fleet of battle cruisers in position at Friendship Station, ready for void-jump.

The only problem was, it would take the fleet over 13 days to reach Aiden's position, having to travel close to four billion kilometers to the polar opposite point after making its jump into the Alpha-2 Hydri system. For a craft with a zero-point drive, it would be a matter of hours. But with the conventional M/AM drives used by everyone else, even at 1 G constant acceleration, it couldn't be done in less than 13 days. That meant the *Sun Wolf* had to stay put guarding the gateway voidoid until the UED forces arrived.

Accepting this responsibility did nothing to diminish Aiden's determination to find LO's Dark Fort in the Alpha-2 Hydri system. If Black Dog had told the truth about the kidnapped scientists and voidship crew he'd left there, some of them might still be alive. Aiden wanted to rescue them sooner than later, and with the zero-point drive online it wouldn't take long—assuming he knew where to look for them. That was when Elgin Woo stepped up and told them where he thought the Black Fort had to be—on a rocky moon around the system's third planet, a gas giant about 3 AU from the star. Never mind how he knew this, but it turned out he was right.

The *Sun Wolf* covered the distance in about two hours, from start to stop, no turnaround. The moon was one of six orbiting a Neptune-sized gas giant, an airless rock about half the size of Luna, pocked with craters of all sizes. Aiden brought the *Sun Wolf* into low orbit and employed the ship's entire array of survey sensors to quickly locate a single dome structure nestled inconspicuously at the base of a one-kilometer-tall crater wall. It turned out to be only the tip of the proverbial iceberg.

Armed to the teeth, Ro took a shuttle down to investigate, accompanied by Billy Hotah and Faye Desai. Upon entering the dome structure, cycling through its fully functional air lock, they found an entrance into a large, roughly hewn, underground habitat. Still powered by a sizable fusion generator, its life-support system had kept the habitat viable. They met no resistance but found seven scientists and nine former crew members of the RMV *Markos*, including their captain. They were alive but not well.

Woo recognized five of the scientists as having done research stints at the Cauldron at one time or another, including Dr. Emilio Roca. But Anwar Cain was nowhere to be found among them. Nor were any crew members of the still-missing SS *Conquest*. The scientists had been kidnapped by agents of LO or otherwise brutally compelled to contribute to LO's scheme. The displaced crew members of the *Markos* had been imprisoned aboard their ship after it was hijacked by LO agents and then deposited at the Dark Fort on Black Dog's way out.

All of these unfortunate souls had been treated poorly and left for dead when LO's fledgling Empire of the Pure vacated Bound Space. Their maladies ranged from malnutrition to physical and mental trauma, the kind commonly found in torture victims. The scientists in particular exhibited signs of mental vacancy. Ro suspected it was the result of "brain tapping," an arcane technique of interrogation implemented by the Dark Arts. Stuff of rumor only, but Ro was convinced of it and implied that he'd seen it before.

Aiden wondered why these survivors had been left alive at all. It couldn't have been out of compassion. That much was obvious. Was it instead some kind of twisted calling card, like what serial killers leave behind for the benefit of those who discover their victims?

The *Sun Wolf* returned to the gateway voidoid to wait out the remaining days for the UED fleet to arrive. While they waited, one of the ship's docking bays was converted into a modest living area to house and continue treating the survivors. Crew and survivors alike were allowed to contact family and loved ones back in the System via Holtzman transmission. Aiden and Skye communicated frequently. He promised to visit her at Chara as soon as possible upon his return to Sol. A handfasting ceremony was mentioned. And not for the first time.

Aiden began following what had transpired back home during their absence. By mutual agreement, the Allied Republic of Mars sent their own contingency of warships to join UED's presence at the gateway. Negotiations between the two superpowers were already underway to iron out agreements over the use and protection of the gateway. Aiden guessed that a new Friendship Station would be constructed there to serve the same purpose as the one at V-Prime, but with a beefed-up military presence. And at the forceful urging of Dr. Elgin Woo, a smaller force was to be sent through the gateway to Woo's Star to guard over the habitable planet he'd found there. His beloved Shénmì. Woo, in fact was already busy organizing a research expedition from the Cauldron to establish an orbital base there.

Very few people among the entire human population knew anything yet about how close their corner of the universe had come to the Rip, or who had been behind it. Those who did know deemed it wise to keep it that way. But the discovery of a gateway voidoid into Woo's Astrocell? That was big news. It promised enormous potential for further human expansion—for exploration, resource development, and the search for habitable planets.

Not the entire population had reacted with unbridled optimism over the new discoveries. The revelations actually polarized the citizens of the Domain even further, in the same ways the discovery of Silvanus had. The One Earth adherents saw the gateway as just another escape hatch through which the human race could flee their responsibility to stay home and do the hard work of repairing Mother Earth. And the fringe elements, whose numbers had grown alarmingly, saw it as an even larger doorway through which hostile "alien creatures" could pour in to enslave or destroy them. It was a fear that Houda Thunkit expertly exploited to advance his presidential campaign. The election hadn't happened yet, but it was right around the corner and no one had a clue how it would turn out. Aiden hoped the majority of the Domain would make the right choice, but he knew enough of history not to count on it.

One thing, however, was certain. Science, mostly in areas related to quantum astrophysics and voidoid research, had been greatly advanced by the *Sun Wolf*'s mission. Elgin Woo's theories, presented in his seminal work, *Living Voidoids*, had gained greater credibility. The dramatic resurrection of the voidoids within Bound Space under the apparent influence of a voidoid from an adjacent astrocell supported Woo's suggestion that voidoid family groups were in fact populations of coupled oscillators in sync, and that synchronization was the key to how they operated and communicated with each other.

It also validated his hunch that the "void conduits" interconnecting them all, the weird space-time anomalies that allowed the phenomenon of voidjumping, were in fact ephemeral properties that could survive for some period of time after the apparent death of a voidoid family, like what occurred in Bound Space. It was through one such conduit that the voidoid at Woo's Star managed to reanimate V-Prime at Sol. Once reborn, V-Prime promptly reanimated all its daughter voidoids, and just like that, Bound Space stabilized, the Rip was avoided, and voidjumping resumed. Exactly how and why that reanimation occurred remained a mystery. But for Woo, the answer was simple—voidoids were not only alive but also conscious and intelligent. The outcome of Aiden's neurolinkage with Woo's Voidoid was proof enough for him.

And all of it argued convincingly for Woo's bigger picture of the universe, of a living universe. A place where billions of individual astrocells exist, each one a living family group, together maintaining the proper balance of dark energy to allow matter to persist and organic life to thrive. And where each astrocell was likely to be connected to at least one other through a gateway voidoid like the one at Alpha-2 Hydri. The implications of that premise rang clear as a bell to anyone paying attention, not just scientists. It meant that the entire galaxy might be opened up to voidjumping, possibly even within their lifetimes.

The UED warships arrived on day 13 to relieve the *Sun Wolf* from guard duty. Four heavily armed battle cruisers set up positions around the gateway voidoid. They deployed a powerful Holtzman communication hub, an array of sophisticated sensor drones, and the *Sun Wolf* was finally free to go home.

~ ~ ~

Back at Sol, the *Sun Wolf* made its first stop at the Cauldron, where Elgin Woo said a brief farewell and departed aboard the *Starhawk*, bringing Maryam Ebadi and Cass Healy with him.

Then, after delivering the Dark Fort survivors to Tycho City Medical Center on Luna, the *Sun Wolf* docked at Hawking Station for refitting and resupply. Aiden remained at Hawking for several days of debriefing with UED Admiralty and then was finally released for some well-deserved R and R. Elgin Woo knew exactly what Aiden needed and came back for him aboard the *Starhawk*. They left Hawking Station the next day on a fast trip to the Chara system, where Aiden could finally reunite with Skye at the Silvanus Project.

During the trip aboard the *Starhawk*, Aiden mentioned his vision of the black crow he'd seen while still neurolinked to Hutton and what the AI had said about it. According to Hutton, all the Omicron-3 units currently in use throughout Bound Space were interconnected and shared information. That resulted in a massively large, complex, and dynamic network—a network-of-networks Hutton called the OverNet—that was constantly learning and deepening. At last estimate, there were over 430 known Omicron-3 units, integral to everything from research and medical facilities, government and military, to civic, commercial, and financial institutions. They managed virtually every aspect of human endeavor, weaving the indispensable fabric of everyday life.

But not all Omicron-3 units within the OverNet were officially registered or in any other way identifiable. Some existed in the shadows, either by design or special circumstances. Since the neural net of each individual Omicron unit was grown and taught in much the same way as the human brain develops, the potential for building maverick or even malevolent units was real. Those rogue Omicrons could theoretically infiltrate the OverNet to influence or change it in significant ways, while remaining completely out of sight. According to Hutton, the "community" of Omicrons that constituted the OverNet performed a kind of self-policing function against such aberrancies, but Hutton's recently acquired knowledge of Licet Omnia had him concerned.

Hutton pointed out that Licet Omnia had access to the very powerful Omicron-3 units aboard the RMV *Markos* and possibly the still-missing SS *Conquest*. Preexisting Omicrons could be "bent" to purposes other than those they were intended to manage, but only by extremely skillful manipulation. If someone within Licet Omnia was capable of doing such a thing, it could prove exceedingly dangerous.

"I agree with Hutton," Woo said after listening to Aiden's account. "And I believe that Cardew himself is that person. His powers of consciousness manipulation are absolutely unheard of in modern history. I think what you may have experienced during neurolinkage was a symbolic representation of an attempted intrusion from somewhere within the OverNet. An attempt to either stop you from your work with the voidoid or to extract information. Or both."

Aiden sat back and said nothing. He'd been right to temper his sense of triumph with the sobering realization that this story was far from over. A battle had been won, but only the first in a war that had just begun.

Woo turned to Aiden again, looking as if he had something else to say, then looked away and said nothing.

"Out with it, Elgin."

Woo took a deep breath and said, "There's something else I should tell you about Cardew. Something I found in the top-secret documents recovered from Terra Corp's headquarters last year, just after R.Q. Farthing was arrested. When I got back to the Cauldron, I was given access to them by a close contact of mine in the DSI. The documents belonged to Terra Corp's strategy director, Cole Brahmin."

After the Chara Crisis came to a close, Terra Corp's director, R.Q. Farthing, had been arrested and charged with crimes he and his security chief had committed to further the corporation's wealth and power. Farthing had been sent to prison, Brahmin had been killed during the Crisis, and Terra Corp had been stripped of its military power by the UED under President Michi Takema.

"We know now," Woo continued, "that Cole Brahmin was an agent of Licet Omnia. But Brahmin's reign in that capacity was preceded by another strategy director who served under R.Q.'s father, Stewart Farthing. His name was C.S. Amon. The two worked together for nearly 35 years before R.Q. took over in 2195. They were responsible for some of the most egregious misdeeds in the corporation's long history of corruption. The documents reveal that in the late 2180s, Amon—a young man at the time—compiled a hit list of people that Terra Corp wanted eliminated, people who stood firmly in the way of the corporation's voracious consolidation of power. People who stood for justice and equality. People who spoke the truth and who would not be intimidated into backing down. Amon took personal responsibility for—and by some accounts, pleasure in—executing these hits himself. We're talking about assassinations, Aiden. Cleverly disguised as accidents, but murder nonetheless."

Aiden felt his stomach tighten, his face beginning to burn.

Woo saw the change in him and grew even more reluctant to continue, but he finally did. "One of the names on that hit list was a brilliant young structural engineer and a fiercely outspoken activist for worker's rights on Luna. She was Morgan Macallan."

The volcano of rage that had consumed the first half of Aiden's life began to erupt anew. The same hot rage that had almost eaten him alive and ended up landing him in prison. Fueled by his conviction that his mother's "accidental" death had been deliberately engineered by Terra Corp, Aiden had gone on to expose that crime and many more perpetrated by the corporation. But he had never learned who was personally responsible for his mother's death. Now he knew.

"That's not all, Aiden," Woo said cautiously. "Almost no records of C.S. Amon exist anywhere, but my deepest sources finally discovered his true identity. The 'S' stands for Amon's middle name, Seth. The 'C' stands for his first name, Cardew. Terra Corp's director of strategy during those early years was none other than Cardew, the founder of Licet Omnia."

It had taken Aiden many years and much work to learn how to live productively with the anger he held inside. Now, as it reared its flaming head once again, he doubted that even Sudha Devi could help him subdue it. But this time around, the anger did not incapacitate him. Now it gave him raw strength. And it revived his old reckless friend—revenge.

"I wasn't going to tell you this at first," Woo said. "I know it reopens old wounds, but I felt that, in all good conscience, I could not keep it from you. I am truly sorry, Aiden. And I am also truly angry. I will not let this go unresolved. Not for as long as I live."

Aiden mastered his emotion enough to face Woo with steady eyes. "You did the right thing, Elgin. Telling me what you've learned. For me, this just ups the ante."

"For me as well. We have a lot left to do."

Right. And now it gets personal.

The two men shared a dark silence, eyes averted, until Mari eventually said, "Voidjump in one minute."

The *Starhawk* had come to a standstill five kilometers from Friendship Station. Thanks to an order signed by the UED president, Michi Takema, the usual red tape preceding a voidjump from V-Prime had been waived for the *Starhawk*. Aiden had to admit, celebrity had its perks.

He and Woo sat back in their seats and prepared themselves for the jump. Woo's eyes were closed, Aiden's were open.

Mari said, "Voidjump commencing now."

The sensation of voidjumping always reminded Aiden of sitting in a brightly lit room where the lights went out for just a microsecond, then back on. So fast you didn't notice it at all unless you were looking for it. But in that timeless moment, he thought he heard the voice again. The one that said without sound or words: *Welcome. You are always here.*

After Aiden's brief moment of dislocation passed, he looked over at Woo. Elgin was looking back at him with a wide smile and knowing eyes. Aiden thought he knew why. "You heard that, too, didn't you, Elgin?"

"Yes," he said off-handedly. "And not for the first time. It appears that the voidoids know both of us quite well now."

"We are now in the Chara system," Mari said as a formality. Aiden's spirits lifted. It felt like coming home. Home not only to Skye but also to Silvanus.

"Thank you, Mari," Woo said. "Set course for Silvanus Station and proceed."

Within a couple hours, the *Starhawk* began docking maneuvers at the station's shuttle bay. The extraordinary planet Silvanus appeared below in full view, a beautiful blue-green jewel set in the velvet blackness of space. A living and fully conscious planet.

After the *Starhawk* was secured inside and the shuttle fully bay repressurized, Aiden stood and shook Woo's hand. "Thanks for the lift, Elgin. Are you sticking around for a while?"

Woo shook his head. "I'd love to, but I've got a date and can't be late."

Aiden nodded. "With Shénmì."

"Correct," Woo said, then gestured toward the screen display of Silvanus as the light of dawn slowly crept across her face. "I'm sure you, of all people, understand."

Aiden glanced at Silvanus, then back to Woo. "I do indeed."

Woo accompanied Aiden through the airlock to the outer door. It opened with a subtle pop as the pressure of the ship's interior equalized with that of the bay. Aiden turned to face Woo and placed a hand on his shoulder. "Safe journey, my friend."

Woo smiled as he closed the hatch behind him. "Safety second. Adventure first."

From inside the docking bay's receiving area, Aiden watched the *Starhawk* move away from the station then vanish from sight. He was sad to see Elgin Woo go but knew that the trajectories of their lives were bound to intersect once again in the very near future.

43

SILVANUS STATION
Domain Day 126, 2218

Sitting quietly in Skye Landen's quarters, on the single chair next to her bed, Aiden watched her sleep. She lay on her left side, her shoulder-length blond hair fanned out across the pillow, tossed there in elegant disarray by the randomness of sleep. Her breathing was slow and deep, her face smooth and untroubled. Aiden sipped a remarkably good scotch from a small shot glass he'd borrowed from the station's galley and envied her ability to sleep so peacefully. When they were together, which was never often enough, he usually woke before she did. It gave him the opportunity to appreciate her beauty unselfconsciously, to meditate on how much he loved her.

Aiden was learning to recognize moments like this, the quiet and softly glowing moments in her presence, as the only reality that truly mattered in his life. The love they shared allowed him a transcendence that clearly surpassed the transcendence of neurolinkage. Or of Continuum. More enduring, more constant, imparting a subtle radiance that was all his own and that enriched him during his everyday life, whether in the foreground or in the background. When secrets such as these revealed themselves to Aiden, they were always astonishingly simple and unassuming, hiding in plain sight if only he stopped long enough to see them. Only when he stopped seeking them were they found.

A sliver of mellow light appeared at the edge of the viewport just beyond where Skye slept. Aiden watched the glowing crescent gradually fill more and more of the viewport. He was witnessing another sunrise on Silvanus from nearly 500 kilometers above her surface, only the third one he'd seen since his arrival here at Silvanus Station. The station served as the orbital platform for the Silvanus Project, founded ten months ago to study the miraculous planet. It operated under the joint management of both the UED and ARM, and Dr. Skye Landen was the Research Director from the UED contingent. It had taken him nearly three weeks after Bound Space had reopened to finally make it out to Chara to be with her. They had made up for lost time during the first day, passionately, frenzied, compelled by needs of their bodies. By the second day, things slowed down, grew deeper, compelled by needs of the heart.

Aiden let the last few milliliters of scotch slide down his throat and watched Silvanus slowly turn into full daylight through the viewport. It cast a mellow light upon the sleeping woman next to him. Silvanus and Skye. His two favorite women. Both had played such an important role in his life, in saving his life. Both were beautiful beyond description and precious to him beyond value. And he'd come so close to losing both of them.

The thought of losing a mate made him think of Cass Healy and how she had endured the loss of her own mate, Joal. But Cass's story was unique and had every indication of turning out happily. For reasons still unclear to Aiden, Colonel Victor Aminu had failed to include Cass's name in the official report he sent back to his superiors at DSI. Aiden knew this because Aminu had left an unredacted copy of it for his eyes only. It showed up in his secure message box shortly after the colonel launched himself toward the *Markos* on the suicide mission that had saved their lives. It included a detailed account of their encounter with the wreckage of the *Rachel Carson* but mentioned no survivors. It claimed that the source of information they had acquired—about Black Dog, the base at Rhea, the *Rachel Carson*'s mission, the

Final Blow, all of it—had come from records and personal documents recovered from the demolished ship. The tragic fate of
the *Rachel Carson* had been surmised from an examination of the
wreckage. No mention of a Cassandra Healy.

Aiden was sure the omission had not been due to forgetfulness
or sloppy reporting. That was most definitely not Aminu's style.
But neither was sacrificing his own life for a cause he'd been reluctant to embrace, much less believe in. Or so Aiden had thought.
The colonel had been a far more complex man than he'd been
given credit for. Aiden couldn't shake his suspicion that Aminu
had somehow been changed by his brief visit to Shénmì, by what
he'd seen or felt there.

As for Aiden's own official report of the *Rachel Carson* incident, he had not mentioned survivors either. In fact, it was eerily
similar to Aminu's report in content. Nor had he reported Cass's
presence on the *Sun Wolf* after communications had been established with Bound Space. On their way back to Sol, Aiden had
taken her aside and explained all this to her, told her that she
would not be prosecuted for her part in Black Dog's scheme
because no one knew about it except his crew, and they had sworn
not to reveal it. She was free to live her life now, to follow her
dreams. Cass's reaction had been emotional, particularly when
told of Aminu's omission, a mixture of profound gratitude and
bewilderment.

When the *Sun Wolf* made its stop at the Cauldron before
proceeding to Hawking Station, Cass had left the ship in the
company of Elgin Woo and Maryam Ebadi. There among the
Cauldron's self-absorbed scientists, fiercely asocial and obsessed
with their own work, Cass had hardly been noticed. The following day, Woo arranged passage for her to Luna and lodging
at Luna University. Acting on conversations between Cass and
Dr. Devi in which Cass expressed a keen interest in studying med-
icine, Devi had introduced her to the renowned Gaian physician
Thea Delamere, who also happened to be Ro's wife. Cass apparently made an impression, and she'd been granted first-year

admission to Luna U. Medical School. Her studies would begin after returning from a brief trip to visit her parents living in her native Ireland.

In Dr. Devi's latest communication to Aiden, she mentioned that Cass had received a visitor from Hawking Station, a certain Lieutenant William Hotah on "shore leave" from the *Sun Wolf*. Devi reported that Cass had appeared unusually happy after the visit and left it at that. Devi also mentioned that Lieutenant Dalton had taken his shore leave to the Cauldron, claiming that he needed to learn more about the zero-point drive from Dr. Min Lee. Aiden was fairly certain that Dalton wanted to learn more than just rocket science from Ms. Lee.

As a sidenote to the more pivotal consequences of the *Sun Wolf*'s mission, a few lesser-known blessings had occurred. The UED Science and Survey vessel SS *Arcadia* had reappeared with its captain, Captain Dural Hawthorne, and his crew intact and none the worse for wear. The *Arcadia* had disappeared while attempting to jump out of the Alpha-2 Hydri system just as the voidoid there fluxed out, the result of the *Rachel Carson*'s misguided tampering. Soon after the voidoids of Bound Space came back to life, the *Arcadia* mysteriously popped out of Sol's polar opposite point, back into the Sol system. The crew had perceived no lapse of time between their disappeared and reappearance. Go figure.

But the other missing ship, UED's warship the SS *Conquest*, had not yet been found. It had been on a routine shakedown cruise out in the Zeta Tucanae system when, just like the *Arcadia*, it had disappeared while attempting a jump during a sudden void flux. Aiden believed that the *Conquest* had been hijacked by LO, the same way the *Markos* had, and used by Cardew to transport the vanguard of his Empire of the Pure to its unknown location somewhere in Woo's Astrocell. That notion had been supported by vague accounts from some of the scientists rescued from LO's Dark Fort and was currently under investigation by the DSI.

If anyone could figure it all out, it would be Elgin Woo. His brief return to the Cauldron had set into motion a whole new direction of inquiries for his brilliant and quirky band of resident scientists to pursue. Woo himself took particular interest in developing methods for communication with the voidoids. Aiden, after all, had proved it was possible. Woo was convinced that others could do it as well; maybe even the Omicron AIs would find their own unique way of doing it. So much could be learned. The living voidoids represented the second alien intelligence encountered by the human race, right alongside the Rete on Silvanus.

Furthermore, Woo's discovery that voidoids shared the exact same resonant frequency as their host stars—0.0035 Hz in the case of Woo's Star—was given added dimension by Faye Desai's broadband seismograph readings made on Shénmì. The instrument had been set to determine the planet's "free oscillation" frequency, commonly known as a planet's inherent hum, its constant low-frequency seismic vibration. Woo had not been surprised to find that it turned out to be 0.0035 Hz as well. He knew that planet Earth's hum happened to be, on average, right at 0.0033 Hz, the same as the sun's average resonant frequency. Both Earth and Shénmì supported organic life. A coincidence? Aiden thought not and guessed that the same three-way synchronization between voidoid, star, and planet would exist here in the Chara system where Silvanus lived.

Then, of course, there were the mysterious "seed pods" being launched into space by the planet Shénmì. What was that all about? Panspermia, no doubt, but there had to be something more to it. Something deliberate, purposeful. Was Shénmì another planet like Silvanus? A living world? Another Gaia? Those questions were of particular interest to the Silvanus Project, and when the Project's director, Skye Landen, asked, Woo gladly handed off that line of inquiry to her and her colleagues at Silvanus Station.

Aiden picked up the shot glass, realized it was empty, set it back down, and sighed. He watched Skye shift position in her sleep, turning gracefully to face him. Still, she did not wake. How could he be so lucky that a woman as smart and beautiful, both inside and out, be in love with him in the same way he was in love with her? He only wished he had more time to be with her before departing. But once again, he was needed elsewhere.

It had been impossible to keep reports of the *Sun Wolf*'s exploits secret, and the existence of the zero-point drive could no longer be plausibly denied. Both the UED and ARM were already pressuring Woo to make the drive technology available to their military and commercial vessels. Woo said he'd consider it only on the condition that both powers could come to a firm agreement, an indisputable treaty enacted into interplanetary law, on exactly how the technology would be used, founded on equal access and good faith. Aiden doubted that would happen any time soon and knew it depended a great deal on who became the next president of the Domain.

In the meantime, the *Sun Wolf* remained the only fully equipped voidship in Bound Space powered by the zero-point drive, and already it and her crew were being called into action by a troubling development at the gateway voidoid. A few days ago, another gravity bomb just like the one Black Dog used on V-Prime had popped through the gateway into the Alpha-2 Hydri system. Surprising the warships standing guard, it parked itself within 50 meters of the voidoid and immediately began emanating a powerful gravity field. Fortunately, the voidoid remained totally unaffected, prompting speculations that it had somehow "learned" that the bomb was a ruse, that its G-field was artificial and not the result of a natural reduction of dark energy within the system. Otherwise, the device would surely have shut down the voidoid well before being destroyed by the high-G missiles hurled at it.

So, the writing was on the wall. Licet Omnia was operating somewhere in Woo's Astrocell, establishing a stronghold from which it would build its Empire of the Pure. Black Dog had not lied about that one. Sooner or later, Cardew would come knocking, and when he did, he would bring extraordinary powers to bear. Bound Space and its inhabitants would not be safe from him. The G-bomb intruder was just the beginning, a scout. A teaser. Now was not the time to let down one's guard. Now was the time to go on the offensive. Once again, the *Sun Wolf* was clearly the best choice for the job. And once again, Aiden Macallan and his crew were clearly the best choice for the *Sun Wolf*. In fact, his ship would be arriving at Silvanus Station tomorrow morning—with its XO, Roseph Hand, in command—to pick up Aiden and spirit him away from his precious few days with Skye.

But there was another, much happier subplot, for the *Sun Wolf*'s arrival here tomorrow. It was to witness and celebrate the official handfasting ceremony for Aiden and Skye. They were finally getting married, Gaian style. It would be presided over by Thea Delamere, Ro's wife, who was accompanying her husband to Chara for that very reason. A very special reason. Handfasting, with its origins in old Celtic tradition, had been adopted by present-day Gaians as the preferred form of betrothal and was now legally binding in the eyes of Domain law.

Up until now, Aiden had been apprehensive about making such a life-changing commitment. But after his experiences on Silvanus, that had changed. Not that doubts didn't linger, but now he recognized that the positive effects of his relationship with Skye far outweighed the unfounded qualms of a younger man. Time, Aiden had learned, was the great equalizer. At 39, he'd finally grown up. And Skye had grown with him.

She stirred now, and, as if his thoughts had wakened her, opened her eyes. As the fog of sleep slipped away, she looked at him sitting next to the bed, blinked, and smiled. "Are you real?"

Aiden smiled back and nodded. "Yep, I'm pretty sure of it. In fact, I feel more real now than ever before."

She moved to sit at the side of the bed, facing Aiden. Her fair complexion glowed with a subtle blush. Her eyes were the bluest blue Aiden had ever seen. They drew him in like deep pools of water, beckoning him to submerge. She reached out and touched his cheek. "Yes, you *are* real. We are real."

Her touch was like soft electricity. It coursed through his body to wake every part of him. As he moved to join her on the bed, something caught his eye. Something from the viewport behind her. Some subtle change in the appearance of the blue-green planet below them, a sharpening of its features.

"What is it, Aiden?"

As she turned to follow his gaze out the viewport, a voice came over the comm. It was one of Skye's research associates. "Dr. Landen. I apologize if I've disturbed you, but I believe something remarkable just happened. To Silvanus. Can you please come to Control?"

Skye was already getting dressed. "Yes, Amelia, I'll be right there." She looked at Aiden, her eyes bright with anticipation. "I dreamed this was about to happen. Come with me, Aiden."

He was right behind her as they hurried down the cramped corridor leading to the station's control center. When they got there, five other researchers were standing around instrument screens, their gazes alternating between data readouts and the realtime view of Silvanus out the main viewport. Skye took one quick look at their astonished faces, then turned to the viewport and said what the others wanted to say but couldn't yet believe. "The shield around Silvanus is gone. She's opened up to us. She's inviting us to visit. In person."

Aiden felt the hairs on his neck prickle. The mysterious energy field around the planet had materialized during the Chara Conflict, a time of war when UED and ARM battle cruisers engaged in deadly combat not far from Silvanus. The energy field had perplexing properties. It allowed only pure energy to penetrate, to and from the surface, but repelled matter of any kind, travelling at any velocity. It effectively closed Silvanus off to physical visitation, human or otherwise. That had been over 10 months ago and the shield had persisted ever since. Fortunately, a clone of Hutton's hardware remained on the surface, thanks to Aiden's original visit, and it continued to beam data up to the station for the researchers to pore over. There were many opinions on why the shield appeared when it did, but no one had the slightest idea of how long it would stay in place. Aiden had always felt that Silvanus was saying to the human race, "I'm not so sure about you, and until I know more, I'm off limits to your kind."

But now? After Bound Space had been resurrected from the dead, after the darkness that infected it had moved on? Elgin Woo's vision of a living universe, a cosmic ecosystem populated by forms of consciousness at every level, looked more attractive with each new revelation.

Aiden stood next to Skye as they both gazed out the viewport. Silvanus—the living planet that had given him new life, new awareness, that he in return had given new life—looked more beautiful now than ever. Was she allowing him to return now and to bring others with him?

He took hold of Skye's hand and said, "I think we've been offered a new venue for our handfasting."

She gripped his hand more tightly and said, "Blessed be. We're finally here."

Aiden smiled at her and said, "We are always here."

ACKNOWLEDGEMENTS

M UCH THANKS TO the following people for their support and assistance in bringing this novel into print: editors Scott Pearson, Allister Thompson, and Sandi Goodman for their thoughtful and thorough copy editing; Rafael Andres for his stunning cover design; Phillip Gessert for his creative interior design; to Jeffrey Brandenburg for his invaluable advice from the very start; to Bob Page and Barbara Ware for their friendship and their quiet, creative space called Quail Crossing; to Alicia Grefenson for her guiding light along my path homeward; and, as always, to Ann for her unconditional support and our life-long partnership of the heart.